OXFORD WORLD'S CLASSICS

THE BEGGAR'S OPERA
AND
POLLY

JOHN GAY (1685–1732) was born in Barnstaple in Devon, to a socially prominent Dissenting family involved in trade with the West Indies. Orphaned at ten, Gay was educated at the Barnstaple Grammar School and later apprenticed to a silk mercer in London, but he broke off his apprenticeship early, and in 1707 joined forces with the literary entrepreneur Aaron Hill. Through Hill, Gay was introduced to the London literary and theatre worlds, and began to make a name for himself as a poet with *The Shepherd's Week* (1714), a set of six comic-pastoral eclogues. In this period he became friends with Alexander Pope and Jonathan Swift, with whom he remained close for the rest of his life. In search of a courtly sinecure, Gay was successively steward to the Duchess of Monmouth and secretary to Lord Clarendon, and was supported by such patrons of the arts as the Duke of Chandos and Richard Boyle, Earl of Burlington, who helped Gay to the post of Commissioner of the State Lottery, which he held from 1723 to 1731. With *Trivia* (1716), a mock-georgic poem on 'the Art of Walking the Streets of London', and *Poems on Several Occasions* (1720), Gay secured his reputation as a poet, although he lost most of the profits from the latter with the collapse of the 'South Sea Bubble' investment scheme. In his parallel career as a playwright, Gay wrote such minor hits as the 'tragi-comi-pastoral farce' *The What D'Ye Call It* (1715), but his greatest theatrical success was *The Beggar's Opera* (1728), a raucous, bitingly satirical 'ballad opera' or comedy with songs, which had a record-breaking first season and proved the most popular play of the century. Its sequel, *Polly*, was barred from the stage for political reasons, but Gay made a small fortune from publishing it; along with his first volume of verse *Fables* (1727), it brought him wealth at last. After three years as the special guest of the Duke and Duchess of Queensberry, Gay died in December 1732.

HAL GLADFELDER is Senior Lecturer in Eighteenth-Century English Literature and Culture at the University of Manchester. His books include *Criminality and Narrative in Eighteenth-Century England: Beyond the Law* (2001) and *Fanny Hill in Bombay: The Making and Unmaking of John Cleland* (2012), as well as the Broadview edition of Cleland's *Memoirs of a Coxcomb* (2005).

OXFORD WORLD'S CLASSICS

*For over 100 years Oxford World's Classics have brought
readers closer to the world's great literature. Now with over 700
titles—from the 4,000-year-old myths of Mesopotamia to the
twentieth century's greatest novels—the series makes available
lesser-known as well as celebrated writing.*

*The pocket-sized hardbacks of the early years contained
introductions by Virginia Woolf, T. S. Eliot, Graham Greene,
and other literary figures which enriched the experience of reading.
Today the series is recognized for its fine scholarship and
reliability in texts that span world literature, drama and poetry,
religion, philosophy, and politics. Each edition includes perceptive
commentary and essential background information to meet the
changing needs of readers.*

OXFORD WORLD'S CLASSICS

JOHN GAY

The Beggar's Opera
and
Polly

Edited with an Introduction and Notes by
HAL GLADFELDER

OXFORD
UNIVERSITY PRESS

OXFORD
UNIVERSITY PRESS

Great Clarendon Street, Oxford OX2 6DP
United Kingdom

Oxford University Press is a department of the University of Oxford.
It furthers the University's objective of excellence in research, scholarship,
and education by publishing worldwide. Oxford is a registered trade mark of
Oxford University Press in the UK and in certain other countries

First published as an Oxford World's Classics paperback 2013
Impression: 12

British Library Cataloguing in Publication Data
Data available

ISBN 978-0-19-964222-9

Printed in Great Britain by
Clays Ltd, Elcograf S.p.A.

CONTENTS

ACKNOWLEDGEMENTS

For help and encouragement of various kinds while I was preparing this volume, I am grateful to Thomas Keymer, Jeffrey Geiger, Noelle Gallagher, and, especially, Judith Luna at Oxford University Press. Jeanne Clegg invited me to present some of the material in its early stages at the Università Ca' Foscari in Venice, and my students at the University of Manchester helped me sharpen my readings, often by resisting them. I am also indebted to numerous previous editors of *The Beggar's Opera*, including John Fuller, Edgar V. Roberts, Bryan Loughrey and T. O. Treadwell, Vivien Jones and David Lindley, and particularly Peter Lewis, whose superb critical edition provided the editorial model for my work on both plays.

INTRODUCTION

SHORTLY before the opening night of *The Beggar's Opera*, 29 January 1728, John Gay's friend Alexander Pope, in a letter to Jonathan Swift, expressed uneasiness as to what audiences would make of it: 'Gay's Opera', he wrote, 'is just on the point of Delivery. It may be call'd (considering its Subject) a Jayl-Delivery. Mr Congreve (with whom I have commemorated you) is anxious as to its Success, and so am I; whether it succeeds or not, it will make a great noise, but whether of Claps or Hisses I know not.'[1] As things turned out, Pope need not have worried: *The Beggar's Opera* was to prove the most successful dramatic work not just of the year but of the century. It did indeed 'make a great noise', and if there was no shortage of hisses, claps far outnumbered them. In its first season, at the Theatre Royal, Lincoln's Inn Fields, it ran for a record-breaking sixty-two nights, and the theatre manager, John Rich, crammed as many spectators into the theatre as he could possibly fit, including, on one night, ninety-eight on stage and two wedged into what Rich labelled 'pidgeon holes'.[2] No wonder that, as the weekly newspaper *The Craftsman* put it on the day of the play's fifth performance, 'the Waggs [wits] say it has made *Rich* very *Gay*, and probably will make *Gay* very *Rich*'.[3]

Despite its runaway success, however, Pope, Swift, and the great Restoration playwright William Congreve were right to be anxious about the play's reception, for Gay had created a work that left even his friends puzzled. Charles Douglas, Duke of Queensberry, who with his wife Catherine was Gay's most loyal patron, was at a loss when he first read the manuscript, remarking, 'This is a very odd thing, Gay; I am satisfied that it is either a very good thing, or a very bad thing.'[4] But oddness was Gay's authorial trademark. His first play, *The Mohocks*, was billed as a 'Tragi-Comical Farce', while his

[1] Alexander Pope, *Correspondence*, ed. George Sherburn (Oxford: Clarendon Press, 1956), 2:469.

[2] Calhoun Winton, *John Gay and the London Theatre* (Lexington: University Press of Kentucky, 1993), 102.

[3] Quoted in William Eben Schultz, *Gay's Beggar's Opera: Its Content, History and Influence* (New Haven: Yale University Press, 1923), 6.

[4] Quoted in James Boswell, *Life of Johnson*, ed. George Birkbeck Hill, rev. L. F. Powell, 6 vols. (Oxford: Clarendon Press, 1934–50), ii. 368.

first theatrical success, the one-act *What D'Ye Call It*—whose title draws attention to its strangeness—was subtitled a 'Tragi-Comi-Pastoral Farce', as if to emphasize its unclassifiability. The collision of incongruous literary forms that these subtitles announce would be most fully realized in *The Beggar's Opera* and its sequel *Polly*, which veer from raucous satire to poignant lyricism, from cynicism to sentimentality, in the space of a few lines, continually wrong-footing their audiences. But it was precisely that unpredictability, the juxta-position of clashing styles and generic expectations, which struck a chord with theatre-goers.

First, they might have wondered, what could a 'beggar's opera' possibly be? Opera, to London audiences in the early decades of the eighteenth century, was a musical and theatrical form for the cultural elite: expensive to produce and attend; composed and performed by foreign artists in a language, Italian, that few but those who had made the grand tour to Italy could understand; musically and dramatically sophisticated and abstruse. Along with its formal complexity and its prohibitively high ticket prices came the elitism of opera's subject matter—stories of gods and heroes taken from classical history and mythology, the worlds of epic and romance. Gay was no enemy of Italian opera, and *The Beggar's Opera* is not an attack, even if it is in part a burlesque of conventional operatic devices and scenes. But opera was not—could not possibly be—either by or for beggars. The very thought was absurd.

No less absurd was the name of the dramatic form that Gay, with *The Beggar's Opera*, invented: the ballad opera. This term only came into common use in the 1730s, and Gay did not coin it, but it was applied retrospectively to *The Beggar's Opera* and *Polly* as the found-ing texts of a new theatrical genre. More than one hundred ballad operas were published or staged in the twenty years after *The Beggar's Opera*'s first performance, many of them slavish imitations, but some the work of major comic authors such as Henry Fielding. Gay him-self wrote a third, *Achilles*, first performed shortly after his death, in 1733. Like 'beggar's opera', the term 'ballad opera' suggests the hybrid, contradictory nature of the form, which mixes high and low, opera and ballad, the antithetical social worlds of the metropolitan elite and the folk. As Gay conceived it, the ballad opera intersperses spoken dialogue with newly written songs set to familiar tunes, chiefly folk tunes or street ballads, but also songs stolen or parodied from other, current plays and operas.[5] While many of the later ballad operas simply copy Gay's formula—the same tunes, the same lowlife settings, the same romantic triangles—his work had wider repercussions over the long term. Gay showed that original work could, paradoxically, be generated out of a dialogic assembly of disparate, incongruous pre-existing materials and forms: comedy, opera, folk song, country dance, pirate tale, tragedy, street ballad, ballet, and farce. Like that other hybrid eighteenth-century genre, the novel, the ballad opera is a form predicated on continual formal recombination and play, a form without form. It would lead, over time, to the German Singspiel, the Savoy operettas of Gilbert and Sullivan, and the twentieth-century musical: from Brecht and Weill's relocation of Macheath to 1920s Berlin in *The Threepenny Opera* to Stephen Sondheim's bitter, bloody horror show *Sweeney Todd*. It could even be claimed that, with *The Beggar's Opera*, Gay invented modern theatre.

Samuel Johnson, in the short life of Gay he wrote in 1780, described 'the Ballad Opera' as 'a mode of comedy which at first was supposed to delight only by its novelty, but has now by the experience of half a century been found so well accommodated to the disposition of a popular audience, that it is likely to keep long possession of the stage'.[6] Johnson's last prophetic words have been borne out over the past 230-odd years by both the ballad opera in general (the musical comedy form) and *The Beggar's Opera* in particular. Although performances became less frequent in the second half of the nineteenth century, it was spectacularly revived by the producer Nigel Playfair at the Lyric Theatre, Hammersmith, in 1920, running for over three years (1,468 performances in all); and even though Playfair and his collaborators, Frederic Austin (music) and Arnold Bennett (script), cut out much of the play's most daring material, their revival proved it had lost none of its ability to entertain and provoke.[7] It was

---

[5] See the Appendix to this edition for notes on the sources of the 140 tunes Gay incorporated into *The Beggar's Opera* and *Polly*.

[6] Samuel Johnson, *Gay* (1780), in *The Lives of the Most Eminent English Poets*, ed. Roger Lonsdale (Oxford: Oxford University Press, 2006), iii. 95–102, at 100.

[7] Cuts were especially severe in the third act. Among the airs absent from the Playfair production were some of the most popular original tunes, including Air 67, perhaps Gay's most politically incisive lyric, set to the most popular tune of all, 'Greensleeves'. See *The Beggar's Opera, as it is performed at the Lyric Theatre, Hammersmith*, with music by Frederic Austin (London: Boosey & Co., 1920).

the success of this staging that inspired Elisabeth Hauptmann to translate the text into German, and then, with Bertolt Brecht and the composer Kurt Weill, to transform it into the corrosively lyrical, cynical, sleazy *Threepenny Opera*, which opened in Berlin exactly 200 years after *The Beggar's Opera*'s first season.[8] Hauptmann, Brecht, and Weill's political updating, set in Victorian London but reflecting the conditions of Weimar Germany, was the model for similar rewritings by such playwrights as the Czech dissident Vaclav Havel and the Nigerian author and activist Wole Soyinka in the 1970s, while Weill's modernist flirtation with American jazz was to be followed by Duke Ellington and Billy Strayhorn's multiracial reimagining of the original as *Beggar's Holiday* (1946; book and lyrics by John Latouche).[9] These and other adaptations attest to *The Beggar's Opera*'s cultural resonance, its continuing power to unsettle and captivate.

The action of the play unfolds in and around Newgate prison in London, and the plot, an uneasy compound of the comic and the tragic, is structured by a pattern of secrets, betrayals, and lies. When the play opens, the female romantic lead, Polly Peachum, has secretly married the charismatic highwayman and gang leader Macheath, and concealed him in her room. Her parents, partners in the business of thief-taking and receiving stolen goods, discover what Polly has done when she is betrayed by their apprentice, Filch. Worried that Macheath might betray them in turn for their money, and avid to get their hands on the reward for having him arrested or 'peached', they resolve to turn him in; but Polly warns him, and the first act ends with his escape from the Peachums' house. The second act opens in a tavern nearby, where Macheath's gang are preparing to take the road. Excusing himself from joining them because of his trouble with Peachum, Macheath stays behind with a select group of his eight favourite whores; but two of them, led by his 'dear Slut' Jenny Diver,

---

[8] See Joseph Roach, *It* (Ann Arbor: University of Michigan Press, 2007), 213–26; Calhoun Winton, '*The Beggar's Opera*: A Case Study', in *The Cambridge History of British Theatre, Volume 2: 1660–1895*, ed. Joseph Donohue (Cambridge: Cambridge University Press, 2004), 126–44, esp. 140–1.

[9] On Havel, see Roach, *It*, 213–14; Winton, 'Case Study', 142–3; Dianne Dugaw, '*Deep Play': John Gay and the Invention of Modernity* (Newark: University of Delaware Press, 2001), 41–7. On Soyinka, see Roach, *It*, 213, 216. On Ellington and Strayhorn, see Winton, 'Case Study', 143–4, and David Hajdu, *Lush Life: A Biography of Billy Strayhorn* (New York: North Point, 1996), 101–5.

betray him to Peachum, who has him arrested and taken to Newgate. Once there he is confronted by Lucy Lockit, the prison-keeper's daughter, whom he has made pregnant and promised to marry. She is enraged at first by news of his marriage to Polly, but even though Polly bursts into his cell and claims him as her husband, Macheath assures Lucy that Polly is 'distracted', and after Peachum carries his daughter away, Lucy steals her father's keys, to finish the second act with Macheath's second escape. In the third act, Lucy, imagining Macheath united with Polly, plots to avenge herself by poisoning her rival; meanwhile, Peachum and Lockit learn where Macheath is hiding from Diana Trapes, another receiver of stolen goods, and have him arrested a second time. As he is brought back to Newgate, Polly, in shock, drops the poisoned glass. She and Lucy plead by turns with their fathers to spare Macheath, but he is tried and convicted on the evidence of one of his gang mates, Jemmy Twitcher. As he awaits execution, Lucy and Polly visit, still vying for his love; but when four more 'wives' show up, each with a child, Macheath declares himself ready to die. No sooner is he carried off, however, than the action is interrupted by the Player, who demands that the play's author, the Beggar, reprieve Macheath and give the audience the happy ending they expect—and so the play ends with Macheath's third escape.

But *The Beggar's Opera* by itself tells only half the story. Within a year of its opening night, Gay and Rich were preparing to start rehearsals of a new play, *Polly*, 'the second part of The Beggar's Opera'. But the Walpole government, stung by what its leader took to be Gay's ad hominem attacks in *The Beggar's Opera*, stopped Rich from rehearsing the new work, and ruled 'that it was not allow'd to be acted, but commanded to be supprest' (p. 75). In the short term, the banning of *Polly* actually worked to Gay's advantage, for within a few months he published the play at his own expense, along with an account of its prohibition, and the scandal of its suppression made it an immediate best-seller. Gay earned £1,200 from subscriptions alone, far more than *The Beggar's Opera* had brought him, and the play's initial print run of 10,000 copies was quickly followed by a spate of pirate editions. Yet in the long term Walpole's ban achieved its aim. *Polly* was not performed until nearly fifty years later, in George Colman's recomposed and defanged version of 1777, and the delay meant that *Polly* had no chance to engage with the audiences it was written for, or to develop a living perform-ance tradition.[10]

But perhaps *Polly*'s time has come round again. With its West Indian setting and its cast of transported outlaws, Indian princes, rebel slaves, rapacious colonials, and cross-dressing female adventur-ers, *Polly* transplants the thieves and whores of *The Beggar's Opera* into the new world of British colonial expansion, and broadens the earlier play's critique of a culture in which all human relationships are reduced to commercial transactions. It also compounds *The Beggar's Opera*'s formal innovations, folding elements of tragedy and masquerade into the first play's mixture of knockabout comedy, popular song, and bleak, even misanthropic satire. Read (or seen in performance) alongside *The Beggar's Opera*, *Polly* compels us to rethink our views of the celebrated captain Macheath and Polly Peachum, calling Macheath's heroic glamour into question while complicating Polly's seemingly artless simplicity. Disrupting any straightforward notions of sexual or racial identity, *Polly* features a romantic heroine passing as a pirate recruit and a white outlaw passing as a black slave leader, and adapts theatrical conventions of travesty and blackface to stage scenes of both same-sex and cross-race erotic desire which challenge the prevailing ethos of commodifica-tion. Diverting and discomfiting in equal measure, *Polly* is both a continuation and an undermining of *The Beggar's Opera*, and only by bringing the two parts together can we get an adequate sense of Gay's theatrical and moral vision, as he explores many of the same issues that Defoe and Swift confront in such contemporaneous works as *Robinson Crusoe* and *Gulliver's Travels*.

John Gay

John Gay's life and authorial career exemplify the variety and hap-hazardness of the writing trade in the eighteenth century. Best known today for such quintessentially urban works as *The Beggar's Opera* and the long poem *Trivia: or the Art of Walking the Streets of London*, Gay was born in the West Country, in the Devonshire market town of Barnstaple, to a socially prominent Dissenting family involved in

---

[10] Following on the success of his 1920 revival of *The Beggar's Opera*, Nigel Playfair produced a new, completely rewritten version of *Polly* at the Kingsway and Savoy Theatres in London, which ran for 324 performances in 1922–3.

trade with the West Indies, among other enterprises.[11] Orphaned at ten, Gay was the youngest of five children; and while he received a good basic education, with an emphasis on Latin and Greek literature, at the Barnstaple grammar school, there was no money to send him to university, nor any property or business to inherit, so in 1702, aged seventeen, he was apprenticed to John Willet, a draper or silk mercer in London. He was evidently unhappy with his work as a shop assistant, for he broke off his apprenticeship in 1706, about halfway through the usual period of seven years, and returned to Devon. But after his uncle's death the next year he took the first opportunity to come back to London, and took on the role of amanuensis—secretary, sidekick, and collaborator—to his former Barnstaple schoolmate, the author, literary entrepreneur, and later theatre manager Aaron Hill. Through Hill, Gay made his way into the thick of the vibrant but often tumultuous and fractious London literary scene, publishing his first poem, *Wine* (characteristically, a burlesque of Milton); writing for Hill's periodical, *The British Apollo* (consisting mainly of answers to readers' questions on topics ranging from mathematics to medical complaints); and meeting Alexander Pope, who was to become his closest literary collaborator, sponsor, and friend. Although he fell into a literary career as much as he deliberately pursued one, within a few years of returning to London, Gay had begun to establish himself as a distinctive new voice in a range of genres.

But authorship for Gay was never only about literature: it was also bound up with the struggle to find a secure social footing. In another of his early works, a pamphlet-length survey of contemporary periodicals titled *The Present State of Wit*, Gay says nothing at all about *The British Apollo*, for which he had only recently stopped writing, until a postscript, in which he claims that he had 'quite forgot' it, but notes, 'I am inform'd however, That it still recommends its self by deciding Wagers at Cards, and giving good Advice to the Shopkeepers, and their Apprentices'.[12] His most recent biographer asserts that this is a 'condescending gesture', which reflects 'the intensity of

[11] Biographical information, unless otherwise noted, is derived from David Nokes, *John Gay: A Profession of Friendship* (Oxford: Oxford University Press, 1995), and William Henry Irving, *John Gay: Favorite of the Wits* (Durham, NC: Duke University Press, 1940). Some of the dates from the years before he became an author are conjectural.

[12] Gay, *The Present State of Wit*, in *John Gay: Poetry and Prose*, ed. Vinton A. Dearing with Charles E. Beckwith, 2 vols. (Oxford: Clarendon Press, 1974), ii. 455–6.

Gay's desire for social status' and misleadingly distances him from the social world and ethos of 'Shop-keepers, and their Apprentices', of which he had been part only five years before.[13] Perhaps so; and Gay may indeed be trying to cover up his own recent past as apprentice and hack author. But it might also be a gesture of self-mockery, a wry acknowledgement of his distinctly unglamorous and even 'low' origins. In later years, Pope tried to play down Gay's time as a draper's apprentice, but the authorial self-portraits in Gay's work—such as the Beggar, and the mercenary Poet in *Polly*—are anything but self-aggrandizing, and suggest that Gay was as ready to turn his satirical lens on himself as on others.

In any case, his letters make clear that Gay saw writing as a means to a particular social end. The end he had in view was a paradoxical kind of independence—paradoxical because it depended on the will of a wealthy or politically powerful patron.[14] Gay, one biographer wrote, 'wasted his life' seeking a well-paid position at court, and he describes himself doing exactly this in *A Letter to a Lady*, a poem of 1714 written in honour of Caroline, Princess of Wales.[15] It is, typically, a work that both praises the princess and mocks the poet for writing such a panegyric. Portraying himself roving from room to room in St James's Palace, Gay writes, 'Still ev'ry one I met in this agreed, | That Writing was my Method to succeed; | But now Preferments so possess'd my Brain, | That scarce I could produce a single Strain'.[16] His failure to write mirrors his failure to find a courtly post: 'Places, I found, were daily giv'n away, | And yet no friendly Gazette mention'd *Gay*' (ll. 95–6). For all his complaining—and his letters dwell obsessively on such frustrated hopes—Gay was actually rather successful in finding patrons: from 1712 to 1714 he was secretary and steward to the Duchess of Monmouth; in July 1714 he became secretary to Lord Clarendon, envoy to the court of Hanover; for much of the time between 1715 and the late 1720s he lived with, or at the expense of, Richard Boyle, Earl of Burlington, who probably

---

[13] Nokes, *John Gay*, 72.

[14] On Gay's search for patrons, see Brean Hammond, '"A Poet, and a Patron, and Ten Pound": John Gay and Patronage', in Peter Lewis and Nigel Wood, eds., *John Gay and the Scriblerians* (London: Vision Press, 1988), 23–43.

[15] Austin Dobson, 'John Gay' (1889), available under 'DNB Archive' in *Oxford Dictionary of National Biography Online* (Oxford University Press, 2004–).

[16] Gay, *A Letter to a Lady*, ll. 127–30, in *Poetry and Prose*, ed. Dearing and Beckwith, i. 133.

secured Gay the lucrative and easy post of Commissioner of the State Lottery which he held from 1723 to 1731. Burlington, along with another patron of the arts, James Brydges, Duke of Chandos, was chief among the subscribers to Gay's *Poems on Several Occasions* (1720), which netted some £1,000, a small fortune at the time. Another aristocrat, the Earl of Lincoln, obtained rent-free lodgings for Gay in 1723 in the gatehouse to the royal garden in Whitehall, where he lived until 1729, by which time *The Beggar's Opera* and *Polly* had made him rich. He then spent the rest of his life as the favoured guest of another aristocratic couple, the Duke and Duchess of Queensberry. By any outward measure, Gay was well provided for, but his very success in securing patronage only underlined his dependency, the slavish obligation to please. And professional authorship was no better: to succeed as playwright or poet he had to comply with the tastes of a paying public, to sell his work at market, turn himself into a hack.

No wonder, then, that Gay's writing is infused with what Margaret Doody has called the 'double-tongued utterance, or quality of double-mindedness' of much Augustan poetry.[17] The poet both seeks a patron and scorns patronage-seekers; both strives to be a courtier and mocks the ways of the court. He denounces others as he unmasks himself. This combination of moral denunciation and self-exposure came to a head in a letter to Pope from October 1727, around the time he was finishing *The Beggar's Opera*. For much of the previous two years he had been writing and overseeing the production of a volume of fifty verse *Fables*, which he dedicated to George II's younger son, Prince William, six years old when the *Fables* appeared. Even though Gay had written to Swift during this period that 'I still despise Court Performents so that I lose no time upon attendance on great men', his dedication of the *Fables* to William was manifestly intended to win him a sinecure at court, and in fact it did so: in October 1727, Gay was offered the post of Gentleman Usher to the two-year-old Princess Louisa, at £150 per year.[18] Along with his Lottery post, this would have brought Gay an income of £300 for very little work, more than enough to make him 'independent'. But Gay found the offer

---

[17] Margaret Anne Doody, *The Daring Muse: Augustan Poetry Reconsidered* (Cambridge: Cambridge University Press, 1985), 211.

[18] Gay, letter to Swift, 22 Oct. 1726, in *The Letters of John Gay*, ed. C. F. Burgess (Oxford: Clarendon Press, 1966), 59.

demeaning, perhaps infantilizing, and was thrown into bitterness and despair. 'There is now what *Milton* says is in Hell,' he wrote to Pope: 'Darkness visible.—O that I had never known what a Court was! . . . Why did I not take your Advice before my writing Fables for the Duke, not to write them?'[19] Gay's rather theatrical outburst conveys both injury and moral outrage at the perfidy of the court: he should never have stooped so low as to place his trust in the nobility. Pope endorsed this view in his reply, urging Gay to 'enjoy . . . your own Integrity, and the satisfactory Consciousness of having *not* merited such Graces from them, as they bestow only on the mean, servile, flattering, interested, and undeserving'.[20] But Gay was too ironically self-aware to fully buy into Pope's stark contrast between courtly servility on the one hand and his 'own Integrity' on the other. Indeed, after regretting that he hadn't taken Pope's advice 'not to write' the *Fables*, he corrects himself: 'Or rather', he asks, why did he not 'write them for some [other] young Nobleman?' His fault was not to have sold his work for a place at court, but to have sold to the wrong buyer. In his next work, *The Beggar's Opera*, he would seek his fortune by selling himself at another market, that of the theatre-going public.

The Beggar's Opera

Gay's recognition—at once ironic and rueful—that he was no less complicit in the culture of the marketplace than the courtiers and politicians he equates with pimps and thieves in *The Beggar's Opera* and *Polly* gives both plays their distinctive tonal complexity, which derives from Gay's practice of taking 'double-mindedness' to its limits. *The Beggar's Opera* signals this from the start, in the dialogue between Beggar and Player who, although collaborators on the performance we are about to watch, represent distinct social worlds, those of the theatre and the prison ('our great Room at St. *Giles*'s' alluding to the Roundhouse or jail in the disreputable St Giles district of London). Introducing a Beggar as his authorial alter ego, Gay affiliates himself with the legion of impoverished hacks who were also compelled to live in St Giles, while the Beggar's 'small Yearly Salary

[19] Gay, letter to Pope, October 1727, ibid. 66.
[20] Pope, letter to Gay, in *Correspondence*, ii. 453.

for my Catches' parallels the political rewards Gay scraped for at court. The very term 'beggar's opera' is oxymoronic, a fusion of contraries, as is the pairing of street-ballad singers with 'our two Ladies', the opera divas parodied in the contest between Polly and Lucy. The Beggar who writes 'Catches' for his 'Dinner', like the Player who agrees to 'push his Play as far as it will go', stand in for Gay and his producer John Rich, but as men of business they also pave the way for Peachum, who opens the play proper sitting at a table with a theatrically oversize 'Book of Accounts' before him.

As we soon discover, Peachum is what audiences of the time would have recognized as a 'thief-taker', who works the reward system then in place, turning in criminals for the forty pounds blood money they brought, but also using the threat of betrayal as a method of control, a form of labour management. All the criminals listed in his account book work on his behalf. If, like Black Moll and Betty Sly, they are 'active and industrious', Peachum will 'soften the Evidence' to spare them from hanging or transportation, for as he says of Betty, 'I can get more by her staying in *England*' (p. 6). But if the thief in question, like Tom Gagg, is a 'lazy Dog' who brings no money in, the price is 'Death without Reprieve'. Playing the parts of both crime boss and police agent, Peachum acts 'in a double Capacity, both against Rogues and for 'em'; but in his case, the 'double Capacity' serves but a single interest, his own.

Through Peachum, then, Gay introduces one of the principal thematic strands running through both parts of *The Beggar's Opera*, the idea that everyone, in all walks of life, acts only out of self-interest, conceived of almost entirely in economic terms; and, intertwined with this, a corollary idea that for each of us, other people exist only as commodities to be bought, sold, or otherwise exploited. Peachum makes this claim in the play's opening lines, the words to its first song: 'Through *all* the Employments of Life | *Each* Neighbour abuses his Brother' (emphasis added). No one is immune, not even those pillars of society, the Statesman, Lawyer, and Priest, for all that they embody the institutions—state, law, and church—on which the whole social order rests. By equating them with rogues, cheats, and knaves, Peachum mocks their moral and social pretensions: the statesman may be 'great' in terms of status or power, but is not even as 'honest' as a thief-taker. And private life is as corrupt as public: the words 'Husband and Wife' are only respectable masks for

'Whore and Rogue'; and marriage is just as much based on the exchange of sexual for economic goods as is prostitution.

But Peachum's cynical, almost morally nihilistic claims merit a closer look. First of all, a line like 'Whore and Rogue they call Husband and Wife' is less simple than it appears. Who, to begin with, are 'they'? Are 'they' giving an actual 'Whore and Rogue' the unmerited titles of 'Husband and Wife', or insulting a true husband and wife by calling them whore and rogue? If the latter, why should we believe the insult? The fact that 'The Priest calls the Lawyer a Cheat' doesn't at all prove that the lawyer *is* a cheat, but it serves Peachum's interests for us to think he is, for by positing a universal moral (or immoral) equivalency, he can claim to justify his own murderous betrayals and extortion of stolen wealth as simply business as usual. In this opening scene, then, Gay too is acting 'in a double Capacity', both exposing the morally corrosive effects of the burgeoning commercial economy, and ideology, of early eighteenth-century England and inviting us to question the validity of Peachum's sweeping, cynical assertions.

Peachum acts in a double capacity in another sense, too, for he is not only an invented character in the Beggar's play but a recognizable dramatic portrait of one of the most hated and intriguing criminal figures of the period, the self-appointed Thief-Taker General of Great Britain, Jonathan Wild. Like Gay, Wild had thrown over his apprenticeship—in Wild's case, to a buckle-maker or 'Hardware Man'—to seek his fortune in London; and after a stint as second in command to the corrupt City Marshal Charles Hitchin, Wild left to set up his own business as receiver of stolen goods and gang boss.[21] He was able to capitalize on the absence of a formal or standing police force to control crime and law enforcement from both sides at once. The first steps towards a professional police force in London were only taken with the founding of the Bow Street Runners (a salaried body of constables) by Henry Fielding around 1750, and it was not until 1829 that Robert Peel established the London Metropolitan Police. In Gay's time, arrests and prosecutions depended on rewards

[21] Daniel Defoe (attrib.), *The True and Genuine Account of the Life and Actions of the Late Jonathan Wild* (1725), reprinted with *Colonel Jack* (Oxford: Basil Blackwell for the Shakespeare Head Press, 1927), ii. 236. The attribution of this text to Defoe is contested but widely accepted as likely. The best study of Wild's career is Gerald Howson, *Thief-Taker General: The Rise and Fall of Jonathan Wild* (New York: St. Martin's, 1971).

for information, but such information tended to come from those closest to the accused: it's no accident that Macheath is betrayed to the police first by his 'dear Slut' Jenny Diver (p. 32) and second by his fellow gang member Jemmy Twitcher. Wild exploited this system by creating a network of information and dependence, bringing London's thieves under his control by organizing a method for disposing of their loot—often acting as a middleman to restore the stolen goods to their original owners, for a generous finder's fee, but never handling the goods himself. He thus provided a service and a form of security to the criminals who worked for him, but only for as long as they brought in goods of greater value than the reward he could get for betraying them. He provided a service to the robbery victims as well, even if he was behind the crime in the first place, for at least theirs was not a total loss if Wild restored what others had stolen. And by regulating the activities of criminals on a business model, he brought a modicum of order to a disorderly city, as well as bringing scores of London's most wanted to justice.

Wild's double-dealing was no secret, but as he served the interests of criminals and the law alike—while of course constantly betraying both—he was tacitly licensed to stay in the role of Thief-Taker General for more than a decade, until his flagrant defiance of legal authority, and widespread outrage at his eagerness to condemn those in his power to death, led to his eventual prosecution and hanging in 1725. In a biography of the same year, probably written by Defoe, he is reviled as a corrupter of 'poor wretched Creatures, like himself; who he having first led them on in the Road of Crime for several Years, as long as they would be subservient to him, and put all their Purchase into his Hands, abandon'd as soon as they offer'd to set up for themselves, and leaving them to the mercy of the Government, made himself the Instrument of their Destruction'.[22] Peachum, looking through his account books and deploring the conduct of Wat Dreary, 'an irregular Dog, who hath an underhand way of disposing of his Goods', or planning to impeach Slippery Sam, 'for the Villain hath the Impudence to have views of following his Trade as a Taylor, which he calls an honest Employment' (p. 7), is a comic theatrical send-up of Wild, who 'abandon'd' his confederates 'as soon as they offer'd to set up for themselves', and 'made himself the Instrument of

---

[22] Defoe (attrib.), *True and Genuine Account*, 264.

their Destruction' for the sake of both short-term profit and long-term rule by intimidation over his criminal subjects.

If Wild as gang boss was a ruthless profiteer, as thief-taker he threatened to grab control of the machinery of the law. In effect, he had assumed the powers of a statesman, overseeing all the operations of the justice system. Gay had for some years been thinking about the parallels between statesmen and outlaws, seeing both as agents of corruption and plunder. In a letter of 1723, he wrote, 'I cannot indeed wonder that the Talents requisite for a great Statesman are so scarce in the world since so many of those who possess them are every month cut off in the prime of their Age at the Old-Baily . . . A Highwayman never picks up an honest man for a companion, but if such a one accidentally falls in his way; if he cannot turn his heart He like a wise Statesman discards him.'[23] If the equation Gay makes here is generic rather than specific, it has long been held that in *The Beggar's Opera* he intended audiences to recognize Peachum not just as a portrait of Wild but, by extension, as a satirical likeness of the then chief Minister of State—in effect, the Prime Minister—Sir Robert Walpole.[24] A consummate political operator, Walpole so dominated British politics from 1721 to 1742 that, as Paul Langford writes, 'he came to stand for an entire system of finance and government' which was viewed by its enemies as no better than a kleptocracy, a government of thieves.[25] Walpole ran the government by way of a canny balancing of competing interests, currying royal favour with George I and George II (with the latter, in part, through his friendship with Queen Caroline) and securing ministerial and parliamentary support via a combination of patronage (or pay-offs), persuasion (or strong-arming), and pragmatism (or unscrupulousness). Like the highwayman in Gay's letter, he would 'discard' any honest man he chanced to meet if he could not 'turn his heart'—that is, make him his accomplice—and he would only patronize those from whom he could expect some material benefit in return. Such, at any rate, was the view of the opposition and of those, like Gay, whose hopes for advancement he had disappointed. Still smarting from what he saw

[23] Gay, letter to Henrietta Howard, *c*.August 1723, in *Letters*, ed. Burgess, 45.
[24] The office of Prime Minister did not exist at this time, but Walpole is generally credited with creating the role.
[25] Paul Langford, *Walpole and the Robinocracy* (Cambridge: Chadwyck-Healey, 1986), 22.

as the demeaning offer to serve as Gentleman Usher to Princess Louisa, which he believed was Walpole's doing, Gay had both personal and ideological reasons to hold up Walpole and his 'corrupt' regime for satiric ridicule in *The Beggar's Opera*.

Yet the more closely one looks at the play and its reception, the less convincing it is to treat it as just an attack on Walpole. The one clear allusion to Walpole comes when Peachum reads out the last of the names from his account book: '*Robin* of *Bagshot*, alias *Gorgon*, alias *Bluff Bob*, alias *Carbuncle*, alias *Bob Booty*' (p. 7). All of these are satirical digs at the Prime Minister, whose government was known by its opponents as a 'Robinocracy' (with a pun on Robin/robbing); 'Bob Booty' even became a popular opposition nickname.[26] But this otherwise insignificant character has only one line (in II.i), which could have been given to any of the gang. Peachum, a master manipulator, has seemed to later commentators the most Walpolean figure in the play; but to writers of the time, it was Lockit, 'the *prime Minister of Newgate*', and Macheath, the gang leader, who were thought to represent '*somebody in Authority*': code for Walpole.[27] To these four supposed stand-ins for the Prime Minister one could add Jemmy Twitcher, who 'peaches' Macheath in Act III; Filch, who, Mrs Peachum claims, 'wilt be a great Man in History' (p. 11; the phrase 'great man', also used of Macheath, was applied satirically to Walpole by the opposition press); and doubtless others. If Walpole were really the target of Gay's satire, this surfeit of mock-Walpoles would surely dilute and confuse the message. Rather than hunt for specific equivalences, it would be truer to Gay's authorial approach to treat these fleeting and multiple allusions to Walpole, Wild, and other contemporary figures as devices for jolting, or comically startling, the audience into recognizing unexpected affinities: between thief-takers and ministers of state, highwaymen and courtiers, executioner and businessman. Cutting across differences of class, power, age, gender, and profession, this network of affinities among diverse characters shapes Gay's depiction of a society in which everyone,

---

[26] For more on these names, see the Explanatory Notes, p. 191.

[27] 'Phil. Harmonicus', letter to *The Craftsman*, 85 (17 Feb. 1728), quoted in Schultz, *Gay's Beggar's Opera*, 181; and Nokes, *John Gay*, 435. See also the discussion in Winton, *John Gay and the London Theatre*, 103–5, and William McIntosh, 'Handel, Walpole, and Gay: The Aims of *The Beggar's Opera*', *Eighteenth-Century Studies*, 7:4 (1974), 415–33, esp. 428–31.

from Polly Peachum to Robert Walpole, is caught up in a nexus of buying and selling, conning and thieving, swindles and cheats.

This disenchanted perspective on all social relationships pervades *The Beggar's Opera* and is woven into almost every character's speech. We find it in Filch's song ''Tis Woman that seduces all Mankind', in which women deploy their beauty for financial gain—'She tricks us of our Money with our Hearts'—while men offer money to buy sexual favours: 'For Suits of Love, like Law, are won by Pay, | And Beauty must be fee'd into our Arms' (p. 6). In this transaction, both parties benefit from their mutual exploitation, and lovers, like lawyers or statesmen, bribe their way to success. Mrs Peachum puts things still more starkly in a characteristically cynical air, singing, 'A Maid is like the golden Oar [ore], | Which hath Guineas intrinsical in't' (p. 11), reducing sexual 'purity' to currency. Macheath, taking advantage of Lucy Lockit's fondness to effect his escape from prison, assures her that 'Money well tim'd, and properly apply'd, will do any thing' (p. 42), equating sexual seduction to bribing a bureaucrat in the song he sings by way of illustration. Lockit, '*prime Minister of Newgate*', attributes this ruthless system of self-interest to human nature, asserting that 'Of all Animals of Prey, Man is the only sociable one. Every one of us preys upon his Neighbour, and yet we herd together' (p. 50). Macheath, by contrast, offers a political explanation, singing, 'The Modes of the Court so common are grown, | That a true Friend can hardly be met; | Friendship for Interest is but a Loan, | Which they let out for what they can get' (p. 52). Although later events will call his boasts into question, Macheath assures his gang mates that he is not 'a meer Court Friend, who professes every thing and will do nothing': only the outlaw, he brags, has 'Honour enough to break through the Corruptions of the World'.

In making this claim, Macheath adopts one of the play's two principal, overlapping, satirical strategies. If the first, as in Peachum's air, is to assert an equivalency between seeming opposites (high and low, statesman and thief-taker, wife and whore), the second is to invert the conventional valuation of contrasting terms, so the outlaw, for example, is more honourable than the courtier. The equation of high and low runs through *Polly* as well, as when the maid Flimzy, accepting a bribe to spy on her mistress, sings, 'My conscience is of courtly mold, | Fit for highest station. | Where's the hand, when touch'd with gold, | Proof against temptation?' (p. 88); while the strategy of inversion is put to more complex use in Gay's staging of the relations among Indians, pirates, and 'lawful' English colonials, through which he tests Lockit's claim that predation is a defining mark of the human.

Against the pervasive sordidness of Lockit's and the Peachums' world—and the offhand betrayals of Jenny Diver, Jemmy Twitcher, and Mrs Trapes—Macheath, Polly, and Lucy appear all the more affecting and alive. Entering halfway through the second act and playing the part of woman wronged to the hilt, Lucy swings wildly from tenderness to fury to grim determination (as when she tries to poison Polly with 'Rats-bane', p. 58); but while she could be played as a comic or even ludicrous figure, her emotional extremes bring a dramatic intensity to the action that catches the audience off-guard. Her scenes are the closest thing in the play to a parody of Italian *opera seria*, with its revenge arias and love-rivalry duets, but Gay's parody is also a kind of homage, and the contrast between Lucy's passion and her father's and the Peachums' coarse calculations of profit works entirely to her advantage.[28]

Polly is a more complex, even troubled figure, but beloved for her supposed simplicity. James Boswell, in his *Life of Johnson*, records a story that on the play's opening night there was 'a disposition to damn it' until Lavinia Fenton sang Polly's touching air 'Oh, ponder well!' (Air 12) whereupon, 'the audience being much affected by the innocent looks of Polly', the play was 'saved'.[29] Although some critics, notably William Empson, have argued that Polly is in truth as duplicitous and self-interested as any character in the play, she has more often been interpreted as genuinely virtuous: naïve perhaps, but innocent, faithful, loving, sincere.[30] In acting contrary to the mercenary ethos of the world around her—as when she says, of Macheath, 'I did not marry him (as 'tis the Fashion) cooly and deliberately for Honour or Money. But, I love him' (p. 15)—she is a figure of moral

---

[28] On some of the operatic antecedents to these scenes in *The Beggar's Opera*, see Bertrand H. Bronson, 'The Beggar's Opera', in *Studies in the Comic*, University of California Publications in English, 8:2 (1941), 197–231. Bronson argues persuasively that the play as a whole 'may more properly be regarded as a testimonial to the strength of opera's appeal to John Gay's imagination than as a deliberate attempt to ridicule it out of existence' (p. 217).

[29] James Boswell, *Life of Johnson*, ed. Hill (ii. 368).

[30] See William Empson, *Some Versions of Pastoral* [1935] (London: Chatto and Windus, 1968), esp. 239–47. Against Empson, see Toni-Lynn O'Shaughnessy, 'A Single Capacity in *The Beggar's Opera*', *Eighteenth-Century Studies*, 21:2 (1987–88), 212–27.

integrity amidst the degraded values most vividly embodied by her parents. Polly's naïveté is suggested by her remark to Macheath, when he avows his fidelity to her: 'Nay, my Dear, I have no Reason to doubt you, for I find in the Romance you lent me, none of the great Heroes were ever false in Love' (p. 22). Her misreading is double, first in believing Macheath to be a great hero, and second in crediting romance as a true reflection of life. But if love at first blinds her to Macheath's real character, she learns from experience, later reflecting, 'When I was forc'd from him, he did not shew the least Tenderness.—But perhaps, he hath a Heart not capable of it' (p. 60). Even if she is initially naïve about Macheath, from the outset she is canny enough to address her father in his terms, reassuring him that 'A Woman knows how to be mercenary, though she hath never been in a Court or at an Assembly. We have it in our Natures, Papa. If I allow Captain *Macheath* some trifling Liberties, I have this Watch and other visible Marks of his Favour to show for it' (p. 13). She deliberately misleads him, both as to the real nature of her relationship with Macheath and as to the fact that she has hidden him in her bedroom, for however heartfelt her pleas to her parents to spare him, she knows how they think, and that her principles are not theirs. She acts the part of one who 'knows how to be mercenary' in order to affirm a contrary set of values.

By the end of *The Beggar's Opera*, Polly sees Macheath clearly. 'The Coquets of both Sexes', she declares, 'are Self-lovers, and that is a Love no other whatever can dispossess. I fear, my dear *Lucy*, our Husband is one of those' (p. 60). Yet as the events of the sequel show, clear-sightedness cannot dictate desire. Polly confesses as much when she says, of Macheath, 'He ran into the madness of every vice. I detest his principles, tho' I am fond of his person to distraction' (p. 155). Even as she seeks to act on virtuous principles, Polly acknowledges that for her, physical desire, a kind of 'distraction' or 'madness', is at the heart of what she calls love. In that respect, she hints that she is more like Macheath than her principles allow her to know.

Macheath is the most problematic character in *The Beggar's Opera* (and becomes even more so in *Polly*). Before he makes an appearance on stage, Mrs Peachum says, 'Sure there is not a finer Gentleman upon the Road than the Captain!' (p. 9). He has become the archetype of the cavalier highwayman: libertine in morality, refined in

manners, courageous in action—a natural if low-born aristocrat.[31]
Peachum calls him 'a great Man' and lauds 'his Personal Bravery' and
'fine Stratagem' (p. 21); and Macheath characterizes himself and his
gang as men of 'Honour'. Yet in the play itself Macheath exhibits no
bravery: indeed, as Pat Rogers notes, 'Macheath is basically a supine
character, bought and sold by other characters, and never seen in the
commission of a successful crime'.[32] He chooses not to join in
the gang's expedition when Peachum is after him, and is curiously
defensive about this, asking, 'Is there any man who suspects my
Courage? . . . My Honour and Truth to the Gang?' (pp. 26–7). At
three different points in the play, he is found hiding from Peachum
in the company of women—with Polly in Act I, with the whores in
Act II, and again with Mrs Coaxer in Act III—which attests to his
libertine sexual appetite but also has the effect of feminizing him. His
'escapes' at the end of each act are engineered by others (Polly, Lucy,
and the Beggar); and the only way he can face his own death is by
drinking himself into oblivion as he waits in the condemned hold,
singing pathetically, 'O Leave me to Thought! I fear! I doubt! |
I tremble! I droop!—See, my Courage is out' (p. 68) as he turns up
the bottle he has emptied.

One could go on: Macheath is a faithless liar to Lucy and Polly;
his repeated uses of the word 'honour' are as duplicitous and
self-serving as Lockit's (see, for example, his dialogue with Lucy
in II.ix); he is no genuine but a strictly counterfeit 'Captain'.[33] As
Steve Newman writes in an incisive reading of the last prison
scene, with its medley of song fragments, 'Just as Macheath can
be seen as a recycled and debased figure patched together from
romances and playbooks, a history of heroism repeated as farce, his
bravery in this scene consists of scraps of low songs stitched
together.'[34] But that is only half the story, for Macheath's medley

---

[31] On Macheath and the figure of the highwayman in general, see Erin Mackie, *Rakes,
Highwaymen, and Pirates: The Making of the Modern Gentleman in the Eighteenth Century*
(Baltimore: Johns Hopkins University Press, 2009), esp. 71–113.

[32] Pat Rogers, 'Macheath and the Gaol-Breakers', *Literature and History*, 14:2 (2005),
14–36 (at 15).

[33] On 'honour' as 'a convenient code of self-interest' in *The Beggar's Opera*, see David
Nokes, *Raillery and Rage: A Study of Eighteenth-Century Satire* (Brighton: Harvester,
1987), 142–4.

[34] Steve Newman, 'The Value of "Nothing": Ballads in *The Beggar's Opera*', *The
Eighteenth Century: Theory and Interpretation*, 45:3 (2004), 265–83 (at 275).

ends with one of the play's two most powerful political statements, his rewriting of the ancient ballad 'Greensleeves'. Comparing his own crimes to those of his social betters, Macheath sings, 'But Gold from Law can take out the Sting; | And if rich Men like us were to swing, | 'Twou'd thin the Land, such Numbers to string | Upon *Tyburn* Tree!' (p. 66). As Newman writes, 'at this moment, we are asked not only to sympathize with him but also to admire his insistent truth-telling in the face of death'—all the more so in light of the play's second key political statement, spoken moments later by Gay's alter ego, the Beggar, who states the play's 'Moral': 'that the lower Sort of People have their Vices in a degree as well as the Rich: And that they'—and *only* they, he implies by omission—'are punish'd for them' (p. 69). Echoing Macheath's devastating critique of the legal system, the Beggar confirms his highwayman's status as a proper hero.

But no sooner does Macheath earn our sympathy and admiration than he reverts to maudlin self-pity ('I tremble! I droop!'). It is a turn characteristic of Gay's dramatic approach, which 'disorients by making its audience sympathize where they also ridicule'.[35] This double, divided response is the keynote of *The Beggar's Opera*, as it will be of *Polly*, and is produced most vividly by the songs that are its most original feature. In a masterful reading of the 'Cotillon' in II.iv ('Youth's the Season made for Joys'), Margaret Doody draws out the song's twofold effect. On the one hand, we are fully aware of the singers' ludicrous posturing. A self-indulgent thief and the group of hard-drinking 'Sluts' he has hired for the night ape the manners of 'fine ladies' and gentlemen, and mask the realities of their degraded lives in the language of a lyric worthy of such Cavalier poets as Robert Herrick:

> Let us drink and sport to-day,
>   Ours is not to-morrow.
> Love with Youth flies swift away,
>   Age is nought but Sorrow.
>   Dance and sing,
>   Time's on the Wing.
>   Life never knows the return of Spring. (p. 30)

---

[35] Howard Erskine-Hill, 'The Significance of Gay's Drama', in Marie Axton and Raymond Williams, eds., *English Drama: Forms and Development* (Cambridge: Cambridge University Press, 1977), 142–63, at 152.

The contrast between the refinement of the lyric and the coarseness of the prose that surrounds it only underlines the squalor of the scene and of the characters' motives. On the other hand, as Doody writes, 'the melody itself touches us . . . We are not allowed to hang on to pure satire and dismiss the song, any more than we can hang on to the loveliness of the song and eliminate the vulgarity and crassness of the characters, or the satire on human nature. One effect does not cancel out the other.'[36] To take another case, Polly's Air 6, following her cynical assurance to her father that 'a Woman knows how to be mercenary', elicits at least three sorts of reaction: first, amusement at her artless use of the trite similes (the bee, the flower) promised in the Beggar's Introduction; second, a recoil from the harshness of her account of what becomes of a fair virgin once she is 'pluck'd' and forced to sell herself in Covent Garden—where, riddled with venereal disease, she 'rots, stinks, and dies, and is trod under feet'; third, a sympathetic melancholy produced by the minor-key beauty of Henry Purcell's melody. The music offers a momentary emotional respite, or refuge, from the surrounding darkness. By way of the various affective responses it elicits, it also makes a more complex character of Polly, who becomes something other than a moral emblem or 'type'; and to varying degrees this is true of all the characters given songs in *The Beggar's Opera*. The music—and the wit and lyricism of the song texts—is not ornamental or decorative, but integral to the meanings of the work as a whole. Reading is not enough; like any play, but more so than most because of the way music shapes our response to the action on stage, *The Beggar's Opera* is only fully realized in performance.

Hence the suppression of *Polly*. Walpole, acting through the Lord Chamberlain, pulled the play from rehearsal, so for the rest of Gay's life and almost half a century after, it languished in a kind of limbo: not banned outright, but not allowed to be brought to life on stage, whence its songs might have been taken up and circulated back into the streets from which they sprang. *Polly*, like the third edition of *The Beggar's Opera*, was published with both the melodies and the accompanying bass lines printed at the end of the volume. The words were printed between the treble and bass staves, so readers who had

---

[36] Doody, *The Daring Muse*, 213. For similarly nuanced readings of the complex effects of other songs in the play, see Newman, 'The Value of "Nothing"', 277–8, and Dugaw, *Deep Play*, 169–85.

some musical training could have sung the airs to a simple keyboard accompaniment, or played the tunes on recorder or violin. But such private performances of the songs must have been relatively rare, and would not have had anything like the impact of hearing the airs sung in character by singer-actors in a crowded, buzzy playhouse in London or Dublin or Bath. Many in the audience—especially those who were seeing the play for a second or third or fourth time—would have hummed along with the actors, for most of the tunes in both plays were from familiar street or folk ballads, often reprinted in such collections of dance tunes and songs as John and Henry Playford's *The Dancing Master*, Thomas D'Urfey's *Wit and Mirth: Or Pills to Purge Melancholy*, and William Thomson's anthology of Scots songs, *Orpheus Caledonius*. A handful of airs in *The Beggar's Opera*, and more in *Polly*, were adapted from the work of such opera and theatre composers as Henry Purcell, Giovanni Bononcini, Attilio Ariosti, and George Frideric Handel, the last of whom had collaborated with Gay on the operatic masque *Acis and Galatea*. These tunes, although not popular in the sense of a folk or broadside ballad, would also have been known to many in the original audience, so Gay could play off their original words and associations to produce complex effects of echo or irony in his new songs. In performance, these effects would be vivid and shared, and any digs at Walpole or other contemporary figures would provoke public laughter and applause. To bar *Polly* from the stage was to mute the political challenge Walpole evidently feared it posed.[37]

Polly

How audiences might have responded to 'the second part of The Beggar's Opera' is, of course, impossible to know. They would

---

[37] In *The Beggar's Opera*'s original production, the songs were provided with accompaniments by the composer Johann Christoph Pepusch (b. 1667, Berlin; d. 1752, London), who also composed the overture. The basses in both the third edition of *The Beggar's Opera* and the first of *Polly* are Pepusch's, but the melodies were selected by Gay from the various sources discussed here and in the Appendix. See Jeremy Barlow, ed., *The Music of John Gay's The Beggar's Opera* (Oxford and New York: Oxford University Press, 1990), esp. pp. ix–xv, 108–16. The overture of *The Beggar's Opera* is scored for 2 oboes, 2 violins, viola, and continuo (harpsichord and cello or other bass instruments), but the songs were probably more simply accompanied, by unison strings and continuo.

probably have been startled by the shift of scene from Newgate to the West Indies, which signals a radical break from the lowlife milieu so integral to the first part's disreputable charm, while the play's title signals another radical shift, from a male to a female protagonist. Between the first part and the second, Macheath has been transported as a slave to the Indies, and Peachum has been hanged. Polly has come to find and reclaim her husband, but learns in the opening scenes that some time since, 'he robb'd his master, ran away from the plantation and turn'd pyrate' (p. 90). Worse yet, he has married Jenny Diver, who had also been transported as a prisoner-slave. The final character carried over from *The Beggar's Opera* is Mrs Trapes: she promises to treat Polly, who was robbed of her money on the voyage out, as a daughter, but instead sells her as a slave to the plantation owner Ducat. Just as he tries to force himself on her, news comes that pirates, led by one Morano, an ex-slave, 'are ravaging and plund'ring the country' (p. 103); in the confusion, Polly, dressed as a man, escapes.

In the second act, set in 'Indian Country', she is captured by some of Morano's pirate crew and taken to his camp, where we discover that, unknown to anyone but Jenny, Morano is really Macheath in blackface. As the pirates, joined by escaped plantation slaves, pursue their campaign of plunder against the colonists and their allies the Indians, Jenny urges Morano to make 'a judicious retreat' (p. 117), rob his own crew, and 'steal off to *England*'. Torn between the pirates' battle-lust and Jenny's blandishments, Morano tries to decide on a course of action, while first Polly and then the Indian prince Cawwawkee are brought before him as prisoners. Just as Polly fails to see through his disguise as an ex-slave, so Morano fails to see through her impersonation of a male. Jenny, attracted to this 'mighty pretty man', kisses and tries to seduce her, but Polly resists her advances. Meanwhile, Morano interrogates Cawwawkee. When the latter refuses to say where the Indians' gold is hidden, he is put in chains, but Polly bribes their guards to free them. Finally bowing to Jenny's advice, Morano and his lieutenant Vanderbluff are about to seize the ships while their comrades are engaged in battle when they learn their path has been cut off, so, having no retreat, they determine to 'conquer or die' (p. 134).

In the play's final act, Polly joins the Indian forces against the rebel slaves and pirates. Morano tries to negotiate a private deal with the Indian king, Pohetohee; but the latter spurns his proposal, and

battle begins. The Indian forces triumph. Cawwawkee, separated
from Polly, fears s/he has been slain, but s/he soon reappears, having
caught Morano just as he was 'flying with all the cowardice of guilt
upon him' (p. 149). In quick succession, Morano is sentenced to
death, Polly reveals she is a woman seeking her unworthy husband,
and Jenny pleads for Morano's life. When she reveals he is no other
than Macheath in disguise, Polly joins in her plea—but too late, for
he has already been executed. As Pohetohee orders the rebel leaders
to be killed and the slaves sent back into slavery, Cawwawkee asks the
grieving Polly to marry him. She in turn asks him to let her devote
'a decent time to my sorrows' (p. 160), and they leave stage before
a final, celebratory dance and hymn to justice.

Unlike *The Beggar's Opera*, with its undeserved reprieve and
its cheerfully amoral final couplet—'But think of this Maxim, and
put off your Sorrow, | The Wretch of To-day, may be happy
To-morrow'—*Polly* really does end as 'a down-right deep Tragedy'
(p. 69). In defying the Player's contention in *The Beggar's Opera* that
such a 'Catastrophe is manifestly wrong, for an Opera must end
happily', the Poet of *Polly* is, at least ostensibly, fulfilling the
Beggar's original intention in the earlier play of 'doing strict poetical
Justice'; as he tells the First Player in *Polly*'s Introduction, 'I will not
so much as seem to give up my moral' (p. 78). The Poet's declaration
is echoed in Howard Erskine-Hill's statement that, with *Polly*, 'Gay
does move in the direction of a more straightforward kind of moral
play . . . a more stable moral fiction than the *Opera*, with a clear and
firm conclusion'.[38] Far from praising Gay for this moral turn, however, many critics have scorned *Polly*'s 'high tone' as 'self-righteous',
and deplored the schematic way in which 'society', in the later work,
'splits into heroes and villains', so that 'there is no doubt at all where
one's sympathies are to lie'.[39] Starting with Dianne Dugaw's
reappraisal of *Polly*, however, this 'second part of The Beggar's
Opera' has begun to be read as in some ways more provocative, more
challenging, more *contemporary* than its more familiar precursor.[40]

[38] Erskine-Hill, 'The Significance of Gay's Drama', 159.

[39] Empson, *Some Versions of Pastoral*, 239; Patricia Meyer Spacks, *John Gay*
(New York: Twayne, 1965), 160.

[40] Dianne Dugaw, *Warrior Women and Popular Balladry, 1650–1850* (Cambridge:
Cambridge University Press, 1989), esp. 191–211. Dugaw offers an abbreviated version
of this argument in *Deep Play*, 185–96.

Dugaw locates the source of *Polly*'s plot in the 'female war-rior' motif so pervasive in the English ballad tradition from the Elizabethan period on. In such ballads, the heroine dresses as a man and goes to sea or to war for the sake of her (male) beloved, with whom in the end she is reunited. By doing so, she affirms the conven-tionally feminine-coded ideal of love—but only, as Dugaw argues, by also appropriating the masculine-coded ideal of martial glory or val-our to win her endangered lover back. In *Polly*, the heroine similarly proves herself both steadfast in love and brave in battle; but Gay almost cruelly denies her, and us, the reward of her simultaneously feminine and masculine virtue. The culmination of her heroic ven-tures is to take her own lover prisoner and so bring about his igno-minious offstage death, while her naïve faith that her 'love might still reclaim' (p. 155) the reprobate Macheath is dashed by her inability even to recognize him in his blackface disguise as Morano. As she asks herself, too late, in anguish, 'Why could not I know him?' (p. 157); and the question pertains not just to his theatrical make-up but more generally to his moral character, to which she has to blind herself in order to sustain the fiction of virtuous love. In truth, there is little to differentiate between Polly and Jenny Diver as far as love goes: Jenny professes to 'have so much power over him, that I can even make him good' (p. 156), but has no more ground for saying so than Polly; while Polly, pressed to explain her love for a man who 'ran into the madness of every vice' (p. 155), is forced to admit that while she 'detests his principles', she is 'fond of his person'—his body, his looks—'to distraction'. But 'distraction' is just another word for 'madness', and Polly is as much in its grip as Macheath.

Unable to redeem, or even know, her beloved, Polly is faced, by the end of the play, with the ruin of her heroic quest and the romantic ideal that inspired it. In light of that ruin, Cawwawkee's verdict that 'Justice hath reliev'd you from the society of a wicked man' (p. 159), leading into his marriage offer, has a nasty, opportunistic ring, while the closing hymn to justice mocks Polly's failure to save Macheath, figured as a hunted animal: 'What tongues then defend him? | Or what hand will succour lend him? | Even his friends attend him, | To foment the chace' (p. 161). It is difficult to read this ending, in which the shattered, defeated Polly has to exit before the 'sports and dances' can begin, as offering 'a clear and firm conclusion'. Even the marriage of Polly and Cawwawkee, which almost every earlier critic has viewed as 'inevitable', is far from certain. Cawwawkee proposes by stating that 'my titles, my treasures, are all at your command' (p. 160), but Polly's response is to sing that she desires neither: 'Frail is ambition, how weak the foundation! | Riches have wings as inconstant as wind; | My heart is proof against either temptation, | Virtue, without them, contentment can find'.[41] Even more than in *The Beggar's Opera*, Gay leaves us torn between the desire for a happy ending and a disenchanted, ironic recognition of the 'absurdity' (p. 77) of such endings, and such desires, in a world where the hunger for 'titles' and 'treasures' overwhelms every other motive.

Polly's West Indian setting affiliates it to a significant line of English plays set in the new world, from Shakespeare's *The Tempest* to Thomas Southerne's *Oroonoko* (based on Aphra Behn's novel-romance) and Behn's own *The Widow Ranter*, all of them playing on the tension between a newly discovered, seemingly natural realm and the political and social corruptions of contemporary England. Like these plays, and such other precursors as Montaigne's essay 'Of Cannibals' (on which Shakespeare drew in *The Tempest*) and Swift's *Gulliver's Travels*, *Polly* stages the confrontation between European colonizers and the other peoples they encounter as a vehicle for satirical reflection on European cultural norms; but it also comments on issues of racial difference, the transatlantic slave trade, and the ethics of colonialist expropriation.[42] Not that Gay ever states outright his position on these issues. Instead, as in *The Beggar's Opera*, he uses irony, inversion, reversals of expectations, and the satirical equation of opposites to jolt the audience out of its taken-for-granted ways of thinking and feeling. So the new world's Indians uphold the classical

---

[41] In a suggestive reading of *Polly*'s ending as 'a ludic dance on the grave of the feudal ethos', J. Douglas Canfield describes Polly and Cawwawkee's marriage as 'inevitable', but also as 'patently absurd', writing that 'Gay's wish-fulfillment ending is thoroughly satirical'. See Canfield, *Heroes and States: On the Ideology of Restoration Tragedy* (Lexington, KY: The University Press of Kentucky, 2000), 197–8.

[42] On racial difference and cross-race mimicry, see Peter P. Reed, 'Conquer or Die: Staging Circum-Atlantic Revolt in *Polly* and *Three-Finger'd Jack*', *Theatre Journal*, 59 (2007), 241–58, and *Rogue Performances: Staging the Underclasses in Early American Theatre Culture* (New York: Palgrave Macmillan, 2009). On issues of slavery and the ethics of colonialism, see Robert G. Dryden, 'John Gay's *Polly*: Unmasking Pirates and Fortune Hunters in the West Indies', *Eighteenth-Century Studies*, 34 (2001), 539–57; John Richardson, 'John Gay and Slavery', *Modern Language Review*, 97 (2002), 15–25; Dugaw, *Warrior Women*, 196–211; and Noelle Chao, 'Music and Indians in John Gay's *Polly*', in Patricia Fumerton and Anita Guerrini with Kris McAbee, eds., *Ballads and Broadsides in Britain, 1500–1800* (Farnham: Ashgate, 2010), 297–316.

Western ideals of justice and honour, only to be derided as 'down-right Barbarians' (p. 127) by a gang of pirates. So the same pirate gang talk of dividing up the new world, 'squabbling' over who shall have Mexico, who Peru, and who Cuba, only to be mocked by Polly as 'those brave spirits, those *Alexanders*, that shall soon by conquest be in possession of the *Indies*' (p. 114).[43] So Macheath, in his great, defiant last scene, having equated piracy and the founding of empires—'*Alexander* the great was more successful. That's all'—then turns the tables on his 'noble' captors, the Indians, singing 'If justice had piercing eyes, | Like ourselves to look within, | She'd find power and wealth a disguise | That shelter the worst of our kin' (p. 152). Here, unexpectedly, it is Macheath who speaks truth to power. His judges do not have 'piercing eyes'; they cannot penetrate his own, literal, blackface disguise (which makes him a doubly marginal or outcast figure, both pirate and slave); nor can they see beneath the disguise of power and wealth to recognize their ally, the grasping, sexually predatory colonial landowner Ducat, as indeed 'the worst' of the pirates' 'kin', guilty of the same crimes, but on a larger scale. Coming so soon after Macheath's last words (which echo the 'Moral' of *The Beggar's Opera*), the Indians' concluding hymn to 'Justice long forbearing' cannot simply be taken at face value, for their 'justice' is as biased towards the powerful and rich as is the legal system so caustically denounced in the earlier play.

Gay's presentation of the Indians in *Polly* is typical of the sly, underhand way he plays with notions of difference—moral, racial, sexual—throughout the play. As Albert Wertheim has noted, 'the three acts of *Polly* take the title character into three sectors of the new world': those of the colonial slave-owners; of the pirates who prey on legitimate traders; and of the Indians who seem to embody 'the moral paradise that Europeans hoped existed across the Atlantic'.[44] Certainly Cawwawkee and Pohetohee are prone to passing imperious judgements on the moral flaws of those they scathingly call 'European', as when Cawwawkee tells Polly that, 'contrary to the *European* custom', he 'will perform' what he has promised (p. 136).[45]

[43] See Dugaw, *Warrior Women*, 200–1.

[44] Albert Wertheim, '*Polly*: John Gay's Image of the West', in Dunbar H. Ogden, Douglas McDermott, and Robert K. Sarlós, eds., *Theatre West: Image and Impact* (Amsterdam: Rodopi, 1990), 195–206, at 196, 206.

[45] For other examples of the use of 'European' as an insult, see pp. 128, 136, 140, 151, and 156.

And clearly it is to his discredit that Morano mocks the Indians as 'Barbarians' for having 'our notional honour still in practice among 'em' (p. 127). Against such morally compromised characters as Morano, Jenny, and Ducat, Cawwawkee and Pohetohee come off well by the comparison, and it may seem that they are meant to serve as the author's moral surrogates. This view has been almost unanimous among the play's critics, and is all the more credible given Polly's many admiring comments on Cawwawkee's 'virtues' (p. 134).

Yet it would be strange for a writer as relentlessly ironic as Gay, in a comedy so teeming with cases of feigned, mistaken, and secret identity, to intend for the Indian characters alone to be taken straight, as if we had to accept them at their solemn word. We have already seen how, in his last song, Morano calls into question the Indians' notion of justice, explicitly equating this to the corrupt Newgate system he knew in another life. But there are signs all through the play that we should be sceptical of any claims that the Indians embody an idealized state of natural virtue, the most damning of which is the fact of their alliance with Ducat and his ilk. For all their contempt of 'Europeans', the Indians are in league with the worst of that race. Indeed, rather than being 'set apart from the mercenary activities of the other characters, the Indians', as Noelle Chao argues, 'are active participants in a global system of corruption'.[46] Their complicity extends to armed support of the colonial slave system, for not only do they defend the colonials' property against the slave uprising occurring offstage, they round up the rebels on Pohetohee's orders, so that they can 'be restor'd to their owners, and return to their slavery' (p. 159). Whatever Gay's views on the colonial slave trade as practised in the 1720s, Pohetohee's complicity with Ducat disturbs the simple, moralistic opposition of European and Indian, and signals that the second term offers no secure ground for critiquing or denouncing the first.[47]

---

[46] Chao, 'Music and Indians', 309.

[47] Dugaw, noting that 'the issue of slavery . . . permeates *Polly*' (*Warrior Women*, 206), insists that Gay writes in opposition to it, and to 'the heroic ideal as an ethos of slavery' (p. 196). John Richardson, by contrast, contends that while the play 'generates sympathy for the enslaved English heroine', it supports 'the systematic enslavement of Africans' ('John Gay and Slavery', 16). See also Richardson, *Slavery and Augustan Literature: Swift, Pope, Gay* (London: Routledge, 2004), esp. 113–20, for a somewhat tempered version of this argument.

Similarly, in one of their quasi-amorous duets, Polly and Cawwawkee sing friendship's praises in terms that suggest the corrupting influence of the same commercial ideology exposed in *The Beggar's Opera*: 'All friendship is a mutual debt, | The contract's inclination: | We never can that bond forget | Of sweet retaliation' (p. 153). On one hand, this can be read as a lyric that undoes the damaging effects of the commercial ethos by using commercial terms—debt, contract, bond—to celebrate a 'mutual', non-exploitative relationship between equals. In that light, the delicate oxymoron of 'sweet retaliation' points to an emotional sincerity and warmth not subject to calculations of profit. On the other hand, and in light of Cawwawkee's attempt to win Polly's hand by offering her 'titles' and 'treasures', the language of contracts and debts insinuates that friendship is not only about sincere feeling, but also implies obligation, the necessity of repaying whatever has been given us: friendship, like love, is for sale. From that angle, Polly's lines later in the duet—'All day, and every day the same | We are paying and still owing'—suggest an endless, unpayable debt, like a mortgage, a 'bond' in the sense of shackles, with a further suggestion of bondservant or slave. None of this is to say that the affective bond (in the sense of friendship) between the two is not genuine, but rather that the 'European' ethos of the marketplace—now including the slave market—can be felt in all areas of life.

Cawwawkee and Polly's duet in praise of friendship contains at least one further twist or strand, however. The melody to which it is sung, 'Prince George', is from a song celebrating the 1683 marriage of Prince George of Denmark and Princess (later Queen) Anne; so that anyone who remembered the original might have picked up on a romantic-erotic second sense running just under the surface of the lyric. Of course, it might be a stretch to suggest that audiences would have recalled the original words to a forty-five-year-old song and, from that, have inferred a coded sexual meaning to this air. But Air 62 is the fourth in a series of songs, three of them duets, in which the melodies Cawwawkee and Polly sing vividly evoke a familiar precursor song of love or erotic longing.[48] In the first, Air 47, the words are typical of Cawwawkee's sententious rhetoric—'Virtue's treasure | Is a pleasure, | Cheerful even amid distress'—but the

---

[48] See the Appendix for further details on Airs 47, 57, 58, and 62.

music, along with the stage image Gay meant the audience to see, playfully undermines the sermonizing. The tune, taken from Attilio Ariosti's 1724 opera *Ataxerxes*, was sung to the words 'T'amo tanto o mio tesoro' ('I love you dearly, O my treasure'), and as Cawwawkee's solo air becomes a duet, the romantic overtone would be unmistakable to those who knew the opera. The effect would have been all the more striking given the stage identities of the singers: a woman dressed as a 'mighty pretty man', and an 'Indian' prince played by a white English actor. Depending on how the viewer 'saw' Polly—as a female character and actor, or as the male she appears to the others on stage to be—this love duet could have looked like an expression of either same-sex or other-sex desire; and, either way, a desire that cuts across racial difference.

The same ambiguous play of sameness and difference colours Polly and Cawwawkee's second duet, Air 58, sung at the moment of their reunion after separation in battle. In this case Cawwawkee's words, even on their own, seem to express sentiments stronger than conventional friendship: '[Polly] *Victory is ours.* [Cawwawkee] *My fond heart is at rest.* [Polly] *Friendship thus receives its guest.* [Cawwawkee] *O what transport fills my breast!*' But this would have been compounded by memories of the original lyric—'Claspt in my dear *Melinda*'s Arms, | Soft engaging, oh how she Charms'—which infuse the characters' embrace with a homoerotic charge at the same time that the music unmasks the visibly male Polly as 'she'. Out of this combination of music, text, and stage image (the two actors embracing), Gay creates a moment of unsettling, but also pleasurable, indeterminacy, in which we are witness at once to a same-sex, other-sex, single-race, and cross-race union of friendship and desire. At such moments the grim economic realities of slavery and colonial exploitation seem far away; or at least it seems possible to imagine an alternative. As with Shakespeare (and before him, Montaigne), the new world of the Americas offers both a position from which to critique European cultural norms and a kind of free space for the play of the theatrical and desiring imagination.

One of the eighteenth century's chief figures for the free play of desire was the pirate.[49] In *Polly*, the romanticized image of the pirate

---

[49] On the pirate as a figure of sexual, economic, and political freedom, see John Richetti, *Popular Fiction Before Richardson: Narrative Patterns 1700–1739* (Oxford: Clarendon Press, 1969), 60–118; Hans Turley, *Rum, Sodomy, and the Lash: Piracy,*

as rebel—transatlantic offspring of *The Beggar's Opera*'s highwayman—is largely debunked, but one character does inhabit the role with gusto: none other than Polly. Hacker, one of the pirate gang, is the first to express the popular fantasy: 'Our profession is great, brothers. What can be more heroic than to have declar'd war with the whole world?' (p. 112). But as he and his 'brothers' fall to drunken bickering, they soon become the objects of Polly's mock-heroic sarcasm, when she calls them 'those *Alexanders*, that shall soon by conquest be in possession of the Indies' (p. 114). Polly, however, in her masculine drag, gives a creditable performance as 'a young fellow, who hath been robb'd by the world', and who 'came on purpose to join you, to rob the world by way of retaliation'. As she puts it, echoing Hacker, 'an open war with the whole world is brave and honourable' (p. 121). But she is the only outlaw character who lives up to this ideal of bravery. As her fellow pirates take bribes, plot mutiny, or try to run off with the others' share of the loot, Polly faces battle and overpowers her foe; while he, the pirate 'captain' Morano, exhibits 'all the cowardice of guilt' (p. 149).[50] Polly, in her male garb, reinvents herself in the new world. She thus embodies the observation that in Gay's work, 'disguise can be . . . a means of revealing rather than concealing truth'.[51] The 'truth' here is that Polly is more of a man than her runaway husband Macheath; indeed, when she returns to being a woman she seems diminished, a figure of virtue in distress, crying out 'Support me!' when she learns that Macheath has died (p. 159).

Macheath, too, reinvents himself in the new world; but just as Polly's pirate act reveals a heroic fortitude not apparent in *The Beggar's Opera*, so his impersonation of a slave alters him beyond recognition while (arguably) revealing the truth of his nature or place in the world. As in *The Beggar's Opera*, however, that truth is open to contrary readings. Does his blackface disguise reveal his 'bravery and audacity', acting as 'a sign of his rebellious class position'?[52] Or does it simply mark him as 'a willing slave', in thrall to Jenny and a debased

---

Sexuality, and Masculine Identity (New York: New York University Press, 1999); and Erin Mackie, *Rakes, Highwaymen, and Pirates*, 114–48.

[50] On Gay's 'debunking' of the pirate myth, see Wertheim, '*Polly*', 201–2. On Polly as 'a more ruthless pirate' than Macheath, see Roach, *It*, 214–15.

[51] Spacks, *John Gay*, 139.

[52] Peter P. Reed, 'Conquer or Die', 250, 243.

ideal of love, a poor man's Antony to her 'arrant *Cleopatra*' (p. 113)?[53] In either case, what is perhaps most striking is that he goes to his death without removing the mask of blackness. Does Morano not remember that he ever was Macheath? Robert Dryden has argued that when he 'approaches the scaffold . . . Morano is no longer disguised as a black pirate; he has *become* a black pirate'. Macheath, like the characters in Shakespeare's *Tempest*, has undergone a 'sea change'.[54]

By the end of *Polly*, the fantasy-ideal of piracy as a radical form of freedom from social or economic constraints has collapsed: the pirate gang is no different in its aims or principles from Ducat and his landowning cronies, and both parties seek to maximize their profits from an emerging global system of exploitation and enslavement. Morano, however, for all his flaws, goes to his death rejecting the moral authority of his judges, and maintaining his self-created identity as black but no longer a slave.[55] Passive for much of the play, he ends as a figure of resistance: resistance both to political authority and to any single, restrictive interpretation. Polly, likewise, assumes multiple identities over the course of three acts, playing by turns a foolishly loving wife, a pursuing spirit—as she says of Macheath, 'I love him, and like a troubled ghost shall never be at rest till I appear to him' (p. 90)—and then, in rapid succession, a female warrior, boy pirate, grieving widow, and, perhaps, Indian princess. When she exits the stage, her identity and her story's ending are unresolved. Rather than join in with the chorus, she leaves us to wonder if there is any space in this new world which has not been colonized, morally as well as physically, by the agents of empire; and if her own opera, as the Player insisted to the Beggar all operas must, could ever, in such a world, 'end happily'.

[53] Dugaw, *Warrior Women*, 202.

[54] Dryden, 'John Gay's *Polly*', 541 (emphasis added); Shakespeare, *The Tempest*, 1.2.401.

[55] As Calhoun Winton and other critics have noted, the name Morano echoes 'Maroon', a term applied to groups of independent and resistant ex-slaves in the Caribbean and the coastal areas of Central and South America from the later 16th century on. Winton, *John Gay*, 141. See also Mackie, *Rakes, Highwaymen, and Pirates*, 127–48.

NOTE ON THE TEXT

THIS edition of *The Beggar's Opera* and *Polly* is based on the first London printed editions of both plays. According to Peter Lewis, who has done the most extensive bibliographical research on the versions of the earlier play published during Gay's lifetime, there were five impressions or issues of the first edition of *The Beggar's Opera* (on sale by 14 February 1728) and nine of the second (on sale from 9 April 1728). I have followed Lewis in adopting the first issue of the first edition as the basis of this text, and have only adopted variants from later issues or editions when these are clearly authorial. Both the first and second editions were in octavo format (somewhat larger than the page size of an Oxford World's Classics edition). There are two major changes introduced in the second edition: the tunes are printed above the text of each song rather than appearing together at the end of the volume, as in the first; and the airs are consecutively numbered I–LXIX (1–69) rather than I–XVIII for Act I, I–XXII for Act II, and so on. In addition, from the second impression on, the second edition also included the score of the Overture composed by Johann Christoph Pepusch. For reasons of space, and because this is a readers' rather than a performing edition, I have not included the music, for which the best source is the 1990 edition by Jeremy Barlow (see Bibliography); but I have followed the consecutive numbering of the airs from Gay's second edition.

This was followed by a third edition in 1729, published as a companion volume to *Polly* (which appeared on 3 April of that year). Like *Polly*, the third edition of *The Beggar's Opera* was issued in the larger and more expensive quarto format, and musically is the most important of the three editions Gay was involved with: it provides a fuller score of the overture than the second, and the words of each air are printed directly below the notes they are sung to, giving a much clearer sense of how music and words fit together. The third edition included the 'basses' for each air as well—that is, simple bass lines indicating the basic harmonic structure of the instrumental accompaniment, which could then be 'realized' or filled in by the musicians in performance. As far as the text is concerned, however, Lewis offers good evidence that it is less authoritative than either the first or second editions, and I have not made use of it here.

When Gay decided to publish *Polly* at his own expense, and for his own profit, after its theatrical prohibition, he correctly predicted that it would sell extremely well, and ordered over 10,000 copies from the printer William Bowyer. This deluxe quarto edition, 'Printed for the Author' and meant to be sold for a rather pricey six shillings, is the basis for this edition, as it is the only edition Gay was involved in producing. The play was almost immediately pirated and printed in cheaper editions (as cheap as one shilling), none of which has textual authority. I have not collated multiple copies of Gay's first edition to look for variant readings, but have consulted John Fuller's 1983 edition and incorporated two of his substantive corrections (breaking 'besure' and 'Introth' into two words in I.ii and I.iv).

Otherwise, apart from technical or typographical changes for the sake of consistency—such as regularizing the use of full stops, the spelling of character names, and the format of speech prefixes and stage directions—I have followed the copy text, with the following modifications: (1) names of the actors in the original cast of *The Beggar's Opera* have been omitted from the page of Dramatis Personae. (2) The direction 'Aside' has been placed before the words to which it applies. (3) A small number of stage directions and speech prefixes have been added where needed for clarity; these are enclosed in angle brackets. (4) The two-column format of 'Errors' and 'Emendations' in the Preface to *Polly* has been eliminated, as has the list of 'Errata' at the end of the Preface. (5) Arabic numerals are used in the numbering of the airs in both plays, in place of roman.

SELECT BIBLIOGRAPHY

Editions

John Gay: Dramatic Works, ed. John Fuller, 2 vols. (Oxford: Clarendon Press, 1983).

The Beggar's Opera, ed. Oswald Doughty (London: Daniel O'Connor, 1922).

The Beggar's Opera, facsimile of 1729 third edn., with commentaries by Louis Kronenberger and Max Goberman (Larchmont, NY: Argonaut, 1961).

The Beggar's Opera, ed. Edgar V. Roberts (Lincoln: University of Nebraska Press, 1969).

The Beggar's Opera, ed. Peter Elfed Lewis (Edinburgh: Oliver and Boyd, 1973).

The Beggar's Opera, ed. Bryan Loughrey and T. O. Treadwell (Harmondsworth: Penguin, 1986).

The Beggar's Opera, ed. Vivien Jones and David Lindley (London: Methuen, 2010).

The Music of John Gay's The Beggar's Opera, ed. Jeremy Barlow (Oxford: Oxford University Press, 1990).

Reference and Background

Burgess, C. F., 'John Gay and *Polly* and a Letter to the King', *Philological Quarterly*, 47 (1968), 596–8.

Conolly, L. W., 'Anna Margaretta Larpent, The Duchess of Queensberry and Gay's *Polly* in 1777', *Philological Quarterly*, 51 (1972), 955–7.

Fiske, Roger, *English Theatre Music in the Eighteenth Century* (London: Oxford University Press, 1973).

Fuller, John, 'Cibber, *The Rehearsal at Goatham*, and the Suppression of *Polly*', *The Review of English Studies*, new series, 13:50 (1962), 125–34.

[Gay, John], *The Letters of John Gay*, ed. C. F. Burgess (Oxford: Clarendon Press, 1966).

—— *John Gay: Poetry and Prose*, ed. Vinton A. Dearing with Charles E. Beckwith, 2 vols. (Oxford: Clarendon Press, 1974).

Howson, Gerald, *Thief-Taker General: The Rise and Fall of Jonathan Wild* (New York: St. Martin's, 1971).

Irving, William Henry, *John Gay: Favorite of the Wits* (Durham, NC: Duke University Press, 1940).

Johnson, Samuel, 'Gay' [1781], in *The Lives of the Most Eminent English Poets*, ed. Roger Lonsdale, 4 vols. (Oxford: Clarendon Press, 2006), iii. 95–102 and 342–53.

Kidson, Frank, *The Beggar's Opera: Its Predecessors and Successors* [1922] (Westport, CT: Greenwood Press, 1971).

Nokes, David, *John Gay: A Profession of Friendship* (Oxford: Oxford University Press, 1995).

Petzold, Jochen, 'Moral Opposition to Gay's *Beggar's Opera*: William Duncombe's "Evidence" Refuted', *Notes and Queries*, 57 (255):1 (2010), 71–3.

Schultz, William Eben, *Gay's Beggar's Opera: Its Content, History and Influence* (New Haven: Yale University Press, 1923).

Simpson, Claude M., *The British Broadside Ballad and Its Music* (New Brunswick: Rutgers University Press, 1966).

Sutherland, James R., '*Polly* among the Pirates', *Modern Language Review*, 37 (1942), 291–303.

Swaen, A. E. H., 'The Airs and Tunes of John Gay's *Beggar's Opera*', *Anglia*, 43 (1919), 152–90.

—— 'The Airs and Tunes of John Gay's *Polly*', *Anglia*, 60 (1936), 403–22.

Westrup, J. A., 'French Tunes in *The Beggar's Opera* and *Polly*', *The Musical Times* 69, no. 1022 (1 Apr. 1928), 320–3.

Criticism

Armens, Sven M., *John Gay, Social Critic* [1954] (New York: Octagon, 1970).

Bender, John, *Imagining the Penitentiary: Fiction and the Architecture of Mind in Eighteenth-Century England* (Chicago: University of Chicago Press, 1987).

Bindman, David, and Wilcox, Scott, eds., *'Among the Whores and Thieves': William Hogarth and The Beggar's Opera* (New Haven: Yale Center for British Art, 1997).

Bronson, Bertrand H., 'The Beggar's Opera', in *Studies in the Comic*, University of California Publications in English, 8:2 (1941), 197–231.

Canfield, J. Douglas, *Heroes and States: On the Ideology of Restoration Tragedy* (Lexington: University Press of Kentucky, 2000).

Canfield, Rob, 'Something's Mizzen: Anne Bonny, Mary Read, *Polly*, and Female Counter-Roles on the Imperialist Stage', *South Atlantic Review*, 66 (2001), 45–63.

Chao, Noelle, 'Music and Indians in John Gay's *Polly*', in Patricia Fumerton and Anita Guerrini with Kris McAbee, eds., *Ballads and Broadsides in Britain, 1500–1800* (Farnham: Ashgate, 2010), 297–316.

Denning, Michael, 'Beggars and Thieves: The Ideology of the Gang', *Literature and History*, 8 (1982), 41–55.

Doody, Margaret Anne, *The Daring Muse: Augustan Poetry Reconsidered* (Cambridge: Cambridge University Press, 1985).

Downie, J. A., 'Gay's Politics', in Peter Lewis and Nigel Wood, eds., *John Gay and the Scriblerians* (London: Vision Press, 1988), 44–61.

Dryden, Robert G., 'John Gay's *Polly*: Unmasking Pirates and Fortune Hunters in the West Indies', *Eighteenth-Century Studies*, 34 (2001), 539–57.

Dugaw, Dianne, *'Deep Play': John Gay and the Invention of Modernity* (Newark: University of Delaware Press, 2001).

——*Warrior Women and Popular Balladry, 1650–1850* (Cambridge: Cambridge University Press, 1989).

Empson, William, *Some Versions of Pastoral* [1935] (London: Chatto and Windus, 1968).

Erskine-Hill, Howard, 'The Significance of Gay's Drama', in Marie Axton and Raymond Williams, eds., *English Drama: Forms and Development* (Cambridge: Cambridge University Press, 1977), 142–63.

Hammond, Brean S., '"A Poet, and a Patron, and Ten Pound": John Gay and Patronage', in Peter Lewis and Nigel Wood, eds., *John Gay and the Scriblerians* (London: Vision Press, 1988), 23–43.

Lewis, Peter, 'The Beggar's Rags to Rich's and Other Dramatic Transformations', in Peter Lewis and Nigel Wood, eds., *John Gay and the Scriblerians* (London: Vision Press, 1988), 122–46.

——*John Gay: The Beggar's Opera* (London: Edward Arnold, 1976).

Mackie, Erin, *Rakes, Highwaymen, and Pirates: The Making of the Modern Gentleman in the Eighteenth Century* (Baltimore: Johns Hopkins University Press, 2009).

McIntosh, William A., 'Handel, Walpole, and Gay: The Aims of *The Beggar's Opera*', *Eighteenth-Century Studies*, 7:4 (1974), 415–33.

Newman, Steve, 'The Value of "Nothing": Ballads in *The Beggar's Opera*', *Eighteenth Century: Theory and Interpretation*, 45 (2004), 265–83.

Nicholson, Colin, *Writing and the Rise of Finance: Capital Satires of the Early Eighteenth Century* (Cambridge: Cambridge University Press, 1994).

Noble, Yvonne, 'Sex and Gender in Gay's *Achilles*', in Peter Lewis and Nigel Wood, eds., *John Gay and the Scriblerians* (London: Vision Press, 1988), 184–215.

Nokes, David, *Raillery and Rage: A Study of Eighteenth-Century Satire* (Brighton: Harvester, 1987).

O'Shaughnessy, Toni-Lynn, 'A Single Capacity in *The Beggar's Opera*', *Eighteenth-Century Studies*, 21:2 (1987–88), 212–27.

Piper, William Bowman, 'Similitude as Satire in *The Beggar's Opera*', *Eighteenth-Century Studies*, 21:3 (1988), 334–51.

Reed, Peter P., 'Conquer or Die: Staging Circum-Atlantic Revolt in *Polly* and *Three-Finger'd Jack*', *Theatre Journal*, 59 (2007), 241–58.

——*Rogue Performances: Staging the Underclasses in Early American Theatre Culture* (New York: Palgrave Macmillan, 2009).

Richardson, John, 'John Gay and Slavery', *Modern Language Review*, 97 (2002), 15–25.

—— 'John Gay, *The Beggar's Opera*, and Forms of Resistance', *Eighteenth-Century Life*, 24 (2000), 19–30.

—— *Slavery and Augustan Literature: Swift, Pope, Gay* (London: Routledge, 2004).

Roach, Joseph, *It* (Ann Arbor: University of Michigan Press, 2007).

Rogers, Pat, 'Gay and the World of Opera', in Peter Lewis and Nigel Wood, eds., *John Gay and the Scriblerians* (London: Vision Press, 1988), 147–62.

—— 'Macheath and the Gaol-Breakers', *Literature and History*, 14 (2005), 14–36.

Spacks, Patricia Meyer, *John Gay* (New York: Twayne, 1965).

Timmons, Gregory, 'Gay's Retreatment of *The Beggar's Opera* in *Polly*', in Debra Taylor Bourdeau and Elizabeth Kraft, eds., *On Second Thought: Updating the Eighteenth-Century Text* (Newark: University of Delaware Press, 2007), 112–22.

Wanko, Cheryl, 'Three Stories of Celebrity: *The Beggar's Opera* "Biographies"', *Studies in English Literature, 1500–1900*, 38 (1998), 481–98.

Wertheim, Albert, '*Polly*: John Gay's Image of the West', in Dunbar H. Ogden with Douglas McDermott and Robert K. Sarlós, eds., *Theatre West: Image and Impact* (Amsterdam and Atlanta: Rodopi, 1990), 195–206.

Williams, Carolyn D., 'The Migrant Muses: A Study of John Gay's Later Drama', in Peter Lewis and Nigel Wood, eds., *John Gay and the Scriblerians* (London: Vision Press, 1988), 163–83.

Winton, Calhoun, *John Gay and the London Theatre* (Lexington: University Press of Kentucky, 1993).

—— '*The Beggar's Opera*: A Case Study'. In *The Cambridge History of British Theatre, Volume 2: 1660–1895*, ed. Joseph Donohue (Cambridge: Cambridge University Press, 2004), 126–44.

Further Reading in Oxford World's Classics

Behn, Aphra, *Oronooko and Other Writings*, ed. Paul Salzman.

Defoe, Daniel, *Moll Flanders*, ed. G. A. Starr and Linda Bree.

—— *Robinson Crusoe*, ed. Thomas Keymer and James Kelly.

Fielding, Henry, *Jonathan Wild*, ed. Claude Rawson and Linda Bree.

Pope, Alexander, *Selected Poetry*, ed. Pat Rogers.

Swift, Jonathan, *Gulliver's Travels*, ed. Claude Rawson and Ian Higgins.

A CHRONOLOGY OF JOHN GAY

1685   Born, 30 June, in Barnstaple, Devon, the youngest of five children of William Gay, a Dissenting merchant, and Katherine Hanmer Gay. Death of Charles II; accession of James II.

1688   Accession of William III.

1694   Death of Katherine Gay. Around this age, JG begins attending Barnstaple Grammar School, where from 1698 the schoolmaster is the would-be poet and classical dramatic amateur Robert Luck.

1695   Death of William Gay, on JG's tenth birthday; JG and his siblings move in with an uncle, probably John Hanmer, who also lives in Barnstaple.

1702   Around this time, becomes apprentice to John Willet, a silk mercer in London. Death of William III; accession of Queen Anne.

1706   Ends apprenticeship by agreement with master; returns to Barnstaple.

1707   Following his uncle's death in July, returns to London and collaborates with the author and literary entrepreneur Aaron Hill, a former Barnstaple schoolmate, on the periodical *British Apollo*. Act of Union between England and Scotland creates the unitary state of Great Britain.

1708   *Wine*, a burlesque-Miltonic poem, published in May.

1711   *The Present State of Wit*, a pamphlet essay on contemporary periodicals, published in May.

1712   *The Mohocks*, a 'Tragi-Comical Farce', published on 10 April, but not performed. In December, assumes post as secretary and domestic steward to the Duchess of Monmouth, which he retains to 1714.

1713   *Rural Sports*, a georgic poem, published in January. *The Wife of Bath*, a neo-Chaucerian comedy, performed at the Theatre Royal, Drury Lane, on 12 May; it runs for only two nights and is published on 22 May. In December, publishes *The Fan*, a mock-epic poem.

1714   Becomes a charter member and secretary of the Martinus Scriblerus Club, along with Alexander Pope, Jonathan Swift, John Arbuthnot, and Thomas Parnell. In April, publishes *The Shepherd's Week*, a set of six comic-pastoral-folkloric eclogues. Resident in Hanover (Germany) from July to September as secretary to Edward Hyde, Earl of Clarendon, on an abortive diplomatic mission. Death of Queen Anne; accession of George I.

1715 *The What D'Ye Call It*, a short two-act 'Tragi-Comi-Pastoral Farce', performed at the Theatre Royal, Drury Lane, 23 February; performed seventeen times in its first season, and published on 19 March.

1716 In January, publishes a three-book mock-georgic poem, *Trivia; or the Art of Walking the Streets of London*.

1717 *Three Hours after Marriage*, a comedy written in collaboration with Pope and Arbuthnot, performed at Drury Lane, 16 January; the object of much critical controversy for its alleged obscenity, it was performed seven times in its first season and published on 21 January.

1719 *Acis and Galatea*, a masque or 'English Pastoral Opera' with music by George Frideric Handel (the composer's first score to an English libretto), performed privately at Cannons, the Duke of Chandos's estate. Daniel Defoe, *Robinson Crusoe*.

1720 Publishes *Poems on Several Occasions* on 12 July, including the unacted 'Pastoral Tragedy' *Dione*, four satirical eclogues, and 'Sweet William's Farewell to Black-Eyed Susan', his most popular ballad. Invests profits from subscriptions to the collection in South Sea Company stock and loses most of those profits when the company's 'bubble' bursts in September.

1721 In Bath seeking to cure the 'colical complaints' that would plague him for the rest of his life, he meets and befriends Catherine Douglas, Duchess of Queensberry, in September.

1722 Assists Pope in collating editions of Shakespeare. Robert Walpole becomes de facto Prime Minister. Daniel Defoe, *Moll Flanders*.

1723 Accepts post as Commissioner of the State Lottery, carrying an annual salary of £150, which he occupies until 1731.

1724 *The Captives*, a tragedy, performed at Drury Lane, 15 January; performed seven times in its first season and published on 23 January, earning Gay a reported (but unlikely) £1,000. Publishes 'Newgate's Garland', a satirical ballad based on the criminal adventures of Jack Sheppard, Jonathan Wild, and Blueskin Blake. (Sheppard, often if disputably regarded as a model for *The Beggar's Opera*'s Macheath, was hanged at Tyburn in November.)

1725 Jonathan Wild, model for *The Beggar's Opera*'s Peachum, hanged at Tyburn in May.

1726 'Molly Mog', a comic-satirical ballad on a low-life lover (written with input from Pope and Swift), published. Jonathan Swift, *Gulliver's Travels*.

1727 Publishes his first series of verse *Fables*, which, along with *The Beggar's Opera*, was to prove his most popular work, appearing in some 350 editions over the following two centuries. After many years seeking a courtly sinecure, is offered the post of Gentleman Usher to the two-year-old Princess Louise; regarding this as an insult (perhaps engineered by the Prime Minister Robert Walpole), he declines the offer. Death of George I; accession of George II.

1728 *The Beggar's Opera* first performed at the Theatre Royal, Lincoln's Inn Fields, 29 January; it runs for an unprecedented 62 performances in its first season, and is published on 14 February. The sequel, *Polly*, is set to begin rehearsals in December, but is 'commanded to be supprest' by the Lord Chamberlain, and never performed during Gay's lifetime.

1729 *Polly* published by subscription in April; brings Gay profits of some £1,200. JG moves in as the permanent guest of the Duke and Duchess of Queensberry, with whom he remains for the rest of his life.

1730 Revised version of *The Wife of Bath* performed at Lincoln's Inn Fields, 19 January; runs for only three performances, and is published in February.

1731 First public performance of Gay and Handel's *Acis and Galatea*, Lincoln's Inn Fields, 26 March; published 11 May 1732.

1732 Death of John Gay, London, 4 December. Buried in the Poet's Corner of Westminster Abbey, 23 December.

1733 First performance of Gay's third and final ballad opera, *Achilles*, Covent Garden, 10 February; it runs for nineteen performances in its first season and is published on 1 March.

1734 *The Distress'd Wife*, a comedy (written *c*.1732), first performed at Covent Garden, 5 May; it receives four performances, but is not published until 1743.

1738 Second series of verse *Fables*, written in 1731–2, and 'graver and more political' than those of the first series, published.

1743 Fielding, *Jonathan Wild*.

1754 *The Rehearsal at Goatham*, an unperformed one-act comedy (written *c*.1730–1), published in April.

1777 First production of *Polly*, revised by George Colman, with music adapted by Samuel Arnold, at the Theatre Royal, Haymarket, 19 June.

THE BEGGAR'S OPERA

Nos haec novimus esse nihil. Mart.*

DRAMATIS PERSONAE*

MEN

PEACHUM*
LOCKIT*
MACHEATH*
FILCH
JEMMY TWITCHER
CROOK-FINGER'D JACK
WAT DREARY
ROBIN OF BAGSHOT
NIMMING NED
HARRY PADINGTON
MATT OF THE MINT
BEN BUDGE
BEGGAR
PLAYER

} Macheath's Gang

Constables, Drawer, Turnkey, &c.

WOMEN

MRS PEACHUM
POLLY PEACHUM
LUCY LOCKIT
DIANA TRAPES
MRS COAXER
DOLLY TRULL
MRS VIXEN
BETTY DOXY
JENNY DIVER
MRS SLAMMEKIN
SUKY TAWDRY
MOLLY BRAZEN

} Women of the Town

INTRODUCTION

BEGGAR, PLAYER.

BEGGAR. If Poverty be a Title to Poetry, I am sure No-body can dispute mine. I own myself of the Company of Beggars; and I make one at their Weekly Festivals at St. *Giles*'s.* I have a small Yearly Salary for my Catches,* and am welcome to a Dinner there whenever I please, which is more than most Poets can say.

PLAYER. As we live by the Muses, 'tis but Gratitude in us to encourage Poetical Merit where-ever we find it. The Muses, contrary to all other Ladies, pay no Distinction to Dress, and never partially mistake the Pertness of Embroidery for Wit, nor the Modesty of Want for Dulness. Be the Author who he will, we push his Play as far as it will go. So (though you are in Want) I wish you Success heartily.

BEGGAR. This Piece I own was originally writ for the celebrating the Marriage of *James Chanter* and *Moll Lay*,* two most excellent Ballad-Singers. I have introduc'd the Similes that are in all your celebrated *Operas*: The *Swallow*, the *Moth*, the *Bee*, the *Ship*, the *Flower*, &c.* Besides, I have a Prison Scene which the Ladies always reckon charmingly pathetick. As to the Parts, I have observ'd such a nice Impartiality to our two Ladies,* that it is impossible for either of them to take Offence. I hope I may be forgiven, that I have not made my Opera throughout unnatural, like those in vogue; for I have no Recitative:* Excepting this, as I have consented to have neither Prologue nor Epilogue, it must be allow'd an Opera in all its forms. The Piece indeed hath been heretofore frequently represented by ourselves in our great Room at St. *Giles*'s, so that I cannot too often acknowledge your Charity in bringing it now on the Stage.

PLAYER. But I see 'tis time for us to withdraw; the Actors are preparing to begin. Play away the Overture.

[*Exeunt.*

THE BEGGAR'S OPERA

ACT I

SCENE I

SCENE *Peachum's House.*

PEACHUM *sitting at a Table with a large Book of Accounts before him.*

AIR I. An old Woman cloathed in Gray, &c.*

> *Through all the Employments of Life*
> *Each Neighbour abuses his Brother;*
> *Whore and Rogue they call Husband and Wife:*
> *All Professions be-rogue one another.*
> *The Priest calls the Lawyer a Cheat,*
> *The Lawyer be-knaves the Divine;*
> *And the Statesman, because he's so great,*
> *Thinks his Trade as honest as mine.*

A Lawyer is an honest Employment, so is mine. Like me too he acts in a double Capacity, both against Rogues and for 'em; for 'tis but fitting that we should protect and encourage Cheats, since we live by them.

SCENE II

PEACHUM, FILCH.

FILCH. Sir, Black *Moll* hath sent word her Tryal comes on in the Afternoon, and she hopes you will order Matters so as to bring her off.*

PEACHUM. Why, she may plead her Belly* at worst; to my Knowledge she hath taken care of that Security. But as the Wench is very active and industrious, you may satisfy her that I'll soften the Evidence.

FILCH. *Tom Gagg,* Sir, is found guilty.

PEACHUM. A lazy Dog! When I took him the time before, I told him what he would come to if he did not mend his Hand. This is Death without Reprieve. I may venture to Book him. [*writes*] For *Tom Gagg,* forty Pounds.* Let *Betty Sly* know that I'll save her from Transportation,* for I can get more by her staying in *England.*

FILCH. *Betty* hath brought more Goods into our Lock* to-year than any five of the Gang; and in truth, 'tis a pity to lose so good a Customer.

PEACHUM. If none of the Gang take her off,* she may, in the common course of Business, live a Twelve-month longer. I love to let Women scape. A good Sportsman always lets the Hen Partridges fly, because the breed of the Game depends upon them. Besides, here the Law allows us no Reward; there is nothing to be got by the Death of Women—except our Wives.

FILCH. Without dispute, she is a fine Woman! 'Twas to her I was oblig'd for my Education, and (to say a bold Word) she hath train'd up more young Fellows to the Business than the Gaming-table.*

PEACHUM. Truly, *Filch,* thy Observation is right. We and the Surgeons are more beholden to Women than all the Professions besides.*

AIR 2. The bonny gray-ey'd Morn, &*c.*

FILCH.
> *'Tis Woman that seduces all Mankind,*
> > *By her we first were taught the wheedling Arts:*
> *Her very Eyes can cheat; when most she's kind,*
> > *She tricks us of our Money with our Hearts.*
> *For her, like Wolves by night we roam for Prey,*
> > *And practise ev'ry Fraud to bribe her Charms;*
> *For Suits of Love, like Law, are won by Pay,*
> > *And Beauty must be fee'd into our Arms.*

PEACHUM. But make haste to *Newgate,* Boy, and let my Friends know what I intend; for I love to make them easy one way or other.

FILCH. When a Gentleman is long kept in suspence, Penitence may break his Spirit ever after. Besides, Certainty gives a Man a good

Air upon his Tryal, and makes him risque another without Fear or Scruple. But I'll away, for 'tis a Pleasure to be the Messenger of Comfort to Friends in Affliction.

SCENE III

PEACHUM.

But 'tis now high time to look about me for a decent Execution against next Sessions.* I hate a lazy Rogue, by whom one can get nothing 'till he is hang'd. A Register of the Gang, [*reading*] Crookfinger'd *Jack*. A Year and a half in the Service; Let me see how much the Stock owes to his Industry; one, two, three, four, five Gold Watches, and seven Silver ones. A mighty clean-handed Fellow! Sixteen Snuff-boxes, five of them of true Gold. Six dozen of Handkerchiefs, four silver-hilted Swords, half a dozen of Shirts, three Tye-Perriwigs, and a Piece of Broad Cloth.* Considering these are only the Fruits of his leisure Hours, I don't know a prettier Fellow, for no Man alive hath a more engaging Presence of Mind upon the Road. *Wat Dreary*, alias *Brown Will*, an irregular Dog, who hath an underhand way of disposing of his Goods. I'll try him only for a Sessions or two longer upon his good Behaviour. *Harry Padington*, a poor petty-larceny Rascal,* without the least Genius; that Fellow, though he were to live these six Months, will never come to the Gallows with any Credit. Slippery *Sam*; he goes off the next Sessions, for the Villain hath the Impudence to have views of following his Trade as a Taylor, which he calls an honest Employment. *Matt* of the *Mint*; listed* not above a Month ago, a promising sturdy Fellow, and diligent in his way; somewhat too bold and hasty, and may raise good Contributions on the Publick, if he does not cut himself short by Murder. *Tom Tipple*, a guzzling soaking Sot, who is always too drunk to stand himself, or to make others stand. A Cart* is absolutely necessary for him. *Robin* of *Bagshot*, alias *Gorgon*, alias *Bluff Bob*, alias *Carbuncle*, alias *Bob Booty*.*

SCENE IV

PEACHUM, MRS PEACHUM.

MRS PEACHUM. What of *Bob Booty*, Husband? I hope nothing bad hath betided him. You know, my Dear, he's a favourite Customer of mine. 'Twas he made me a Present of this Ring.

PEACHUM. I have set his Name down in the Black-List,* that's all, my Dear; he spends his Life among Women, and as soon as his Money is gone, one or other of the Ladies will hang him for the Reward, and there's forty Pound lost to us for-ever.

MRS PEACHUM. You know, my Dear, I never meddle in matters of Death; I always leave those Affairs to you. Women indeed are bitter bad Judges in these cases, for they are so partial to the Brave that they think every Man handsome who is going to the Camp* or the Gallows.

AIR 3. Cold and Raw, &c.

If any Wench Venus's *Girdle* wear,*
Though she be never so ugly;
Lillys and Roses will quickly appear,
And her Face look wond'rous smuggly.
Beneath the left Ear so fit but a Cord,
(A Rope so charming a Zone is!)
The Youth in his Cart hath the Air of a Lord,
And we cry, There dies an Adonis!*

But really, Husband, you should not be too hard-hearted, for you never had a finer, braver set of Men than at present. We have not had a Murder among them all, these seven Months. And truly, my Dear, that is a great Blessing.

PEACHUM. What a dickens is the Woman always a whimpring about Murder for? No Gentleman is ever look'd upon the worse for killing a Man in his own Defence; and if Business cannot be carried on without it, what would you have a Gentleman do?

MRS PEACHUM. If I am in the wrong, my Dear, you must excuse me, for No-body can help the Frailty of an over-scrupulous Conscience.

PEACHUM. Murder is as fashionable a Crime as a Man can be guilty of. How many fine Gentlemen have we in *Newgate* every Year, purely upon that Article! If they have wherewithal to persuade the Jury to bring it in Manslaughter, what are they the worse for it? So, my Dear, have done upon this Subject. Was Captain *Macheath* here this Morning, for the Bank-notes* he left with you last Week?

MRS PEACHUM. Yes, my Dear; and though the Bank hath stopt Payment, he was so cheerful and so agreeable! Sure there is not a finer Gentleman upon the Road than the Captain! If he comes from *Bagshot* at any reasonable Hour he hath promis'd to make one this Evening with *Polly* and me, and *Bob Booty*, at a Party of Quadrille.* Pray, my Dear, is the Captain rich?

PEACHUM. The Captain keeps too good Company ever to grow rich. *Mary-bone* and the Chocolate-houses* are his undoing. The Man that proposes to get Money by Play should have the Education of a fine Gentleman, and be train'd up to it from his Youth.

MRS PEACHUM. Really, I am sorry upon *Polly*'s Account the Captain hath not more Discretion. What business hath he to keep Company with Lords and Gentlemen? he should leave them to prey upon one another.

PEACHUM. Upon *Polly*'s Account! What, a Plague, does the Woman mean?—Upon *Polly*'s Account!

MRS PEACHUM. Captain *Macheath* is very fond of the Girl.

PEACHUM. And what then?

MRS PEACHUM. If I have any Skill in the Ways of Women, I am sure *Polly* thinks him a very pretty Man.

PEACHUM. And what then? You would not be so mad to have the Wench marry him! Gamesters and Highwaymen are generally very good to their Whores, but they are very Devils to their Wives.

MRS PEACHUM. But if *Polly* should be in love, how should we help her, or how can she help herself? Poor Girl, I am in the utmost Concern about her.

AIR 4. Why is your faithful Slave disdain'd? &c.

> *If Love the Virgin's Heart invade,*
> *How, like a Moth, the simple Maid*
> *Still plays about the Flame!*
> *If soon she be not made a Wife,*
> *Her Honour's sing'd, and then for Life,*
> *She's—what I dare not name.*

PEACHUM. Look ye, Wife. A handsome Wench in our way of Business is as profitable as at the Bar of a *Temple* Coffee-House,* who looks upon it as her Livelihood to grant every Liberty but one. You see I would indulge the Girl as far as prudently we can. In any thing, but Marriage! After that, my Dear, how shall we be safe? Are we not then in her Husband's Power? For a Husband hath the absolute Power over all a Wife's Secrets but her own. If the Girl had the Discretion of a Court Lady, who can have a dozen young Fellows at her Ear without complying with one, I should not matter it; but *Polly* is Tinder, and a Spark will at once set her on a Flame. Married! If the Wench does not know her own Profit, sure she knows her own Pleasure better than to make herself a Property!* My Daughter to me should be, like a Court Lady to a Minister of State,* a Key to the whole Gang. Married! If the Affair is not already done, I'll terrify her from it, by the Example of our Neighbours.

MRS PEACHUM. May-hap, my Dear, you may injure the Girl. She loves to imitate the fine Ladies, and she may only allow the Captain Liberties in the View of Interest.

PEACHUM. But 'tis your Duty, my Dear, to warn the Girl against her Ruin, and to instruct her how to make the most of her Beauty. I'll go to her this moment, and sift her. In the mean time, Wife, rip out the Coronets and Marks of these dozen of Cambric Handkerchiefs,* for I can dispose of them this Afternoon to a Chap* in the City.

SCENE V

MRS PEACHUM.

Never was a Man more out of the way in an Argument than my Husband! Why must our *Polly*, forsooth, differ from her Sex, and love only her Husband? And why must *Polly*'s Marriage, contrary to all Observation, make her the less followed by other Men? All Men are Thieves in Love, and like a Woman the better for being another's Property.

AIR 5. Of all the simple Things we do, *&c.*

> *A Maid is like the golden Oar,**
> *Which hath Guineas intrinsical in't,*
> *Whose Worth is never known, before*
> *It is try'd and imprest* in the Mint.*
> *A Wife's like a Guinea in Gold,*
> *Stampt with the Name of her Spouse;*
> *Now here, now there; is bought, or is sold;*
> *And is current in every House.*

SCENE VI

MRS PEACHUM, FILCH.

MRS PEACHUM. Come hither *Filch*. I am as fond of this Child, as though my Mind misgave me he were my own. He hath as fine a Hand at picking a Pocket as a Woman, and is as nimble-finger'd as a Juggler.* If an unlucky Session does not cut the Rope of thy Life, I pronounce, Boy, thou wilt be a great Man in History. Where was your Post last Night, my Boy?

FILCH. I ply'd at the Opera,* Madam; and considering 'twas neither dark nor rainy, so that there was no great Hurry in getting Chairs* and Coaches, made a tolerable hand on't. These seven Handkerchiefs, Madam.

MRS PEACHUM. Colour'd ones, I see. They are of sure Sale from our Ware-house at *Redriff** among the Seamen.

FILCH. And this Snuff-box.

MRS PEACHUM. Set in Gold! A pretty Encouragement this to a young Beginner.

FILCH. I had a fair tug at a charming Gold Watch. Pox take the Taylors for making the Fobs* so deep and narrow! It stuck by the way, and I was forc'd to make my Escape under a Coach. Really, Madam, I fear I shall be cut off in the Flower of my Youth, so that every now and then (since I was pumpt)* I have thoughts of taking up and going to Sea.

MRS PEACHUM. You should go to *Hockley in the Hole*,* and to *Marybone*, Child, to learn Valour. These are the Schools that have bred so many brave Men. I thought, Boy, by this time, thou hadst lost Fear as well as Shame. Poor Lad! how little does he know as yet of the *Old-Baily*!* For the first Fact I'll insure thee from being hang'd; and going to Sea, *Filch*, will come time enough upon a Sentence of Transportation. But now, since you have nothing better to do, ev'n go to your Book, and learn your Catechism; for really a Man makes but an ill Figure in the Ordinary's Paper,* who cannot give a satisfactory Answer to his Questions. But, hark you, my Lad. Don't tell me a Lye; for you know I hate a Lyar. Do you know of any thing that hath past between Captain *Macheath* and our *Polly*?

FILCH. I beg you, Madam, don't ask me; for I must either tell a Lye to you or to Miss *Polly*; for I promis'd her I would not tell.

MRS PEACHUM. But when the Honour of our Family is concern'd—

FILCH. I shall lead a sad Life with Miss *Polly*, if ever she come to know that I told you. Besides, I would not willingly forfeit my own Honour by betraying any body.

MRS PEACHUM. Yonder comes my Husband and *Polly*. Come, *Filch*, you shall go with me into my own Room, and tell me the whole Story. I'll give thee a Glass of a most delicious Cordial that I keep for my own drinking.

SCENE VII

PEACHUM, POLLY.

POLLY. I know as well as any of the fine Ladies how to make the most of my self and of my Man too. A Woman knows how to be mercenary, though she hath never been in a Court or at an Assembly.* We have it in our Natures, Papa. If I allow Captain *Macheath* some trifling Liberties, I have this Watch and other visible Marks of his Favour to show for it. A Girl who cannot grant some Things, and refuse what is most material, will make but a poor hand of her Beauty, and soon be thrown upon the Common.*

AIR 6. What shall I do to show how much I love her, *&c.*

> *Virgins are like the fair Flower in its Lustre,*
>   *Which in the Garden enamels the Ground;*
> *Near it the Bees in Play flutter and cluster,*
>   *And gaudy Butterflies frolick around.*
> *But, when once pluck'd, 'tis no longer alluring,*
>   *To* Covent-Garden* *'tis sent, (as yet sweet,)*
> *There fades, and shrinks, and grows past all enduring,*
>   *Rots, stinks, and dies, and is trod under feet.*

PEACHUM. You know, *Polly*, I am not against your toying and trifling with a Customer in the way of Business, or to get out a Secret, or so. But if I find out that you have play'd the fool and are married, you Jade* you, I'll cut your Throat, Hussy. Now you know my Mind.

SCENE VIII

PEACHUM, POLLY, MRS PEACHUM.

AIR 7. Oh *London* is a fine Town.

MRS PEACHUM [*in a very great Passion*].

> *Our* Polly *is a sad Slut! nor heeds what we have taught her.*
> *I wonder any Man alive will ever rear a Daughter!*

For she must have both Hoods and Gowns, and Hoops to
   swell her Pride,
With Scarfs and Stays, and Gloves and Lace; and she
   will have Men beside;
And when she's drest with Care and Cost, all-tempting,
   fine and gay,
*As Men should serve a Cowcumber, she flings herself away.**

Our Polly *is a sad Slut,* &c.

You Baggage! you Hussy! you inconsiderate Jade! had you been hang'd, it would not have vex'd me, for that might have been your Misfortune; but to do such a mad thing by Choice! The Wench is married, Husband.

PEACHUM.   Married! The Captain is a bold Man, and will risque any thing for Money; to be sure he believes her a Fortune. Do you think your Mother and I should have liv'd comfortably so long together, if ever we had been married? Baggage!

MRS PEACHUM.   I knew she was always a proud Slut; and now the Wench hath play'd the Fool and married, because forsooth she would do like the Gentry. Can you support the Expence of a Husband, Hussy, in gaming, drinking and whoring? have you Money enough to carry on the daily Quarrels of Man and Wife about who shall squander most? There are not many Husbands and Wives, who can bear the Charges of plaguing one another in a handsome way. If you must be married, could you introduce no-body into our Family but a Highwayman? Why, thou foolish Jade, thou wilt be as ill-us'd, and as much neglected, as if thou hadst married a Lord!

PEACHUM.   Let not your Anger, my Dear, break through the Rules of Decency, for the Captain looks upon himself in the Military Capacity, as a Gentleman by his Profession. Besides what he hath already, I know he is in a fair way of getting,* or of dying; and both these ways, let me tell you, are most excellent Chances for a Wife. Tell me Hussy, are you ruin'd* or no?

MRS PEACHUM.   With *Polly*'s Fortune, she might very well have gone off to a Person of Distinction. Yes, that you might, you pouting Slut!

PEACHUM. What, is the Wench dumb? Speak, or I'll make you plead by squeezing out an Answer from you.* Are you really bound Wife to him, or are you only upon liking?*

> [*Pinches her.*

POLLY [*screaming*]. Oh!

MRS PEACHUM. How the Mother is to be pitied who hath hand-some Daughters! Locks, Bolts, Bars, and Lectures of Morality are nothing to them: They break through them all. They have as much Pleasure in cheating a Father and Mother, as in cheating at Cards.

PEACHUM. Why, *Polly*, I shall soon know if you are married, by *Macheath*'s keeping from our House.

AIR 8. Grim King of the Ghosts, &c.

POLLY.   *Can Love be controul'd by Advice?*
  Will Cupid our Mothers obey?
  Though my Heart were as frozen as Ice,
   At his Flame 'twould have melted away.

  When he kist me so closely he prest,
   'Twas so sweet that I must have comply'd:
  So I thought it both safest and best
   To marry, for fear you should chide.

MRS PEACHUM. Then all the Hopes of our Family are gone for ever and ever!

PEACHUM. And *Macheath* may hang his Father and Mother-in-Law, in hope to get into their Daughter's Fortune.

POLLY. I did not marry him (as 'tis the Fashion) cooly and deliber-ately for Honour or Money. But, I love him.

MRS PEACHUM. Love him! worse and worse! I thought the Girl had been better bred. Oh Husband, Husband! her Folly makes me mad! my Head swims! I'm distracted! I can't support myself—Oh!

> [*Faints.*

PEACHUM. See, Wench, to what a Condition you have reduc'd your poor Mother! a Glass of Cordial, this instant. How the poor Woman takes it to Heart!

[POLLY *goes out, and returns with it.*

Ah, Hussy, now this is the only Comfort your Mother has left!

POLLY. Give her another Glass, Sir; my Mama drinks double the Quantity whenever she is out of Order. This, you see, fetches her.

MRS PEACHUM. The Girl shows such a Readiness, and so much Concern, that I could almost find in my Heart to forgive her.

AIR 9. O *Jenny*, O *Jenny*, where hast thou been.

POLLY.

> O Polly, *you might have toy'd and kist.*
> *By keeping Men off, you keep them on.*
> *But he so teaz'd me,*
> *And he so pleas'd me,*
> *What I did, you must have done.*

MRS PEACHUM. Not with a Highwayman.—You sorry Slut!

PEACHUM. A Word with you, Wife. 'Tis no new thing for a Wench to take Man without consent of Parents. You know 'tis the Frailty of Woman, my Dear.

MRS PEACHUM. Yes, indeed, the Sex is frail. But the first time a Woman is frail she should be somewhat nice* methinks, for then or never is the time to make her Fortune. After that, she hath nothing to do but to guard herself from being found out, and she may do what she pleases.

PEACHUM. Make your self a little easy; I have a Thought shall soon set all Matters again to rights. Why so melancholy, *Polly*? since what is done cannot be undone, we must all endeavour to make the best of it.

MRS PEACHUM. Well, *Polly*; as far as one Woman can forgive another, I forgive thee.—Your Father is too fond of you, Hussy.

POLLY. Then all my Sorrows are at an end.

MRS PEACHUM. A mighty likely Speech in troth, for a Wench who is just married!

AIR 10. *Thomas, I cannot, &c.*

POLLY.

I, like a Ship in Storms, was tost;
Yet afraid to put in to Land;
For seiz'd in the Port the Vessel's lost,
Whose Treasure is contreband.
  The Waves are laid,
  My Duty's paid.
O Joy beyond Expression!
  Thus, safe a-shore,
  I ask no more,
My All is in my Possession.

PEACHUM. I hear Customers* in t'other Room; Go, talk with 'em, *Polly*; but come to us again, as soon as they are gone.—But, heark ye, Child, if 'tis the Gentleman who was here Yesterday about the Repeating-Watch;* say, you believe we can't get Intelligence of it, till to-morrow. For I lent it to *Suky Straddle*, to make a Figure with it to-night at a Tavern in *Drury-Lane.** If t'other Gentleman calls for the Silver-hilted Sword; you know Beetle-brow'd *Jemmy* hath it on, and he doth not come from *Tunbridge** till *Tuesday* Night; so that it cannot be had till then.

SCENE IX

PEACHUM, MRS PEACHUM.

PEACHUM. Dear Wife, be a little pacified. Don't let your Passion run away with your Senses. *Polly*, I grant you, hath done a rash thing.

MRS PEACHUM. If she had had only an Intrigue with the Fellow, why the very best Families have excus'd and huddled up a Frailty of that sort. 'Tis Marriage, Husband, that makes it a Blemish.

PEACHUM. But Money, Wife, is the true Fuller's Earth* for Reputations, there is not a Spot or a Stain but what it can take out. A rich Rogue now-a-days is fit Company for any Gentleman; and the World, my Dear, hath not such a Contempt for Roguery as you imagine. I tell you, Wife, I can make this Match turn to our Advantage.

MRS PEACHUM. I am very sensible, Husband, that Captain *Macheath* is worth Money, but I am in doubt whether he hath not two or three Wives already, and then if he should dye in a Session or two, *Polly*'s Dower would come into Dispute.

PEACHUM. That, indeed, is a Point which ought to be consider'd.

AIR 11. A Soldier and a Sailor.

A Fox may steal your Hens, Sir,
A Whore your Health and Pence, Sir,
Your Daughter rob your Chest, Sir,
Your Wife may steal your Rest, Sir,
A Thief your Goods and Plate.
But this is all but picking,
With Rest, Pence, Chest and Chicken;
It ever was decreed, Sir,
If Lawyer's Hand is fee'd, Sir,
He steals your whole Estate.

The Lawyers are bitter Enemies to those in our Way. They don't care that any Body should get a Clandestine Livelihood but themselves.

SCENE X

MRS PEACHUM, PEACHUM, POLLY.

POLLY. 'Twas only Nimming *Ned*. He brought in a Damask Window-Curtain, a Hoop-Petticoat, a Pair of Silver Candlesticks, a Perriwig, and one Silk Stocking, from the Fire that happen'd last Night.

PEACHUM. There is not a Fellow that is cleverer in his way, and saves more Goods out of the Fire than *Ned*. But now, *Polly*, to your Affair; for Matters must not be left as they are. You are married then, it seems?

POLLY. Yes, Sir.

PEACHUM. And how do you propose to live, Child?

POLLY. Like other Women, Sir, upon the Industry of my Husband.

MRS PEACHUM. What, is the Wench turn'd Fool? A Highwayman's Wife, like a Soldier's, hath as little of his Pay, as of his Company.

PEACHUM. And had not you the common Views of a Gentlewoman in your Marriage, *Polly?*

POLLY. I don't know what you mean, Sir.

PEACHUM. Of a Jointure,* and of being a Widow.

POLLY. But I love him, Sir: how then could I have Thoughts of parting with him?

PEACHUM. Parting with him! Why, that is the whole Scheme and Intention of all Marriage Articles. The comfortable Estate of Widow-hood, is the only Hope that keeps up a Wife's Spirits. Where is the Woman who would scruple to be a Wife, if she had it in her Power to be a Widow whenever she pleas'd? If you have any Views of this sort, *Polly,* I shall think the Match not so very unreasonable.

POLLY. How I dread to hear your Advice! Yet I must beg you to explain yourself.

PEACHUM. Secure what he hath got, have him peach'd* the next Sessions, and then at once you are made a rich Widow.

POLLY. What, murder the Man I love! The Blood runs cold at my Heart with the very Thought of it.

PEACHUM. Fye, *Polly!* What hath Murder to do in the Affair? Since the thing sooner or later must happen, I dare say, the Captain himself would like that we should get the Reward for his Death sooner than a Stranger. Why, *Polly,* the Captain knows, that as 'tis his Employment to rob, so 'tis ours to take Robbers; every Man in his Business. So that there is no Malice in the Case.

MRS PEACHUM. Ay, Husband, now you have nick'd the Matter.* To have him peach'd is the only thing could ever make me forgive her.

AIR 12. Now ponder well, ye Parents dear.

POLLY.   *Oh, ponder well! be not severe;*
                    So save a wretched Wife!

> *For on the Rope that hangs my Dear*
> *Depends poor* Polly's *Life.**

MRS PEACHUM. But your Duty to your Parents, Hussy, obliges you to hang him. What would many a Wife give for such an Opportunity!

POLLY. What is a Jointure, what is Widow-hood to me? I know my Heart. I cannot survive him.

AIR 13. Le printemps rappelle aux armes.

The Turtle* thus with plaintive crying,
   Her Lover dying,
The Turtle thus with plaintive crying,
   Laments her Dove.
Down she drops quite spent with sighing,
Pair'd in Death, as pair'd in Love.

Thus, Sir, it will happen to your poor *Polly*.

MRS PEACHUM. What, is the Fool in Love in earnest then? I hate thee for being particular:* Why, Wench, thou art a Shame to thy very Sex.

POLLY. But hear me, Mother.—If you ever lov'd—

MRS PEACHUM. Those cursed Play-books she reads have been her Ruin. One Word more, Hussy, and I shall knock your Brains out, if you have any.

PEACHUM. Keep out of the way, *Polly*, for fear of Mischief, and consider of what is propos'd to you.

MRS PEACHUM. Away, Hussy. Hang your Husband, and be dutiful.

SCENE XI

MRS PEACHUM, PEACHUM.

[POLLY *listning.*

MRS PEACHUM. The Thing, Husband, must and shall be done. For the sake of Intelligence* we must take other Measures, and have him peach'd the next Session without her Consent. If she will not know her Duty, we know ours.

PEACHUM. But really, my Dear, it grieves one's Heart to take off a great Man. When I consider his Personal Bravery, his fine Stratagem,* how much we have already got by him, and how much more we may get, methinks I can't find in my Heart to have a Hand in his Death. I wish you could have made *Polly* undertake it.

MRS PEACHUM. But in a Case of Necessity—our own Lives are in danger.

PEACHUM. Then, indeed, we must comply with the Customs of the World, and make Gratitude give way to Interest.—He shall be taken off.

MRS PEACHUM. I'll undertake to manage *Polly*.

PEACHUM. And I'll prepare Matters for the *Old-Baily*.

SCENE XII

POLLY.

Now I'm a Wretch, indeed.—Methinks I see him already in the Cart, sweeter and more lovely than the Nosegay in his Hand!*— I hear the Crowd extolling his Resolution and Intrepidity!—What Vollies of Sighs are sent from the Windows of *Holborn*,* that so comely a Youth should be brought to disgrace!—I see him at the Tree!* The whole Circle are in Tears!—even Butchers weep!—*Jack Ketch** himself hesitates to perform his Duty, and would be glad to lose his Fee, by a Reprieve. What then will become of *Polly*!—As yet I may inform him of their Design, and aid him in his Escape.—It shall be so.—But then he flies, absents himself, and I bar my self from his dear dear Conversation!* That too will distract me.—If he keep out of the way, my Papa and Mama may in time relent, and we may be happy.—If he stays, he is hang'd, and then he is lost for ever!—He intended to lye conceal'd in my Room, 'till the Dusk of the Evening: If they are abroad, I'll this Instant let him out, lest some Accident should prevent him.

[*Exit, and returns.*

SCENE XIII

POLLY, MACHEATH.

AIR 14. Pretty Parrot, say—

MACHEATH.   *Pretty* Polly, *say,*
                            When I was away,
                            Did your Fancy never stray
                            To some newer Lover?

POLLY.   *Without Disguise,*
                            Heaving Sighs,
                            Doating Eyes,
                            My constant Heart discover.
                            Fondly let me loll!

MACHEATH.   *O pretty, pretty* Poll.

POLLY.   And are *you* as fond as ever, my Dear?

MACHEATH.   Suspect my Honour, my Courage, suspect any thing
but my Love.—May my Pistols miss Fire, and my Mare slip her
Shoulder while I am pursu'd, if I ever forsake thee!

POLLY.   Nay, my Dear, I have no Reason to doubt you, for I find in
the Romance you lent me, none of the great Heroes were ever false
in Love.

AIR 15. Pray, Fair One, be kind—

MACHEATH.   *My Heart was so free,*
                            It rov'd like the Bee,
                            'Till Polly *my Passion requited;*
                            I sipt each Flower,
                            I chang'd ev'ry Hour,
                            But here ev'ry Flower is united.

POLLY.   Were you sentenc'd to Transportation, sure, my Dear, you
could not leave me behind you—could you?

MACHEATH.   Is there any Power, any Force that could tear me from
thee? You might sooner tear a Pension out of the Hands of a Courtier,*
a Fee from a Lawyer, a pretty Woman from a Looking-glass, or any
Woman from *Quadrille*.—But to tear me from thee is impossible!

AIR 16. Over the Hills and far away.

Were I laid on Greenland's Coast,
And in my Arms embrac'd my Lass;
Warm amidst eternal Frost,
Too soon the Half Year's Night would pass.

POLLY.   *Were I sold on Indian Soil,*
Soon as the burning Day was clos'd,
I could mock the sultry Toil,
When on my Charmer's Breast repos'd.

MACHEATH. *And I would love you all the Day,*

POLLY.   *Every Night would kiss and play,*

MACHEATH. *If with me you'd fondly stray*

POLLY.   *Over the Hills and far away.*

Yes, I would go with thee. But oh!—how shall I speak it? I must be torn from thee. We must part.

MACHEATH. How! Part!

POLLY. We must, we must.—My Papa and Mama are set against thy Life. They now, even now are in Search after thee. They are preparing Evidence against thee. Thy Life depends upon a Moment.

AIR 17. Gin thou wert mine awn thing—

O what Pain it is to part!
Can I leave thee, can I leave thee?
O what Pain it is to part!
Can thy Polly ever leave thee?
But lest Death my Love should thwart,
And bring thee to the fatal Cart,
Thus I tear thee from my bleeding Heart!
    Fly hence, and let me leave thee.

One Kiss and then—one Kiss—begone—farewell.

MACHEATH. My Hand, my Heart, my Dear, is so rivited to thine, that I cannot unloose my Hold.

POLLY. But my Papa may intercept thee, and then I should lose the very glimmering of Hope. A few Weeks, perhaps, may reconcile us all. Shall thy *Polly* hear from thee?

MACHEATH.   Must I then go?

POLLY.   And will not Absence change your Love?

MACHEATH.   If you doubt it, let me stay—and be hang'd.

POLLY.   O how I fear! how I tremble!—Go—but when Safety will give you leave, you will be sure to see me again; for 'till then *Polly* is wretched.

AIR 18. O the Broom, &c.

[Parting, and looking back at each other with fondness;
he at one Door, she at the other.

MACHEATH.   *The Miser thus a Shilling sees,*
    Which he's oblig'd to pay,
    With Sighs resigns it by degrees,
    And fears 'tis gone for aye.

POLLY.   *The Boy, thus, when his Sparrow's flown,*
    The Bird in Silence eyes;
    But soon as out of Sight 'tis gone,
    Whines, whimpers, sobs and cries.

ACT II

SCENE I

A Tavern near Newgate.

JEMMY TWITCHER, CROOK-FINGER'D JACK, WAT DREARY,
ROBIN OF BAGSHOT, NIMMING NED, HENRY PADINGTON,
MATT OF THE MINT, BEN BUDGE, *and the rest of the Gang, at the
Table, with Wine, Brandy and Tobacco.*

BEN BUDGE. But pr'ythee, *Matt*, what is become of thy Brother
Tom? I have not seen him since my Return from Transportation.

MATT OF THE MINT. Poor Brother *Tom* had an Accident this time
Twelve-month, and so clever a made Fellow he was, that I could
not save him from those fleaing Rascals the Surgeons; and now,
poor Man, he is among the Otamys at *Surgeon's Hall.**

BEN BUDGE. So it seems, his Time was come.

JEMMY TWITCHER. But the present Time is ours, and no Body alive
hath more. Why are the Laws levell'd at us? are we more dishonest
than the rest of Mankind? What we win, Gentlemen, is our own by
the Law of Arms, and the Right of Conquest.

CROOK-FINGER'D JACK. Where shall we find such another Set of
practical Philosophers, who to a Man are above the Fear of Death?

WAT DREARY. Sound Men, and true!

ROBIN OF BAGSHOT. Of try'd Courage, and indefatigable Industry!

NIMMING NED. Who is there here that would not dye for his Friend?

HARRY PADINGTON. Who is there here that would betray him for
his Interest?

MATT OF THE MINT. Show me a Gang of Courtiers that can say as
much.

BEN BUDGE. We are for a just Partition of the World, for every Man
hath a Right to enjoy Life.

MATT OF THE MINT. We retrench the Superfluities of Mankind. The World is avaritious, and I hate Avarice. A covetous fellow, like a Jack-daw, steals what he was never made to enjoy, for the sake of hiding it. These are the Robbers of Mankind, for Money was made for the Free-hearted and Generous, and where is the Injury of taking from another, what he hath not the Heart to make use of?

JEMMY TWITCHER. Our several Stations for the Day are fixt. Good luck attend us all. Fill the Glasses.

AIR 19. Fill ev'ry Glass, &c.

MATT OF THE MINT.

> *Fill ev'ry Glass, for Wine inspires us,*
> *And fires us*
> *With Courage, Love and Joy.*
> *Women and Wine should Life employ.*
> *Is there ought else on Earth desirous?*

CHORUS.   *Fill ev'ry Glass, &c.*

SCENE II

To them enter MACHEATH.

MACHEATH. Gentlemen, well met. My Heart hath been with you this Hour; but an unexpected Affair hath detain'd me. No Ceremony, I beg you.

MATT OF THE MINT. We were just breaking up to go upon Duty. Am I to have the Honour of taking the Air with you, Sir, this Evening upon the Heath? I drink a Dram now and then with the Stage-Coachmen in the way of Friendship and Intelligence; and I know that about this Time there will be Passengers upon the Western Road,* who are worth speaking with.

MACHEATH. I was to have been of that Party—but—

MATT OF THE MINT. But what, Sir?

MACHEATH. Is there any man who suspects my Courage?

MATT OF THE MINT. We have all been witnesses of it.

MACHEATH. My Honour and Truth to the Gang?

MATT OF THE MINT. I'll be answerable for it.

MACHEATH. In the Division of our Booty, have I ever shown the least Marks of Avarice or Injustice?

MATT OF THE MINT. By these Questions something seems to have ruffled you. Are any of us suspected?

MACHEATH. I have a fixt Confidence, Gentlemen, in you all, as Men of Honour, and as such I value and respect you. *Peachum* is a Man that is useful to us.

MATT OF THE MINT. Is he about to play us any foul Play? I'll shoot him through the Head.

MACHEATH. I beg you, Gentlemen, act with Conduct and Discretion. A Pistol is your last resort.

MATT OF THE MINT. He knows nothing of this Meeting.

MACHEATH. Business cannot go on without him. He is a Man who knows the World, and is a necessary Agent to us. We have had a slight Difference, and till it is accommodated I shall be oblig'd to keep out of his way. Any private Dispute of mine shall be of no ill consequence to my Friends. You must continue to act under his Direction, for the moment we break loose from him, our Gang is ruin'd.

MATT OF THE MINT. As a Bawd* to a Whore, I grant you, he is to us of great Convenience.

MACHEATH. Make him believe I have quitted the Gang, which I can never do but with Life. At our private Quarters I will continue to meet you. A Week or so will probably reconcile us.

MATT OF THE MINT. Your Instructions shall be observ'd. 'Tis now high time for us to repair to our several Duties; so till the Evening at our Quarters in *Moor-fields** we bid you farewell.

MACHEATH. I shall wish my self with you. Success attend you.

[*Sits down melancholy at the Table.*

AIR 20. March in *Rinaldo*, with Drums and Trumpets.

MATT OF THE MINT.

> Let us take the Road.
> Hark! I hear the sound of Coaches!
> The hour of Attack approaches,
> To your Arms, brave Boys, and load.
> See the Ball I hold!
> Let the Chymists toil like Asses,
> Our Fire their Fire surpasses,
> And turns all our Lead to Gold.*

[*The Gang, rang'd in the Front of the Stage, load their Pistols, and stick them under their Girdles; then go off singing the first Part in Chorus.*

SCENE III

MACHEATH.

What a Fool is a fond Wench! *Polly* is most confoundedly bit.*— I love the Sex. And a Man who loves Money, might as well be contented with one Guinea, as I with one Woman. The Town perhaps hath been as much oblig'd to me, for recruiting it with free-hearted Ladies, as to any Recruiting Officer in the Army. If it were not for us and the other Gentlemen of the Sword, *Drury Lane* would be uninhabited.*

AIR 21. Would you have a Young Virgin, &c.

> If the Heart of a Man is deprest with Cares,
> The Mist is dispell'd when a Woman appears;
> Like the Notes of a Fiddle, she sweetly, sweetly
> Raises the Spirits, and charms our Ears,
> Roses and Lillies her Cheeks disclose,
> But her ripe Lips are more sweet than those.
> Press her,
> Caress her
> With Blisses,
> Her Kisses
> Dissolve us in Pleasure, and soft Repose.

I must have Women. There is nothing unbends the Mind like them. Money is not so strong a Cordial for the Time.* Drawer.—

[*Enter* DRAWER.

Is the Porter gone for all the Ladies, according to my directions?

DRAWER. I expect him back every Minute. But you know, Sir, you sent him as far as *Hockley in the Hole*, for three of the Ladies, for one in *Vinegar Yard*, and for the rest of them somewhere about *Lewkner's Lane*.* Sure some of them are below, for I hear the Barr Bell. As they come I will show them up. Coming, Coming.

<*Exit.*>

SCENE IV

MACHEATH, MRS COAXER, DOLLY TRULL, MRS VIXEN,
BETTY DOXY, JENNY DIVER, MRS SLAMMEKIN, SUKY TAWDRY,
and MOLLY BRAZEN.

MACHEATH. Dear Mrs *Coaxer*, you are welcome. You look charmingly to-day. I hope you don't want the Repairs of Quality, and lay on *Paint*.*—*Dolly Trull*! kiss me, you Slut; are you as amorous as ever, Hussy? You are always so taken up with stealing Hearts, that you don't allow your self Time to steal any thing else.—Ah *Dolly*, thou wilt ever be a Coquette!—Mrs *Vixen*, I'm yours, I always lov'd a Woman of Wit and Spirit; they make charming Mistresses, but plaguy Wives.—*Betty Doxy*! Come hither, Hussy. Do you drink as hard as ever? You had better stick to good wholesome Beer; for in troth, *Betty*, Strong-Waters* will in time ruin your Constitution. You should leave those to your Betters.—What! and my pretty *Jenny Diver* too! As prim and demure as ever! There is not any Prude, though ever so high bred, hath a more sanctify'd Look, with a more mischievous Heart. Ah! thou art a dear artful Hypocrite.—Mrs *Slammekin*! as careless and genteel as ever! all you fine Ladies, who know your own Beauty, affect an Undress.*—But see, here's *Suky Tawdry* come to contradict what I was saying. Every thing she gets one way she lays out upon her Back. Why, *Suky*, you must keep at least a dozen Tally-men.* *Molly Brazen*!

> [*She kisses him.*

That's well done. I love a free-hearted Wench. Thou hast a most agreeable Assurance, Girl, and art as willing as a Turtle.*—But hark! I hear musick. The Harper is at the Door. *If Musick be the Food of Love, play on.** E'er you seat your selves, Ladies, what think you of a Dance? Come in.

> [*Enter* HARPER.

Play the *French* Tune, that Mrs *Slammekin* was so fond of.

> [*A Dance* a la ronde *in the* French *Manner;** near the End of it this Song and Chorus.*

AIR 22. Cotillon.

<MACHEATH.>   *Youth's the Season made for Joys,*
>   *Love is then our Duty,*
>   *She alone who that employs,*
>   *Well deserves her Beauty.*
>   *Let's be gay,*
>   *While we may,*
>   *Beauty's a Flower, despis'd in decay.*

<CHORUS.>   *Youth's the Season* &c.

<MACHEATH.>   *Let us drink and sport to-day,*
>   *Ours is not to-morrow.*
>   *Love with Youth flies swift away,*
>   *Age is nought but Sorrow.*
>   *Dance and sing,*
>   *Time's on the Wing,*
>   *Life never knows the return of Spring.*

CHORUS.   *Let us drink* &c.

MACHEATH.   Now, pray Ladies, take your Places. Here Fellow [*Pays the* HARPER]. Bid the Drawer bring us more Wine.

> [*Exit* HARPER.

If any of the Ladies chuse Ginn, I hope they will be so free to call for it.

JENNY DIVER. You look as if you meant me. Wine is strong enough for me. Indeed, Sir, I never drink Strong-Waters, but when I have the Cholic.*

MACHEATH. Just the Excuse of the fine Ladies! Why, a Lady of Quality is never without the Cholic. I hope, Mrs *Coaxer*, you have had good Success of late in your Visits among the Mercers.*

MRS COAXER. We have so many Interlopers—Yet with Industry, one may still have a little Picking. I carried a silver flower'd Lutestring, and a Piece of black Padesoy* to Mr *Peachum*'s Lock but last Week.

MRS VIXEN. There's *Molly Brazen* hath the Ogle of a Rattle-Snake.* She rivetted a Linnen-draper's Eye so fast upon her, that he was nick'd of three Pieces of Cambric before he could look off.

MOLLY BRAZEN. Oh dear Madam!—But sure nothing can come up to your handling of Laces! And then you have such a sweet deluding Tongue! To cheat a Man is nothing; but the Woman must have fine Parts indeed who cheats a Woman!

MRS VIXEN. Lace, Madam, lyes in a small Compass, and is of easy Conveyance. But you are apt, Madam, to think too well of your Friends.

MRS COAXER. If any Woman hath more Art than another, to be sure, 'tis *Jenny Diver*. Though her Fellow be never so agreeable, she can pick his Pocket as cooly, as if Money were her only Pleasure. Now that is a Command of the Passions uncommon in a Woman!

JENNY DIVER. I never go to the Tavern with a Man, but in the View of Business. I have other Hours, and other sort of Men for my Pleasure. But had I your Address,* Madam—

MACHEATH. Have done with your Compliments, Ladies; and drink about: You are not so fond of me, *Jenny*, as you use to be.

JENNY DIVER. 'Tis not convenient, Sir, to show my Fondness among so many Rivals. 'Tis your own Choice, and not the warmth of my Inclination that will determine you.

AIR 23. All in a misty Morning, &c.

Before the Barn-door crowing,
The Cock by Hens attended,
His Eyes around him throwing,
Stands for a while suspended.
Then One he singles from the Crew,
And cheers the happy Hen;
With how do you do, and how do you do,
And how do you do again.

MACHEATH. Ah *Jenny*! thou art a dear Slut.

DOLLY TRULL. Pray, Madam, were you ever in keeping?*

SUKY TAWDRY. I hope, Madam, I ha'nt been so long upon the Town, but I have met with some good Fortune as well as my Neighbours.

DOLLY TRULL. Pardon me, Madam, I meant no harm by the Question; 'twas only in the way of Conversation.

SUKY TAWDRY. Indeed, Madam, if I had not been a Fool, I might have liv'd very handsomely with my last Friend. But upon his missing five Guineas, he turn'd me off. Now I never suspected he had counted them.

MRS SLAMMEKIN. Who do you look upon, Madam, as your best sort of Keepers?

DOLLY TRULL. That, Madam, is thereafter as they be.*

MRS SLAMMEKIN. I, Madam, was once kept by a *Jew*; and bating* their Religion, to Women they are a good sort of People.

SUKY TAWDRY. Now for my part, I own I like an old Fellow: for we always make them pay for what they can't do.

MRS VIXEN. A spruce Prentice, let me tell you, Ladies, is no ill thing, they bleed freely. I have sent at least two or three dozen of them in my time to the Plantations.*

JENNY DIVER. But to be sure, Sir, with so much good Fortune as you have had upon the Road, you must be grown immensely rich.

MACHEATH. The Road, indeed, hath done me justice, but the Gaming-Table hath been my ruin.

AIR 24. When once I lay with another Man's Wife, &c.

JENNY DIVER.   *The Gamesters and Lawyers are Jugglers alike,*
If they meddle your All is in danger.
Like Gypsies, if once they can finger a Souse,*
Your Pockets they pick, and they pilfer your House,
And give your Estate to a Stranger.

A Man of Courage should never put any Thing to the Risque, but his Life. These* are the Tools of a Man of Honour. Cards and Dice are only fit for cowardly Cheats, who prey upon their Friends.

[*She takes up his Pistol.* SUKY TAWDRY *takes up the other.*

SUKY TAWDRY.   This, Sir, is fitter for your Hand. Besides your Loss of Money, 'tis a Loss to the Ladies. Gaming takes you off from Women. How fond could I be of you! but before Company, 'tis ill bred.

MACHEATH.   Wanton Hussies!

JENNY DIVER.   I must and will have a Kiss to give my Wine a zest.

[*They take him about the Neck, and make Signs to*
PEACHUM *and Constables, who rush in upon him.*

SCENE V

To them, PEACHUM *and Constables.*

PEACHUM.   I seize you, Sir, as my Prisoner.

MACHEATH.   Was this well done, *Jenny?*—Women are Decoy Ducks; who can trust them! Beasts, Jades, Jilts, Harpies, Furies, Whores!

PEACHUM.   Your Case, Mr *Macheath*, is not particular. The greatest Heroes have been ruin'd by Women. But, to do them justice, I must own they are a pretty sort of Creatures, if we could trust them. You must now, Sir, take your leave of the Ladies, and if they have a Mind to make you a Visit, they will be sure to find you at home. The Gentleman, Ladies, lodges in *Newgate.* Constables, wait upon the Captain to his Lodgings.

AIR 25. When first I laid Siege to my *Chloris*, &c.

MACHEATH. *At the Tree I shall suffer with pleasure,*
At the Tree I shall suffer with pleasure,
Let me go where I will,
In all kinds of Ill,
I shall find no such Furies as these are.

PEACHUM. Ladies, I'll take care the Reckoning shall be discharg'd.

[*Exit* MACHEATH, *guarded with* PEACHUM *and Constables.*

SCENE VI

The Women remain.

MRS VIXEN. Look ye, Mrs *Jenny*, though Mr *Peachum* may have made a private Bargain with you and *Suky Tawdry* for betraying the Captain, as we were all assisting, we ought all to share alike.

MRS COAXER. I think Mr *Peachum*, after so long an acquaintance, might have trusted me as well as *Jenny Diver*.

MRS SLAMMEKIN. I am sure at least three Men of his hanging, and in a Year's time too, (if he did me justice) should be set down to my account.

DOLLY TRULL. Mrs *Slammekin*, that is not fair. For you know one of them was taken in Bed with me.

JENNY DIVER. As far as a Bowl of Punch or a Treat, I believe Mrs *Suky* will join with me.— As for any thing else, Ladies, you cannot in conscience expect it.

MRS SLAMMEKIN. Dear Madam—

DOLLY TRULL. I would not for the World—

MRS SLAMMEKIN. 'Tis impossible for me—

DOLLY TRULL. As I hope to be sav'd, Madam—

MRS SLAMMEKIN. Nay, then I must stay here all Night—

DOLLY TRULL. Since you command me.*

[*Exeunt with great Ceremony.*

SCENE VII

Newgate.

LOCKIT, *Turnkeys,** MACHEATH, *Constables.*

LOCKIT. Noble Captain, you are welcome. You have not been
a Lodger of mine this Year and half. You know the custom,
Sir. Garnish, Captain, Garnish.* Hand me down those Fetters there.

MACHEATH. Those, Mr *Lockit*, seem to be the heaviest of the whole
sett. With your leave, I should like the further pair better.

LOCKIT. Look ye, Captain, we know what is fittest for our Prisoners.
When a Gentleman uses me with Civility, I always do the best I can
to please him.—Hand them down I say.—We have them of all
Prices, from one Guinea to ten, and 'tis fitting every Gentleman
should please himself.

MACHEATH. I understand you, Sir.

[*Gives Money.*

The Fees here are so many, and so exorbitant, that few Fortunes
can bear the Expence of getting off handsomly, or of dying like a
Gentleman.

LOCKIT. Those, I see, will fit the Captain better.—Take down the
further Pair. Do but examine them, Sir.—Never was better work.
How genteely they are made!—They will sit as easy as a Glove, and
the nicest* Man in *England* might not be asham'd to wear them.

[*He puts on the Chains.*

If I had the best Gentleman in the Land in my Custody I could not
equip him more handsomly. And so, Sir—I now leave you to your
private Meditations.

SCENE VIII

MACHEATH.

AIR 26. Courtiers, Courtiers think it no harm, &c.

Man may escape from Rope and Gun;
Nay, some have out-liv'd the Doctor's Pill;
Who takes a Woman must be undone,
*   That Basilisk* is sure to kill.*
The Fly that sips Treacle is lost in the Sweets,
So he that tastes Woman, Woman, Woman,
He that tastes Woman, Ruin meets.

To what a woful plight have I brought my self! Here must I (all day long, 'till I am hang'd) be confin'd to hear the Reproaches of a Wench who lays her Ruin at my Door.—I am in the Custody of her Father, and to be sure if he knows of the matter, I shall have a fine time on't betwixt this and my Execution.—But I promis'd the Wench Marriage.—What signifies a Promise to a Woman? Does not Man in Marriage itself promise a hundred things that he never means to perform? Do all we can, Women will believe us; for they look upon a Promise as an Excuse for following their own Inclinations.—But here comes *Lucy*, and I cannot get from her—Wou'd I were deaf!

SCENE IX

MACHEATH, LUCY.

LUCY. You base Man you,—how can you look me in the Face after what hath past between us?—See here, perfidious Wretch, how I am forc'd to bear about the load of Infamy* you have laid upon me—O *Macheath*! thou hast robb'd me of my Quiet—to see thee tortur'd would give me pleasure.

AIR 27. A lovely Lass to a Friar came, &c.

Thus when a good Huswife sees a Rat
In her Trap in the Morning taken,

> *With pleasure her Heart goes pit a pat,*
> *In Revenge for her loss of Bacon.*
> *Then she throws him*
> *To the Dog or Cat,*
> *To be worried, crush'd and shaken.*

MACHEATH. Have you no Bowels,* no Tenderness, my dear *Lucy*, to see a Husband in these Circumstances?

LUCY. A Husband!

MACHEATH. In ev'ry respect but the Form, and that, my Dear, may be said over us at any time.——Friends should not insist upon Ceremonies. From a Man of Honour, his Word is as good as his Bond.

LUCY. 'Tis the Pleasure of all you fine Men to insult the Women you have ruin'd.

AIR 28. *'Twas when the Sea was roaring, &c.*

> *How cruel are the Traytors,*
> *Who lye and swear in jest,*
> *To cheat unguarded Creatures*
> *Of Virtue, Fame, and Rest!*
> *Whoever steals a Shilling,*
> *Through Shame the Guilt conceals:*
> *In Love the perjur'd Villain*
> *With Boasts the Theft reveals.*

MACHEATH. The very first Opportunity, my Dear, (have but Patience) you shall be my Wife in whatever manner you please.

LUCY. Insinuating Monster! And so you think I know nothing of the Affair of Miss *Polly Peachum*.——I could tear thy Eyes out!

MACHEATH. Sure *Lucy*, you can't be such a Fool as to be jealous of *Polly*!

LUCY. Are you not married to her, you Brute, you?

MACHEATH. Married! Very good. The Wench gives it out only to vex thee, and to ruin me in thy good Opinion. 'Tis true, I go to the House; I chat with the Girl, I kiss her, I say a thousand things to her (as all Gentlemen do) that mean nothing, to divert my self; and now the silly Jade hath set it about that I am married to her, to let me know what she would be at. Indeed, my dear *Lucy*, these violent Passions may be of ill consequence to a Woman in your condition.

LUCY.   Come, come, Captain, for all your Assurance, you know that Miss *Polly* hath put it out of your power to do me the Justice you promis'd me.

MACHEATH.   A jealous Woman believes ev'ry thing her Passion suggests. To convince you of my Sincerity, if we can find the Ordinary, I shall have no Scruples of making you my Wife; and I know the consequence of having two at a time.

LUCY.   That you are only to be hang'd, and so get rid of them both.

MACHEATH.   I am ready, my dear *Lucy*, to give you satisfaction—if you think there is any in Marriage.—What can a Man of Honour say more?

LUCY.   So then it seems, you are not married to Miss *Polly*.

MACHEATH.   You know, *Lucy*, the Girl is prodigiously conceited. No Man can say a civil thing to her, but (like other fine Ladies) her Vanity makes her think he's her own for ever and ever.

AIR 29.   *The Sun had loos'd his weary Teams, &c.*

> *The first time at the Looking-glass*
> *The Mother sets her Daughter,*
> *The Image strikes the smiling Lass*
> *With Self-love ever after.*
> *Each time she looks, she, fonder grown,*
> *Thinks ev'ry Charm grows stronger.*
> *But alas, vain Maid, all Eyes but your own*
> *Can see you are not younger.*

When Women consider their own Beauties, they are all alike unreasonable in their demands; for they expect their Lovers should like them as long as they like themselves.

LUCY.   Yonder is my Father—perhaps this way we may light upon the Ordinary, who shall try if you will be as good as your Word.—For I long to be made an honest Woman.

SCENE X

PEACHUM, LOCKIT *with an Account-Book.*

LOCKIT. In this last Affair, Brother *Peachum*,* we are agreed. You have consented to go halves in *Macheath.*

PEACHUM. We shall never fall out about an Execution.—But as to that Article, pray how stands our last Year's account?

LOCKIT. If you will run your Eye over it, you'll find 'tis fair and clearly stated.

PEACHUM. This long Arrear of the Government* is very hard upon us! Can it be expected that we should hang our Acquaintance for nothing, when our Betters will hardly save theirs without being paid for it. Unless the People in employment pay better, I promise them for the future, I shall let other Rogues live besides their own.

LOCKIT. Perhaps, Brother, they are afraid these matters may be carried too far. We are treated too by them with Contempt, as if our Profession were not reputable.

PEACHUM. In one respect indeed, our Employment may be reckon'd dishonest, because, like Great Statesmen, we encourage those who betray their Friends.

LOCKIT. Such Language, Brother, any where else, might turn to your prejudice. Learn to be more guarded, I beg you.

AIR 30. How happy are we, *&c.*

> When you censure the Age,
> Be cautious and sage,
> Lest the Courtiers offended should be:
> If you mention Vice or Bribe,
> 'Tis so pat to all the Tribe;
> Each crys—That was levell'd at me.

PEACHUM. Here's poor *Ned Clincher*'s Name,* I see. Sure, Brother *Lockit*, there was a little unfair proceeding in *Ned*'s case: for he told me in the Condemn'd Hold,* that for Value receiv'd, you had promis'd him a Session or two longer without Molestation.

LOCKIT. Mr *Peachum*,—This is the first time my Honour was ever call'd in Question.

PEACHUM. Business is at an end—if once we act dishonourably.

LOCKIT. Who accuses me?

PEACHUM. You are warm, Brother.

LOCKIT. He that attacks my Honour, attacks my Livelyhood.—And this Usage—Sir—is not to be born.

PEACHUM. Since you provoke me to speak—I must tell you too, that Mrs *Coaxer* charges you with defrauding her of her Information-Money, for the apprehending of curl-pated *Hugh*. Indeed, indeed, Brother, we must punctually pay our Spies, or we shall have no Information.

LOCKIT. Is this Language to me, Sirrah—who have sav'd you from the Gallows, Sirrah!

[*Collaring each other.*

PEACHUM. If I am hang'd, it shall be for ridding the World of an arrant Rascal.

LOCKIT. This Hand shall do the office of the Halter* you deserve, and throttle you—you Dog!—

PEACHUM. Brother, Brother,—We are both in the Wrong—We shall be both Losers in the Dispute—for you know we have it in our Power to hang each other. You should not be so passionate.

LOCKIT. Nor you so provoking.

PEACHUM. 'Tis our mutual Interest; 'tis for the Interest of the World we should agree. If I said any thing, Brother, to the Prejudice of your Character, I ask pardon.

LOCKIT. Brother *Peachum*—I can forgive as well as resent.—Give me your Hand. Suspicion does not become a Friend.

PEACHUM. I only meant to give you occasion to justifie yourself: But I must now step home, for I expect the Gentleman about this Snuff-box, that *Filch* nimm'd* two Nights ago in the Park. I appointed him at this hour.

SCENE XI

LOCKIT, LUCY.

LOCKIT. Whence come you, Hussy?

LUCY. My Tears might answer that Question.

LOCKIT. You have then been whimpering and fondling, like a Spaniel, over the Fellow that hath abus'd you.

LUCY. One can't help Love; one can't cure it. 'Tis not in my Power to obey you, and hate him.

LOCKIT. Learn to bear your Husband's Death like a reasonable Woman. 'Tis not the fashion, now-a-days, so much as to affect Sorrow upon these Occasions. No Woman would ever marry, if she had not the Chance of Mortality for a Release. Act like a Woman of Spirit, Hussy, and thank your Father for what he is doing.

AIR 31. Of a noble Race was *Shenkin*.

LUCY.   *Is then his Fate decreed, Sir?*
           Such a Man can I think of quitting?
           When first we met, so moves me yet,
           O see how my Heart is splitting!

LOCKIT. Look ye, *Lucy*—There is no saving him.—So, I think, you must ev'n do like other Widows—Buy your self Weeds,* and be cheerful.

AIR 32.

You'll think e'er many Days ensue
This Sentence not severe;
I hang your Husband, Child, 'tis true,
But with him hang your Care.
Twang dang dillo dee.

Like a good Wife, go moan over your dying Husband. That, Child, is your Duty—Consider, Girl, you can't have the Man and the Money too—so make yourself as easy as you can, by getting all you can from him.

SCENE XII

LUCY, MACHEATH.

LUCY. Though the Ordinary was out of the way to-day, I hope, my Dear, you will, upon the first opportunity, quiet my Scruples—Oh Sir!—my Father's hard Heart is not to be soften'd, and I am in the utmost Despair.

MACHEATH. But if I could raise a small Sum—Would not twenty Guineas, think you, move him?—Of all the Arguments in the way of Business, the Perquisite* is the most prevailing.—Your Father's Perquisites for the Escape of Prisoners must amount to a considerable Sum in the Year. Money well tim'd, and properly apply'd, will do any thing.

AIR 33. *London* Ladies.

If you at an Office solicit your Due,
  And would not have Matters neglected;
You must quicken the Clerk with the Perquisite too,
  To do what his Duty directed.
Or would you the Frowns of a Lady prevent,
  She too has this palpable Failing,
The Perquisite softens her into Consent;
  That Reason with all is prevailing.

LUCY. What Love or Money can do shall be done: for all my Comfort depends upon your Safety.

SCENE XIII

LUCY, MACHEATH, POLLY.

POLLY. Where is my dear Husband?—Was a Rope ever intended for this Neck!—O let me throw my Arms about it, and throttle thee with Love!—Why dost thou turn away from me?—'Tis thy *Polly*—'Tis thy Wife.

MACHEATH. Was ever such an unfortunate Rascal as I am!

LUCY. Was there ever such another Villain!

POLLY. O *Macheath*! was it for this we parted? Taken! Imprison'd! Try'd! Hang'd!—cruel Reflection! I'll stay with thee 'till Death— no Force shall tear thy dear Wife from thee now.—What means my Love?—Not one kind Word! not one kind Look! think what thy *Polly* suffers to see thee in this Condition.

AIR 34. All in the Downs, &c.

Thus when the Swallow, seeking Prey,
  Within the Sash* is closely pent,
His Consort, with bemoaning Lay,
  Without sits pining for th' Event.*
Her chatt'ring Lovers all around her skim;
She heeds them not (poor Bird!) her Soul's with him.

MACHEATH [*aside*]. I must disown her. <*Aloud.*> The Wench is distracted.

LUCY. Am I then bilk'd of my Virtue? Can I have no Reparation? Sure Men were born to lye, and Women to believe them! O Villain! Villain!

POLLY. Am I not thy Wife?—Thy Neglect of me, thy Aversion to me too severely proves it.—Look on me.—Tell me, am I not thy Wife?

LUCY. Perfidious Wretch!

POLLY. Barbarous Husband!

LUCY. Hadst thou been hang'd five Months ago, I had been happy.

POLLY. And I too—If you had been kind to me 'till Death, it would not have vex'd me—And that's no very unreasonable Request, (though from a Wife) to a Man who hath not above seven or eight Days to live.

LUCY. Art thou then married to another? Hast thou two Wives, Monster?

MACHEATH. If Women's Tongues can cease for an Answer— hear me.

LUCY. I won't.—Flesh and Blood can't bear my Usage.

POLLY. Shall I not claim my own? Justice bids me speak.

AIR 35. Have you heard of a frolicksome Ditty, &c.

MACHEATH.   *How happy could I be with either,*
Were t'other dear Charmer away!
But while you thus teaze me together,
To neither a Word will I say;
But tol de rol, &c.

POLLY. Sure, my Dear, there ought to be some Preference shown to a Wife! At least she may claim the Appearance of it. He must be distracted with his Misfortunes, or he could not use me thus!

LUCY. O Villain, Villain! thou hast deceiv'd me—I could even inform against thee with Pleasure. Not a Prude wishes more heartily to have Facts* against her intimate Acquaintance, than I now wish to have Facts against thee. I would have her Satisfaction, and they should all out.

AIR 36. *Irish* Trot.

POLLY.   *I'm bubbled.**

LUCY.   —————*I'm bubbled.*

POLLY.   *Oh how I am troubled!*

LUCY.   *Bambouzled, and bit!*

POLLY.   —————————*My Distresses are doubled.*

LUCY.   *When you come to the Tree, should the Hangman refuse,*
These Fingers, with Pleasure, could fasten the Noose.

POLLY.   *I'm bubbled,* &c.

MACHEATH. Be pacified, my dear Lucy—This is all a Fetch* of *Polly*'s, to make me desperate with you in case I get off. If I am hang'd, she would fain have the Credit of being thought my Widow—Really, *Polly*, this is no time for a Dispute of this sort; for whenever you are talking of Marriage, I am thinking of Hanging.

POLLY. And hast thou the Heart to persist in disowning me?

MACHEATH. And hast thou the Heart to persist in persuading me that I am married? Why, *Polly*, dost thou seek to aggravate my Misfortunes?

LUCY.   Really, Miss *Peachum*, you but expose yourself. Besides, 'tis barbarous in you to worry a Gentleman in his Circumstances.

AIR 37.

POLLY.

> *Cease your Funning;*
> *Force or Cunning*
> *Never shall my Heart trapan.**
> *All these Sallies*
> *Are but Malice*
> *To seduce my constant Man.*
> *'Tis most certain,*
> *By their flirting*
> *Women oft' have Envy shown;*
> *Pleas'd, to ruin*
> *Others wooing;*
> *Never happy in their own!*

Decency, Madam, methinks might teach you to behave yourself with some Reserve with the Husband, while his Wife is present.

MACHEATH.   But seriously, *Polly*, this is carrying the Joke a little too far.

LUCY.   If you are determin'd, Madam, to raise a Disturbance in the Prison, I shall be oblig'd to send for the Turnkey to show you the Door. I am sorry, Madam, you force me to be so ill-bred.

POLLY.   Give me leave to tell you, Madam; These forward Airs don't become you in the least, Madam. And my Duty, Madam, obliges me to stay with my Husband, Madam.

AIR 38. Good-morrow, Gossip Joan.

LUCY.

> *Why how now, Madam* Flirt?
> *If you thus must chatter;*
> *And are for flinging Dirt,*
> *Let's try who best can spatter;*
> *Madam* Flirt!

POLLY.

> *Why how now, saucy Jade;*
> *Sure the Wench is Tipsy!*
> *How can you see me made*   [*To him.*
> *The Scoff of such a Gipsy?*
> *Saucy Jade!*   [*To her.*

SCENE XIV

LUCY, MACHEATH, POLLY, PEACHUM.

PEACHUM. Where's my Wench? Ah Hussy! Hussy!—Come you home, you Slut; and when your Fellow is hang'd, hang yourself, to make your Family some amends.

POLLY. Dear, dear Father, do not tear me from him—I must speak; I have more to say to him—Oh! twist thy Fetters about me, that he may not haul me from thee!

PEACHUM. Sure all Women are alike! If ever they commit the Folly,* they are sure to commit another by exposing themselves— Away—Not a Word more—You are my Prisoner now, Hussy.

AIR 39. *Irish* Howl.

POLLY.   *No Power on Earth can e'er divide,*
            The Knot that Sacred Love hath ty'd.
            When Parents draw against our Mind,
            The True-love's Knot they faster bind.
            Oh, oh ray, oh Amborah—oh, oh, &c.

                    [*Holding* MACHEATH, PEACHUM *pulling her.*

SCENE XV

LUCY, MACHEATH.

MACHEATH. I am naturally compassionate, Wife; so that I could not use the Wench as she deserv'd; which made you at first suspect there was something in what she said.

LUCY. Indeed, my Dear, I was strangely puzzled.

MACHEATH. If that had been the Case, her Father would never have brought me into this Circumstance—No, *Lucy*,—I had rather dye than be false to thee.

LUCY. How happy am I, if you say this from your Heart! For I love thee so, that I could sooner bear to see thee hang'd than in the Arms of another.

MACHEATH. But couldst thou bear to see me hang'd?

LUCY. O *Macheath*, I can never live to see that Day.

MACHEATH. You see, *Lucy*; in the Account of Love you are in my debt, and you must now be convinc'd, that I rather chuse to die than be another's.—Make me, if possible, love thee more, and let me owe my Life to thee—If you refuse to assist me, *Peachum* and your Father will immediately put me beyond all means of Escape.

LUCY. My Father, I know, hath been drinking hard with the Prisoners: and I fancy he is now taking his Nap in his own Room—If I can procure the Keys, shall I go off with thee, my Dear?

MACHEATH. If we are together, 'twill be impossible to lye conceal'd. As soon as the Search begins to be a little cool, I will send to thee—'Till then my Heart is thy Prisoner.

LUCY. Come then, my dear Husband—owe thy Life to me—and though you love me not—be grateful—But that *Polly* runs in my Head strangely.

MACHEATH. A Moment of time may make us unhappy for-ever.

AIR 40. The Lass of Patie's Mill, &c.

LUCY.   *I like the Fox shall grieve,*
                Whose Mate hath left her side,
                Whom Hounds, from Morn to Eve,
                Chase o'er the Country wide.
                Where can my Lover hide?
                Where cheat the weary Pack?
                If Love be not his Guide,
                He never will come back!

ACT III

SCENE I

SCENE *Newgate.*

LOCKIT, LUCY.

LOCKIT. To be sure, Wench, you must have been aiding and abetting to help him to this Escape.

LUCY. Sir, here hath been *Peachum* and his Daughter *Polly*, and to be sure they know the Ways of *Newgate* as well as if they had been born and bred in the Place all their Lives. Why must all your Suspicion light upon me?

LOCKIT. *Lucy, Lucy,* I will have none of these shuffling Answers.

LUCY. Well then—If I know any Thing of him I wish I may be burnt!*

LOCKIT. Keep your Temper, *Lucy,* or I shall pronounce you guilty.

LUCY. Keep yours, Sir,—I do wish I may be burnt. I do—And what can I say more to convince you?

LOCKIT. Did he tip handsomely?—How much did he come down with? Come Hussy, don't cheat your Father; and I shall not be angry with you—Perhaps, you have made a better Bargain with him than I could have done—How much, my good Girl?

LUCY. You know, Sir, I am fond of him, and would have given Money to have kept him with me.

LOCKIT. Ah *Lucy*! thy Education might have put thee more upon thy Guard; for a Girl in the Bar of an Ale-house is always besieg'd.

LUCY. Dear Sir, mention not my Education—for 'twas to that I owe my Ruin.

AIR 41. If Love's a sweet Passion, &c.

When young at the Bar you first taught me to score,*
And bid me be free of my Lips, and no more;
I was kiss'd by the Parson, the Squire, and the Sot.
When the Guest was departed, the Kiss was forgot.
But his Kiss was so sweet, and so closely he prest,
That I languish'd and pin'd 'till I granted the rest.

If you can forgive me, Sir, I will make a fair Confession, for to be sure he hath been a most barbarous Villain to me.

LOCKIT. And so you have let him escape, Hussy—Have you?

LUCY. When a Woman loves; a kind Look, a tender Word can persuade her to any thing—And I could ask no other Bribe.

LOCKIT. Thou wilt always be a vulgar Slut, *Lucy.*—If you would not be look'd upon as a Fool, you should never do any thing but upon the Foot of Interest. Those that act otherwise are their own Bubbles.*

LUCY. But Love, Sir, is a Misfortune that may happen to the most discreet Woman, and in Love we are all Fools alike.—Notwithstanding all he swore, I am now fully convinc'd that *Polly Peachum* is actually his Wife.—Did I let him escape, (Fool that I was!) to go to her?—*Polly* will wheedle herself into his Money, and then *Peachum* will hang him, and cheat us both.

LOCKIT. So I am to be ruin'd, because, forsooth, you must be in Love!—a very pretty Excuse!

LUCY. I could murder that impudent happy Strumpet:—I gave him his Life, and that Creature enjoys the Sweets of it.—Ungrateful *Macheath*!

AIR 42. *South-Sea* Ballad.

My Love is all Madness and Folly,
Alone I lye,
Toss, tumble, and cry,
What a happy Creature is Polly!
Was e'er such a Wretch as I!
With Rage I redden like Scarlet,

> That my dear inconstant Varlet,
>   Stark blind to my Charms,
>   Is lost in the Arms
> Of that Jilt, that inveigling Harlot!
>   Stark blind to my Charms,
>   Is lost in the Arms
> Of that Jilt, that inveigling Harlot!
> This, this my Resentment alarms.

LOCKIT. And so, after all this Mischief, I must stay here to be entertain'd with your catterwauling, Mistress Puss!—Out of my Sight, wanton Strumpet! you shall fast and mortify yourself into Reason, with now and then a little handsome Discipline to bring you to your Senses.—Go.

SCENE II

LOCKIT.

Peachum then intends to outwit me in this Affair; but I'll be even with him.—The Dog is leaky in his Liquor,* so I'll ply him that way, get the Secret from him, and turn this Affair to my own Advantage.—Lions, Wolves, and Vulturs don't live together in Herds, Droves or Flocks.—Of all Animals of Prey, Man is the only sociable one. Every one of us preys upon his Neighbour, and yet we herd together.—*Peachum* is my Companion, my Friend—According to the Custom of the World, indeed, he may quote thousands of Precedents for cheating me—And shall not I make use of the Privilege of Friendship to make him a Return?

AIR 43. *Packington's* Pound.

> Thus Gamesters united in Friendship are found,
> Though they know that their Industry all is a Cheat;
> They flock to their Prey at the Dice-Box's Sound,
> And join to promote one another's Deceit.
>   But if by mishap
>   They fail of a Chap,*
> To keep in their Hands, they each other entrap.

Like Pikes, lank with Hunger, who miss of their Ends,
They bite their Companions, and prey on their Friends.

Now, *Peachum*, you and I, like honest Tradesmen, are to have a fair Tryal which of us two can over-reach the other.—*Lucy*.—

[*Enter* LUCY.

Are there any of *Peachum*'s People now in the House?

LUCY. *Filch*, Sir, is drinking a Quartern of Strong-Waters* in the next Room with Black *Moll*.

LOCKIT. Bid him come to me.

SCENE III

LOCKIT, FILCH.

LOCKIT. Why, Boy, thou lookest as if thou wert half starv'd; like a shotten Herring.*

FILCH. One had need have the Constitution of a Horse to go thorough the Business.—Since the favourite Child-getter was disabled by a Mis-hap, I have pick'd up a little Money by helping the Ladies to a Pregnancy against their being call'd down to Sentence.*—But if a Man cannot get an honest Livelyhood any easier way, I am sure, 'tis what I can't undertake for another Session.

LOCKIT. Truly, if that great Man should tip off,* 'twould be an irreparable Loss. The Vigor and Prowess of a Knight-Errant never sav'd half the Ladies in Distress that he hath done.—But, Boy, can'st thou tell me where thy Master is to be found?

FILCH. At his Lock, Sir, at the *Crooked Billet*.*

LOCKIT. Very well.—I have nothing more with you.

[*Exit* FILCH.

I'll go to him there, for I have many important Affairs to settle with him; and in the way of those Transactions, I'll artfully get into his Secret.—So that *Macheath* shall not remain a Day longer out of my Clutches.

SCENE IV

A Gaming-House.

MACHEATH *in a fine tarnish'd Coat*, BEN BUDGE,
MATT OF THE MINT.

MACHEATH. I am sorry, Gentlemen, the Road was so barren of
Money. When my Friends are in Difficulties, I am always glad that
my Fortune can be serviceable to them.

[*Gives them Money.*

You see, Gentlemen, I am not a meer Court Friend, who professes
every thing and will do nothing.

AIR 44. Lillibullero.

> *The Modes of the Court so common are grown,*
>   *That a true Friend can hardly be met;*
> *Friendship for Interest is but a Loan,*
>   *Which they let out for what they can get.*
>   *'Tis true, you find*
>   *Some Friends so kind,*
> *Who will give you good Counsel themselves to defend.*
>   *In sorrowful Ditty,*
>   *They promise, they pity,*
> *But shift you for Money, from Friend to Friend.*

But we, Gentlemen, have still Honour enough to break through
the Corruptions of the World.—And while I can serve you, you
may command me.

BEN BUDGE. It grieves my Heart that so generous a Man should be
involv'd in such Difficulties, as oblige him to live with such ill
Company, and herd with Gamesters.

MATT OF THE MINT. See the Partiality of Mankind!—One Man
may steal a Horse, better than another look over a Hedge*—Of all
Mechanics, of all servile Handycrafts-men, a Gamester is the
vilest. But yet, as many of the Quality are of the Profession, he is
admitted amongst the politest Company. I wonder we are not more
respected.

MACHEATH. There will be deep Play* to-night at *Marybone*, and consequently Money may be pick'd up upon the Road. Meet me there, and I'll give you the Hint who is worth Setting.*

MATT OF THE MINT. The Fellow with a brown Coat with a narrow Gold Binding, I am told, is never without Money.

MACHEATH. What do you mean, *Matt?*—Sure you will not think of meddling with him!—He's a good honest kind of a Fellow, and one of us.

BEN BUDGE. To be sure, Sir, we will put our selves under your Direction.

MACHEATH. Have an Eye upon the Money-Lenders.—A *Rouleau,** or two, would prove a pretty sort of an Expedition. I hate Extortion.

MATT OF THE MINT. Those *Rouleaus* are very pretty Things.—I hate your Bank Bills.—There is such a Hazard in putting them off.

MACHEATH. There is a certain Man of Distinction, who in his Time hath nick'd me out of a great deal of the Ready. He is in my Cash,* *Ben*;—I'll point him out to you this Evening, and you shall draw upon him for the Debt.—The Company are met; I hear the Dice-box in the other Room. So, Gentlemen, your Servant. You'll meet me at *Marybone*.

SCENE V

Peachum's *Lock*.

A Table with Wine, Brandy, Pipes and Tobacco.

PEACHUM, LOCKIT.

LOCKIT. The Coronation Account,* Brother *Peachum*, is of so intri-cate a Nature, that I believe it will never be settled.

PEACHUM. It consists indeed of a great Variety of Articles.—It was worth to our People, in Fees of different Kinds, above ten Instalments.*—This is part of the Account, Brother, that lies open before us.

LOCKIT. A Lady's Tail* of rich Brocade—that, I see, is dispos'd of.

PEACHUM. To Mrs *Diana Trapes*, the Tally-woman, and she will make a good Hand on't in Shoes and Slippers, to trick out young Ladies, upon their going into Keeping.—*

LOCKIT. But I don't see any Article of the Jewels.

PEACHUM. Those are so well known, that they must be sent abroad—You'll find them enter'd under the Article of Exportation.—As for the Snuff-Boxes, Watches, Swords, &c.—I thought it best to enter them under their several Heads.

LOCKIT. Seven and twenty Women's Pockets* compleat; with the several things therein contain'd; all Seal'd, Number'd, and enter'd.

PEACHUM. But, Brother, it is impossible for us now to enter upon this Affair.—We should have the whole Day before us.—Besides, the Account of the last Half Year's Plate* is in a Book by it self, which lies at the other Office.

LOCKIT. Bring us then more Liquor.—To-day shall be for Pleasure—To-morrow for Business.—Ah Brother, those Daughters of ours are two slippery Hussies—Keep a watchful Eye upon *Polly*, and *Macheath* in a Day or two shall be our own again.

AIR 45. Down in the North Country, &c.

> *What Gudgeons* are we Men!*
> *Ev'ry Woman's easy Prey.*
> *Though we have felt the Hook, agen*
> *We bite and they betray.*
>
> *The Bird that hath been trapt,*
> *When he hears his calling Mate,*
> *To her he flies, again he's clapt*
> *Within the wiry Grate.*

PEACHUM. But what signifies catching the Bird, if your Daughter *Lucy* will set open the Door of the Cage?

LOCKIT. If Men were answerable for the Follies and Frailties of their Wives and Daughters, no Friends could keep a good Correspondence together for two Days.—This is unkind of you,

Brother; for among good Friends, what they say or do goes for nothing.

[*Enter a* SERVANT.

SERVANT. Sir, here's Mrs *Diana Trapes* wants to speak with you.

PEACHUM. Shall we admit her, Brother *Lockit*?

LOCKIT. By all means—She's a good Customer, and a fine-spoken Woman—And a Woman who drinks and talks so freely, will enliven the Conversation.

PEACHUM. Desire her to walk in.

[*Exit* SERVANT.

SCENE VI

PEACHUM, LOCKIT, MRS TRAPES.

PEACHUM. Dear Mrs *Dye*, your Servant—One may know by your Kiss, that your Ginn is excellent.

MRS TRAPES. I was always very curious* in my Liquors.

LOCKIT. There is no perfum'd Breath like it—I have been long acquainted with the Flavour of those Lips—Han't I, Mrs *Dye*?

MRS TRAPES. Fill it up.—I take as large Draughts of Liquor, as I did of Love.—I hate a Flincher in either.

AIR 46. A Shepherd kept Sheep, &c.

In the Days of my Youth I could bill like a Dove, fa, la, la, &c.
Like a Sparrow at all times was ready for Love, fa, la, la, &c.
The Life of all Mortals in Kissing should pass,
Lip to Lip while we're young—then the Lip to the Glass, fa, &c.

But now, Mr *Peachum*, to our Business.—If you have Blacks* of any kind, brought in of late; Mantoes*—Velvet Scarfs—Petticoats—Let it be what it will—I am your Chap—for all my Ladies are very fond of Mourning.

PEACHUM. Why, look ye, Mrs *Dye*—you deal so hard with us, that we can afford to give the Gentlemen, who venture their Lives for the Goods, little or nothing.

MRS TRAPES. The hard Times oblige me to go very near in my Dealing.—To be sure, of late Years I have been a great Sufferer by the Parliament.—Three thousand Pounds would hardly make me amends.—The Act for destroying the Mint,* was a severe Cut upon our Business—'Till then, if a Customer stept out of the way—we knew where to have her—No doubt you know Mrs *Coaxer*—there's a Wench now ('till to-day) with a good Suit of Cloaths of mine upon her Back, and I could never set Eyes upon her for three Months together.—Since the Act too against Imprisonment for small Sums,* my Loss there too hath been very considerable, and it must be so, when a Lady can borrow a handsome Petticoat, or a clean Gown, and I not have the least Hank upon her!* And, o' my Conscience, now-a-days most Ladies take a Delight in cheating, when they can do it with Safety.

PEACHUM. Madam, you had a handsome Gold Watch of us t'other Day for seven Guineas.—Considering we must have our Profit—To a Gentleman upon the Road, a Gold Watch will be scarce worth the taking.

MRS TRAPES. Consider, Mr *Peachum*, that Watch was remarkable, and not of very safe Sale.—If you have any black Velvet Scarfs—they are a handsome Winter-wear; and take with most Gentlemen who deal with my Customers.—'Tis I that put the Ladies upon a good Foot. 'Tis not Youth or Beauty that fixes their Price. The Gentlemen always pay according to their Dress, from half a Crown to two Guineas; and yet those Hussies make nothing of bilking of me.—Then too, allowing for Accidents.—I have eleven fine Customers now down under the Surgeon's Hands,—*what with Fees and other Expences, there are great Goings-out, and no Comings-in, and not a Farthing to pay for at least a Month's cloathing.—We run great Risques—great Risques indeed.

PEACHUM. As I remember, you said something just now of Mrs *Coaxer.*

MRS TRAPES. Yes, Sir.—To be sure I stript her of a Suit of my own

Cloaths about two hours ago; and have left her as she should be, in her Shift, with a Lover of hers at my House. She call'd him up Stairs, as he was going to *Marybone* in a Hackney Coach.—And I hope, for her own sake and mine, she will perswade the Captain to redeem her, for the Captain is very generous to the Ladies.

LOCKIT. What Captain?

MRS TRAPES. He thought I did not know him—An intimate Acquaintance of yours, Mr *Peachum*—Only Captain *Macheath*—as fine as a Lord.

PEACHUM. To-morrow, dear Mrs *Dye*, you shall set your own Price upon any of the Goods you like—We have at least half a dozen Velvet Scarfs, and all at your service. Will you give me leave to make you a Present of this Suit of Night-cloaths for your own wearing?—But are you sure it is Captain *Macheath*?

MRS TRAPES. Though he thinks I have forgot him; no Body knows him better. I have taken a great deal of the Captain's Money in my Time at second-hand, for he always lov'd to have his Ladies well drest.

PEACHUM. Mr *Lockit* and I have a little business with the Captain;—You understand me—and we will satisfye you for Mrs *Coaxer's* Debt.

LOCKIT. Depend upon it—we will deal like Men of Honour.

MRS TRAPES. I don't enquire after your Affairs—so whatever happens, I wash my Hands on't.—It hath always been my Maxim, that one Friend should assist another—But if you please—I'll take one of the Scarfs home with me, 'Tis always good to have something in Hand.

SCENE VII

Newgate.

LUCY. Jealousy, Rage, Love and Fear are at once tearing me to pieces. How I am weather-beaten and shatter'd with distresses!

AIR 47. One Evening, having lost my Way, &c.

I'm like a Skiff on the Ocean tost,
   Now high, now low, with each Billow born,
With her Rudder broke, and her Anchor lost,
   Deserted and all forlorn.
While thus I lye rolling and tossing all Night,
That Polly *lyes sporting on Seas of Delight!*
   Revenge, Revenge, Revenge,
   Shall appease my restless Sprite.

I have the Rats-bane* ready.—I run no Risque; for I can lay her Death upon the Ginn, and so many dye of that naturally that I shall never be call'd in Question.*—But say, I were to be hang'd—I never could be hang'd for any thing that would give me greater Comfort, than the poysoning that Slut.

[*Enter* FILCH.

FILCH. Madam, here's our Miss *Polly* come to wait upon you.

LUCY. Show her in.

SCENE VIII

LUCY, POLLY.

LUCY. Dear Madam, your Servant.—I hope you will pardon my Passion, when I was so happy to see you last.—I was so over-run with the Spleen,* that I was perfectly out of my self. And really when one hath the Spleen, every thing is to be excus'd by a Friend.

AIR 48. Now *Roger*, I'll tell thee, because thou'rt my Son.

When a Wife's in her Pout,
(As she's sometimes, no doubt;)
   The good Husband as meek as a Lamb,
      Her Vapours to still,*
      First grants her her Will,
And the quieting Draught is a Dram.
Poor Man! And the quieting Draught is a Dram.

—I wish all our Quarrels might have so comfortable a Reconciliation.

POLLY. I have no Excuse for my own Behaviour, Madam, but my Misfortunes.—And really, Madam, I suffer too upon your Account.

LUCY. But, Miss *Polly*—in the way of Friendship, will you give me leave to propose a Glass of Cordial to you?

POLLY. Strong-Waters are apt to give me the Head-ache—I hope, Madam, you will excuse me.

LUCY. Not the greatest Lady in the Land could have better in her Closet,* for her own private drinking.—You seem mighty low in Spirits, my Dear.

POLLY. I am sorry, Madam, my Health will not allow me to accept of your Offer.—I should not have left you in the rude Manner I did when we met last, Madam, had not my Papa haul'd me away so unexpectedly—I was indeed somewhat provok'd, and perhaps might use some Expressions that were disrespectful.— But really, Madam, the Captain treated me with so much Contempt and Cruelty, that I deserv'd your Pity, rather than your Resentment.

LUCY. But since his Escape, no doubt all Matters are made up again.—Ah *Polly*! *Polly*! 'tis I am the unhappy Wife; and he loves you as if you were only his Mistress.

POLLY. Sure, Madam, you cannot think me so happy as to be the Object of your Jealousy.—A Man is always afraid of a Woman who loves him too well—so that I must expect to be neglected and avoided.

LUCY. Then our Cases, my dear *Polly*, are exactly alike. Both of us indeed have been too fond.

AIR 49. O *Bessy Bell*.

POLLY.   *A Curse attends that Woman's Love,*
                    Who always would be pleasing.
LUCY.   *The Pertness of the billing Dove,*
                    Like tickling, is but teazing.
POLLY.   *What then in Love can Woman do?*

LUCY.   *If we grow fond they shun us.*
POLLY.   *And when we fly them, they pursue.*
LUCY.   *But leave us when they've won us.*

Love is so very whimsical in both Sexes, that it is impossible to be lasting.—But my Heart is particular,* and contradicts my own Observation.

POLLY. But really, Mistress *Lucy*, by his last Behaviour, I think I ought to envy you.—When I was forc'd from him, he did not shew the least Tenderness.—But perhaps, he hath a Heart not capable of it.

AIR 50. Would Fate to me *Belinda* give—

Among the Men, Coquets* we find,
Who Court by turns all Woman-kind;
And we grant all their Hearts desir'd,
When they are flatter'd, and admir'd.

The Coquets of both Sexes are Self-lovers, and that is a Love no other whatever can dispossess. I fear, my dear *Lucy*, our Husband is one of those.

LUCY. Away with these melancholy Reflections,—indeed, my dear *Polly*, we are both of us a Cup too low.—Let me prevail upon you, to accept of my Offer.

AIR 51. Come, sweet Lass, *&c.*

Come, sweet Lass,
Let's banish Sorrow
'Till To-morrow;
Come, sweet Lass,
Let's take a chirping* Glass.
Wine can clear
The Vapours of Despair;
And make us light as Air;
Then drink, and banish Care.

I can't bear, Child, to see you in such low Spirits.—And I must persuade you to what I know will do you good.— [*Aside*] I shall now soon be even with the hypocritical Strumpet.

<Exit.>

SCENE IX

POLLY.

All this wheedling of *Lucy* cannot be for nothing.—At this time too! when I know she hates me!—The Dissembling of a Woman is always the Fore-runner of Mischief.—By pouring Strong-Waters down my Throat, she thinks to pump some Secrets out of me.—I'll be upon my Guard, and won't taste a Drop of her Liquor, I'm resolv'd.

SCENE X

LUCY, *with Strong-Waters*, POLLY.

LUCY. Come, Miss *Polly*.

POLLY. Indeed, Child, you have given yourself trouble to no purpose.—You must, my Dear, excuse me.

LUCY. Really, Miss *Polly*, you are so squeamishly affected about taking a Cup of Strong-Waters as a Lady before Company. I vow, *Polly*, I shall take it monstrously ill if you refuse me.—Brandy and Men (though Women love them never so well) are always taken by us with some Reluctance—unless 'tis in private.

POLLY. I protest, Madam, it goes against me.—What do I see! *Macheath* again in Custody!—Now every glimm'ring of Happiness is lost.

[*Drops the Glass of Liquor on the Ground.*

LUCY [*aside*]. Since things are thus, I'm glad the Wench hath escap'd: for by this Event, 'tis plain, she was not happy enough to deserve to be poison'd.

SCENE XI

LOCKIT, MACHEATH, PEACHUM, LUCY, POLLY.

LOCKIT. Set your Heart to rest, Captain.—You have neither the Chance of Love or Money for another Escape,—for you are order'd to be call'd down upon your Tryal immediately.

PEACHUM. Away, Hussies!—This is not a time for a Man to be hamper'd with his Wives.—You see, the Gentleman is in Chains already.

LUCY. O Husband, Husband, my Heart long'd to see thee; but to see thee thus distracts me!

POLLY. Will not my dear Husband look upon his *Polly*? Why hadst thou not flown to me for Protection? with me thou hadst been safe.

AIR 52. The last time I went o'er the Moor.

POLLY.	*Hither, dear Husband, turn your Eyes.*
LUCY.	*Bestow one Glance to cheer me.*
POLLY.	*Think with that Look, thy* Polly *dyes.*
LUCY.	*O shun me not—but hear me.*
POLLY.	*'Tis* Polly *sues.*
LUCY.	——————*'Tis* Lucy *speaks.*
POLLY.	*Is thus true Love requited?*
LUCY.	*My Heart is bursting.*
POLLY.	————————*Mine too breaks.*
LUCY.	*Must I*
POLLY.	————*Must I be slighted?*

MACHEATH. What would you have me say, Ladies?—You see, this Affair will soon be at an end, without my disobliging either of you.

PEACHUM. But the settling this Point, Captain, might prevent a Law-suit between your two Widows.

AIR 53. *Tom Tinker's* my true Love.

MACHEATH. *Which way shall I turn me?*—*How can I decide?*
Wives, the Day of our Death, are as fond as a Bride.

One Wife is too much for most Husbands to hear,
But two at a time there's no Mortal can bear.
This way, and that way, and which way I will,
What would comfort the one, t'other Wife would take ill.

POLLY. But if his own Misfortunes have made him insensible to mine—A Father sure will be more compassionate.—Dear, dear Sir, sink* the material Evidence, and bring him off at his Tryal—*Polly* upon her Knees begs it of you.

AIR 54. I am a poor Shepherd undone.

When my Hero in Court appears,
    And stands arraign'd for his Life;
Then think of poor Polly's *Tears;*
    For Ah! Poor Polly's *his Wife.*
Like the Sailor he holds up his Hand,
    Distrest on the dashing Wave.
To die a dry Death at Land,
    Is as bad as a watry Grave.
And alas, poor Polly!
Alack, and well-a-day!
Before I was in Love,
    Oh! every Month was May.

LUCY. If *Peachum*'s Heart is harden'd; sure you, Sir, will have more Compassion on a Daughter.—I know the Evidence is in your Power.—How then can you be a Tyrant to me?

[*Kneeling.*

AIR 55. *Ianthe the lovely, &c.*

When he holds up his Hand arraign'd for his Life,
O think of your Daughter, and think I'm his Wife!
What are Cannons, or Bombs, or clashing of Swords?
For Death is more certain by Witnesses Words.
Then nail up their Lips; that dread Thunder allay;
And each Month of my Life will hereafter be May.

LOCKIT. *Macheath*'s time is come, Lucy.—We know our own Affairs, therefore let us have no more Whimpering or Whining.

AIR 56. A Cobler there was, &c.

Our selves, like the Great, to secure a Retreat,
When Matters require it, must give up our Gang:
And good reason why,
*   Or, instead of the Fry,**
*   Ev'n Peachum and I,*
Like poor petty Rascals, might hang, hang;
Like poor petty Rascals, might hang.

PEACHUM. Set your Heart at rest, *Polly.*—Your Husband is to dye to-day.—Therefore, if you are not already provided, 'tis high time to look about for another. There's Comfort for you, you Slut.

LOCKIT. We are ready, Sir, to conduct you to the *Old-Baily.*

AIR 57. Bonny *Dundee.*

MACHEATH.   *The Charge is prepar'd; The Lawyers are met,*
The Judges all rang'd (a terrible Show!)
I go, undismay'd.—For Death is a Debt,
A Debt on demand.—So, take what I owe.
Then farewell, my Love—Dear Charmers, adieu.
Contented I die—'Tis the better for you.
Here ends all Dispute the rest of our Lives.
For this way at once I please all my Wives.

Now, Gentlemen, I am ready to attend you.

SCENE XII

LUCY, POLLY, FILCH.

POLLY. Follow them, *Filch,* to the Court. And when the Tryal is over, bring me a particular Account of his Behaviour, and of every thing that happen'd.—You'll find me here with Miss *Lucy.*

[*Exit* FILCH.

But why is all this Musick?

LUCY. The Prisoners, whose Tryals are put off till next Session, are diverting themselves.

POLLY. Sure there is nothing so charming as Musick! I'm fond of it to distraction!—But alas!—now, all Mirth seems an Insult upon my Affliction.—Let us retire, my dear *Lucy*, and indulge our Sorrows.—The noisy Crew, you see, are coming upon us.

[*Exeunt.*

A Dance of Prisoners in Chains, &c.

SCENE XIII

The Condemn'd Hold.

MACHEATH, *in a melancholy Posture.*

AIR 58. Happy Groves.

O cruel, cruel, cruel Case!
Must I suffer this Disgrace?

AIR 59. Of all the Girls that are so smart.

Of all the Friends in time of Grief,
When threatning Death looks grimmer,
Not one so sure can bring Relief,
*As this best Friend, a Brimmer.**

[*Drinks.*

AIR 60. *Britons* strike home.

Since I must swing,—I scorn, I scorn to wince or whine.

[*Rises.*

AIR 61. Chevy Chase.

But now again my Spirits sink;
I'll raise them high with Wine.

[*Drinks a Glass of Wine.*

AIR 62. To old Sir *Simon* the King.

But Valour the stronger grows,
The stronger Liquor we're drinking.

And how can we feel our Woes,
When we've lost the Trouble of Thinking?

[*Drinks.*

AIR 63. Joy to great *Caesar.*

If thus—A Man can die
Much bolder with Brandy.

[*Pours out a Bumper of Brandy.*

AIR 64. There was an Old Woman.

So I drink off this Bumper.—And now I can stand the Test.
And my Comrades shall see, that I die as brave as the Best.

[*Drinks.*

AIR 65. Did you ever hear of a gallant Sailor.

But can I leave my pretty Hussies,
Without one Tear, or tender Sigh?

AIR 66. Why are mine Eyes still flowing.

*Their Eyes, their Lips, their Busses**
Recall my Love.—Ah must I die!

AIR 67. Green Sleeves.

Since Laws were made for ev'ry Degree,
To curb Vice in others, as well as me,
I wonder we han't better Company,
Upon Tyburn *Tree!*
But Gold from Law can take out the Sting;
And if rich Men like us were to swing,
'Twou'd thin the Land, such Numbers to string
Upon Tyburn *Tree!*

<*Enter* JAILOR.>

JAILOR. Some Friends of yours, Captain, desire to be admitted.—
I leave you together.

SCENE XIV

MACHEATH, BEN BUDGE, MATT OF THE MINT.

MACHEATH. For my having broke Prison, you see, Gentlemen, I am order'd immediate Execution.—The Sheriffs Officers, I believe, are now at the Door.—That *Jemmy Twitcher* should peach me, I own surpriz'd me!*—'Tis a plain Proof that the World is all alike, and that even our Gang can no more trust one another than other People. Therefore, I beg you, Gentlemen, look well to yourselves, for in all probability you may live some Months longer.

MATT OF THE MINT. We are heartily sorry, Captain, for your Misfortune.—But 'tis what we must all come to.

MACHEATH. *Peachum* and *Lockit*, you know, are infamous Scoundrels. Their Lives are as much in your Power, as yours are in theirs.—Remember your dying Friend!—'Tis my last Request.—Bring those Villains to the Gallows before you, and I am satisfied.

MATT OF THE MINT. We'll do't.

<Enter JAILOR.>

JAILOR. Miss *Polly* and Miss *Lucy* intreat a Word with you.

MACHEATH. Gentlemen, adieu.

SCENE XV

LUCY, MACHEATH, POLLY.

MACHEATH. My dear *Lucy*—My dear *Polly*—Whatsoever hath past between us is now at an end.—If you are fond of marrying again, the best Advice I can give you, is to Ship yourselves off for the *West-Indies*, where you'll have a fair chance of getting a Husband a-piece;* or by good Luck, two or three, as you like best.

POLLY. How can I support this Sight!

LUCY. There is nothing moves one so much as a great Man in Distress.

AIR 68. All you that must take a Leap,* &c.

LUCY.   *Would I might be hang'd!*
POLLY.   ————————————*And I would so too!*
LUCY.   *To be hang'd with you.*
POLLY.   ————————————*My Dear, with you.*
MACHEATH. *O Leave me to Thought! I fear! I doubt!*
             I tremble! I droop!—See, my Courage is out.

                              [*Turns up the empty Bottle.*

POLLY.   *No token of Love?*
MACHEATH. ————————————*See, my Courage is out.*

                              [*Turns up the empty Pot.*

LUCY.   *No token of Love?*
POLLY.   ————————————*Adieu.*
LUCY.   ————————————*Farewell.*
MACHEATH. *But hark! I hear the Toll of the Bell.**
CHORUS.   *Tol de rol lol,* &c.

                              <*Enter* JAILOR.>

JAILOR. Four Women more, Captain, with a Child a-peice! See, here they come.

                              [*Enter Women and Children.*

MACHEATH. What—four Wives more!—This is too much.— Here—tell the Sheriffs Officers I am ready.

                              [*Exit* MACHEATH *guarded.*

SCENE XVI

To them, Enter PLAYER *and* BEGGAR.

PLAYER. But, honest Friend, I hope you don't intend that *Macheath* shall be really executed.

BEGGAR. Most certainly, Sir.—To make the Piece perfect, I was for doing strict poetical Justice.—*Macheath* is to be hang'd; and for the other Personages of the Drama, the Audience must have suppos'd they were all either hang'd or transported.

PLAYER. Why then, Friend, this is a down-right deep Tragedy. The Catastrophe is manifestly wrong, for an Opera must end happily.

BEGGAR. Your Objection, Sir, is very just; and is easily remov'd. For you must allow, that in this kind of Drama,* 'tis no matter how absurdly things are brought about.—So—you Rabble there—run and cry a Reprieve—let the Prisoner be brought back to his Wives in Triumph.

PLAYER. All this we must do, to comply with the Taste of the Town.

BEGGAR. Through the whole Piece you may observe such a similitude of Manners in high and low Life, that it is difficult to determine whether (in the fashionable Vices) the fine Gentlemen imitate the Gentlemen of the Road, or the Gentlemen of the Road the fine Gentlemen.—Had the Play remain'd, as I at first intended, it would have carried a most excellent Moral. 'Twould have shown that the lower Sort of People have their Vices in a degree as well as the Rich: And that they are punish'd for them.

SCENE XVII

To them, MACHEATH *with Rabble,* &c.

MACHEATH. So, it seems, I am not left to my Choice, but must have a Wife at last.—Look ye, my Dears, we will have no Controversie now. Let us give this Day to Mirth, and I am sure she who thinks herself my Wife will testifie her Joy by a Dance.

ALL. Come, a Dance—a Dance.

MACHEATH. Ladies, I hope you will give me leave to present a Partner to each of you. And (if I may without Offence) for this time, I take *Polly* for mine.—<*To* POLLY> And for Life, you Slut,—for we were really marry'd.—<*Aloud*> As for the rest.— [*To* POLLY] But at present keep your own Secret.

A DANCE.

AIR 69. Lumps of Pudding, &c.

Thus I stand like the Turk, *with his Doxies* around;*
From all Sides their Glances his Passion confound;
For black, brown, and fair, his Inconstancy burns,
And the different Beauties subdue him by turns:
Each calls forth her Charms, to provoke his Desires:
Though willing to all; with but one he retires.
But think of this Maxim, and put off your Sorrow,
The Wretch of To-day, may be happy To-morrow.

CHORUS.   *But think of this Maxim,* &c.

FINIS

POLLY

AN OPERA

BEING THE SECOND PART OF
THE BEGGAR'S OPERA

Raro antecedentem scelestum
Deseruit pede pœna claudo. Hor.*

PREFACE

After Mr Rich *and I were agreed upon terms and conditions for bringing this Piece on the stage, and that every thing was ready for a Rehearsal; The Lord Chamberlain* sent an order from the country to prohibit Mr* Rich *to suffer any Play to be rehears'd upon his stage till it had been first of all supervis'd by his Grace. As soon as Mr* Rich *came from his Grace's secretary (who had sent for him to receive the before-mentioned order) he came to my lodgings and acquainted me with the orders he had received.*

Upon the Lord Chamberlain's coming to town, I was confined by sickness, but in four or five days I went abroad on purpose to wait upon his Grace with a faithful and genuine copy of this Piece, excepting the erratas of the transcriber.

It was transcribed in great haste by Mr Stede *the Prompter of the Playhouse, that it might be ready against his Grace's return from the country. As my illness at that time would not allow me to read it over, I since find in it many small faults, and here and there a line or two omitted. But lest it should be said I had made any one alteration from the copy I deliver'd to the Lord Chamberlain: I have caused every error in the said copy to be printed (litteral faults* excepted) and have taken notice of every omission. I have also pointed out every amendment I have made upon the revisal of my own copy for the Press, that the reader may at one view see what alterations and amendments have been made.*

ERRORS *as they stood in the copy delivered to the* Lord Chamberlain *(occasion'd by the haste of the transcriber) corrected in this edition; by which will appear the most minute difference between that and my own copy.*

P for page. l for line. sc. for scene. what was added mark'd thus *. What was left out, thus †.

The names of all the tunes †. The scenes not divided and number'd. The marginal directions for the Actors were often omitted.

ACT I. p. 84. l. 4. *ever* †. l. 7. after more, *too* *. p. 85. l. 25. before part *not* *. p. 86. l. 4. *take* †. sc. 2. l. 12. *to* †. Air 5. l. 10. *thus* instead of

they. p. 91. l. 18. *wherewith* for *wherewithal.* l. 17. *my* †. l. 24. *will* †.
l. 35. *you* for *it.* p. 93. l. 22. *no* †. Air 10. l. 5. *with a twinkum twankum*
†. p. 96. l. 32. *complaisance* for *compliance.* sc. 9. l. 1. *part from.*
p. 101. l. 3. *surely* for *sure.* l. 7. *And* †. sc. 14. l. 20. insult me *thus.*
p. 108. l. 25. *her* †. l. 28. young and handsome. Act 2. Air 25.
l. 8. *charms* for *arms.* p. 113. the speech between Air 25 and Air
26. †. Air 27. l. 2. *why* for *who.* Air 29. with a mirleton, *&c.* †. sc.
7. l. 2. a bawdyhouse bully. p. 128. l. 9 is †. Air 42. l. 6. *is* for *are.*
p. 129. 1. 32. *none* for *no more.* Act 3. p. 138. l. 18. are *all* at stake.
p. 139. l. 14. *ever* †. p. 140. l. 15. *found* †. Air 51. Thus to battle
we will go †. Air 52. with a fa, la, la †. sc. 8. l. 4. *prey* for *pay.*
p. 151. l. 5, *no* notions. p. 153. l. 21. or redress 'em †. Air 71. the
repetition of the Chorus †.

EMENDATIONS *of my own copy on revising it for the Press.*
* Is the mark for any thing added.
† The mark for what is left out.
‡ The mark of what stood in the original Copy.

ACT I. p. 84. l. 25. *pictures* *. sc. 4. l. 2. *thousand* *. p. 101. l. 20. *But
unhappy love, the more virtuous that is* ‡. Air 21. 1. 13. *my steps
direct, my truth protect, a faithful,* &c. ‡. Act 2. Air 23. l. 3. *sick
imagination* ‡. l. 4. then *alone I forget* to weep ‡. l. 7. for *whole
years* ‡. l. 11. '*Tis* a dream ‡. 1. 12. '*Tis* our utmost ‡. Air 27. l. 9.
you ne'er were drawn to cringe and fawn among the spawn who
&c. ‡. Air 28. l. 2. *for* *. l. 4. *alike* for *both.* p. 125. l. 22. all women
expect ‡. Air 39. l. 3. thus colts let loose, by want of use grow ‡.
Air 40. *unextinguished* ray ‡. Recitative. *Away* for *Hence.* ‡. p. 132.
l. 2. *pardons* for *persons* ‡. Air 45. l. 1. when as ambition's ‡. l. 2.
mighty *. l. 4. *fraud and* *. Air 48. l. 2. *Thus* *. l. 3. what expence
and what care ‡. l. 7. *sage* politicians ‡. Act 3. sc. 1, 2, 3, 4, 5, 6. are
transpos'd with no alteration of the words, but instead of *On then*;
hope and conquer, is put p. 141. l. 13. *let us then to our posts.* p. 144
l. 12. *after* enterprize, *let us now to our posts* ‡. Air 58. l. 4. *cheers* my
breast ‡. Air 62. l. 7. by turns we *take* ‡. Air 63. l. 7. 'Tis jealous
rage ‡. Air 64. l. 3. is of *the* noxious ‡. folded arms hide its charms,
all the night free from blight, *&c.* ‡. *Polly's* speech before Air 64
was plac'd after it, but without any alteration ‡. Air 69. l. 7. *sure* to
virtue ‡.

Excepting these errors and emendations, this Edition is a true and faithful Copy as I my-self in my own hand writing delivered it to Mr Rich, *and afterwards to the Lord Chamberlain, for the truth of which I appeal to his Grace.*

As I have heard several suggestions and false insinuations concerning the copy, I take this occasion in the most solemn manner to affirm, that the very copy I delivered to Mr Rich *was written in my own hand some months before at the* Bath *from my own first foul blotted papers;* from this, that for the Playhouse was transcribed, from whence the above-mention'd Mr* Stede *copied that which I delivered to the Lord Chamberlain, and excepting my own foul blotted papers; I do protest I know of no other copy whatsoever, than those I have mention'd.*

The Copy I gave into the hands of Mr Rich *had been seen before by several Persons of the greatest distinction and veracity, who will be ready to do me the honour and justice to attest it; so that not only by them, but by Mr* Rich *and Mr* Stede, *I can (against all insinuation or positive affirmation) prove in the most clear and undeniable manner, if occasion required, what I have here upon my own honour and credit asserted. The Introduction indeed was not shown to the Lord Chamberlain, which, as I had not then quite settled, was never transcribed in the Play-house copy.*

'Twas on Saturday *morning* December 7th, 1728, *that I waited upon the Lord Chamberlain; I desir'd to have the honour of reading the Opera to his Grace, but he order'd me to leave it with him, which I did upon expectation of having it return'd on the Monday following, but I had it not 'till* Thursday December 12, *when I receiv'd it from his Grace with this answer; that it was not allow'd to be acted, but commanded to be supprest. This was told me in general without any reasons assign'd, or any charge against me of my having given any particular offence.*

Since this prohibition I have been told that I am accused, in general terms, of having written many disaffected libels and seditious pamphlets. As it hath ever been my utmost ambition (if that word may be us'd upon this occasion) to lead a quiet and inoffensive life, I thought my innocence in this particular would never have requir'd a justification; and as this kind of writing is, what I have ever detested and never practic'd, I am persuaded so groundless a calumny can never be believ'd but by those who do not know me. But when general aspersions of this sort have been cast upon me, I think my-self call'd upon to declare my principles; and I do with the strictest truth affirm, that I am as loyal a subject and as firmly attach'd to the present happy establishment* as any of those who have the *greatest places or pensions. I have been inform'd too, that in the following Play, I have been charg'd with writing immoralities; that it is fill'd with slander and calumny against particular great persons, and that Majesty it-self is endeavour'd to be brought into ridicule and contempt.*

As I know every one of these charges was in every point absolutely false and without the least grounds, at first I was not at all affected by them; but when I found they were still insisted upon, and that particular passages which were not in the Play were quoted and propagated to support what had been suggested, I could no longer bear to lye under these false accusations; so by printing it, I have submitted and given up all present views of profit which might accrue from the stage, which undoubtedly will be some satisfaction to the worthy gentlemen who have treated me with so much candour and humanity, and represented me in such favourable colours.

But as I am conscious to my-self that my only intention was to lash in general the reigning and fashionable vices, and to recommend and set virtue in as amiable a light as I could; to justify and vindicate my own character, I thought my-self obliged to print the Opera without delay in the manner I have done.

As the Play was principally design'd for representation,* I hope when it is read it will be considered in that light: And when all that hath been said against it shall appear to be intirely misunderstood or misrepresented; if, some time hence, it should be permitted to appear on the stage, I think it necessary to acquaint the publick, that as far as a contract of this kind can be binding; I am engag'd to Mr Rich *to have it represented upon his Theatre.**

March 25. 1729.

INTRODUCTION

POET, <*FIRST*> PLAYER.

POET. A Sequel to a Play is like more last words. 'Tis a kind of absurdity; and really, Sir, you have prevail'd upon me to pursue this subject against my judgment.

FIRST PLAYER. Be the success as it will, you are sure of what you have contracted for; and upon the inducement of gain no body can blame you for undertaking it.

POET. I know, I must have been look'd upon as whimsical, and particular if I had scrupled to have risqu'd my reputation for my profit; for why should I be more squeamish than my betters? and so, Sir, contrary to my opinion I bring *Polly* once again upon the Stage.

FIRST PLAYER. Consider, Sir, you have prepossession on your side.

POET. But then the pleasure of novelty is lost; and in a thing of this kind I am afraid I shall hardly be pardon'd for imitating my-self, for sure pieces of this sort are not to be followed as precedents. My dependance, like a tricking bookseller's, is, that the kind reception the first part met with will carry off the second be it what it will.

FIRST PLAYER. You should not disparage your own works; you will have criticks enough who will be glad to do that for you: and let me tell you, Sir, after the success you have had, you must expect envy.

POET. Since I have had more applause than I can deserve, I must, with other authors, be content, if criticks allow me less. I should be an arrant courtier or an arrant beggar indeed, if as soon as I have receiv'd one undeserved favour I should lay claim to another; I don't flatter my-self with the like success.

FIRST PLAYER. I hope, Sir, in the catastrophe you have not run into the absurdity of your last Piece.*

POET. I know that I have been unjustly accus'd of having given up my moral for a joke, like a fine gentleman in conversation; but whatever be the event now, I will not so much as seem to give up my moral.

FIRST PLAYER. Really, Sir, an author should comply with the customs and taste of the town.—I am indeed afraid too that your Satyr here and there is too free. A man should be cautious how he mentions any vice whatsoever before good company, lest somebody present should apply it to himself.

POET. The Stage, Sir, hath the privilege of the pulpit to attack vice however dignified or distinguish'd, and preachers and poets should not be too well bred upon these occasions: Nobody can overdo it when he attacks the vice and not the person.

FIRST PLAYER. But how can you hinder malicious applications?

POET. Let those answer for 'em who make 'em. I aim at no particular persons; my strokes are at vice in general: but if any men particularly vicious are hurt, I make no apology, but leave them to the cure of their flatterers. If an author write in character,* the lower people reflect on the follies and vices of the rich and great, and an *Indian* judges and talks of *Europeans* by those he hath seen and convers'd with, *&c.* And I will venture to own that I wish every man of power or riches were really and apparently virtuous, which would soon amend and reform the common people who act by imitation.

FIRST PLAYER. But a little indulgence and partiality to the vices of your own country without doubt would be look'd upon as more discreet. Though your Satyr, Sir, is on vices in general, it must and will give offence; every vicious man thinks you particular, for conscience will make self-application. And why will you make your-self so many enemies? I say no more upon this head. As to us I hope you are satisfy'd we have done all we could for you; for you will now have the advantage of all our best singers.

[*Enter* SECOND PLAYER.

SECOND PLAYER. 'Tis impossible to perform the Opera to night, all the fine singers within are out of humour with their parts. The Tenor, says he was never offer'd such an indignity, and in a rage flung his clean lambskin gloves into the fire; he swears that in his whole life he never did sing, would sing, or could sing but in true kid.*

FIRST PLAYER. Musick might tame and civilize wild beasts, but 'tis evident it never yet could tame and civilize musicians.

[*Enter* THIRD PLAYER.

THIRD PLAYER. Sir, *Signora Crotchetta** says she finds her character so low that she had rather dye than sing it.

FIRST PLAYER. Tell her by her contract I can make her sing it.

[*Enter* SIGNORA CROTCHETTA.

CROTCHETTA. Barbarous Tramontane!* Where are all the lovers of *Virtu*? Will they not all rise in arms in my defence? make me sing it! good Gods! should I tamely submit to such usage I should debase my-self through all *Europe*.

FIRST PLAYER. In the Opera nine or ten years ago, I remember, Madam, your appearance in a character little better than a fish.*

CROTCHETTA. A fish! monstrous! Let me inform you, Sir, that a Mermaid or Syren is not many removes from a sea-Goddess; or I had never submitted to be that fish which you are pleas'd to call me by way of reproach. I have a cold, Sir; I am sick. I don't see, why I may not be allowed the privilege of sickness now and then as well as others. If a singer may not be indulg'd in her humours, I am sure she will soon become of no consequence with the town. And so, Sir, I have a cold; I am hoarse. I hope now you are satisfied.

[*Exit* CROTCHETTA *in a fury.*

[*Enter* FOURTH PLAYER.

FOURTH PLAYER. Sir, the base voice insists upon pearl-colour'd stockings and red-heel'd shoes.

FIRST PLAYER. There is no governing caprice. But how shall we make our excuses to the house?

FOURTH PLAYER. Since the town was last year so good as to encourage an Opera without singers;* the favour I was then shown obliges me to offer my-self once more, rather than the audience should be dismiss'd. All the other Comedians upon this emergency are willing to do their best, and hope for your favour and indulgence.

FIRST PLAYER. Ladies and Gentlemen, as we wish to do every thing for your diversion, and that singers only will come when they will come, we beg you to excuse this unforseen accident, and to accept the proposal of the Comedians, who relye wholly on your courtesie and protection.

[*Exeunt.*

The OUVERTURE.

DRAMATIS PERSONAE*

DUCAT
MORANO
VANDERBLUFF
CAPSTERN
HACKER
CULVERIN
LAGUERRE
CUTLACE
POHETOHEE
CAWWAWKEE

Servants, Indians, Pyrates, Guards, &c.

POLLY
MRS DUCAT
TRAPES
JENNY DIVER
FLIMZY
DAMARIS

SCENE. *In the* WEST-INDIES.

ACT I

SCENE I

SCENE *Ducat's House.*

DUCAT, TRAPES.

TRAPES. Though you were born and bred and live in the *Indies*, as you are a subject of *Britain* you shou'd live up to our customs. Prodigality there, is a fashion that is among all ranks of people. Why, our very younger brothers* push themselves into the polite world by squandering more than they are worth. You are wealthy, very wealthy, Mr *Ducat*; and I grant you the more you have, the taste of getting more should grow stronger upon you. 'Tis just so with us. But then the richest of our Lords and Gentlemen, who live elegantly, always run out. 'Tis genteel to be in debt. Your luxury should distinguish you from the vulgar. You cannot be too expensive in your pleasures.

AIR I. The disappointed Widow.*

> *The manners of the Great affect;*
> *Stint not your pleasure:*
> *If conscience had their genius checkt,*
> *How got they treasure?*
> *The more in debt, run in debt the more,*
> *Careless who is undone;*
> *Morals and honesty leave to the poor,*
> *As they do at* London.

DUCAT. I never thought to have heard thrift laid to my charge. There is not a man, though I say it, in all the *Indies* who lives more plentifully than my self; nor, who enjoys the necessaries of life in so handsome a manner.

TRAPES. There it is now. Who ever heard a man of fortune in *England* talk of the necessaries of life? If the necessaries of life would have satisfied such a poor body as me, to be sure I had never come to mend my fortune to the Plantations.* Whether we can afford it or no, we must have superfluities. We never stint our expence to our own fortunes, but are miserable if we do not live up to the profuseness of our neighbours. If we could content our selves with the necessaries of Life, no man alive ever need be dishonest. As to woman now; why, look ye, Mr *Ducat*, a man hath what we may call every thing that is necessary in a wife.

DUCAT. Ay, and more!

TRAPES. But for all that, d'ye see, your married men are my best customers. It keeps wives upon their good behaviours.

DUCAT. But there are jealousies and family lectures,* Mrs *Trapes*.

TRAPES. Bless us all! how little are our customs known on this side the herring-pond?* Why, jealousy is out of fashion even among our common country-gentlemen. I hope you are better bred than to be jealous. A husband and wife should have a mutual complaisance for each other. Sure, your wife is not so unreasonable to expect to have you always to her self.

DUCAT. As I have a good estate, Mrs *Trapes*, I would willingly run into every thing that is suitable to my dignity and fortune. No body throws himself into the extravagancies of life with a freer spirit. As to conscience and musty morals, I have as few drawbacks upon my profits or pleasures as any man of quality in *England*; in those I am not in the least vulgar. Besides, Madam, in most of my expences I run into the polite taste. I have a fine library of books that I never read; I have a fine stable of horses that I never ride; I build, I buy plate, jewels, pictures, or any thing that is valuable and curious, as your great men do, merely out of ostentation. But indeed I must own, I do still cohabit with my wife; and she is very uneasy and vexatious upon account of my visits to you.

TRAPES. Indeed, indeed, Mr *Ducat*, you shou'd break through all this usurpation at once, and keep——.* Now too is your time; for I have a fresh cargo of ladies just arriv'd: no body alive shall set eyes upon 'em till you have provided your self. You should keep your lady in awe by her maid; place a handsome, sprightly wench near your wife, and she will be a spy upon her into the bargain. I would have you show your self a fine gentleman in every thing.

DUCAT. But I am somewhat advanc'd in life, Mrs *Trapes*, and my duty to my wife lies very hard upon me;* I must leave keeping to younger husbands and old batchelors.

TRAPES. There it is again now! Our very vulgar pursue pleasures in the flush of youth and inclination, but our great men are modishly profligate when their appetite hath left 'em.

AIR 2. *The* Irish *ground.*

BASS.

DUCAT.
What can wealth
When we're old?
Youth and health
Are not sold.

TREBLE.

TRAPES.
When love in the pulse beats low,
(As haply* it may with you)
A girl can fresh youth bestow,
And kindle desire anew.
Thus, numm'd in the brake,*
Without motion, the snake
Sleeps cold winter away;
But in every vein
Life quickens again
On the bosom of May.

We are not here, I must tell you, as we are at *London*, where we can have fresh goods every week by the waggon.* My maid is again gone aboard the vessel; she is perfectly charm'd with one of the ladies; 'twill be a credit to you to keep her. I have obligations to you, Mr *Ducat*, and I would part with her to no man alive but your self. If I had her at *London*, such a lady would be sufficient to make my fortune; but, in truth, she is not impudent enough to make herself agreeable to the sailors in a publick-house in this country. By all accounts, she hath a behaviour only fit for a private family.

DUCAT. But how shall I manage matters with my wife?

TRAPES. Just as the fine gentlemen do with us. We could bring you many great precedents for treating a wife with indifference, contempt, and neglect; but that, indeed, would be running into too high life. I would have you keep some decency, and use her with civility. You should be so obliging as to leave her to her liberties and take them too yourself. Why, all our fine ladies, in what they call pin-money,* have no other views; 'tis what they all expect.

DUCAT. But I am afraid it will be hard to make my wife think like a gentlewoman upon this subject; so that if I take her, I must act discreetly and keep the affair a dead secret.

TRAPES. As to that, Sir, you may do as you please. Should it ever come to her knowledge, custom and education perhaps may make her at first think it somewhat odd. But this I can affirm with a safe conscience, that many a lady of quality have servants of this sort in their families, and you can afford an expence as well as the best of 'em.

DUCAT. I have a fortune, Mrs *Trapes*, and would fain make a fashionable figure in life; if we can agree upon the price I'll take her into the family.

TRAPES. I am glad to see you fling your self into the polite taste with a spirit. Few, indeed, have the turn or talents to get money; but fewer know how to spend it handsomely after they have got it. The elegance of luxury consists in variety, and love requires it as much as any of our appetites and passions, and there is a time of life when a man's appetite ought to be whetted by a delicacy.

DUCAT. Nay, Mrs *Trapes*, now you are too hard upon me. Sure, you cannot think me such a clown as to be really in love with my Wife! We are not so ignorant here as you imagine; why, I married her in a reasonable way, only for her money.

AIR 3. Noel *Hills*.

He that weds a beauty
Soon will find her cloy;
When pleasure grows a duty,
Farewell love and joy:
He that weds for treasure
(Though he hath a wife)
Hath chose one lasting pleasure
In a married life.

SCENE II

DUCAT, TRAPES, DAMARIS.

DUCAT [*calling at the door*]. *Damaris, Damaris,* I charge you not to stir from the door, and the instant you see your lady at a distance returning from her walk, be sure to give me notice.

TRAPES. She is in most charming rigging; she won't cost you a penny, Sir, in cloaths at first setting out. But, alack-a-day! no bargain could ever thrive with dry lips: a glass of liquor makes every thing go so glibly.

DUCAT. Here, *Damaris*; a glass of Rum for Mrs *Dye.*

[DAMARIS *goes out and returns with a bottle and glass.*

TRAPES. But as I was saying, Sir, I would not part with her to any body alive but your self; for, to be sure, I could turn her to ten times the profit by jobbs and chance customers. Come, Sir, here's to the young lady's health.

SCENE III

DUCAT, TRAPES, FLIMZY.

TRAPES. Well, *Flimzy*; are all the ladies safely landed, and have you done as I order'd you?

FLIMZY. Yes, Madam. The three ladies for the run of the house are safely lodg'd at home; the other is without in the hall to wait your commands. She is a most delicious creature, that's certain. Such lips, such eyes, and such flesh and blood! If you had her in *London* you could not fail of the custom of all the foreign Ministers. As I hope to be sav'd, Madam, I was forc'd to tell her ten thousand lyes before I could prevail upon her to come with me. Oh Sir, you are the most lucky, happy man in the world! Shall I go call her in?

TRAPES. 'Tis necessary for me first to instruct her in her duty and the ways of the family. The girl is bashful and modest, so I must

beg leave to prepare her by a little private conversation, and afterwards, Sir, I shall leave you to your private conversations.*

FLIMZY. But I hope, Sir, you won't forget poor *Flimzy*; for the richest man alive could not be more scrupulous than I am upon these
occasions, and the bribe only can make me excuse it to my conscience. I hope, Sir, you will pardon my freedom.

[He gives her money.

AIR 4. Sweetheart, think upon me.

> *My conscience is of courtly mold,*
>   *Fit for highest station.*
> *Where's the hand, when touch'd with gold,*
>   *Proof against temptation?*

[Exit FLIMZY.

DUCAT. We can never sufficiently encourage such useful qualifications. You will let me know when you are ready for me.

<div align="right"><<em>Exit.</em>></div>

SCENE IV

TRAPES.

I wonder I am not more wealthy; for, o' my conscience, I have as few
scruples as those that are ten thousand times as rich. But, alack-a-
day! I am forc'd to play at small game. I now and then betray and
ruine an innocent girl. And what of that? Can I in conscience expect
to be equally rich with those who betray and ruine provinces and
countries? In troth, all their great fortunes are owing to situation; as
for genius and capacity I can match them to a hair: were they in my
circumstance they would act like me; were I in theirs, I should be
rewarded as a most profound penetrating politician.

AIR 5. 'Twas within a furlong.

> *In pimps and politicians*
>   *The genius is the same;*
> *Both raise their own conditions*
>   *On others guilt and shame:*

With a tongue well-tipt with lyes
Each the want of parts* supplies,
And with a heart that's all disguise
Keeps his schemes unknown.
Seducing as the devil,
They play the tempter's part,
And have, when most they're civil,
Most mischief in their heart.
Each a secret commerce drives,
First corrupts and then connives,
And by his Neighbours' vices thrives,
For they are all his own.

SCENE V

TRAPES, FLIMZY, POLLY.

TRAPES. Bless my eye-sight! what do I see? I am in a dream, or it is Miss *Polly Peachum*! mercy upon me! Child, what brought you on this side of the water?

POLLY. Love, Madam, and the misfortunes of our family. But I am equally surpris'd to find an acquaintance here; you cannot be ignorant of my unhappy story, and perhaps from you, Mrs *Dye*, I may receive some information that may be useful to me.

TRAPES. You need not be much concern'd, Miss *Polly*, at a sentence of transportation, for a young lady of your beauty hath wherewithal to make her fortune in any country.

POLLY. Pardon me, Madam; you mistake me. Though I was educated among the most profligate in low life, I never engag'd in my father's affairs as a thief or a thief-catcher, for indeed I abhorr'd his profession. Would my Papa had never taken it up, he then still had been alive and I had never known *Macheath*!

AIR 6. Sortez des vos retraites.

She who had felt a real pain
By Cupid's dart,

> *Finds that all absence is in vain*
> *To cure her heart.*
> *Though from my lover cast*
> *Far as from Pole to Pole,*
> *Still the pure flame must last,*
> *For the love is in the Soul.*

You must have heard, Madam, that I was unhappy in my marriage. When *Macheath* was transported all my peace was banished with him; and my Papa's death hath now given me liberty to pursue my inclinations.

TRAPES. Good lack-a-day! poor Mr *Peachum*! Death was so much oblig'd to him that I wonder he did not allow him a reprieve for his own sake. Truly, I think he was oblig'd to no-body more except the physicians: but they dye it seems too.* Death is very impartial; he takes all alike, friends and foes.

POLLY. Every monthly Sessions-paper* like the apothecary's files (if I may make the comparison) was a record of his services. But my Papa kept company with gentlemen, and ambition is catching. He was in too much haste to be rich. I wish all great men would take warning. 'Tis now seven months since my Papa was hang'd.

TRAPES. This will be a great check indeed to your men of enterprizing genius; and it will be unsafe to push at making a great fortune, if such accidents grow common. But sure, Child, you are not so mad as to think of following *Macheath*.

POLLY. In following him I am in pursuit of my quiet. I love him, and like a troubled ghost shall never be at rest till I appear to him. If I can receive any information of him from you, it will be a cordial to a wretch in despair.

TRAPES. My dear Miss *Polly*, you must not think of it. 'Tis now above a year and a half since he robb'd his master, ran away from the plantation and turn'd pyrate. Then too what puts you beyond all possibility of redress, is that since he came over he married a transported slave, one *Jenny Diver*, and she is gone off with him.* You must give over all thoughts of him for he is a very devil to our sex; not a woman of the greatest vivacity shifts her inclinations half so fast as he can. Besides, he would disown you, for like an upstart he hates an old acquaintance. I am sorry to see those tears, Child, but I love you too well to flatter you.

POLLY. Why have I a heart so constant? cruel love!

AIR 7. *O Waly, Waly, up the bank.*

Farewell, farewell, all hope of bliss!
For Polly *always must be thine.*
Shall then my heart be never his,
Which never can again be mine?
O Love, you play a cruel part,
Thy shaft* still festers in the wound;
You should reward a constant heart,
Since 'tis, alas, so seldom found!

TRAPES. I tell you once again, Miss *Polly*, you must think no more of him. You are like a child who is crying after a butterfly that is hopping and fluttering upon every flower in the field; there is not a woman that comes in his way but he must have a taste of; besides there is no catching him. But, my dear girl, I hope you took care, at your leaving *England*, to bring off wherewithal to support you.

POLLY. Since he is lost, I am insensible of every other misfortune. I brought indeed a summ of money with me, but my chest was broke open at sea, and I am now a wretched vagabond expos'd to hunger and want, unless charity relieve me.

TRAPES. Poor child! your father and I have had great dealings together, and I shall be grateful to his memory. I will look upon you as my daughter; you shall be with me.

POLLY. As soon as I can have remittances from *England*, I shall be able to acknowledge your goodness: I have still five hundred pounds there which will be return'd to me upon demand; but I had rather undertake any honest service that might afford me a main-tenance than be burthensome to my friends.

TRAPES. Sure never anything happen'd so luckily! Madam *Ducat* just now wants a servant, and I know she will take my recommen-dation; and one so tight* and handy as you must please her: then too, her husband is the civilest, best-bred man alive. You are now in her house and I won't leave it 'till I have settled you. Be cheerful, my dear Child, for who knows but all these misfortunes may turn to your advantage? You are in a rich creditable family, and I dare say your person and behaviour will soon make you a favourite. As to captain *Macheath*, you may now safely look upon your self as a widow, and who knows, if Madam *Ducat* should tip off, what may happen? I shall recommend you, Miss *Polly*, as a gentlewoman.

AIR 8. O Jenny come tye me.

> *Despair is all folly;*
> *Hence, melancholy,*
> *Fortune attends you while youth is in flower.*
> *By beauty's possession*
> *Us'd with discretion,*
> *Woman at all times hath joy in her power.*

POLLY. The service, Madam, you offer me, makes me as happy as I can be in my circumstance, and I accept of it with ten thousand obligations.

TRAPES. Take a turn in the hall with my maid for a minute or two, and I'll take care to settle all matters and conditions for your reception. Be assur'd, Miss *Polly*, I'll do my best for you.

<*Exeunt* POLLY *and* FLIMZY.>

SCENE VI

TRAPES, DUCAT.

TRAPES. Mr *Ducat*, Sir. You may come in. I have had this very girl in my eye for you ever since you and I were first acquainted; and to be plain with you, Sir, I have run great risques for her: I had many a stratagem, to be sure, to inveigle her away from her relations! she too herself was exceeding difficult. And I can assure you, to ruine a girl of severe education is no small addition to the pleasure of our fine gentlemen. I can be answerable for it too, that you will have the first of her. I am sure I could have dispos'd of her upon the same account for at least a hundred guineas to an alderman* of *London*; and then too I might have had the disposal of her again as soon as she was out of keeping; but you are my friend, and I shall not deal hard with you.

DUCAT. But if I like her I would agree upon terms beforehand; for should I grow fond of her, I know you have the conscience of other trades-people and would grow more imposing; and I love to be upon a certainty.

TRAPES. Sure you cannot think a hundred pistoles* too much; I mean for me. I leave her wholly to your generosity. Why your fine men, who never pay any body else, pay their pimps and bawds well; always ready money. I ever dealt conscientiously, and set the lowest price upon my ladies; when you see her, I am sure you will allow her to be as choice a piece of beauty as ever you laid eyes on.

DUCAT. But, dear Mrs *Dye*, a hundred pistoles say you? why, I could have half a dozen negro princesses for the price.

TRAPES. But sure you cannot expect to buy a fine handsome christian at that rate. You are not us'd to see such goods on this side of the water. For the women, like the cloaths, are all tarnish'd and half worn out before they are sent hither. Do but cast your eye upon her, Sir; the door stands half open; see, yonder she trips in conversation with my maid *Flimzy* in the hall.

DUCAT. Why truly I must own she is handsome.

TRAPES. Bless me, you are no more mov'd by her than if she were your wife. Handsom! what a cold husband-like expression is that! nay, there is no harm done. If I take her home, I don't question the making more money of her. She was never in any body's house but your own since she was landed. She is pure, as she was imported, without the least adulteration.

DUCAT. I'll have her. I'll pay you down upon the nail.* You shall leave her with me. Come, count your money, Mrs *Dye*.

TRAPES. What a shape is there! she's of the finest growth.

DUCAT. You make me mis-reckon. She even takes off my eyes from gold.

TRAPES. What a curious pair of sparkling eyes!

DUCAT. As vivifying as the sun. I have paid you ten.

TRAPES. What a racy* flavour must breath from those lips!

DUCAT. I want no provoking commendations. I'm in youth; I'm on fire! twenty more makes it thirty; and this here makes it just fifty.

TRAPES. What a most inviting complexion! how charming a colour! In short, a fine woman has all the perfections of fine wine, and is a cordial that is ten times as restorative.

DUCAT. This fifty then makes it just the sum. So now, Madam, you may deliver her up.

SCENE VII

DUCAT, TRAPES, DAMARIS.

DAMARIS. Sir, Sir, my Mistress is just at the door.

[*Exit.*

DUCAT. Get you out of the way this moment, dear Mrs *Dye*; for I would not have my wife see you. But don't stir out of the house till I am put in possession. I'll get rid of her immediately.

[*Exit* TRAPES.

SCENE VIII

DUCAT, MRS DUCAT.

MRS DUCAT. I can never be out of the way, for an hour or so, but you are with that filthy creature. If you were young, and I took liberties, you could not use me worse; you could not, you beastly fellow. Such usage might force the most vertuous woman to resentment. I don't see why the wives in this country should not put themselves upon as easy a foot as in *England*. In short, Mr *Ducat*, if you behave your self like an *English* husband, I will behave my self like an *English* wife.

AIR 9. Red House.

I will have my humours, I'll please all my senses,
I will not be stinted—in love or expences.
I'll dress with profusion, I'll game without measure;
You shall have the business, I will have the pleasure:
   Thus every day I'll pass my life,
   My home shall be my least resort;*
   For sure 'tis fitting that your wife
   Shou'd copy ladies of the court.

DUCAT. All these things I know are natural to the sex, my dear. But husbands like colts, are restif,* and they require a long time to break 'em. Besides, 'tis not the fashion as yet, for husbands to be govern'd in this country. That tongue of yours, my dear, hath not eloquence enough to persuade me out of my reason. A woman's tongue, like a trumpet, only serves to raise my courage.

AIR 10. Old *Orpheus* tickl'd, &c.

When billows come breaking on the strand,
The rocks are deaf and unshaken stand:
Old oaks can defy the thunder's roar,
And I can stand woman's tongue—that's more,
   With a twinkum, twankum, &c.

With that weapon, women, like pyrates, are at war with the whole world. But I thought, my dear, your pride would have kept you from being jealous. 'Tis the whole business of my life to please you; but wives are like children, the more they are flatter'd and humour'd the more perverse they are. Here now have I been laying out my money, purely to make you a present, and I have nothing but these freaks* and reproaches in return. You wanted a maid, and I have bought you the handiest creature; she will indeed make a very creditable servant.

MRS DUCAT. I will have none of your hussies about me. And so, Sir, you would make me your convenience, your bawd. Out upon it!

DUCAT. But I bought her on purpose for you, Madam.

MRS DUCAT. For your own filthy inclinations, you mean. I won't bear it. What keep an impudent strumpet under my nose! Here's fine doings indeed!

DUCAT. I will have the directions of my family. 'Tis my pleasure it shall be so. So, Madam, be satisfy'd.

AIR 11. *Christ-Church Bells.*

When a woman Jealous grows,
  Farewell all peace of life!

MRS DUCAT. *But e'er man roves, he should pay what he owes.*
  And with her due content his wife.

DUCAT. *'Tis man's the weaker sex to sway.*

MRS DUCAT. *We too, whene'er we list, obey.*

DUCAT.   *'Tis just and fit*
    You should submit.

MRS DUCAT. *But sweet kind husband—not to day.*

DUCAT. *Let your clack be still.*

MRS DUCAT. *Not till I have my will.*
  If thus you reason slight,
  There's never an hour
  While breath has power:
  But I will assert my right.

Would I had you in *England*; I should have all the women there rise in arms in my defence. For the honour and prerogative of the sex, they would not suffer such a precedent of submission. And so Mr *Ducat*, I tell you once again, that you shall keep your trollops out of the house, or I will not stay in it.

DUCAT. Look'ee, Wife; you will be able to bring about nothing by pouting and vapours. I have resolution enough to withstand either obstinacy or stratagem. And I will break this jealous spirit of yours before it gets a head. And so, my dear, I order that upon my account you behave your self to the girl as you ought.

MRS DUCAT. I wish you would behave your self to your Wife as you ought; that is to say, with good manners, and complaisance. And so, Sir, I leave you and your minx together. I tell you once again, that I would sooner dye upon the spot, than not be mistress in my own house.

[*Exit in a passion.*

SCENE IX

DUCAT.

If by these perverse humours, I should be forc'd to part with her, and allow her a separate maintenance;* the thing is so common among people of condition, that it could not prove to my discredit. Family divisions, and matrimonial controversies are a kind of proof of a man's riches; for the poor people are happy in marriage out of necessity, because they cannot afford to disagree.

[*Enter* DAMARIS.

Damaris, saw you my Wife? Is she in her own room? What said she? Which way went she?

DAMARIS.   Bless me, I was perfectly frighten'd, she look'd so like a fury! Thank my stars, I never saw her look so before in all my life; tho' mayhap you may have seen her look so before a thousand times. Woe be to the servants that fall in her way! I'm sure I'm glad to be out of it.

AIR 12. Cheshire-rounds.

When kings by their huffing*
Have blown up a squabble,
All the charge and cuffing*
Light upon the rabble.
Thus when Man and Wife
By their mutual snubbing,
Kindle civil strife,
Servants get the drubbing.

DUCAT.   I would have you, *Damaris*, have an eye upon your mistress. You should have her good at heart, and inform me when she has any schemes a-foot; it may be the means to reconcile us.

DAMARIS.   She's wild, Sir. There's no speaking to her. She's flown into the garden! Mercy upon us all, say I! How can you be so unreasonable to contradict a woman, when you know we can't bear it?

DUCAT.   I depend upon you, *Damaris*, for intelligence. You may observe her at a distance; and as soon as she comes into her own

room, bring me word. [*Aside*] There is the sweetest pleasure in the
revenge that I have now in my head! I'll this instant go and take
my charge from Mrs *Trapes*. <*Aloud*> *Damaris*, you know your
instructions.

[*Exit.*

SCENE X

DAMARIS.

Sure all masters and mistresses, like politicans, judge of the conscience of mankind by their own, and require treachery of their
servants as a duty! I am employ'd by my master to watch my mistress, and by my mistress to watch my master. Which party shall
I espouse? To be sure my mistress's. For in hers, jurisdiction
and power, the common cause of the whole sex, are at stake. But
my master I see is coming this way. I'll avoid him, and make my
observations.

[*Exit.*

SCENE XI

DUCAT, POLLY.

DUCAT. Be cheerful, *Polly*, for your good fortune hath thrown you
   into a family, where, if you rightly consult your own interest, as
   every body now-a-days does, you may make your self perfectly
   easy. Those eyes of yours, *Polly*, are a sufficient fortune for any
   woman, if she have but conduct and know how to make the most
   of 'em.

POLLY. As I am your servant, Sir, my duty obliges me not to contradict you; and I must hear your flattery tho' I know my self undeserving. But sure Sir, in handsome women, you must have observ'd
   that their hearts often oppose their interest; and beauty certainly
   has ruin'd more women than it has made happy.

AIR 13. The bush a boon traquair.

The crow or daw* thro' all the year
No fowler seeks to ruin;
But birds of voice or feather rare
He's all day long persuing.
Beware, fair maids; so scape the net
That other beauties fell in;
For sure at heart was never yet
So great a wretch as Helen!

If my Lady, Sir, will let me know my duty, gratitude will make me study to please her.

DUCAT. I have in mind to have a little conversation with you, and I would not be interrupted.

[*Bars the door.*

POLLY. I wish, Sir, you would let me receive my Lady's commands.

DUCAT. And so, *Polly*, by these downcast looks of yours you would have me believe you don't know you are handsome, and that you have no faith in your looking-glass. Why, every pretty woman studies her face, and a looking-glass to her is what a book is to a Pedant; she is poring upon it all day long. In troth, a man can never know how much love is in him by conversations with his Wife. A kiss on those lips would make me young again.

[*Kisses her.*

AIR 14. Bury Fair.

POLLY.   *How can you be so teazing?**
DUCAT.   *Love will excuse my fault.*
                   How can you be so pleasing!

[*Going to kiss her.*

POLLY.   *I vow I'll not be naught.**

[*Struggling.*

DUCAT.   *All maids I know at first resist.*
                   A master may command.
POLLY.   *You're monstrous rude; I'll not be kiss'd:*
                   Nay, fye, let go my hand.

DUCAT.   *'Tis foolish pride—*
POLLY.   *'Tis vile, 'tis base*
              Poor innocence to wrong;
DUCAT.   *I'll force you,*
POLLY.   *Guard me from disgrace.*
              You find that vertue's strong.

                                        [*Pushing him away.*

'Tis barbarous in you, Sir, to take the occasion of my necessities to insult me.

DUCAT. Nay, hussy, I'll give you money.

POLLY. I despise it. No, Sir, tho' I was born and bred in *England*, I can dare to be poor, which is the only thing now-a-days men are asham'd of.

DUCAT. I shall humble these saucy airs of your, Mrs *Minx*. Is this language from a servant! from a slave!

POLLY. Am I then betray'd and sold!

DUCAT. Yes, hussy, that you are; and as legally my property, as any woman is her husband's, who sells her self in marriage.

POLLY. Climates that change constitutions have no effect upon manners. What a profligate is that *Trapes*!

DUCAT. Your fortune, your happiness depends upon your compliance. What, proof against a bribe! Sure, hussy, you belye your country, or you must have had a very vulgar education. 'Tis unnatural.

AIR 15. Bobbing Joan.

Maids like courtiers must be woo'd,
Most by flattery are subdu'd;
Some capricious, coy or nice
Out of pride protract the vice;
   But they fall,
   One and all,
When we bid up to their price.

Besides, hussy, your consent may make me your slave; there's power to tempt you into the bargain. You must be more than woman if you can stand that too.

POLLY.   Sure you only mean to try me! but 'tis barbarous to trifle with my distresses.

DUCAT.   I'll have none of these airs. 'Tis impertinent in a servant, to have scruples of any kind. I hire honour, conscience and all, for I will not be serv'd by halves. And so, to be plain with you, you obstinate slut, you shall either contribute to my pleasure or my profit; and if you refuse play in the bed-chamber, you shall go work in the fields among the planters. I hope now I have explain'd my self.

POLLY.   My freedom may be lost, but you cannot rob me of my vertue and integrity: and whatever is my lot, having that, I shall have the comfort of hope, and find pleasure in reflection.

AIR 16. A Swain long tortur'd with Disdain.

Can I or toil or hunger fear?
For love's a pain that's more severe.
The slave, with vertue in his breast,
Can wake in peace, and sweetly rest.

[*Aside*] But love, when unhappy, the more vertuous it is, the more it suffers.

DUCAT.   What noise is that?

DAMARIS [*without*]. Sir, Sir.

DUCAT.   Step into the closet; I'll call you out immediately to present you to my wife. Don't let bashfulness ruin your fortune. The next opportunity I hope you will be better dispos'd.

[*Exit* POLLY.

DAMARIS.   Open the door, Sir. This moment, this moment.

SCENE XII

DUCAT, DAMARIS.

DUCAT. What's the matter? Was any body about to ravish you? Is the house o' fire? Or my Wife in a passion?

DAMARIS. O Sir, the whole country is in an uproar! The pyrates are all coming down upon us; and if they should raise the militia, you are an officer you know. I hope you have time enough to fling up your commission.*

[*Enter* FIRST FOOTMAN.

FIRST FOOTMAN. The neighbours, Sir, are all frighted out of their wits; they leave their houses, and fly to yours for protection. Where's my Lady, your Wife? Heaven grant, they have not taken her!

DUCAT. If they only took what one could spare.

FIRST FOOTMAN. That's true, there were no great harm done.

DUCAT. How are the musquets?

FIRST FOOTMAN. Rusty Sir, all rusty and peaceable! For we never clean 'em but against training-day.

DAMARIS. Then, Sir, your honour is safe, for now you have just excuse against fighting.

[*Enter* SECOND FOOTMAN.

SECOND FOOTMAN. The *Indians*, Sir, with whom we are in alliance are all in arms; there will be bloody work to be sure. I hope they will decide the matter before we can get ready.

[*Enter* MRS DUCAT.

MRS DUCAT. O dear Husband, I'm frighten'd to death! What will become of us all! I thought a punishment for your wicked lewdness would light upon you at last.

DUCAT. Presence of mind, my dear, is as necessary in dangers as courage.

DAMARIS. But you are too rich to have courage. You should fight by deputy. 'Tis only for poor people to be brave and desperate, who cannot afford to live.

[*Enter* MAIDS, &c. *one after another.*

FIRST MAID. The pyrates, Sir, the pyrates! Mercy upon us, what will become of us poor helpless women!

SECOND MAID. We shall all be ravish'd.

FIRST OLD WOMAN. All be ravish'd.

SECOND OLD WOMAN. Ay to be sure, we shall be ravish'd; all be ravish'd!

FIRST OLD WOMAN. But if fortune will have it so, patience is a vertue, and we must undergo it.

SECOND OLD WOMAN. Ay, for certain we must all bear it, Mrs *Damaris.*

THIRD FOOTMAN. A soldier, Sir, from the *Indian* Camp, desires admittance. He's here, Sir.

[*Enter* INDIAN.

INDIAN. I come, Sir, to the *English* colony, with whom we are in alliance, from the mighty King *Pohetohee*, my lord and master, and address my self to you, as you are of the council, for succours.* The pyrates are ravaging and plund'ring the country, and we are now in arms ready for battle, to oppose 'em.

DUCAT. Does *Macheath* command the enemy?

INDIAN. Report says he is dead. Above twelve moons are pass'd since we heard of him. *Morano*, a Negro villain, is their chief, who in rapine* and barbarities is even equal to him.

DUCAT. I shall inform the council, and we shall soon be ready to joyn you. So acquaint the King your master.

[*Exit* INDIAN.
<*Exeunt* MAIDS *and* OLD WOMEN.>

AIR 17. March in *Scipio*.

	Brave boys prepare.	[*to the men.*
	Ah! Cease, fond Wife to cry.	[*to her.*
SERVANT.	*For when the danger's near,*	
	We've time enough to fly.	
MRS DUCAT.	*How can you be disgrac'd!*	
	For wealth secures your fame.	
SERVANT.	*The rich are always plac'd*	
	Above the sense of shame.	
MRS DUCAT.	*Let honour spur the slave,*	
	To fight for fighting's sake:	
DUCAT.	*But even the rich are brave*	
	When money is at stake.	

Be satisfy'd, my dear, I shall be discreet. My servants here will take care that I be not over-rash, for their wages depend upon me. But before I go to council—come hither *Polly*; I intreat you, Wife, to take her into your service. [*Enter* POLLY] And use her civilly. Indeed, my dear, your suspicions are very frivolous and unreasonable.

MRS DUCAT. I hate to have a handsome wench about me. They are always so saucy!

DUCAT. Women, by their jealousies, put one in mind of doing that which otherwise we should never think of. Why you are a proof, my dear, that a handsome woman may be honest.

MRS DUCAT. I find you can say a civil thing to me still.

DUCAT. Affairs, you see, call me hence. And so I leave her under your protection.

<*Exeunt* DUCAT *and* FOOTMEN.>

SCENE XIII

MRS DUCAT, DAMARIS, <POLLY>.

MRS DUCAT. Away, into the other room again. When I want you, I'll call you.

[*Exit* POLLY.

Well, *Damaris*, to be sure you have observ'd all that has pass'd. I will know all. I'm sure she's a hussy.

DAMARIS. Nay, Madam, I can't say so much. But—

MRS DUCAT. But what?

DAMARIS. I hate to make mischief.

AIR 18. Jig-it-o'Foot.

Better to doubt
All that's doing,
Than to find out
Proofs of ruin.
What servants hear and see
Should they tattle,
Marriage all day would be
Feuds and battle.

A servant's legs and hands should be under your command, but, for the sake of quiet, you should leave their tongues to their own discretion.

MRS DUCAT. I vow, *Damaris*, I will know it.

DAMARIS. To be sure, Madam, the door was bolted, and I could only listen. There was a sort of a bustle between 'em, that's certain. What past I know not. But the noise they made, to my thinking, did not sound very honest.

MRS DUCAT. Noises that did not sound very honest, said you?

DAMARIS. Nay, Madam, I am a maid,* and have no experience. If you had heard them, you would have been a better judge of the matter.

MRS DUCAT. An impudent slut! I'll have her before me. If she be not a thorough profligate, I shall make a discovery by her behaviour. Go call her to me.

[*Exit* DAMARIS *and returns.*

SCENE XIV

MRS DUCAT. In my own house! Before my face! I'll have you sent to the house of correction, strumpet. By that over-honest look, I guess her to be a horrid jade. A mere hypocrite, that is perfectly white-wash'd with innocence. My blood rises at the sight of all strumpets, for they are smuglers in love, that ruin us fair traders in matrimony.* Look upon me, Mrs brazen. She has no feeling of shame. She is so us'd to impudence, that she has not a blush within her. Do you know, madam, that I am Mr *Ducat*'s wife?

POLLY. As your servant, Madam, I think my self happy.

MRS DUCAT. You know Mr *Ducat*, I suppose. She has beauty enough to make any woman alive hate her.

AIR 19. Trumpet Minuet.

Abroad after misses most husbands will roam,
Tho' sure they find woman sufficient at home.
To be nos'd* by a strumpet! Hence, hussy you'd best.
Would he give me my due, I wou'd give her the rest.

I vow I had rather have a thief in my house. For to be sure she is that besides.

POLLY. If you were acquainted with my misfortunes, Madam, you could not insult me.

MRS DUCAT. What does the wench mean?

DAMARIS. There's not one of these common creatures, but, like common beggars, hath a moving story at her finger's ends, which they tell over, when they are maudlin,* to their lovers. I had a sweetheart, Madam, who was a rake, and I know their ways very well, by hearsay.

POLLY. What villains are hypocrites! For they rob those of relief, who are in real distress. I know what it is to be unhappy in marriage.

MRS DUCAT. Married!

POLLY. Unhappily.

MRS DUCAT. When, where, to whom?

POLLY. If woman can have faith in woman, may my words find belief. Protestations are to be suspected, so I shall use none. If truth can prevail, I know you will pity me.

MRS DUCAT. Her manner and behaviour are so particular, that is to say, so sincere, that I must hear her story. Unhappily married! That is a misfortune not to be remedied.

POLLY. A constant woman hath but one chance to be happy; an inconstant woman, tho' she hath no chance to be very happy, can never be very unhappy.

DAMARIS. Believe me, Mrs *Polly*, as to pleasures of all sorts, 'tis a much more agreeable way to be inconstant.

> AIR 20. *Polwart* on the Green.
>
> *Love now is nought but art,*
>   *'Tis who can juggle best;*
> *To all men seem to give your heart,*
>   *But keep it in your breast.*
> *What gain and pleasure do we find,*
>   *Who change whene'er we list!*
> *The mill that turns with every wind*
>   *Must bring the owner grist.**

POLLY. My case, Madam, may in these times be look'd upon as singular; for I married a man only because I lov'd him. For this I was look'd upon as a fool by all my acquaintance; I was us'd inhumanly by my father and mother; and to compleat my misfortunes, my husband, by his wild behaviour, incurr'd the sentence of the law, and was separated from me by banishment. Being inform'd he was in this country, upon the death of my father and mother, with most of my small fortune, I came here to seek him.

MRS DUCAT. But how then fell you into the hands of that consummate bawd, *Trapes*?

POLLY. In my voyage, Madam, I was robb'd of all I had. Upon my landing in a strange country, and in want, I was found out by this inhuman woman, who had been an acquaintance of my father's: She offer'd me at first the civilities of her own house. When she was inform'd of my necessities, she propos'd to me the service of a Lady; of which I readily accepted. 'Twas under that pretence that she treacherously sold me to your husband as a mistress. This, Madam, is in short the whole truth. I fling my self at your feet for protection. By relieving me, you make your self easy.

MRS DUCAT.   What is't you propose?

POLLY.   In conniving at my escape, you save me from your husband's worrying me with threats and violence, and at the same time quiet your own fears and jealousies. If it is ever in my power, Madam, with gratitude I will repay you my ransom.

DAMARIS.   Besides, Madam, you will effectually revenge your self upon your husband; for the loss of the money he paid for her will touch him to the quick.

MRS DUCAT.   But have you consider'd what you request? We are invaded by the pyrates: The *Indians* are in arms; the whole country is in commotion, and you will every where be expos'd to danger.

DAMARIS.   Get rid of her at any rate. For such is the vanity of man, that when once he has begun with a woman, out of pride he will insist upon his point.

POLLY.   In staying with you, Madam, I make two people unhappy. And I chuse to bear my own misfortunes, without being the cause of another's.

MRS DUCAT.   If I let her escape before my husband's return, he will imagine she got off by the favour of this bustle and confusion.

POLLY.   May heaven reward your charity.

MRS DUCAT.   A woman so young and so handsome must be expos'd to continual dangers. I have a suit of cloaths by me of my nephew's, who is dead. In a man's habit* you will run fewer risques. I'll assist you too for the present with some money; and, as a traveller, you may with greater safety make enquiries after your husband.

POLLY.   How shall I ever make a return for so much goodness?

MRS DUCAT. May love reward your constancy. As for that perfidious monster *Trapes*, I will deliver her into the hands of the magistrate. Come, *Damaris*, let us this instant equip her for her adventures.

DAMARIS. When she is out of the house, without doubt, Madam, you will be more easy. And I wish she may be so too.

POLLY. May vertue be my protection; for I feel within me hope, cheerfulness, and resolution.

AIR 21. St. *Martin*'s Lane.

As pilgrims thro' devotion
To some shrine pursue their way,
They tempt the raging ocean,
And thro' desarts stray.
With zeal their hope desiring,
The saint their breast inspiring
With cheerful air,
Devoid of fear,
They every danger bear.
Thus equal zeal possessing,
I seek my only blessing.
O love, my honest vow regard!
My truth protect,
My steps direct,
His flight detect,
A faithful wife reward.

[*Exit.*

ACT II

SCENE I

The View of an INDIAN *Country.*

POLLY *in Boy's Cloaths.*

AIR 22. La Villanella.

Why did you spare him,
  O'er seas to bear him,
Far from his home, and constant bride?
  When Papa 'peach'd him,
  If death had reach'd him,
I then had only sigh'd, wept, and dy'd!

If my directions are right, I cannot be far from the village. With the habit, I must put on the courage and resolution of a man; for I am every where surrounded with dangers. By all I can learn of these pyrates, my dear *Macheath* is not of the crew. Perhaps I may hear of him among the slaves of the next plantation. How sultry is the day! the cool of this shade will refresh me. I am jaded too with reflection. How restless is love! [*Musick, two or three bars of the dead March**] My imagination follows him every where, would my feet were as swift. The world then could not hide him from me. [*Two or three bars more*] Yet even thought is now bewilder'd in pursuing him. [*Two or three bars more*] I'm tir'd, I'm faint.

*The Symphony.**

AIR 23. Dead March in *Coriolanus.*

  Sleep, O sleep,
*With thy rod of incantation,**
Charm my imagination.
Then, only then, I cease to weep.
  By thy power,
The virgin, by time o'ertaken,
For years forlorn, forsaken,
Enjoys the happy hour.

> *What's to sleep?*
> *'Tis a visionary blessing;*
> *A dream that's past expressing;*
> *Our utmost wish possessing;*
> *So may I always keep.*

[*Falls asleep.*

SCENE II

CAPSTERN, HACKER, CULVERIN, LAGUERRE, CUTLACE.

POLLY *asleep in a distant part of the stage.*

HACKER. We shall find but cool reception from *Morano*, if we return without either booty or intelligence.

CULVERIN. A man of invention hath always intelligence ready. I hope we are not exempted from the privilege of travellers.*

CAPSTERN. If we had got booty, you know we had resolv'd to agree in a lye. And, gentlemen, we will not have our diligence and duty call'd in question for that which every common servant has at his fingers end for his justification.

LAGUERRE. Alack, gentlemen, we are not such bunglers in love or politicks, but we must know that either to get favour or keep it, no man ever speaks what he thinks, but what is convenient.

AIR 24. Three Sheep-skins.

CUTLACE.   *Of all the sins that are money-supplying;*
              Consider the world, 'tis past all denying,
                  With all sorts,
                  In towns or courts,
              The richest sin is lying.

CULVERIN. Fatigue, gentlemen, should have refreshment. No man is requir'd to do more than his duty. Let us repose our selves a-while. A sup or two of our cag* would quicken invention.

ALL. Agreed.

[*They sit and drink.*

HACKER. I had always a genius* for ambition. Birth and education cannot keep it under. Our profession is great, brothers. What can be more heroic than to have declar'd war with the whole world?

CULVERIN. 'Tis a pleasure to me to recollect times past, and to observe by what steps a genius will push his fortune.

HACKER. Now as to me, brothers, mark you me. After I had rubb'd through* my youth with variety of adventures, I was prefer'd* to be footman to an eminent gamester, where, after having improv'd my self by his manners and conversation, I left him, betook my self to his politer profession, and cheated like a gentleman. For some time I kept a *Pharaon*-Bank* with success, but unluckily in a drunken bout* was stript by a more expert brother of the trade. I was now, as 'tis common with us upon these occasions, forc'd to have recourse to the highway for a recruit* to set me up; but making the experiment once too often, I was try'd, and receiv'd sentence; but got off for transportation. Which hath made me the man I am.

LAGUERRE. From a footman I grew to be a pimp to a man of quality. Considering I was for sometime in that employment, I look upon my self as particularly unlucky, that I then miss'd making my fortune. But, to give him his due, only his death could have prevented it. Upon this, I betook my self to another service, where my wages not being sufficient for my pleasures, I robb'd my master, and retir'd to visit foreign parts.

CAPSTERN. Now, you must know, I was a drawer* of one of the fashionable taverns, and of consequence was daily in the politest conversations. Tho' I say it, no body was better bred. I often cheated my master, and as a dutiful servant, now and then cheated for him. I had always my gallantries with the ladies that the lords and gentlemen brought to our house. I was ambitious too of a gentleman's profession, and turn'd gamester. Tho' I had great skill and no scruples, my play would not support my extravagancies: So that now and then I was forc'd to rob with pistols too. So I also owe my rank in the world to transportation.

CULVERIN. Our chief, *Morano*, brothers, had never been the man he is, had he not been train'd up in *England*. He has told me, that from his infancy he was the favourite page of a lady. He had a genius too above service, and, like us, ran into higher life. And, indeed, in manners and conversation, tho' he is black, no body has more the air of a great man.*

HACKER. He is too much attach'd to his pleasures. That mistress of his is a clog to his ambition. She's an arrant *Cleopatra*.*

LAGUERRE. If it were not for her, the *Indies* would be our own.

AIR 25. Rigadoon.

By women won,
We're all undone,
Each wench hath a Syren's *charms.*
The lover's deeds
Are good or ill,
As whim succeeds
In woman's will;
Resolution is lull'd in her arms.

HACKER. A man in love is no more to be depended on than a man in liquor, for he is out of himself.

AIR 26. Ton humeur est Catharine.

Woman's like the flatt'ring ocean,
Who her pathless ways can find?
Every blast directs her motion
Now she's angry, now she's kind.
What a fool's the vent'rous lover,
Whirl'd and toss'd by every wind!
Can the bark the port recover
*When the silly Pilot's blind?**

HACKER. A good horse is never turn'd loose among mares, till all his good deeds are over. And really your heroes should be serv'd the same way; for after they take to women, they have no good deeds to come. That inviegling gipsey, brothers, must be hawl'd from him by force. And then—the kingdom of *Mexico* shall be mine. My lot shall be the kingdom of *Mexico*.

CAPSTERN. Who talks of *Mexico*? [*All rise*] I'll never give it up. If you outlive me, brother, and I dye without heirs, I'll leave it to you for a legacy. I hope now you are satisfy'd. I have set my heart upon it, and no body shall dispute it with me.

LAGUERRE. The island of *Cuba*, methinks, brother, might satisfy any reasonable man.

CULVERIN. That I had allotted for you. *Mexico* shall not be parted with without my consent, captain *Morano* to be sure will choose *Peru*; that's the country of gold, and all your great men love gold. *Mexico* hath only silver, nothing but silver. Governor of *Cartagena*,* brother, is a pretty snug employment. That I shall not dispute with you.

CAPSTERN. Death, Sir,—I shall not part with *Mexico* so easily.

HACKER. Nor I.

CULVERIN. Nor I.

LAGUERRE. Nor I.

CULVERIN. Nor I.

HACKER. Draw then, and let the survivor take it.

[*They fight.*

POLLY. Bless me, what noise was that! Clashing of swords and fighting! Which way shall I fly, how shall I escape?

CAPSTERN. Hold, hold, gentlemen, let us decide our pretensions some other time. I see booty. A prisoner. Let us seize him.

CULVERIN. From him we will extort both ransom and intelligence.

POLLY. Spare my life gentlemen. If you are the men I take you for, I sought you to share your fortunes.

HACKER. Why, who do you take us for, friend?

POLLY. For those brave spirits, those *Alexanders*,* that shall soon by conquest be in possession of the *Indies*.

LAGUERRE. A mettl'd* young fellow.

CAPSTERN. He speaks with respect too, and gives us our titles.

CULVERIN. Have you heard of captain *Morano*?

POLLY. I came hither in meer ambition to serve under him.

AIR 27. Ye nymphs and sylvan gods.

I hate those coward tribes,
Who by mean sneaking bribes,
By tricks and disguise,
By flattery and lies,
To power and grandeur rise.
Like heroes of old
You are greatly bold,
The sword your cause supports.
Untaught to fawn,
You ne'er were drawn
Your truth to pawn
Among the spawn,*
Who practise the frauds of courts.

I would willingly choose the more honourable way of making a fortune.

HACKER. The youth speaks well. Can you inform us, my lad, of the disposition of the enemy? Have the *Indians* joyn'd the factory?* We should advance towards 'em immediately. Who knows but they may side with us? May-hap they may like our tyranny better.

POLLY. I am a stranger, gentlemen, and entirely ignorant of the affairs of this country: But in the most desperate undertaking, I am ready to risque your fortunes.*

HACKER. Who, and what are you, friend!

POLLY. A young fellow, who has genteely run out his fortune with a spirit, and would now with more spirit retrieve it.

CULVERIN. The lad may be of service. Let us bring him before *Morano*, and leave him to his disposal.

POLLY. Gentlemen, I thank you.

AIR 28. Minuet.

CULVERIN. *Cheer up my lads, let us push on the fray.*
For battles, like women, are lost by delay.
Let us seize victory while in our power;

> *Alike war and love have their critical hour.*
> *Our hearts bold and steady*
> *Should always be ready,*
> *So, think war a widow, a kingdom the dower.**

[*Exeunt.*

SCENE III

Another Country Prospect.

MORANO, JENNY.

MORANO. Sure, hussy, you have more ambition and more vanity than to be serious in persuading me to quit my conquests. Where is the woman who is not fond of title? And one bold step more, may make you a queen, you gipsy. Think of that.

AIR 29. Mirleton.

> *When I'm great, and flush of treasure,*
> *Check'd by neither fear or shame,*
> *You shall tread a round of pleasure,*
> *Morning, noon, and night the same.*
> *With a Mirleton, &c.*
> *Like a city wife or beauty*
> *You shall flutter life away;*
> *And shall know no other duty,*
> *But to dress, eat, drink, and play*
> *With a Mirleton, &c.*

When you are a queen, *Jenny*, you shall keep your coach and six, and shall game as deep as you please.* So, there's the two chief ends of woman's ambition satisfy'd.

AIR 30. Sawny was tall, and of noble race.

> *Shall I not be bold when honour calls?*
> *You've a heart that would upbraid me then.*
> JENNY. *But, ah, I fear, if my hero falls,*
> *Thy Jenny shall ne'er know pleasure again.*

MORANO.   *To deck their wives fond tradesmen cheat;*
          I conquer but to make thee great.
JENNY.   *But if my hero falls,—ah then*
          Thy Jenny *shall ne'er know pleasure again!*

MORANO. Insinuating creature! but you must own *Jenny*, you have had convincing proofs of my fondness; and if you were reasonable in your love, you should have some regard to my honour, as well as my person.

JENNY. Have I ever betray'd you, since you took me to your self?* That's what few women can say, who ever were trusted.

MORANO. In love, *Jenny*, you cannot out-do me. Was it not entirely for you that I disguis'd my self as a black, to skreen my self from women who laid claim to me where-ever I went? Is not the rumour of my death, which I purposely spread, credited thro' the whole country? *Macheath* is dead to all the world but you. Not one of the crew have the least suspicion of me.

JENNY. But, dear captain, you would not sure persuade me that I have all of you. For tho' women cannot claim you, you now and then lay claim to other women. But my jealousy was never teazing or vexatious. You will pardon me, my dear.

MORANO. Now you are silly, *Jenny*. Pr'ythee—poh! Nature girl is not to be corrected at once. What do you propose? What would you have me do? Speak out, let me know your mind.

JENNY. Know when you are well.

MORANO. Explain your self; speak your sentiments freely.

JENNY. You have a competence* in your power. Rob the crew, and steal off to *England*. Believe me, Captain, you will be rich enough to be respected by your neighbours.

MORANO. Your opinion of me startles me. For I never in my life was treacherous but to women; and you know men of the nicest punctilio* make nothing of that.

JENNY. Look round among all the snug fortunes that are made, and you will find most of 'em were secur'd by a judicious retreat. Why will you bar your self from the customs of the times?

AIR 31. Northern *Nancy*.

How many men have found the skill
Of power and wealth acquiring?
But sure there's a time to stint the will
And the judgment is in retiring.
For to be displac'd,
For to be disgrac'd,
Is the end of too high aspiring.

[*Enter* SAILOR.

SAILOR. Sir, Lieutenant *Vanderbluff* wants to speak with you. And he hopes your honour will give him the hearing.

[*Exit.*

MORANO. Leave me, *Jenny*, for a few minutes. Perhaps he would speak with me in private.

JENNY. Think of my advice before it is too late. By this kiss I beg it of you.

[*Exit.*

SCENE IV

MORANO, VANDERBLUFF.

VANDERBLUFF. For shame, Captain; what, hamper'd in the arms of a woman, when your honour and glory are all at stake! while a man is grappling with these gil-flirts,* pardon the expression, Captain, he runs his reason a-ground; and there must be a woundy* deal of labour to set it a-float again.

AIR 32. Amante fuggite cadente belta.

Fine women are devils, compleat* in their way,
They always are roving and cruising for prey.
When we flounce on their hook, their views they obtain,
Like those too their pleasure is giving us pain.

Excuse my plain speaking, Captain; a boatswain must swear in a storm,* and a man must speak plain, when he sees foul weather a-head of us.

MORANO. D'you think me like the wheat-ear,* only fit for sunshine, who cannot bear the least cloud over him? No *Vanderbluff*, I have a heart that can face a tempest of dangers. Your blust'ring will but make me obstinate. You seem frighten'd, Lieutenant.

VANDERBLUFF. From any body but you, that speech should have had another-guess* answer than words. Death, Captain, are not the *Indies* in dispute? an hour's delay may make their hands too many for us. Give the word, Captain, this hand shall take the *Indian* King pris'ner, and keel-hawl* him afterwards, 'till I make him discover his gold. I have known you eager to venture your life for a less prize.

MORANO. Are *Hacker*, *Culverin*, *Capstern*, *Laguerre* and the rest, whom we sent out for intelligence, return'd, that you are under this immediate alarm?

VANDERBLUFF. No, Sir; but from the top of yon' hill, I my self saw the enemy putting themselves in order of battle.

MORANO. But we have nothing at all to apprehend; for we have still a safe retreat to our ships.

VANDERBLUFF. To our woman, you mean. Furies! you talk like one. If our Captain is bewitch'd, shall we be be-devil'd, and lose the footing we have got?

[*Draws.*

MORANO. Take care, Lieutenant. This language may provoke me. I fear no man. I fear nothing, and that you know. Put up your cutlace, Lieutenant, for I shall not ruin our cause by a private quarrel.

VANDERBLUFF. Noble Captain, I ask pardon.

MORANO. A brave man should be cool till action, Lieutenant; when danger presses us, I am always ready. Be satisfy'd, I'll take my leave of my wife, and then take the command.

VANDERBLUFF. That's what you can never do till you have her

leave. She is but just gone from you, Sir. See her not; hear her not; the breath of a woman has ever prov'd a contrary wind to great actions.

MORANO. I tell you I will see her. I have got rid of many a woman in my time, and you may trust me—

VANDERBLUFF. With any woman but her. The husband that is govern'd is the only man that never finds out that he is so.

MORANO. This then, Lieutenant, shall try my resolution. In the mean time, send out parties and scouts to observe the motions of the *Indians*.

AIR 33. Since all the world's turn'd upside down.

> *Tho' different passions rage by turns,*
> *Within my breast fermenting;*
> *Now blazes love, now honour burns,*
> *I'm here, I'm there consenting.*
> *I'll each obey, so keep my oath,*
> *That oath by which I won her:*
> *With truth and steddiness in both,*
> *I'll act like a man of honour.*

Doubt me not, Lieutenant. But I'll now go with you, to give the necessary commands, and after that return to take my leave before the battle.

SCENE V

MORANO, VANDERBLUFF, JENNY, CAPSTERN, CULVERIN, HACKER, LAGUERRE, POLLY.

JENNY. *Hacker*, Sir, and the rest of the party are return'd with a prisoner. Perhaps from him you may learn some intelligence that may be useful. See, here they are. [*Aside*]—A clever sprightly young fellow! I like him.

VANDERBLUFF. What cheer, my lads? has fortune sent you a good prize?

JENNY. He seems some rich planter's son.

VANDERBLUFF. In the common practice of commerce you should never slip an opportunity, and for his ransome, no doubt, there will be room for comfortable extortion.

MORANO. Hath he inform'd you of any thing that may be of service? where pick'd you him up? whence is he?

HACKER. We found him upon the road. He is a stranger it seems in these parts. And as our heroes generally set out, extravagance, gaming and debauchery have qualify'd him for a brave man.

MORANO. What are you, friend?

POLLY. A young fellow, who hath been robb'd by the world; and I came on purpose to join you, to rob the world by way of retaliation. An open war with the whole world is brave and honourable. I hate the clandestine pilfering war that is practis'd among friends and neighbours in civil societies. I would serve, Sir.

AIR 34. Hunt the Squirrel.

The world is always jarring;*
This is pursuing
T'other man's ruin,
Friends with friends are warring,
In a false cowardly way.
Spurr'd on by emulations,
Tongues are engaging,
Calumny, raging
Murthers reputations,
Envy keeps up the fray.
Thus, with burning hate,
Each, returning hate,
Wounds and robs his friends.
In civil life,
Even man and wife
Squabble for selfish ends.

JENNY [aside]. He really is a mighty pretty man.

VANDERBLUFF. The lad promises well, and has just notions of the world.

MORANO. Whatever other great men do, I love to encourage merit. The youth pleases me; and if he answers in action—d'you hear me, my lad?—your fortune is made. Now Lieutenant *Vanderbluff*, I am for you.

VANDERBLUFF. Discipline must not be neglected.

MORANO. When every thing is settled, my dear *Jenny*, I will return to take my leave. After that, young gentleman, I shall try your mettle.* In the mean time, *Jenny*, I leave you to sift him with farther questions. He has liv'd in the world, you find, and may have learnt to be treacherous.

SCENE VI

JENNY, POLLY.

JENNY. How many women have you ever ruin'd, young gentleman!

POLLY. I have been ruin'd by women, madam. But I think indeed a man's fortune cannot be more honourably dispos'd of; for those have always a kind of claim to their protection, who have been ruin'd in their service.*

JENNY. Were you ever in love?

POLLY. With the sex.*

JENNY. Had you never a woman in love with you?

POLLY. All the women that ever I knew were mercenary.

JENNY. But sure you cannot think all women so.

POLLY. Why not as well as all men? The manners of courts are catching.

JENNY. If you have found only such usage, a generous woman can the more oblige you. Why so bashful, young spark? You don't look as if you would revenge your self on the sex.

POLLY. I lost my impudence with my fortune. Poverty keeps down assurance.

JENNY. I am a plain-spoken woman, as you may find, and I own I like you. And, let me tell you, to be my favourite may be your best step to preferment.

AIR 35. Young *Damon* once the loveliest swain.

> *In love and life the present use.*
> *One hour we grant, the next refuse;*
> *Who then would risque a nay?*
> *Were lovers wise they would be kind,*
> *And in our eyes the moment find;*
> *For only then they may.*

Like other women I shall run to extremes. If you won't make me love you, I shall hate you. There never was a man of true courage who was a coward in love. Sure you are not afraid of me, stripling?*

[*Taking* POLLY *by the hand.*]

POLLY. I know you only railly* me. Respect, madam, keeps me in awe.

JENNY. By your expression and behaviour, one would think I were your wife. If so, I may make use of her freedoms, and do what I please without shame or restraint.

[*Kisses her.*]

Such raillery as this, my dear, requires replication.

POLLY. You'll pardon me then, Madam.

[*Kisses her.*]

JENNY. What, my cheek! let me dye, if by your kiss, I should not take you for my brother or my father.

POLLY [*aside*]. I must put on more assurance, or I shall be discover'd. <*Aloud*> Nay then, Madam, if a woman will allow me liberties, they are never flung away upon me. If I am too rude—

[*Kisses her.*]

JENNY. A woman never pardons the contrary fault.

AIR 36. Catharine Ogye.

We never blame the forward swain,
  Who puts us to the tryal.
POLLY.   *I know you first would give me pain,*
  Then baulk me with denial.
JENNY.   *What mean we then by being try'd?*
POLLY.   *With scorn and slight to use us.*
  Most beauties, to indulge their pride,
  Seem kind but to refuse us.

JENNY. Come then, my dear, let us take a turn in yonder grove. A woman never shews her pride but before witnesses.

POLLY [*aside*]. How shall I get rid of this affair? <*Aloud*> *Morano* may surprize us.

JENNY. That is more a wife's concern. Consider, young man, if I have put my self in your power, you are in mine.

POLLY. We may have more easy and safe opportunities. Besides, I know, Madam, you are not serious.

JENNY. To a man who loses one opportunity, we never grant a second. Excuses! consideration! he hath not a spark of love in him. I must be his aversion! go, monster, I hate you, and you shall find I can be reveng'd.

AIR 37. Roger a Coverly.

My heart is by love forsaken,
  I feel the tempest growing.
A fury the place hath taken,
  I rage, I burn, I'm glowing.
Tho' Cupid's arrows are erring,
  Or indifference may secure ye,
When woman's revenge is stirring,
  You cannot escape that fury.

I could bear your excuses, but those looks of indifference kill me.

SCENE VII

JENNY, POLLY, MORANO.

JENNY. Sure never was such insolence! how can you leave me with this bawdy-house bully? for if he had been bred a page, he must have made his fortune.* If I had given him the least encouragement, it would not have provok'd me. Odious creature!

MORANO. What-a-vengeance is the matter?

JENNY. Only an attempt upon your wife. So ripe an assurance! he must have suck'd in impudence from his mother.

MORANO. An act of friendship only. He meant to push his fortune with the husband. 'Tis the way of the town, my dear.

AIR 38. Bacchus m'a dit.

By halves no friend
Now seeks to do you pleasure.
Their help they lend
In every part of life;
If husbands part,
The friend hath always leisure;
Then all his heart
Is bent to please the wife.

JENNY. I hate you for being so little jealous.

MORANO. Sure, *Jenny*, you know the way of the world better, than to be surpriz'd at a thing of this kind. 'Tis a civility that all you fine ladies expect; and, upon the like occasion, I could not have answer'd for my self. I own, I have a sort of partiality to impudence. Perhaps too, his views might be honourable. If I had been kill'd in battle, 'tis good to be beforehand. You know 'tis a way often practis'd to make sure of a widow.

JENNY. If I find you so easy in these affairs, you may make my vertue less obstinate.

AIR 39. Health to *Betty*.

If husbands sit unsteady,
Most wives for freaks are ready.
Neglect the rein
The steed again
Grows skittish, wild and heady.

Your behaviour forces me to say, what my love for you will never
let me put in practice. You are too safe, too secure, to think of pleas-
ing me.

MORANO. Tho' I like impudence, yet 'tis not so agreeable when put
in practice upon my own wife: and jesting apart, young fellow, if I
ever catch you thinking this way again, a cat-o'-nine-tails* shall
cool your courage.

SCENE VIII

MORANO, JENNY, POLLY, VANDERBLUFF, CAPSTERN,
LAGUERRE, &c. *with* CAWWAWKEE *Prisoner.*

VANDERBLUFF. The party, captain, is return'd with success. After a
short skirmish, the *Indian* prince *Cawwawkee* here was made prisoner, and we want your orders for his disposal.

MORANO. Are all our troops ready and under arms?

VANDERBLUFF. They wait but for your command. Our numbers
are strong. All the ships crews are drawn out, and the slaves that
have deserted to us from the plantations are all brave determin'd
fellows, who must behave themselves well.

MORANO. Look'e lieutenant, the trussing up this prince, in my
opinion, would strike a terror among the enemy. Besides, dead
men can do no mischief. Let a gibbet* be set up, and swing him off
between the armies before the onset.

VANDERBLUFF. By your leave, captain, my advice blows directly
contrary. Whatever may be done hereafter, I am for putting him
first of all upon examination. The *Indians* to be sure have hid their
treasures, and we shall want a guide to shew us the best plunder.

MORANO. The counsel is good. I will extort intelligence from him. Bring me word when the enemy are in motion, and that instant I'll put myself at your head.

[*Exit* SAILOR.

Do you know me, prince?

CAWWAWKEE. As a man of injustice I know you, who covets and invades the properties of another.

MORANO. Do you know my power?

CAWWAWKEE. I fear it not.

MORANO. Do you know your danger?

CAWWAWKEE. I am prepar'd to meet it.

AIR 40. Cappe de bonne Esperance.

The body of the brave may be taken,
    If chance bring on our adverse hour;
But the noble soul is unshaken,
    For that still is in our power:
'Tis a rock whose firm foundation
    Mocks the waves of perturbation;
'Tis a never-dying ray,
    Brighter in our evil Day.

MORANO. Meer downright Barbarians,* you see lieutenant. They have our notional honour still in practice among 'em.

VANDERBLUFF. We must beat civilizing into 'em, to make 'em capable of common society, and common conversation.

MORANO. Stubborn prince, mark me well. Know you, I say, that your life is in my power?

CAWWAWKEE. I know too, that my virtue is in my own.

MORANO. Not a mule, or an old out-of-fashion'd philosopher could be more obstinate. Can you feel pain?

CAWWAWKEE. I can bear it.

MORANO. I shall try you.

CAWWAWKEE. I speak truth, I never affirm but what I know.

MORANO. In what condition are your troops? What numbers have you? How are they dispos'd? Act reasonably and openly, and you shall find protection.

CAWWAWKEE. What, betray my friends! I am no coward, *European.**

MORANO. Torture shall make you squeak.

CAWWAWKEE. I have resolution; and pain shall neither make me lie or betray. I tell thee once more *European*, I am no coward.

VANDERBLUFF. What, neither cheat nor be cheated! There is no having either commerce or correspondence with these creatures.

JENNY. We have reason to be thankful for our good education. How ignorant is mankind without it!

CAPSTERN. I wonder to hear the brute speak.

LAGUERRE. They would make a shew of him in *England*.

JENNY. Poh, they would only take him for a fool.

CAPSTERN. But how can you expect any thing else from a creature, who hath never seen a civiliz'd country? Which way should he know mankind?

JENNY. Since they are made like us, to be sure, were they in *England* they might be taught.

LAGUERRE. Why we see country gentlemen grow into courtiers, and country gentlewomen, with a little polishing of the town, in a few months become fine ladies.

JENNY. Without doubt, education and example can do much.

POLLY [*aside*]. How happy are these savages! Who would not wish to be in such ignorance.

MORANO. Have done, I beg you, with your musty reflections: You but interrupt the examination. You have treasures, you have gold and silver among you, I suppose.

CAWWAWKEE. Better it had been for us if that shining earth had never been brought to light.

MORANO. That you have treasures then you own, it seems. I am glad to hear you confess something.

CAWWAWKEE. But out of benevolence we ought to hide it from you. For, as we have heard, 'tis so rank a poison to you *Europeans*, that the very touch of it makes you mad.

AIR 41. When bright Aurelia tripp'd the plain.

For gold you sacrifice your fame,
Your honour, life and friend:
You war, you fawn, you lie, you game,
And plunder without fear or shame;
Can madness this transcend?*

MORANO. Bold savage, we are not to be insulted with your ignorance. If you would save your lives, you must, like the beaver, leave behind you what we hunt you for, or we shall not quit the chase.* Discover your treasures, your hoards, for I will have the ransacking of 'em.

JENNY. By his seeming to set some value upon gold, one would think that he had some glimmering of sense.

AIR 42. *Peggy's* Mill.

When gold is in hand,
It gives us command;
It makes us lov'd and respected.
'Tis now, as of yore,
Wit and sense, when poor,
Are scorn'd, o'erlook'd and neglected.
Tho' peevish and old,
If women have gold,
They have youth, good-humour and beauty:
Among all mankind
Without it we find
Nor love, nor favour nor duty.

MORANO. I will have no more of these interruptions. Since women will be always talking, one would think they had a chance now and then to talk in season. Once more I ask you, obstinate, audacious savage, if I grant you your life, will you be useful to us? For you shall find mercy upon no other terms. I will have immediate compliance, or you shall undergo the torture.

CAWWAWKEE. With dishonour life is nothing worth.

MORANO. Furies! I'll trifle no longer.

> RECITATIVE. Sia suggetta la plebe in *Coriolan*.
>
> *Hence let him feel his sentence.*
> *Pain brings repentance.*

LAGUERRE. You would not have us put him to death, captain?

MORANO. Torture him leisurely, but severely. I shall stagger your resolution, *Indian*.

> RECITATIVE.
>
> *Hence let him feel his sentence.*
> *Pain brings repentance.*

But hold, I'll see him tortur'd. I will have the pleasure of extorting answers from him myself. So keep him safe till you have my directions.

LAGUERRE. It shall be done.

MORANO. As for you, young gentleman, I think it not proper to trust you till I know you farther. Let him be your prisoner too till I give order how to dispose of him.

> [*Exeunt* CAWWAWKEE *and* POLLY *guarded.*

SCENE IX

MORANO, JENNY, VANDERBLUFF.

VANDERBLUFF. Come, noble captain, take one hearty smack upon her lips, and then steer off; for one kiss requires another, and you will never have done with her. If once a man and woman come to grappling, there's no hawling of 'em asunder. Our friends expect us.

JENNY. Nay, lieutenant *Vanderbluff*, he shall not go yet.

VANDERBLUFF. I'm out of all patience. There is a time for all things,
Madam. But a woman thinks all times must be subservient to her
whim and humour. We should be now upon the spot.

JENNY. Is the captain under your command, lieutenant?

VANDERBLUFF. I know women better than so. I shall never dispute
the command with any gentleman's wife. Come captain, a woman
will never take the last kiss; she will always want another. Break
from her clutches.

MORANO. I must go—But I cannot.*

AIR 43. Excuse me.

Honour calls me from thy arms,	<*To her.*>*
With glory my bosom is beating.	
Victory summons to arms: then to arms	<*To him.*>
Let us haste, for we're sure of defeating.	
One look more—and then—	[*To her.*
Oh, I am lost again!	
What a Power has beauty!	
But honour calls, and I must away.	[*To him.*
But love forbids, and I must obey.	[*To her.*
You grow too bold;	[VANDERBLUFF *pulling him away.*
Hence, loose your hold,	[*To him.*
For love claims all my duty.	[*To her.*

They will bring us word when the enemy is in motion. I know my
own time, lieutenant.

VANDERBLUFF. Lose the *Indies* then, with all my heart. Lose the
money, and you lose the woman, that I can tell you, captain. Furies,
what would the woman be at!

JENNY. Not so hasty and choleric, I beg you, lieutenant. Give me
the hearing, and perhaps, whatever you may think of us, you may
once in your life hear a woman speak reason.

VANDERBLUFF. Dispatch then. And if a few words can satisfy you,
be brief.

JENNY. Men only slight women's advice thro' an over-conceit of
their own opinions. I am against hazarding a battle. Why should

we put what we have already got to the risque? We have money enough on board our ships to secure our persons, and can reserve a comfortable subsistance besides. Let us leave the *Indies* to our comrades.

VANDERBLUFF. Sure you are the first of the sex that ever stinted herself in love or money. If it were consistent with our honour, her counsel were worth listening to.

JENNY. Consistent with our honour! For shame, lieutenant; you talk downright *Indian*. One would take you for the savage's brother or cousin-german at least. You may talk of honour, as other great men do: But when interest comes in your way, you should do as other great men do.

AIR 44. Ruben.

*Honour plays a bubble's part;**
Ever bilk'd and cheated;
Never in ambition's heart,
Int'rest there is seated.
*Honour was in use of yore,**
Tho' by want attended:
Since 'twas talk'd of, and no more;
Lord, how times are mended!

VANDERBLUFF. What think you of her proposal, noble captain? We may push matters too far.

JENNY. Consider, my dear, the *Indies* are only treasures in expectation. All your sensible men, now a days, love the ready.* Let us seize the ships then, and away for *England*, while we have the opportunity.

VANDERBLUFF. Sure you can have no scruple against treachery, captain. 'Tis as common a money-getting vice as any in fashion; for who now-a-days ever boggles at giving up his crew?

MORANO. But the baulking of a great design—

VANDERBLUFF. 'Tis better baulking our own designs, than have 'em baulked by others; for then our designs and our lives will be cut short together.

AIR 45. Troy Town.

When ambition's ten years toils
Have heap'd up mighty hoards of gold;
Amid the harvest of the spoils,
Acquired by fraud and rapin bold,
Comes justice. The great scheme is crost,
At once wealth, life, and fame, are lost.

This is a melancholy reflection for ambition, if it ever could think reasonably.

MORANO. If you are satisfy'd, and for your security, *Jenny*. For any man may allow that he has money enough, when he hath enough to satisfy his wife.

VANDERBLUFF. We may make our retreat without suspicion, for they will readily impute our being mist to the accidents of war.

SCENE X

MORANO, JENNY, VANDERBLUFF, SAILOR.

SAILOR. There is just now news arriv'd, that the troops of the plantation have intercepted the passage to our ships; so that victory is our only hope. The *Indian* forces too are ready to march, and ours grow impatient for your presence, noble captain.

MORANO. I'll be with 'em. Come, then, lieutenant, for death or the world.

JENNY. Nay then, if affairs are desperate, nothing shall part me from you. I'll share your dangers.

MORANO. Since I must have an empire, prepare yourself, *Jenny*, for the cares of royalty. Let us on to battle, to victory.

[*Trumpet sounds.*

Hark the trumpet.

AIR 46. We've cheated the Parson.

> *Despair leads to battle, no courage so great.*
> *They must conquer or die who've no retreat.*

VANDERBLUFF.   *No retreat.*

JENNY.   *No retreat.*

MORANO.   *They must conquer or die who've no retreat.*

[*Exeunt.*

SCENE XI

A room of a poor cottage.

CAWWAWKEE *in chains,* POLLY.

POLLY. Unfortunate prince! I cannot blame your disbelief, when I tell you that I admire your virtues, and share in your misfortunes.

CAWWAWKEE. To be oppress'd by an *European* implies merit. Yet you are an *European*. Are you fools? Do you believe one another? Sure speech can be of no use among you.

POLLY. There are constitutions that can resist a pestilence.

CAWWAWKEE. But sure vice must be inherent in such constitutions. You are asham'd of your hearts, you can lie. How can you bear to look into yourselves?

POLLY. My sincerity could even bear your examination.

CAWWAWKEE. You have cancell'd faith.* How can I believe you? You are cowards too, for you are cruel.

POLLY. Would it were in my power to give you proofs of my compassion.

CAWWAWKEE. You can be avaritious. That is a complication of all vices. It comprehends them all. Heaven guard our country from the infection.

POLLY. Yet the worst men allow virtue to be amiable, or there would be no hypocrites.

CAWWAWKEE. Have you then hypocrisy still among you? For all

that I have experienc'd of your manners is open violence, and barefac'd injustice. Who that had ever felt the satisfaction of virtue would ever part with it?

AIR 47. T'amo tanto.

> *Virtue's treasure*
> *Is a pleasure,*
> *Cheerful even amid distress;*
> *Nor pain nor crosses,*
> *Nor grief nor losses,*
> *Nor death itself can make it less:*
> *Here relying,*
> *Suff'ring, dying,*
> *Honest souls find all redress.*

POLLY. My heart feels your sentiments, and my tongue longs to join in 'em.

CAWWAWKEE.	*Virtue's treasure*
	Is a pleasure,
POLLY.	*Cheerful even amid distress;*
CAWWAWKEE.	*Nor pain nor crosses,*
POLLY.	*Nor grief nor losses,*
CAWWAWKEE.	*Nor death itself can make it less.*
POLLY.	*Here relying,*
CAWWAWKEE.	*Suff'ring, dying,*
POLLY.	*Honest souls find all redress.*

CAWWAWKEE. Having this, I want no other consolation. I am prepar'd for all misfortune.

POLLY. Had you means of escape, you could not refuse it. To preserve your life is your duty.

CAWWAWKEE. By dishonest means, I scorn it.

POLLY. But stratagem is allow'd in war; and 'tis lawful to use all the weapons employ'd against you. You may save your friends from affliction, and be the instrument of rescuing your country.

CAWWAWKEE. Those are powerful inducements. I seek not voluntarily to resign my life. While it lasts, I would do my duty.

POLLY. I'll talk with our guard. What induces them to rapin and murther, will induce 'em to betray. You may offer them what they want; and from no hands, upon no terms, corruption can resist the temptation.

CAWWAWKEE. I have no skill. Those who are corrupt themselves know how to corrupt others. You may do as you please. But whatever you promise for me, contrary to the *European* custom, I will perform. For tho' a knave may break his word with a knave, an honest tongue knows no such distinctions.

POLLY <*calls off stage*>. Gentlemen, I desire some conference with you, that may be for your advantage.

SCENE XII

POLLY, CAWWAWKEE, LAGUERRE, CAPSTERN.

POLLY. Know you that you have the *Indian* prince in your custody?

LAGUERRE. Full well.

POLLY. Know you the treasures that are in his power?

LAGUERRE. I know too that they shall soon be ours.

POLLY. In having him in our possession they are yours.

LAGUERRE. As how, friend?

POLLY. He might well reward you.

LAGUERRE. For what?

POLLY. For his liberty.

CAWWAWKEE. Yes, *European*, I can and will reward you.

CAPSTERN. He's a great man, and I trust no such promises.

CAWWAWKEE. I have said it, *European*: And an *Indian*'s heart is always answerable for his words.

POLLY. Think of the chance of war, gentlemen. Conquest is not so sure when you fight against those who fight for their liberties.

LAGUERRE. What think you of the proposal?

CAPSTERN. The prince can give us places; he can make us all great men. Such a prospect I can tell you, *Laguerre*, would tempt our betters.

LAGUERRE. Besides, if we are beaten, we have no retreat to our ships.

CAPSTERN. If we gain our ends what matter how we come by it?

LAGUERRE. Every man for himself, say I. There is no being even with mankind, without that universal maxim. Consider, brother, we run no risque.

CAPSTERN. Nay, I have no objections.

LAGUERRE. If we conquer'd, and the booty were to be divided among the crews, what would it amount to? Perhaps this way we might get more than would come to our shares.

CAPSTERN. Then too, I always lik'd a place at court. I have a genius to get, keep in, and make the most of an employment.

LAGUERRE. You will consider, prince, our own politicians would have rewarded such meritorious services: We'll go off with you.

CAPSTERN. We want only to be known to be employ'd.

LAGUERRE. Let us unbind him then.

POLLY. 'Tis thus one able politician outwits another; and we admire their wisdom. You may rely upon the prince's word as much as if he was a poor man.

CAPSTERN. Our fortunes then are made.

AIR 48. Down in a meadow.

POLLY. *The sportsmen keep hawks, and their quarry they gain;*
Thus the woodcock, the partridge, the pheasant is slain.
What care and expence for their hounds are employ'd!
Thus the fox, and the hare, and the stag are destroy'd.
The spaniel they cherish, whose flattering way
Can as well as their masters cringe, fawn and betray.
Thus stanch* politicians, look all the world round,
Love the men who can serve as hawk, spaniel or hound.

[*Exeunt.*

ACT III

SCENE I

The Indian Camp.*

POHETOHEE, *Attendants*.

INDIAN. Sir, a party from the *British* factory have join'd us. Their chief attends your majesty's orders for their disposition.

POHETOHEE. Let them be posted next my command; for I would be witness of their bravery. But first let their officer know I would see him.

[*Exit* INDIAN.

[*Enter* DUCAT.

DUCAT. I would do all in my power to serve your majesty. I have brought up my men, and now, Sir,—I would fain give up. I speak purely upon your majesty's account. For as to courage and all that—I have been a colonel of the militia these ten years.

POHETOHEE. Sure, you have not fear. Are you a man?

DUCAT. A married man, Sir, who carries his wife's heart about him, and that indeed is a little timorous. Upon promise to her, I am engag'd to quit in case of a battle; and her heart hath ever govern'd me more than my own. Besides, Sir, fighting is not our business; we pay others for fighting; and yet 'tis well known we had rather part with our lives than our money.

POHETOHEE. And have you no spirit then to defend it? Your families, your liberties, your properties are at stake. If these cannot move you, you must be born without a heart.

DUCAT. Alas, Sir, we cannot be answerable for human infirmities.

AIR 49. There was an old man, and he liv'd.

What man can on virtue or courage repose,
Or guess if the touch 'twill abide?*

Like gold, if intrinsick sure no body knows,
Till weigh'd in the ballance and try'd.

POHETOHEE. How different are your notions from ours! We think virtue, honour, and courage as essential to man as his limbs, or senses; and in every man we suppose the qualities of a man, till we have found the contrary. But then we regard him only as a brute in disguise. How custom can degrade nature!

DUCAT. Why should I have any more scruples about myself, than about my money? If I can make my courage pass currant,* what matter is it to me whether it be true or false? 'Tis time enough to own a man's failings when they are found out. If your majesty then will not dispense with my duty to my wife,* with permission, I'll to my post. 'Tis wonderful to me that kings ever go to war, who have so much to lose, and nothing essential to get.

[*Exit.*

SCENE II

POHETOHEE, *Attendants.*

POHETOHEE. My Son a Prisoner! Tortur'd perhaps and inhumanly butcher'd! Human nature cannot bear up against such afflictions. The war must suffer by his absence. More then is requir'd from me. Grief raises my resolution, and calls me to relieve him, or to a just revenge. What mean those shouts?

[*Enter* INDIAN.

INDIAN. The prince, Sir, is return'd. The troops are animated by his presence. With some of the pyrates in his retinue, he waits your majesty's commands.

SCENE III

POHETOHEE, CAWWAWKEE, POLLY, LAGUERRE,
CAPSTERN, &c.

POHETOHEE. Victory then is ours. Let me embrace him. Welcome, my son. Without thee my heart could not have felt a triumph.

CAWWAWKEE. Let this youth then receive your thanks. To him are owing my life and liberty. And the love of virtue alone gain'd me his friendship.

POHETOHEE. This hath convinc'd me that an *European* can be generous and honest.

CAWWAWKEE. These others, indeed, have the passion of their country. I owe their services to gold, and my promise is engag'd to reward them. How it gauls* honour to have obligations to a dishonourable man!

LAGUERRE. I hope your majesty will not forget our services.

POHETOHEE. I am bound for my son's engagements.

CAWWAWKEE. For this youth, I will be answerable. Like a gem found in rubbish, he appears the brighter among these his country men.

AIR 50. Iris la plus charmante.

> *Love with beauty is flying,*
> *At once 'tis blooming and dying,*
> *But all seasons defying,*
> *Friendship lasts on the year.*
> *Love is by long enjoying,*
>   *Cloying;*
> *Friendship, enjoy'd the longer,*
>   *Stronger.*
> *O may the flame divine*
> *Burn in your breast like mine!*

POLLY. Most noble prince, my behaviour shall justify the good opinion you have of me; and my friendship is beyond professions.

POHETOHEE. Let these men remain under guard, till after the battle. All promises shall then be made good to you.

[*Exeunt* PYRATES *guarded.*]

SCENE IV

POHETOHEE, CAWWAWKEE, POLLY.

CAWWAWKEE. May this young man be my companion in the war. As a boon I request it of you. He knows our cause is just, and that is sufficient to engage him in it.

POHETOHEE. I leave you to appoint him his command. Dispose of him as you judge convenient.

POLLY. To fall into their hands is certain torture and death. As far as my youth and strength will permit me, you may rely upon my duty.

[*Enter* INDIAN.]

INDIAN. Sir, the enemy are advancing towards us.

POHETOHEE. Victory then is at hand. Justice protects us, and courage shall support us. Let us then to our posts.

[*Exeunt.*

SCENE V

The field of battle.

CULVERIN, HACKER, PYRATES.

AIR 51. There was a Jovial Beggar.

FIRST PYRATE.   *When horns,* with cheerful sound,*
Proclaim the active day;
Impatience warms the hound,
He burns to chase the prey.

CHORUS.   *Thus to battle we will go, &c.*

SECOND PYRATE. *How charms the trumpet's breath!*
The brave, with hope possess'd,
Forgetting wounds and death,
Feel conquest in their breast.

CHORUS.   *Thus to battle, &c.*

CULVERIN. But yet I don't see, Brother *Hacker*, why we should be commanded by a Neger.* 'Tis all along of him that we are led into these difficulties. I hate this land fighting. I love to have searoom.

HACKER. We are of the council, brother. If ever we get on board again, my vote shall be for calling of him to account for these pranks. Why should we be such fools to be ambitious of satisfying another's ambition?

CULVERIN. Let us mutiny. I love mutiny as well as my wife.

FIRST PYRATE. Let us mutiny.

SECOND PYRATE. Ay, let us mutiny.

HACKER. Our Captain takes too much upon him. I am for no engrosser* of power. By our articles he hath no command but in a fight or in a storm. Look'ee, brothers, I am for mutiny as much as any of you, when occasion offers.

CULVERIN. Right, brother, all in good season. The pass to our ships is cut off by the troops of the Plantation. We must fight the *Indians* first, and we have a mutiny good afterwards.*

HACKER. Is *Morano* still with his doxy?

CULVERIN. He's yonder on the right, putting his troops in order for the onset.

HACKER. I wish this fight of ours were well over. For, to be sure, let soldiers say what they will, they feel more pleasure after a battle than in it.

CULVERIN. Does not the drum-head here, quarter-master, tempt you to fling a merry main or two?*

[*Takes dice out of his pocket.*

HACKER. If I lose my money, I shall reimburse myself from the *Indians*. I have set.

CULVERIN. Have at you. A nick.

[*Flings.*

HACKER. Throw the dice fairly out. Are you at me again!

CULVERIN. I'm at it. Seven or eleven. [*Flings*] Eleven.

HACKER. Furies! A manifest cog! I won't be bubbled, Sir. This would not pass upon a drunken country gentleman. Death, Sir, I won't be cheated.

CULVERIN. The money is mine. D'you take me for a sharper, Sir?

HACKER. Yes, Sir.

CULVERIN. I'll have satisfaction.

HACKER. With all my heart.

[*Fighting.*

SCENE VI

HACKER, CULVERIN, PYRATES, MORANO, VANDERBLUFF, &c.

MORANO. For shame, gentlemen! [*Parting them*] Is this a time for private quarrel? What do I see! Dice upon the drum-head! If you have not left off those cowardly tools, you are unworthy your profession. The articles you have sworn to, prohibit gaming for money. Friendship and society cannot subsist where it is practis'd. As this is the day of battle, I remit your penalties. But let me hear no more of it.

CULVERIN. To be call'd sharper, captain! is a reproach that no man of honour can put up.

HACKER. But to be one, is what no man of honour can practice.

MORANO. If you will not obey orders, quarter-master, this pistol shall put an end to the dispute. [*Claps it to his head*] The common cause now requires your agreement. If gaming is so rife, I don't wonder that treachery still subsists among you.

HACKER. Who is treacherous?

MORANO. *Capstern* and *Laguerre* have let the prince and the stripling you took prisoner escape, and are gone off with them to the *Indians*. Upon your duty, gentlemen, this day depends our all.

CULVERIN. Rather than have ill blood among us, I return the money. I value your friendship more. Let all animosities be forgot.

MORANO. We should be *Indians* among ourselves, and shew our breeding and parts* to every body else. If we cannot be true to one another, and false to all the world beside, there is an end of every great enterprize.

HACKER. We have nothing to trust to but death or victory.

MORANO. Then hey for victory and plunder, my lads!

AIR 52. To you fair ladies.

	By bolder steps we win the race.
FIRST PYRATE.	*Let's haste where danger calls.*
MORANO.	*Unless ambition mend its pace,**
	It totters, nods and falls.
FIRST PYRATE.	*We must advance or be undone.*
MORANO.	*Think thus, and then the battle's won.*
CHORUS.	*With a fa la la,* &c.

MORANO. You see your booty, your plunder, gentlemen. The *Indians* are just upon us. The great must venture death some way or other, and the less ceremony about it, in my opinion, the better. But why talk I of death! Those only talk of it, who fear it. Let us all live, and enjoy our conquests. Sound the charge.

AIR 53. Prince Eugene's march.

> *When the tyger roams*
> *And the timorous flock is in his view,*
> *Fury foams,*
> *He thirsts for the blood of the crew.*
> *His greedy eyes he throws,*
> *Thirst with their number grows,*

> On he pours, with a wide waste pursuing,*
>> Spreading the plain with a general ruin,
>> Thus let us charge, and our foes o'erturn:

VANDERBLUFF. *Let us on one and all!*

FIRST PYRATE. *How they fly, how they fall!*

MORANO. *For the war, for the prize I burn.*

VANDERBLUFF. Were they dragons, my lads, as they sit brooding upon treasure, we would fright them from their nests.

MORANO. But see, the enemy are advancing to close engagement. Before the onset, we'll demand a parley,* and if we can, obtain honourable terms—We are overpower'd by numbers, and our retreat is cut off.

SCENE VII

Enter POHETOHEE, CAWWAWKEE, POLLY, *&c.* with the Indian *Army drawn up against the Pyrates.*

POHETOHEE. Our hearts are all ready. The enemy halts. Let the trumpets give the signal.

AIR 54. The marlborough.

CAWWAWKEE. *We the sword of justice drawing,*
>> *Terror cast in guilty eyes;*
>> *In its beam false courage dies;*
>> *'Tis like lightning keen and awing.*
>>> *Charge the foe,*
>>> *Lay them low,*
>> *On then and strike the blow.*
>> *Hark, victory calls us. See, guilt is dismay'd:*
>> *The villain is of his own conscience afraid.*
>> *In your hands are your lives and your liberties held,*
>> *The courage of virtue was never repell'd.*

PYRATE. Our chief demands a parley.

POHETOHEE. Let him advance.

> *Art thou,* Morano, *that fell man of prey?*
> *That foe to justice?*

MORANO.   *Tremble and obey.*
> *Art thou great* Pohetohee *styl'd?*

POHETOHEE.   *the same.*
> *I dare avow my actions and my name.*

MORANO. Thou know'st then, king, thy son there was my prisoner. Pay us the ransom we demand, allow us safe passage to our ships, and we will give you your lives and liberties.

POHETOHEE. Shall robbers and plunderers prescribe rules to right and equity? Insolent madman! Composition* with knaves is base and ignominious. Tremble at the sword of justice, rapacious brute.

AIR 55. Les rats.

MORANO.   *Know then, war's my pleasure.*
> *Am I thus controll'd?**
> *Both thy heart and treasure*
> *I'll at once unfold.**
> *You, like a miser, scraping, hiding,*
> *Rob all the world; you're but mines of gold.*
> *Rage my breast alarms:*
> *War is by kings held right-deciding;*
> *Then to arms, to arms;*
> *With this sword I'll force your hold.*

By thy obstinacy, king, thou hast provok'd thy fate; and so expect me.

POHETOHEE. Rapacious fool; by thy avarice thou shalt perish.

MORANO. Fall on.

POHETOHEE. For your lives and liberties.

[Fight, PYRATES beat off.

SCENE VIII

DUCAT.

A slight wound now would have been a good certificate; but who dares contradict a soldier? 'Tis your common soldiers who must content themselves with mere fighting; but 'tis we officers that run away with the most fame as well as pay. Of all fools, the fool-hardy are the greatest, for they are not even to be trusted with themselves. Why should we provoke men to turn again upon us, after they are run away? For my own part, I think it wiser to talk of fighting, than only to be talk'd of. The fame of a talking hero will satisfy me; the sound of whose valour amazes and astonishes all peaceable men, women, and children. Sure a man may be allow'd a little lying in his own praise, when there's so much going about to his discredit. Since every other body gives a man less praise than he deserves, a man, in justice to himself, ought to make up deficiencies. Without this privilege, we should have fewer good characters in the world than we have.

AIR 56. Mad Robin.

How faultless does the nymph appear,
When her own hand the picture draws!
But all others only smear
Her wrinckles, cracks and flaws.
Self-flattery is our claim and right,
Let men say what they will;
Sure we may set our good in sight,
When neighbours set our ill.

So, for my own part, I'll no more trust my reputation in my neighbours hands than my money. But will turn them both myself to the best advantage.

SCENE IX

POHETOHEE, CAWWAWKEE, DUCAT, INDIANS.

POHETOHEE. Had *Morano* been taken or slain, our victory had been compleat.

DUCAT. A hare may escape from a mastiff. I could not be a grey-hound too.

POHETOHEE. How have you dispos'd of the prisoners?

CAWWAWKEE. They are all under safe guard, till the king's justice, by their exemplary punishment, deters others from the like barbarities.

POHETOHEE. But all our troops are not as yet return'd from the pursuit: I am too for speedy justice, for in that there is a sort of clemency. Besides, I would not have my private thoughts worried by mercy to pardon such wretches. I cannot be answerable for the frailties of my nature.

CAWWAWKEE. The youth who rescu'd me from these cruel men is missing; and amidst all our successes I cannot feel happiness. I fear he is among the slain. My gratitude interested itself so warmly in his safety that you must pardon my concern. What hath victory done for me? I have lost a friend.

AIR 57. Thro' the wood laddy.

> *As sits the sad turtle alone on the spray;**
>   *His heart sorely beating,*
>   *Sad murmur repeating,*
> *Indulging his grief for his consort astray;*
>   *For force or death only could keep her away.*
> *Now he thinks of the fowler,* and every snare;*
>   *If guns have not slain her,*
>   *The net must detain her,*
> *Thus he'll rise in my thoughts, every hour with a tear,*
> *If safe from the battle he do not appear.*

POHETOHEE. Dead or alive, bring me intelligence of him; for I share in my son's affliction.

[Exit INDIAN.

DUCAT. I had better too be upon the spot, or my men may embezzle some plunder which by right should be mine.

[Exit.

[Enter INDIAN.

INDIAN. The youth, Sir, with a party is just return'd from the pursuit. He's here to attend your majesty's commands.

SCENE X

POHETOHEE, CAWWAWKEE, POLLY, INDIANS.

CAWWAWKEE. Pardon, Sir, the warmth of my friendship, if I fly to meet him, and for a moment intercept his duty.

[*Embracing.*

AIR 58. Clasp'd in my dear Melinda's arms.

POLLY.	*Victory is ours.*
CAWWAWKEE.	*My fond heart is at rest.*
POLLY.	*Friendship thus receives its guest.*
CAWWAWKEE.	*O what transport fills my breast!*
POLLY.	*Conquest is compleat,*
CAWWAWKEE.	*Now the triumph's great.*
POLLY.	*In your life is a nation blest.*
CAWWAWKEE.	*In your life I'm of all possess'd.*

POHETOHEE. The obligations my son hath receiv'd from you, makes me take a part in his friendship. In your safety victory has been doubly kind to me. If *Morano* hath escap'd, justice only reserves him to be punish'd by another hand.

POLLY. In the rout, Sir, I overtook him, flying with all the cowardice of guilt upon him. Thousands have false courage enough to be vicious; true fortitude is founded upon honour and virtue; that only can abide all tests. I made him my prisoner, and left him without under strict guard, till I receiv'd your majesty's commands for his disposal.

POHETOHEE. Sure this youth was sent me as a guardian. Let your prisoner be brought before us.

SCENE XI

POHETOHEE, CAWWAWKEE, POLLY, MORANO *guarded.*

MORANO. Here's a young treacherous dog now, who hangs the husband to come at the wife. There are wives in the world, who would have undertaken that affair to have come at him. Your son's liberty, to be sure, you think better worth than mine; so that I allow you a good bargain if I take my own for his ransom, without a gratuity. You know, king, he is my debtor.

POHETOHEE. He hath the obligations to thee of a sheep who hath escap'd out of the jaws of the wolf, beast of prey!

MORANO. Your great men will never own their debts, that's certain.

POHETOHEE. Trifle not with justice, impious man. Your barbarities, your rapin, your murthers are now at an end.

MORANO. Ambition must take its chance. If I die, I die in my vocation.

AIR 59. Parson upon Dorothy.

The soldiers, who by trade must dare
The deadly cannon's sounds;
You may be sure, betimes* prepare
For fatal blood and wounds.
The men, who with adventrous dance,
Bound from the cord on high,*
Must own they have the frequent chance
By broken bones to die.
Since rarely then
Ambitious men
Like others lose their breath;
Like these, I hope,
They know a rope
Is but their natural death.

We must all take the common lot of our professions.

POHETOHEE. Would your *European* laws have suffer'd crimes like these to have gone unpunish'd!

MORANO. Were all I am worth safely landed, I have wherewithal to make almost any crime sit easy upon me.

POHETOHEE. Have ye notions of property?

MORANO. Of my own.

POHETOHEE. Would not your honest industry have been sufficient to have supported you?

MORANO. Honest industry! I have heard talk of it indeed among the common people, but all great genius's are above it.

POHETOHEE. Have you no respect for virtue?

MORANO. As a good phrase, Sir. But the practicers of it are so insignificant and poor, that they are seldom found in the best company.

POHETOHEE. Is not wisdom esteem'd among you?

MORANO. Yes, Sir: But only as a step to riches and power; a step that raises ourselves, and trips up our neighbours.

POHETOHEE. Honour, and honesty, are not those distinguish'd?

MORANO. As incapacities and follies. How ignorant are these *Indians*! But indeed I think honour is of some use; it serves to swear upon.

POHETOHEE. Have you no consciousness?* Have you no shame?

MORANO. Of being poor.

POHETOHEE. How can society subsist with avarice! Ye are but the forms of men. Beasts would thrust you out of their herd upon that account, and man should cast you out for your brutal dispositions.

MORANO. *Alexander* the great was more successful. That's all.

AIR 60. The collier has a daughter.

When right or wrong's decided
In war or civil causes,
We by success are guided
To blame or give applauses.

Thus men exalt ambition,
In power by all commended,
But when it falls from high condition,
Tyburn *is well attended.*

POHETOHEE. Let justice then take her course, I shall not interfere with her decrees. Mercy too obliges me to protect my country from such violences. Immediate death shall put a stop to your further mischiefs.

MORANO. This sentence indeed is hard. Without the common forms of trial! Not so much as the counsel of a newgate attorney!* Not to be able to lay out my money in partiality and evidence! Not a friend perjur'd for me! This is hard, very hard.

POHETOHEE. Let the sentence be put in execution. Lead him to death. Let his accomplices be witnesses of it, and afterwards let them be securely guarded till farther orders.

AIR 61. Mad Moll.

MORANO.   *All crimes are judg'd like fornication;*
                   While rich we are honest no doubt.
               Fine ladies can keep reputation,
                   Poor lasses alone are found out.
               If justice had piercing eyes,
               Like ourselves to look within,
               She'd find power and wealth a disguise
               That shelter the worst of our kin.

[*Exit guarded.*

SCENE XII

POHETOHEE, CAWWAWKEE, POLLY.

POHETOHEE. How shall I return the obligations I owe you? Every thing in my power you may command. In making a request, you confer on me another benefit. For gratitude is oblig'd by occasions of making a return: And every occasion must be agreeable, for a grateful mind hath more pleasure in paying than receiving.

CAWWAWKEE. My friendship too is impatient to give you proofs of it. How happy would you make me in allowing me to discharge that duty!

AIR 62. Prince George.

	All friendship is a mutual debt,
POLLY.	*The contract's inclination:*
CAWWAWKEE.	*We never can that bond forget*
	Of sweet retaliation.
POLLY.	*All day, and every day the same*
	We are paying and still owing;
CAWWAWKEE.	*By turns we grant by turns we claim*
	The pleasure of bestowing.
BOTH.	*By turns we grant, &c.*

POLLY. The pleasure of having serv'd an honourable man is a sufficient return. My misfortunes, I fear, are beyond relief.

CAWWAWKEE. That sigh makes me suffer. If you have a want let me know it.

POHETOHEE. If it is in a king's power, my power will make me happy.

CAWWAWKEE. If you believe me a friend, you are unjust in concealing your distresses from me. You deny me the privilege of friendship; for I have a right to share them, or redress them.

POHETOHEE. Can my treasures make you happy?

POLLY. Those who have them not think they can; those who have them know they cannot.

POHETOHEE. How unlike his countrymen!

CAWWAWKEE. While you conceal one want from me, I feel every want for you. Such obstinacy to a friend is barbarity.

POLLY. Let not my reflection interrupt the joys of your triumph. Could I have commanded my thoughts, I would have reserv'd them for solitude.

CAWWAWKEE. Those sighs and that reservedness are symptoms of a heart in love. A pain that I am yet a stranger to.

POLLY. Then you have never been compleatly wretched.

AIR 63. Blithe Jockey young and gay.

Can words the pain express
Which absent lovers know?
He only mine can guess
Whose heart hath felt the woe.
'Tis doubt, suspicion, fear,
Seldom hope, oft' despair;
'Tis jealousy, 'tis rage, in brief
'Tis every pang and grief.

CAWWAWKEE. But does not love often deny itself aid and comfort, by being too obstinately secret?

POLLY. One cannot be too open to generosity; that is a sun, of universal benignity. In concealing ourselves from it we but deny ourselves the blessings of its influence.

AIR 64. In the fields in frost and snow.

The modest lilly, like the maid,
Its pure bloom defending,
Is of noxious dews afraid,
Soon as even's descending.
Clos'd all night,
Free from blight,
It preserves the native white
But at morn unfolds its leaves,
And the vital sun receives.

Yet why should I trouble your majesty with the misfortunes of so inconsiderable a wretch as I am?

POHETOHEE. A king's beneficence should be like the sun. The most humble weed should feel its influence as well as the most gaudy flower. But I have the nearest concern in any thing that touches you.

POLLY. You see then at your feet the most unhappy of women.

[*Kneels, he raises her.*

CAWWAWKEE. A woman! Oh my heart!

POHETOHEE. A woman!

POLLY. Yes, Sir, the most wretched of her sex. In love! married! abandon'd, and in despair!

POHETOHEE. What brought you into these countries?

POLLY. To find my husband. Why had not the love of virtue directed my heart? But, alas, 'tis outward appearance alone that generally engages a woman's affections! And my heart is in the possession of the most profligate of mankind.

POHETOHEE. Why this disguise?

POLLY. To protect me from the violences and insults to which my sex might have expos'd me.

CAWWAWKEE [*aside*]. Had she not been married, I might have been happy.

POLLY. He ran into the madness of every vice. I detest his principles, tho' I am fond of his person to distraction. Could your commands for search and enquiry restore him to me, you reward me at once with all my wishes. For sure my love still might reclaim him.

CAWWAWKEE. Had you conceal'd your sex, I had been happy in your friendship; but now, how uneasy, how restless is my heart!

AIR 65. Whilst I gaze on Chloe.

Whilst I gaze in fond desiring,
Every former thought is lost.
Sighing, wishing and admiring,
How my troubled soul is tost!
Hot and cold my blood is flowing,
How it thrills in every vein!
Liberty and life are going,
Hope can ne'er relieve my pain.

[*Enter* INDIAN.

INDIAN. The rest of the troops, Sir, are return'd from the pursuit with more prisoners. They attend your majesty's commands.

POHETOHEE. Let them be brought before us.

[*Exit* INDIAN.

[*To* POLLY] Give not yourself up to despair; for every thing in my
power you may command.

CAWWAWKEE. And every thing in mine. But, alas, I have none; for
I am not in my own!

SCENE XIII

POHETOHEE, CAWWAWKEE, POLLY, DUCAT,
JENNY *guarded*, &c.

JENNY. Spare my husband, *Morano* is my husband.

POHETOHEE. Then I have reliev'd you from the society of a monster.

JENNY. Alas, Sir, there are many husbands who are furious mon-
sters to the rest of mankind, that are the tamest creatures alive to
their wives. I can be answerable for his duty and submission to
your majesty, for I know I have so much power over him, that I can
even make him good.

POHETOHEE. Why then had you not made him so before?

JENNY. I was, indeed, like other wives, too indulgent to him, and as
it was agreeable to my own humour, I was loth to baulk his ambition. I must, indeed, own too that I had the frailty of pride. But
where is the woman who hath not an inclination to be as great and
rich as she can be?

POHETOHEE. With how much ease and unconcern these *Europeans*
talk of vices, as if they were necessary qualifications.

AIR 66. The Jamaica.

JENNY.
> *The sex, we find,*
> *Like men inclin'd*
> *To guard against reproaches;*
> *And none neglect*
> *To pay respect*
> *To rogues who keep their coaches.*

Indeed, Sir, I had determin'd to be honest myself, and to have
made him so too, as soon as I had put myself upon a reasonable

foot in the world; and that is more self-denial than is commonly practis'd.

POHETOHEE. Woman, your profligate sentiments offend me; and you deserve to be cut off from society, with your husband. Mercy would be scarce excusable in pardoning you. Have done then. *Morano* is now under the stroke of justice.

JENNY. Let me implore your majesty to respite his sentence. Send me back again with him into slavery, from whence we escap'd. Give us an occasion of being honest, for we owe our lives and liberties to another.

DUCAT. Yes, Sir, I find some of my run-away slaves among the crew; and I hope my services at least will allow me to claim my own again.

JENNY. *Morano*, Sir, I must confess hath been a free liver, and a man of so many gallantries, that no woman could escape him. If *Macheath*'s misfortunes were known, the whole sex would be in tears.

POLLY. *Macheath*!

JENNY. He is no black, Sir, but under that disguise, for my sake, skreen'd himself from the claims and importunities of other women. May love intercede for him?

POLLY. *Macheath*! Is it possible? Spare him, save him, I ask no other reward.

POHETOHEE. Haste, let the sentence be suspended.

[*Exit* INDIAN.

POLLY. Fly; a moment may make me miserable. Why could not I know him? All his distresses brought upon him by my hand! Cruel love, how could'st thou blind me so?

AIR 67. Tweed Side.

The stag, when chas'd all the long day
*O'er the lawn, thro' the forest and brake;**
Now panting for breath and at bay,
Now stemming the river or lake;*

When the treacherous scent is all cold,
And at eve he returns to his hind,
Can her joy, can her pleasure be told?
Such joy and such pleasure I find.

But, alas, now again reflection turns fear upon my heart. His pardon may come too late, and I may never see him more.

POHETOIIEE. Take hence that profligate woman. Let her be kept under strict guard till my commands.

JENNY. Slavery, Sir, slavery is all I ask. Whatever becomes of him, spare my life; spare an unfortunate woman. What can be the meaning of this sudden turn! Consider, Sir, if a husband be never so bad, a wife is bound to duty.

POHETOHEE. Take her hence, I say; let my orders be obey'd.

[*Exit* JENNY *guarded.*

SCENE XIV

POHETOHEE, CAWWAWKEE, POLLY, DUCAT, &c.

POLLY. What, no news yet? Not yet return'd!

CAWWAWKEE. If justice hath overtaken him, he was unworthy of you.

POLLY. Not yet! Oh how I fear.

AIR 68. One Evening as I lay.

My Heart forebodes he's dead,
That thought how can I bear?
He's gone, for ever fled,
My soul is all despair!
I see him pale and cold,
The noose hath stop'd his breath,
Just as my dream foretold,
Oh had that sleep been death!

SCENE XV

POHETOHEE, CAWWAWKEE, POLLY, DUCAT, INDIANS.

[*Enter* INDIANS.

POLLY. He's dead, he's dead! Their looks confess it. Your tongues have no need to give it utterance to confirm my misfortunes! I know, I see, I feel it! Support me! O *Macheath*!

DUCAT. Mercy upon me! Now I look upon her nearer, bless me, it must be *Polly*. This woman, Sir, is my slave, and I claim her as my own. I hope, if your majesty thinks of keeping her, you will reimburse me, and not let me be a loser. She was an honest girl to be sure, and had too much virtue to thrive, for, to my knowledge, money could not tempt her.

POHETOHEE. And if she is virtuous, *European*, dost thou think I'll act the infamous part of a ruffian, and force her? 'Tis my duty as a king to cherish and protect virtue.

CAWWAWKEE. Justice hath reliev'd you from the society of a wicked man. If an honest heart can recompense your loss, you would make me happy in accepting mine. I hope my father will consent to my happiness.

POHETOHEE. Since your love of her is founded upon the love of virtue and gratitude, I leave you to your own disposal.

CAWWAWKEE. What, no reply?

POLLY. Abandon me to my sorrows. For in indulging them is my only relief.

POHETOHEE. Let the chiefs have immediate execution. For the rest, let 'em be restor'd to their owners, and return to their slavery.

AIR 69. Buff-coat.

CAWWAWKEE.	*Why that languish!*
POLLY.	*Oh he's dead! O he's lost for ever!*
CAWWAWKEE.	*Cease your anguish, and forget your grief.*
POLLY.	*Ah, never!*
	What air, grace and stature!

CAWWAWKEE.	*How false in his nature!*
POLLY.	*To virtue my love might have won him.*
CAWWAWKEE.	*How base and deceiving!*
POLLY.	*But love is believing.*
CAWWAWKEE.	*Vice, at length, as 'tis meet,* hath undone him.*

By your consent you might at the same time give me happiness, and procure your own. My titles, my treasures, are all at your command.

AIR 70. An *Italian* Ballad.

POLLY.   *Frail is ambition, how weak the foundation!*
             Riches have wings as inconstant as wind;
             My heart is proof against either temptation,
             Virtue, without them, contentment can find.

I am charm'd, Prince, with your generosity and virtues. 'Tis only by the pursuit of those we secure real happiness. Those that know and feel virtue in themselves, must love it in others. Allow me to give a decent time to my sorrows. But my misfortunes at present interrupt the joys of victory.

CAWWAWKEE. Fair princess, for so I hope shortly to make you, permit me to attend you, either to divide your griefs, or, by conversation, to soften your sorrows.

POHETOHEE. 'Tis a pleasure to me by this alliance to recompense your merits.

[*Exeunt* CAWWAWKEE *and* POLLY.

Let the sports and dances then celebrate our victory.

[*Exit.*

DANCE

AIR 71. The temple.

FIRST INDIAN.   *Justice long forbearing,*
                    Power or riches never fearing,
                    Slow, yet persevering,
                    Hunts the villain's pace.
CHORUS.   Justice long, &c.

SECOND INDIAN.   *What tongues then defend him?*
                    Or what hand will succour lend him?
                    Even his friends attend him,
                    To foment the chace.*
CHORUS.   Justice long, *&c.*
THIRD INDIAN.   *Virtue, subduing,*
                           Humbles in ruin
                    All the proud wicked race.
                           Truth, never-failing,
                           Must be prevailing,
                    Falsehood shall find disgrace.
CHORUS.   Justice long forbearing, *&c.*

FINIS

APPENDIX

THE SOURCES OF GAY'S AIRS

All of the songs or airs in *The Beggar's Opera* and *Polly* adapt existing tunes, most of them from well-known broadside ballads or folk songs, but some from theatre songs or recent operas. In many cases, Gay alludes, often ironically, to the original words in his lyrics; I give examples of this in the notes below. Among the sources Gay probably drew on in selecting material to adapt were such collections of dance tunes and songs as John and Henry Playford's *The Dancing Master* (eighteen editions between 1651 and 1728), Thomas D'Urfey's *Wit and Mirth: Or Pills to Purge Melancholy* (six-volume final edition, 1719–20), and two collections of Scottish songs: Allan Ramsay's *The Tea-Table Miscellany* (1724; published without music), and William Thomson's *Orpheus Caledonius* (1725). Gay would also have made use of single-sheet songs, a common form of publication in the period.

The fullest discussion of Gay's use of his musical sources is found in Jeremy Barlow's edition of *The Music of John Gay's The Beggar's Opera*; further details on the tunes Gay may have taken from broadside ballad versions can be found in Claude Simpson's *The British Broadside Ballad and Its Music* (see details on both in the list below). William Eben Schultz and A. E. H. Swaen, in the early decades of the twentieth century, tracked down earlier versions of most of the songs Gay cites in the headings of his airs and along with Barlow and Simpson are my main sources on *The Beggar's Opera*. No one other than Swaen has looked into the originals of the songs in *Polly*, and these sources were more varied than those Gay had used in the earlier play, including more songs of Scottish, French, and Italian origin as well as more opera numbers and instrumental pieces, so I have had to range more widely to locate information on the songs Gay included in his second ballad opera.

In the following entries, I have summarized existing scholarship and where relevant emphasized thematic connections or contrasts between the original texts and Gay's rewritten versions. Each entry cites the sources I have drawn on and the page on which discussion of that particular song begins; sources are listed in order of relevance to what I have highlighted. For works cited more than once, I have used the following abbreviations:

Barlow *The Music of John Gay's The Beggar's Opera*, ed. Jeremy Barlow
(Oxford: Oxford University Press, 1990).

Dugaw   Dianne Dugaw, *'Deep Play': John Gay and the Invention of Modernity* (Newark: University of Delaware Press, 2001).

Fiske   Roger Fiske, *English Theatre Music in the Eighteenth Century* (London: Oxford University Press, 1973).

Grove   *Grove Music Online* (part of *Oxford Music Online*).

Pills   Thomas D'Urfey, *Wit and Mirth, or Pills to Purge Melancholy* (six-volume final edition, London: Jacob Tonson, 1719–20).

Schultz   William Eben Schultz, *Gay's Beggar's Opera: Its Content, History and Influence* (New Haven: Yale University Press, 1923).

Simpson   Claude M. Simpson, *The British Broadside Ballad and Its Music* (New Brunswick: Rutgers University Press, 1966).

Swaen   A. E. H. Swaen, 'The Airs and Tunes of John Gay's *Beggar's Opera*', *Anglia*, 43 (1919), 152–90; and 'The Airs and Tunes of John Gay's *Polly*', *Anglia* 60 (1936), 403–22.

Tea-Table   Allan Ramsay, *The Tea-Table Miscellany* (Edinburgh, 1724).

Westrup   J. A. Westrup, 'French Tunes in *The Beggar's Opera* and *Polly*', *The Musical Times* 69, no. 1022 (1 April 1928), 320–3.

THE BEGGAR'S OPERA

AIR 1. **An old Woman cloathed in Gray.** As with most of the headings Gay provides for each air, this is the first line of a song whose tune he borrowed for his own lyrics. The original song, a seventeenth-century ballad also known as 'Unconstant Roger', tells of the seduction of a 'charming and young' country girl by 'Roger's false flattering tongue'. It may thus allude to Macheath's seductions of Polly and Lucy, as well as suggesting parallels between sexual seduction and the professional deceptions that Peachum details. [Schultz 307; Simpson 405]

AIR 2. **The bonny gray-ey'd Morn.** The tune, credited to Jeremiah Clarke and dating from 1696, was originally used for 'A New Scotch Song', a seduction lyric probably composed for the theatre. Filch's lyrics reverse the sexual dynamics of the original, whose female singer says, of her lover Jockey, 'My yielding Heart at ev'ry word he said, | Did flutter up and down and strangly move'. [Swaen 155; Simpson 51]

AIR 3. **Cold and Raw.** A very popular tune, dating back to at least the earlier seventeenth century and originally used for a song in praise of strong drink titled 'Stingo, or the Oyle of Barley'. Thomas D'Urfey set it to new lyrics, beginning 'Cold and Raw the North did blow', in 1688: a wooing song to which Mrs Peachum's words give a macabre twist. [Swaen 155; Schultz 308; Simpson 687]

AIR 4. **Why is your faithful Slave disdain'd?** The tune has been attributed to the Italian opera composer Giovanni Bononcini (1670–1747), who lived in London in the 1720s. This may have been his setting of a song with the above title from 1688, whose male singer entreats his female listener to grant him possession 'of what I dare not name'—a euphemism for the woman's body which Mrs Peachum uses as a euphemism for 'harlot'. [Schultz 309; Barlow 110]

AIR 5. **Of all the simple Things we do.** The original words, probably written by D'Urfey for Thomas Doggett's 1696 comedy *The Country Wake*, were given the title 'The Mouse Trap' and offered a comically disenchanted view of marriage: 'We're just like a Mouse in a Trap, | Or Vermin caught in a Gin; | We Sweat and Fret, and try to Escape, | And Curse the sad Hour we came in'. The theme of female commodification, however, is Mrs Peachum's own. [Swaen 157; Barlow 110; Simpson 540]

AIR 6. **What shall I do to show how much I love her.** The tune, by Henry Purcell, was written for the opera *Dioclesian, or The Prophetess* (1690) adapted by Betterton and/or Dryden from Fletcher and Massinger's 1622 play *The Prophetess*. Polly's view of love is harsher than in the original, though Gay alludes to the earlier lyrics: 'In fair Aurelia's Arms, leave me expiring, | To be Imbalm'd with the sweets of her Breath; | To the last moment I'll still be desiring; | Never had Hero so glorious a Death'. In 1789, the musician Charles Burney wrote that it 'became the favourite tune in the *Beggar's Opera*'. [Swaen 158; Barlow 110; Simpson 754]

AIR 7. **Oh London is a fine Town.** The tune is known under many names and was used for many song texts from the early seventeenth century on. One of its popular early versions was 'Watten town's end' ('At every Door, there stands a Whore, at Watten Towns end'), whose words add an extra twist to Mrs Peachum's lyric. As 'Oh *London* is a fine Town', the ballad was a burlesque of the Lord Mayor's office, and so resonates with the sexual and political themes that run through *The Beggar's Opera*. [Swaen 159, Simpson 460]

AIR 8. **Grim King of the Ghosts.** The opening line of another popular and often-used tune, titled 'The Frantick [or 'Lunatick'] Lover'. It was most familiar as the melody of 'Collin's Complaint', a pastoral-themed lyric by Nicholas Rowe ('Despairing, beside a clear stream, | A Shepherd forsaken was laid'), but there were also many parodic and satirical versions. [Swaen 160; Simpson 280]

AIR 9. **O Jenny, O Jenny, where has thou been.** The first line of 'The Willoughby Whim', a bawdy dialogue between two sisters in which one confesses to 'playing the Wanton' ('For the Miller has taken his Toll of me'). D'Urfey's original words reinforce Gay's characterization of Polly not as virginal innocent but as a sexually desiring woman. [Schultz 312]

AIR 10. **Thomas, I cannot.** Also known as 'Thomas, you cannot', a bawdy story-song beginning 'Thomas: untied his points apace' (*points* meaning fastenings for clothes). The title comes from the refrain: 'But then shee Cryes "Thomas! You Cannott, you Cannott!!"'. As with many of the airs Gay adopts, the audience's knowledge of the original lyrics might have suggested a ribald second meaning to lines such as 'I, like a Ship in Storms, was tost'. [Barlow 110; Simpson 703]

AIR 11. **A Soldier and a Sailor.** The tune was written by John Eccles for Congreve's song of this title in Act III of his comedy *Love for Love* (1695). Congreve's lyric involves a contest among a soldier, a sailor, a tinker, and a tailor for the love of 'buxom Joan', who 'no more intended, | To lick her lips at men, sir, | And gnaw the sheets in vain, sir, | And lie o'nights alone'. [Swaen 161; Simpson 670]

AIR 12. **Now ponder well, ye Parents dear.** The opening line of 'The Children in the Wood', a sixteenth-century ballad telling the story of two children abandoned by their wicked uncle to die in the forest. Addison wrote that this 'old ballad' was 'one of the Darling Songs of the Common People' (*Spectator* 85), and Polly's words convey a similar poignancy, undercut only slightly by the pun in her last two lines. [Schultz 314; Simpson 103]

AIR 13. **Le printemps rappelle aux armes.** Like Polly's song, the original is a female lover's lament for her departing male beloved: in the French text, a soldier recalled to military duty. The song first appeared in the French song collection *La Clef des chansonniers* (1717), and then (without music) in *Pills* (1719–20). Gay may have got the tune from the untitled version in *The Bird Fancyer's Delight*, a 1717 collection of tunes for flute meant to be taught to various kinds of songbirds—in this case to skylarks (11). [Schultz 314; Barlow 111]

AIR 14. **Pretty Parrot, say.** Also known as 'Pretty Poll' (*Polly* and *Poll* being common names for a parrot), the tune was written by John Freeman for a song translated from French. In the original English text, the 'pretty parrot' tells its master that while he was away, 'We are gay, | Night and Day, | Good Chear and Mirth Renewing; | Singing, Laughing all, Singing Laughing all, like pretty pretty Poll'. In the context of Macheath asking *his* Polly if she has been unfaithful to him, the audience's knowledge of the original lyrics might underline his worries about Polly's 'constant Heart' in his absence. [Schultz 314; Swaen 163; Simpson 579; Barlow 111]

AIR 15. **Pray, Fair One, be kind.** The tune, as 'Come Fair one be kind', was most likely written by Richard Leveridge for performance in George Farquhar's comedy *The Recruiting Officer* (1706). A rather bullying seduction song, it is changed in Macheath's version into something far more delicate and flattering, but still retains, perhaps, an undercurrent of manipulation. [Swaen 164; Barlow 111]

AIR 16. **Over the Hills and far away.** This phrase is the refrain both of Gay's duet and of the song it was taken from, 'Jockey's Lamentation'. In that song, possibly of Scottish origin (*Jockey* or *Jock* being a stock slang name for a Scotsman, often a yokel or a rascal), Jockey's beloved Jenny, 'Altho' she promis'd to be true, | She proven has, alake! unkind'—which may, as with 'Pretty Polly', suggest some uncertainty as to Polly's and Macheath's present and future fidelity. The music was also used for a number of political broadside ballads, including D'Urfey's 'The Hubble Bubbles', a satirical commentary on the financial speculations that led to the collapse of the South Sea Company (the so-called 'South Sea Bubble'), in which Gay lost a considerable sum of money himself. [Simpson 561; Swaen 164]

AIR 17. **Gin thou wert mine awn thing.** The oldest known version, from *c*.1700, is just titled 'A Scotch Song', and is a simple love lyric: 'Gin [if] thou wert my en'e Thing, | So Dearly I wou'd Love thee | I wou'd take thee in my Arms | I'd secure thee From all Harms'. Gay's lyric offers an equally heartfelt expression of love, but instead of taking her beloved into her arms, in order to save him Polly insists that Macheath 'fly hence, and let me leave thee'. [Schultz 316]

AIR 18. **O the Broom.** From at least the early seventeenth century there were many versions of this song: Robert Burton cites 'O the Broom, the bonny, bonny broom' as a familiar 'rustick' tune in his *Anatomy of Melancholy* (1621), and it may be much older. One of the best known versions, 'The Broom of Cowdenknows', has a Scottish setting and may be of Scottish origin; it was the basis of the Scottish poet Allan Ramsay's more sentimental adaptation of 1724. [Swaen 166; Schultz 317; Simpson 68; Barlow 111]

AIR 19. **Fill ev'ry Glass.** A drinking song translated from French ('Que chacun remplisse son verre') by D'Urfey around 1710. The original featured a toast to three generals, and so is suited to the equation of military valour and criminal enterprise that runs through this scene, although Gay here focuses on the association of wine with eros. [Schultz 318; Barlow 111]

AIR 20. **March in *Rinaldo*, with Drums and Trumpets.** The music is adapted from the march in Act III of Handel's 1711 opera *Rinaldo*—his first for the English stage—produced (possibly with Gay's assistance) by Gay's boyhood friend Aaron Hill. Gay's mock-heroic lyrics play off the grandeur of the music, which, however, had already been turned into a drinking song ('Let the waiter bring clean glasses') before Gay incorporated it in *The Beggar's Opera*.

AIR 21. **Would you have a young Virgin.** Also known under the title 'Poor Robin's Maggot' (*maggot* being a common term for a dance tune in the period, from a word meaning whim or quirk), the original song was written for D'Urfey's 1709 comedy *The Modern Prophets* and is a blunt guide to seduction: 'Would you have a young Virgin of fifteen years, | You must tickle her fancy, with sweets and dear's, | Ever toying, and playing, and sweetly, sweetly, | Sing a love sonnet, and charm her Ears'. Gay retains some of the original phrases, but not the rather coarse ending to the first verse: 'teize her, and please her, | And touch but her smicket, and all's your own'— a *smicket* being a woman's shift or undergarment. [Schultz 319; Swaen 169]

AIR 22. **Cotillon.** The *cotillon* or *cotillion* was a French dance introduced to England in the 1720s. The name may come from a song, to the tune Gay uses, from Alain-René Le Sage's play *Télémaque* (1715): 'Ma commère quand je danse, | Mon cotillon va-t-il bien' (My gossip [old friend] when I dance, do my petticoats look well?)—the words suggesting a saucier sort of dance than a formal round. [Barlow 112]

AIR 23. **All in a misty Morning.** The tune for this ballad, also known as 'The Wiltshire Wedding', derives from an older ballad, 'The Friar and the Nun'. The 'how do you do' refrain, which Gay takes from 'The Wiltshire Wedding', has, in both songs, a bawdy implied meaning. [Simpson 238; Swaen 169; Schultz 320]

AIR 24. **When once I lay with another Man's Wife.** This is from the refrain of a song titled 'The Benefit of Marriage', set to an older tune, 'The King's Delight', popular in the Restoration period (1660–88). Audiences familiar with Gay's source could have registered one of the play's recurrent motifs, the equation of sexual with professional and political forms of cheating. [Simpson 414; Barlow 112]

AIR 25. **When first I laid Siege to my Chloris.** The first line of a song by Sir Charles Sedley, from his 1687 comedy *Bellamira*, which equates a man's seduction of a woman with laying siege to a fortified town ('Cannon Oaths I brought down, | To batter the Town, | And boom'd her with amorous Stories'). Here, the seduced women have become vengeful 'Furies'. [Schultz 320; Simpson 11]

AIR 26. **Courtiers, Courtiers think it no harm.** The opening line of a song titled (fittingly for Gay) 'The Beggar's Delight', which may have been written in the 1680s for performances of Richard Brome's older comedy *The Jovial Crew*. In that song, rich and poor are equals in love: 'For the Beggar he loves his Lass as dear, | As he that hath thousands, thousands, thousands, | He that has thousand Pounds a Year'. Macheath's cynically misogynist lyrics present a reversal of the sentiment of his own Air 21. [Schultz 321; Simpson 137]

AIR 27. **A lovely Lass to a Friar came.** The opening line to a song called 'The Fair Penitent', included in Ramsay's *Tea-Table Miscellany*. It tells of a 'fallen' lass's confession to a friar, who pardons her on condition she repeat her sin with him. Gay transforms the last lines of the first stanza—'I've done, Sir, what I dare not name, | With a Lad, who loves me dearly' (72)—to words that express the full force of Lucy's ire. [Schultz 321, Simpson 474]

AIR 28. **'Twas when the Sea was roaring.** The song Gay appropriates here is his own, from his 1715 'Tragi-Comi-Pastoral Farce' *The What D'Ye Call It*; the music was attributed in 1729 to Handel. In the earlier play it is a woman's lament for her beloved at sea; it is changed here to a song of hate. [Schultz 321; Simpson 719]

AIR 29. **The Sun had loos'd his weary Teams.** The first line of a song of 1685 by D'Urfey, 'The Winchester Christening', itself an adaptation of an older ballad, 'The Hemp-Dresser, or The London Gentlewoman'. [Simpson 302; Schultz 322]

AIR 30. **How happy are we.** A song in praise of mindlessness—'How happy are we, | Who from thinking are free'—from Thomas Baker's comedy *The Fine Lady's Airs* (1708), with music by John Barrett. Both the original and Gay's reworking are concerned with reputation: but whereas Baker's singer celebrates the freedom to 'Love where we like best, | Not by dull reputation Confin'd', Gay's courtiers are so anxious about their reputations that they imagine every general 'censure' is aimed at them. [Barlow 112, Schultz 322]

AIR 31. **Of a noble Race was Shenkin.** The original was written by D'Urfey for his play *The Richmond Heiress* (1693) to a tune of unknown origin. It was meant to be accompanied by a 'Welch Harp', and the lyrics have a Welsh (or faux-Welsh) flavour. As the subject is a noble man brought down by love, it could be seen as suited to Macheath's position at this point in the play. [Simpson 541; Schultz 323]

AIR 32. Gay cites no original for this air, which is similar but not identical to 'Walsingham', a popular sixteenth-century ballad best known today in settings for lute (by John Dowland) and keyboard (by John Bull and William Byrd). The tune used here has also been associated with Ophelia's song 'How should I your true love know' in *Hamlet*, although it is not known whether that was true in Gay's time. [Simpson 741, Barlow 113]

AIR 33. **London Ladies.** Another song by D'Urfey, titled 'Advice to the Ladies' (first published 1687). The tune was used for some thirty ballads over the following few years, and appeared in at least seven ballad operas. Gay adapts the original's 'advice' structure: while D'Urfey's song gives advice to the ladies of London on how to choose suitable husbands, Gay's offers advice on how to use 'perquisites' or bribes for political or sexual favours. [Simpson 421; Schultz 324]

AIR 34. **All in the Downs.** Opening phrase of 'Sweet William's Farewell to Black-ey'd Susan' by Gay himself (from *Poems on Several Occasions*, 1720). One of Gay's most popular songs, it was set to music by several composers, including Pietro Sandoni, whose version was used here. A delicately sentimental ballad of two lovers' parting; the same sentiments are carried over into Polly's version. [Barlow 113]

AIR 35. **Have you heard of a frolicksome Ditty.** As 'Give ear to my Frolicsome Ditty', this is the opening line of 'The Jolly Gentleman's Frolick', a broadside ballad from the 1680s. There is no connection between Gay's text and the original, but he plays with the tension between the 'frolicsome' tune and Macheath's exasperated state of mind. [Barlow 113; Simpson 596]

AIR 36. **Irish Trot.** The Irish trot was a lively dance akin to the jig; in fact Gay's tune is that of a ballad titled 'The Irish Jig or, The Night Ramble', beginning 'One night in my ramble', from *c.*1710. The fourth stanza gives the flavour of the song as a whole: 'Then nothing but dancing our fancy could please, | We lay on the grass and danced at our ease, | I down'd with my breeches and off with my wig, | And we fell a-dancing the Irish jigg'. The song celebrates the kind of male sexual freedom Macheath also embodies—at the end, the male singer leaves his partner to deal with her pregnancy on her own—but Lucy and Polly, in Gay's duet, refuse to let Macheath off the hook. [Lucy Skeaping, ed., *Broadside Ballads* (London: Faber Music, 2005), 72; Barlow 113]

AIR 37. As with Air 32, Gay cites no source for this tune, but Barlow has identified it as the tune for 'Charming Billy' (also known as 'Constant Billy') from *c.*1725. In that song, which begins 'When the hills and lofty mountains . . .', 'fair Flora' laments her lover's absence, crying, 'Billy, constant Billy, | Must we never meet again?'; but by the end of the song she is reassured that her 'charming Billy' will soon return to her. Polly also calls Macheath her 'constant man' in her version of the song, but this echo of the original ironically underlines Macheath's inconstancy. [Barlow 113; Schultz 325]

AIR 38. **Good-morrow, Gossip Joan.** The first line to a song of the same title from *c*.1705. Gay transforms a chat between two neighbours (the song was also known as 'The Woman's Complaint to her Neighbour') into a duel between rival singers—hence the melismas (single syllables sung to many notes) on 'dirt' and 'name'. [Schultz 326; Barlow 113]

AIR 39. **Irish Howl.** Composed by George Vanbrughe *c*.1710, the melody was originally used to set a lyric about a woman abandoned by her lover: 'Remember Damon you did tell, | In Chastity you lov'd me well, | But now alass I am undone, | And here am left to make my Moan'—a lyric at odds with Polly's perhaps naïve affirmation of 'Sacred Love'. [Barlow 113; Schultz 326]

AIR 40. **The Lass of Patie's Mill.** A love song written by Ramsay to a tune first recorded in the seventeenth century. In the *Tea-Table Miscellany*, it opens, 'The Lass of *Peatie's* Mill, | So bonny, blyth and gay, | In Spite of all my Skill, | Hath stole my Heart away' (75). Lucy's lyric changes the sex of the beloved and echoes the sentiments of loss and apprehension at Macheath's parting that Polly expressed at the close of Act I. [Barlow 113; Schultz 327]

AIR 41. **If Love's a sweet Passion.** A song from Henry Purcell's 1692 opera-masque *The Fairy Queen* (based on Shakespeare's *A Midsummer Night's Dream*), with words attributed to either Thomas Betterton or Elkanah Settle. The tune was used for dozens of broadside ballads. Gay's lyric emphasizes the links between sex and commerce, but Lucy's last couplet is in keeping with this from the original: 'Yet so pleasing the Pain is, so soft is the Dart, | That at once it both wounds me and tickles my Heart'. [Schultz 327; Barlow 113; Simpson 359]

AIR 42. **South-Sea Ballad.** Although there were several ballads with this title on the 'bursting' of the South Sea Bubble in 1720, none has been located with this tune. The same tune appears in the last edition of *The Dancing Master*—a collection of dance tunes and instructions first published by John Playford in 1651, and updated by his son Henry, and later by John Young, from 1690 to 1728—with the title 'South Sea'; but given the timing, it is not clear this was Gay's source. [Barlow vii, 113; Schultz 328]

AIR 43. **Packington's Pound.** According to Claude Simpson, 'This is the most popular single tune associated with ballads before 1700', and it dates back to at least the mid-sixteenth century. If any particular song to this tune was Gay's source, it might have been a ballad by Ben Jonson from his 1614 comedy *Bartholomew Fair*, whose refrain links it to the criminal setting of *The Beggar's Opera*: 'Youth, youth, thou hadst better bin starv'd by thy Nurse, | Than live to be hanged for cutting a purse'. Gay had already used the tune, also known as 'Cutpurse', for his 1725 ballad about Jonathan Wild, 'Newgate's Garland'. [Simpson 564; Barlow 114]

AIR 44. **Lillibullero.** The title is taken from the original ballad's non-sense refrain: 'Lero, lero, lilli burlero | Lilli burlero, bullen a la'. Those nonsense words have been claimed to have been passwords used by some Irish Catholics during a 1641 massacre of Protestants; the ballad itself is overtly (if jovially) anti-Catholic and anti-Irish, and was taken up by those who opposed the Catholic Stuart monarch James II and supported the anti-Stuart Glorious Revolution of 1688. The tune has been ascribed to Henry Purcell, who published a setting for harpsichord in 1689; but Purcell was most likely arranging a tune already in circulation. Gay may have chosen it just because it was catchy and popular, but may also have had an ironic aim in setting a lyric critical of the 'Modes of the [Hanoverian] Court' to a tune so strongly associated with the Hanoverian cause. [Simpson 449; Barlow 114; Schultz 329]

AIR 45. **Down in the North Country.** First line of a ballad from *c*.1705, 'The Farmer's Daughter of Merry Wakefield'. Gay characteristically reverses the gender dynamics, so that in Lockit's song it is men who are seduced and entrapped by women, as opposed to the original ballad story. [Barlow 114; Schultz 330]

AIR 46. **A Shepherd kept Sheep.** First words of a song from *Pills* (from 1707) although Gay's tune is quite different. The original is an anti-courtship song: 'A Shepherd kept sheep on a hill so high, | And there came a pretty maid passing by, | Shepherd, quoth she, dost thou want e'er a wife, | No by my troth I'm not weary of my life'. Peachum and Lockit may join in on the 'fa, la, la' refrains. [Barlow 114; Schultz 330]

AIR 47. **One Evening, having lost my Way.** First line of a song attrib-uted to Matthew Birkhead (as is *Polly* Air 58) titled 'The Happy Clown', from *c*.1720. It was also known as 'Wallpoole; or the happy Clown', and as the tune is prominently featured in the overture that Pepusch adapted from some of the ballad tunes, it has been suggested that this was meant as a satirical allusion to Sir Robert Walpole. [Barlow 114; Schultz 330; Swaen 179]

AIR 48. **Now Roger, I'll tell thee, because thou'rt my Son.** No source for the words or tune has been located, although Jeremy Barlow suggests that the tune is related to a popular sixteenth-century Italian 'ground' (a musical form based on a repeating bass line), the *passamezzo antico*, as are several other airs in *The Beggar's Opera*. [Barlow 114]

AIR 49. **O Bessy Bell.** The tune comes from Ramsay's version ('Bessy Bell and Mary Gray') of an older ballad. In it, the singer is unable to choose which of the two women he loves better, anticipating Lucy's statement immediately after Gay's song, that 'Love is so very whimsical in both Sexes, that it is impossible to be lasting'. [*Tea-Table* 104; Schultz 331; Barlow 114]

AIR 50. **Would Fate to me Belinda give.** First line of a song (*c*.1705) with text by Mary Child, set to music by John Wilford. Gay changes the original's conventional love sentiments ('Nor with her cou'd I more require, | Nor a greater Bliss desire') into a wry commentary on male vanity. [Schultz 332; Barlow 114]

AIR 51. **Come, sweet Lass.** First line of a song originally titled 'An Excellent New Scotch Song, Cald, Jockey's Complaint for His beloved Moggy', written for performance in an unknown play in the 1690s. The tune was also known as 'Greenwich Park'. Gay retains the repeated opening line, which acquires a sinister inflection in Lucy's version. [Barlow 114; Schultz 332]

AIR 52. **The last time I went o'er the Moor.** A love song by Ramsay from the 1724 *Tea-Table Miscellany*, possibly set to an older ballad tune, which Gay transforms into a duet of rivalry. [Barlow 114; Schultz 332]

AIR 53. **Tom Tinker's my true Love.** A bawdy song first recorded in 1714: 'Tom Tinker's my true love, and I am his Dear, | And I will go with him his Budget to bear; | For of all the young Men he has the best luck, | All the Day he will Fuddle [drink], at night he will ———'. As the missing rhyme word suggests, the original was, in Swaen's words, 'excessively coarse'. [Swaen 182]

AIR 54. **I am a poor Shepherd undone.** First line of a song titled 'The Distress'd Shepherd', set to an older tune known as 'Hey ho my Honey' to which many different ballad texts were set in the period. Polly's sorrowful sentiments are not unlike those of the shepherd in the original, but along with Gay's characteristic gender reversal, the relocation from a pastoral landscape to a London courtroom radically transforms the song's effect, even though the last four lines are the same. [Simpson 116; Schultz 333; Swaen 182; Barlow 115]

AIR 55. **Ianthe the lovely.** Opening words of a song titled 'The Happy Pair' from 1705; words by John Glanville, music by John Barrett. The first stanza of the original concludes, 'But the longer they liv'd, | Still the fonder they grew'—a sentiment Lucy's harder-edged lyric still echoes. [Schultz 334; Simpson 357]

AIR 56. **A Cobler there was.** Opening words of a song titled 'The Cobler's End', first printed in 1729, and said to be set to music by Richard Leveridge, although versions of the tune date back to before 1700; it was most commonly known as 'Derry down' (from the words of the original refrain) and 'The Abbot of Canterbury'. This air was not included in the first four impressions of the play's first edition, but was added as an unnumbered air to the fifth; presumably it had been omitted by mistake, as it was retained in later editions. [Simpson 172; Barlow 115; Schultz 335]

AIR 57. **Bonny Dundee.** The full title tells the story: 'Bonny Dundee: or Jockey's Deliverance, being his Valiant Escape from Dundee and the Parson's Daughter, whom he had Mow'd'—*mow* being 'A Scotch word for the act of copulation' (Francis Grose, *Dictionary of the Vulgar Tongue*). The parallels to Macheath's efforts to escape the women he has 'married' are evident, but the context is much grimmer. The ballad was first printed *c*.1690; the earliest recorded version of the tune is from *The Dancing Master*, 1688. [Simpson 49; Barlow 115; Swaen 184]

AIR 58. **Happy Groves.** From a song titled 'The Pilgrim' with music by John Barrett, from John Vanbrugh's 1700 comedy *The Pilgrim*. The contrast between Macheath's words and the original song's 'Oh! Happy, happy Groves, | Witness of our tender loves' is clear; but by the end of the original's first stanza the singer is lamenting, 'But *Corinna* perjur'd proves, and forsakes the shady Groves', evoking a melancholy sense of abandonment similar to Macheath's. [Swaen 185; Barlow 115]

AIR 59. **Of all the Girls that are so smart.** Opening line of Henry Carey's 'Sally in our Alley' (*c*.1715), one of the most popular tunes of the period, often adapted and parodied: 'Of all the Girls that are so smart | There's none like pretty Sally, | She is the Darling of my Heart, | And she lives in our Alley'. Macheath's praise of wine parallels Carey's celebration of Sally, but the undercurrents of despair are far from the original's naïve simplicity. [Schultz 336; Barlow 115]

AIR 60. **Britons strike home.** The tune was written by Henry Purcell for a song in the tragedy *Bonduca* (1695; adapted by George Powell from an older play by Beaumont and Fletcher). The original is a call to arms: 'Britons strike Home, revenge, revenge your country's wrongs'. [Barlow 115; Schultz 336]

AIR 61. **Chevy Chase.** A ballad dating back to the mid-sixteenth century; the oldest surviving version is titled 'A memorable song upon the unhappy hunting in Chevy Chase', from the first half of the seventeenth. In *Spectator* 70, Addison wrote, 'The old Song of *Chevy-Chase* is the favourite Ballad of the common people of *England*.' [Schultz 337; Barlow 115; Simpson 96]

AIR 62. **To old Sir Simon the King.** Another ballad dating to the sixteenth century, usually known as 'Old Simon the King' or 'And never be drunk again'. Although it was used for a wide range of political songs in the seventeenth and eighteenth centuries, Gay was most likely alluding to its original subject, drunkenness, as in this 1682 version: 'No company I could find | Till I came to the sign of the Crown; | My hostess was sick of the Mumps, | The Maid was ill at ease, | The Tapster was drunk in his Dumps, | They all were of one disease | Says old Simon the King'. [Schultz 337; Simpson 545; Barlow 115; Swaen 186]

AIR 63. **Joy to great Caesar.** First line of a Royalist song, 'The King's Health', by D'Urfey, first printed in 1684, taking the side of the Catholic-tending Stuarts against the staunchly Protestant Whigs. There may be a hint at Macheath's political sympathies—the Cavalier highwayman was a stock character in popular criminal narrative, often linked to the pro-Stuart Jacobite cause after the Glorious Revolution of 1688—but Gay may just be thinking of it as another drinking song: 'Joy to great *Caesar*, | Long Life, Love & Pleasure; | 'Tis a Health that Divine is, | Fill the Bowl high as mine is'. The tune, 'Farinel's Ground', was a version of the much older dance 'ground' or bass pattern, 'La Folia', from fifteenth-century Portugal. [Schultz 338; Swaen 187; Barlow xii, 115; Simpson 216]

AIR 64. **There was an Old Woman.** First line of 'The Old Pudding-pye Woman', a ballad first recorded in 1675; the tune was generally known as 'Puddings and Pies'. [Barlow 116]

AIR 65. **Did you ever hear of a gallant Sailor.** The first line (but with 'not' in place of 'ever') of 'The Unconstant Woman', a ballad printed in 1707, probably based on a seventeenth-century tune. The refrain— 'Unconstant Woman proves true to no Man, | She has gone and left me all alone'—is suited to Macheath's turn here from singing of drink to singing of love. [Barlow 116; Simpson 336; Schultz 339]

AIR 66. **Why are mine Eyes still flowing.** First line of a song by Thomas D'Urfey, published in 1687, and said to have been 'set to a famous Italian Ayre'. Macheath's sentiments echo the last couplet of the original's first stanza: 'There is no Life like to that she can give, | Nor any Death like taking my leave'. [Schultz 339; Barlow 116; Simpson 781]

AIR 67. **Green Sleeves.** One of the most popular ballad tunes of the period, 'Greensleeves' was first recorded in 1580. The earliest surviving lyric—beginning 'Alas! My love, you do me wrong, | To cast me off discourteously'—dates from 1584. The version of the tune most familiar today, taken from William Ballet's late sixteenth-century manuscript Lute Book, is slightly different from the version Gay uses, from the 1686 7th edition of *The Dancing Master*. [Simpson 268; Barlow 116; Schultz 340]

AIR 68. **All you that must take a Leap.** First line of 'A Hymn upon the Execution of two Criminals', by the opera singer and songwriter Lewis Ramondon, from *c.*1710. The subject matter of this hanging ballad— 'All you that must take a leap in the Dark, | Pity the Fate of Lawson and Clark'—is obviously suited to the dramatic situation at this point of *The Beggar's Opera*, but Gay's treatment, balancing the disparate perspectives of the play's three principal characters, is much more complex. [Barlow 116; Swaen 190]

AIR 69. **Lumps of Pudding.** First printed in the 1714 edition of *Pills*; the tune is found in *The Dancing Master* from 1701. Macheath's paean to female beauty and the inconstancy of male desire is quite far removed from the opening stanzas of the original lyric: 'My Mother she kill'd a good fat Hog, | She made such Puddings wou'd Choak a dog'. By the end of the original song, however, the female singer has met a man who offers her a different kind of 'pudding': 'He gave me a lump which did so agree— | One bit was worth all my mother gave me!' [Schultz 340; Barlow 116]

POLLY

AIR 1. **The disappointed Widow.** Gay uses what is probably the original tune to a ballad also known as 'The slow Men of London: Or, the Widow Brown', which was later set to a different tune titled 'Jamaica'. The words concern a Welsh man who outwits three Londoners who are all making a play for the widow Brown; he seduces her but, having no money, 'disappoints' her. Gay's rhyme of 'undone' and 'London' is taken from the original, as here: 'For wooing tricks he quite put down, | The Slow-men of *London* | He over-reached the Widow *Brown* | That had so many undone'. [*Pills* VI, 93]

AIR 2. **The Irish ground.** A dance tune based on a repeating bass pattern (as in Airs 48 and 63 from *The Beggar's Opera*), from *The Dancing Master* (1721). Ducat's and Trapes's musical lines correspond to the bass and treble (or melody) lines of the original; he most likely carries on singing when she enters, so that his 'Youth and health' is heard under her 'A girl can fresh youth bestow' and is heard again under her 'in every vein | Life quickens again'. [Swaen 405]

AIR 3. **Noel Hills.** Another dance tune in the *Dancing Master* from 1713 on, where it is titled 'Nowil Hills: Or Love neglected'. [Swaen 405]

AIR 4. **Sweetheart, think upon me.** Not yet traced.

AIR 5. **'Twas within a furlong.** A rustic seduction song, titled 'The Scotch Haymakers', written by D'Urfey for Thomas Scott's 1696 play *The Mock-Marriage*, to a tune probably by Charles Powell. Beginning "Twas within a furlong of *Edinborough* Town', it tells of Jockey's efforts to woo Jenny: 'But Jockey was a Wag and would ne'er consent to Wed; | Which made her pish and phoo, and cry out it will not do, | I cannot, cannot, cannot, wonnot, wonnot Buckle too'. Trapes's lyric also concerns seduction, but 'pimps and politicians' have replaced the original's waggish rustics. [Swaen 405; Simpson 635]

AIR 6. **Sortez de vos retraites.** A French lyric set to music by Henry Carey, who may or may not have written the English translation of the words: 'Come from the Groves each Goddess, tune up your sweet Hoboys [oboes]; | And to the voice of muses make an harmonious noise: | Sing Her for whom I languish, Ye charming song approve; | Sing on till Jove is Jealous, and envy me my Love'. [Westrup 322]

AIR 7. **O Waly, Waly, up the bank.** Unlike Air 5, this is a genuine Scottish tune ('waly' is Scots for 'alas') and, like Polly's, a song of lost love. One stanza from Allan Ramsay's version: 'O waly, waly, but love [is] bonny | A little time while it is new, | But when 'tis auld it waxeth cauld, | And fades away like the morning dew'. While Ramsay's words emphasize the male lover's inconstancy, Gay's focus by contrast on Polly's 'constant heart'. [Swaen 406; *Tea-Table Miscellany*, 9th edn., in 3 vols. (London, 1733), 186]

AIR 8. **O Jenny come tye me.** This song heading is an abbreviated version of the line by which the tune was generally known, 'Jenny, come tie me my bonny cravat', from John Wade's 'The Scotch Currant; Or, The Tying of Johnny's Cravat', *c.*1675—'currant' meaning 'courante' or 'coranto', a lively dance in triple time (from French *courant*, running). The tune was also printed as an 'Additional Sheet' to *The Dancing Master*, *c.*1687. [Simpson 378; Swaen 421]

AIR 9. **Red House.** A dance tune from *The Dancing Master*, from 1695 on. Ramsay used it for his 1724 song 'Where wad bonny Annie ly', and it was also used for the hunting song 'John Peel'.

AIR 10. **Old Orpheus tickl'd.** An obscure song, also called 'When Orpheus tickl'd his harp', which evidently began, 'Then come to thy own poor Hut again'—but I have not located this.

AIR 11. **Christ-Church Bells.** A three-part, three-voice 'catch'—a song in which each voice enters in turn, the second singing what the first has just sung, and so on (examples include 'Row, row, row your boat' and 'Frère Jacques')—this was also a popular dance tune. It was written by Henry Aldrich around 1673. Although there are only two singers here, the three-part form may, as Dianne Dugaw suggests, allude to the sexual triangle that has triggered the argument. As a dance, too, the couples, like the Ducats here, are set at odds: 'at no time in the three sections', Dugaw writes, 'does a person dance with his or her own partner'. [Dugaw 200; Swaen 406]

AIR 12. **Cheshire-rounds.** Another popular dance tune; included in the 1701 11th edition of *The Dancing Master*. [Swaen 406]

AIR 13. **The bush a boon traquair.** A song included in the *Tea-Table Miscellany*—a pastoral love lament with a Scottish setting: 'Hear me, ye Nymphs, and every Swain, | I'll tell how *Peggy* grieves me; | Tho' thus I languish, thus complain, | Alas, She ne'er believes me. | My Vows and Sighs, like silent Air, | Unheeded never move her; | At the bonny Bush aboon *Traquair*, | 'Twas there I first did love her'. The tune was used in at least six other ballad operas between 1729 and 1735; Gay characteristically reverses the gender dynamics of the original. [Swaen 407]

AIR 14. **Bury Fair.** A dance tune; included in the supplement to the 9th edition of *The Dancing Master* (1696). [Swaen 407]

AIR 15. **Bobbing Joan.** A popular dance tune, found in every edition of *The Dancing Master* from 1651 on, among other collections. The title comes from a seventeenth-century song, 'Bobbin Jo: Or; The Longing Lass Satisfied at last', beginning 'There was a Maid liv'd in the North, | which had of late a sore mischance'. As the song's subtitle implies, 'bobbin jo' is a euphemism for sex; and in the narrative context of Ducat's purchase of Polly from Mrs Trapes, Gay's lyric points to the parallels between slavery, prostitution/marriage, political flattery, and commerce, playing off the original's bawdy refrain: 'The bobbin jo, the bobbin jo, | And canst thou dance the bobbin jo'. [Simpson 46; Swaen 408; Dugaw 204]

AIR 16. **A Swain long tortur'd with Disdain.** Opening line of a song titled 'The Way to Win Her', a love lament with an alcoholic twist: 'A swain, long tortur'd with disdain, | That daily sigh'd, but sigh'd in vain, | At length the god of wine addrest, | The refuge of a wounded breast'. Gay's final couplet echoes the language of the original, but turns the original's 'god of wine' into Polly's comforting assurance of her own 'vertue'—although her aside after the song undercuts the promise of comfort. [Swaen 408; Dugaw 206]

AIR 17. **March in** *Scipio*. From the overture to Handel's opera *Scipione* (English *Scipio*; 1726), to a libretto by Paolo Antonio Rolli. As in *The Beggar's Opera*'s Air 20, set to another march by Handel, there is an obvious ironic gap between the grandeur of the music and the venality of the singers' motives (emphasized by the Servant's cynical asides). But while Matt, like Ducat here, may be motivated by greed, he at least risks his own life, and so has a better claim to the phrase 'Brave boys', which they both use. [Swaen 408]

AIR 18. **Jig-it-o'Foot**. Lively dance tune; found in the 1718 3rd edition of the second volume of *The Dancing Master*, and in the 1728 edition. [Swaen 408]

AIR 19. **Trumpet Minuet**. The melody is adapted from the second Minuet in F from George Frideric Handel's *Water Music* of 1717—the minuet being a slow to moderate dance in triple time.

AIR 20. **Polwart on the Green**. Song by Allan Ramsay, sung by a 'lass' to the 'lad' she fancies: 'At *Polwart* on the Green, | If you'll meet me the Morn, | Where Lasses do conveen | To dance about the thorn, | A kindly Welcome you shall meet, | Frae her wha likes to view | A Lover and a Lad complete, | The Lad and Lover you'. The tune was used in many later ballad operas. [*Tea-Table* 129; Swaen 409]

AIR 21. **St. Martin's Lane**. Dance tune, found in the 1721 *Dancing Master*. This may originally have been a theatre tune by Henry Purcell, but I have not yet traced this. [Barlow xiv]

AIR 22. **La Villanella**. The villanella was a popular song form originating in Naples in southern Italy in the mid-sixteenth century, often with a rustic feel (It. *villanello*, rustic or rural), although it was a form of composition rather than a folk form. The specific source of this air has not yet been traced.

AIR 23. **Dead March in** *Coriolanus*. Ariosti's very successful opera *Caio Marzio Coriolano*, his first for the Royal Academy, opened on 19 February 1723 at the King's Theatre, Haymarket. The libretto was adapted by Nicola Haym from the original text by Pietro Pariati. See also the 'Recitative' between Airs 42 and 43 below. [Grove, entry for 'Ariosto, Attilio']

AIR 24. **Three Sheep-skins**. An English country dance, in *The Dancing Master* from 1698, with roots in the rural morris dance tradition. The title suggests that this tune was associated with sheep-skinners, and traditionally the dancer who loses his way and falls out of the pattern has to buy drinks for the others. For a discussion of parallels between the dance and this scene, in which the pirates drink and argue over which of them has 'rights' to which stolen territory in the Americas, see Dugaw 206–11.

AIR 25. **Rigadoon.** From the 1721 *Dancing Master*. The rigadoon began as a lively jig-like folk dance for couples, but was later adopted by the court of Louis XIV. [Swaen 409]

AIR 26. **Ton humeur est Catharine.** A French song, 'Reproches à Catherine', attributed to a Monsieur Desroches (1686–1735). The singer complains to a woman about her bad temper: 'Ton himeur est, Catheraine, | Plus aigre qu'un citron vard . . . | Comme un vrai fagot d'épaine | Tu piques par tous les bouts' [Your mood, Catherine, is sourer than a lime . . . Like a real bundle of thorns, you prick all over]. The tune was printed in the 1724 collection *Les rondes, chansons à danser*. [Swaen 409; Westrup 322]

AIR 27. **Ye nymphs and sylvan gods.** First line of a song, 'The Bonny Milk-Maid', by Thomas D'Urfey, written for his play *Don Quixote*, Part II (1694). D'Urfey's lyric is based on an older ballad, 'The Milkmaids' or 'The Merry Milkmaids', but he commissioned new music by John Eccles, and this is the version Gay uses here. The same tune was used in a dozen other ballad operas. [Simpson 490; Swaen 410]

AIR 28. **Minuet.** The melody is taken from the Minuet in D from Handel's 1717 *Water Music* (see also Air 19 above).

AIR 29. **Mirleton.** A mirleton or mirliton is a little reed pipe, the sound of which this dance tune is meant to evoke. Gay uses the original refrain: 'With a Mirliton, Mirliton, Mirlitaine | With a Mirliton, don don'. [Swaen 410]

AIR 30. **Sawny was tall, and of noble race.** First line of a song written by D'Urfey for his comedy *The Virtuous Wife* (1679). The tune, possibly written by Thomas Farmer, was usually known by the song's refrain, 'Sawney will never be my love again', which the final line of Gay's version echoes. Many ballads (including political parodies) and ballad operas made use of the tune. [Simpson 632; Swaen 410]

AIR 31. **Northern Nancy.** The tune appears in *The Dancing Master* from 1670 on—sometimes in major mode (as in *Polly*) and sometimes in minor. It was probably used for a number of ballads dating back to *c*.1635, but the title was often confused with that of another, unrelated, ballad tune, 'Northern Nanny'. Gay probably had no earlier words in mind when he wrote his. [Simpson 517]

AIR 32. **Amante fuggite cadente belta.** Not yet traced—perhaps the opening line of an operatic number?

AIR 33. **Since all the world's turn'd upside down.** First line (substituting 'all' for 'now') of a song titled 'The Dame of Honour', written by Thomas D'Urfey for his 1706 opera *Wonders in the Sun, or, The Kingdom of the Birds* (see also Air 64 below). The composer of the tune is unknown. The theme of the opening lines—'Since now the world's turn'd upside down, | And all things chang'd in Nature'—is suited to the inversions and alterations of identity in *Polly*, as is the substitution of 'Man' for 'Dame' in Gay's version of the original last line: 'When I was a Dame of Honour'. But D'Urfey had already included an alternate version of the song in *Pills* (1719–20) with the title 'The Man of Honour: Or, the Unconstant World turn'd upside down', which made the same gender substitution as Gay's. [Simpson 155; Swaen 411; Dugaw 193]

AIR 34. **Hunt the Squirrel.** The tune is found in *The Dancing Master* (1721) and was used in several other ballad operas. For *The Spectator* no. 67 (17 May 1711) Eustace Budgell wrote a letter supposed to have been written by 'a man in years' on the subject of the new craze for country dancing. 'Among the rest', the gentleman writes, 'I observed one, which I think, they call *Hunt the Squirrel*, in which while the woman flies, the man pursues her; but as soon as she turns, he runs away, and she is obliged to follow'. [See Dugaw 211 for an intriguing reading of the dance associated with this tune as an enactment of Polly's simultaneous transgression and entrapment.]

AIR 35. **Young Damon once the loveliest swain.** First line (substituting 'loveliest' for 'happiest') of a song titled 'Confidence *Essential* to a Lover'; the tune has been attributed to Giovanni Battista Grano. The song treats of the ill effects of love: 'Young *Damon* once the happiest swain, | The pride and glory of the plain; | But see th'effects of love! | Depriv'd of all his former rest, | Shun'd company, with grief opprest; | And sought the thickest grove'. [Swaen 412]

AIR 36. **Catharine Ogye.** Also known as 'Bonny Kathern Oggy' (and in many variant spellings), the best-known version was written to an existing tune by Thomas D'Urfey and published in *Pills*. The tune was published in 1687 as 'Lady Catherine Ogie, a new Dance'. In D'Urfey's lyric, 'Catherine Logy' is just a pretty maid the singer meets while out walking; but in another version included in *Pills*, she is portrayed very differently: 'And had I kend shaw had been a Whore, | I had ne'r Lov'd Kathern Loggy'. [Simpson 54; Swaen 412]

AIR 37. **Roger a Coverly.** Popular dance tune from the 1696 *Dancing Master*. The character Sir Roger de Coverley, introduced by Richard Steele in the second issue of *The Spectator* (2 March 1711), was supposed to be the great-grandson of the man who invented the dance. [Swaen 413]

AIR 38. **Bacchus m'a dit**. Not yet traced—as Bacchus was the Roman god of wine, perhaps a drinking song?

AIR 39. **Health to Betty**. A dance tune in every edition of *The Dancing Master* from 1651. Set to words by D'Urfey in the 1719–20 *Pills* as 'The Female Quarrel ... to the Tune of a Country Dance, call'd, A Health to Betty'. In another version, 'Advice or, an Heroic Epistle to Mr. Fra. Villers', the titular Francis Villers is warned to keep an eye on his sister Nancy: 'She's quite undone | If once King John | Shou'd get between her Haunches'—a raunchy verse Gay may be alluding to here with his image of the unrestrained wife as a wild steed. [Simpson 298; Swaen 413].

AIR 40. **Cappe de bonne Esperance [Cape of Good Hope]**. The tune is similar to one in the French song collection *La Clef des chansonniers* titled 'En deuil et fort afligée' [In grief and sore distressed]. Also used in the 1735 ballad opera *The Merry Cobbler*. [Westrup 322]

AIR 41. **When bright Aurelia tripp'd the plain**. First line of 'The bright Aurelia', a pastoral song dating to 1710. In a version from the 1729 *Tea-Table Miscellany*: 'When bright *Aurelia* trip'd the Pla[i]n, | How chearful then were seen | The Looks of every jolly Swain, | That strove *Aurelia*'s Heart to gain, | With Gambols on the Green!' [Swaen 414]

AIR 42. **Peggy's Mill**. A song by Allan Ramsay, also known as 'The Mill, Mill—O', opening 'Beneath a green Shade I fand [found] a fair Maid | Was sleeping sound and still—O'. On the eve of going to war, the singer is so struck by the fair maid's beauty that, while she sleeps, he has sex with her ('While kindly she slept, close to her I crept, | And kiss'd, and kiss'd her my fill—O'). When he returns two years later, he finds her in disgrace, having given birth without knowing 'wha'd done her the Ill—O'; but, 'Mair fond of her Charms, with my Son in her arms', he promises, 'If I did Offence, I'se make ye Amends | Before I leave *Peggy's-Mill*—O'. The cynical claim in Jenny's song that all men care for in women is their gold contradicts the fondness Ramsay's singer expresses (although we shouldn't overlook the fact that he raped his 'fair Maid' in the song's first stanza). [*Tea-Table* 153]

Recitative. Sia suggetta la plebe in *Coriolan*. From *Caio Marzio Coriolano* by Attilio Ariosti, first performed in London in 1723 (see Air 23 above).

AIR 43. **Excuse me**. A country dance tune first published in *The Dancing Master* in 1686, it was most likely adapted by Thomas Robinson from a song by John Dowland, 'Can she excuse my wrongs with vertue's cloake'

(1597), also known in an instrumental version as 'The Earle of Essex Galliard'. D'Urfey used the tune for his song, 'The Crafty Mistris's Resolution', which he published in *Pills* in 1700. Morano's self-portrait, in Gay's lyric, as a heroic figure torn between love and honour would have been tainted, for those who knew D'Urfey's song, by the memory of its singer's caustic words: 'All the Town So lewd are grown | Hereafter you must excuse me | If when you discover your Self a lover | I think itt is all a lye'. [John M. Ward, '"Excuse Me": A Dance to a Tune of John Dowland's Making', in Israel J. Katz, ed., *Libraries, History, Diplomacy, and the Performing Arts: Essays in Honor of Carleton Sprague Smith* (Hillsdale, NY: Pendragon, 1991), 379–88.]

AIR 44. **Ruben.** As 'Reuben', this tune is printed in the 1728 *Dancing Master*. [Swaen 415]

AIR 45. **Troy Town.** A tune also known as 'Queen Dido', dating back to *c.*1611. The version Gay follows was printed in *Pills* (1719–20). Used for many ballads in the seventeenth and eighteenth centuries; the original ballad text was most likely 'The wandring Prince of Troye', based on the Dido and Aeneas story from Virgil's *Aeneid*. Macheath's attachment to Jenny echoes or parodies the love of the Trojan prince Aeneas for Dido, which he has to renounce in order to fulfil his empire-founding destiny (burlesqued in the pirates' bickering over 'the kingdom of *Mexico*'). [Simpson 587; Swaen 415]

AIR 46. **We've cheated the Parson.** Opening line of the second stanza of a song written by John Dryden for his opera *King Arthur* (1691). The tune, by Henry Purcell, was generally known as 'Harvest Home', from the refrain: 'Harvest home, harvest home, and merrily roar out our harvest home'. Cheating the parson refers to the tithe (one part in ten) of the harvest that was supposed to be given as a contribution or tax to the church. But as the singer in Dryden's text puts it, 'We've cheated the parson, we'll cheat him again, | For why should a blockhead have one in ten?' [Swaen 416; Simpson 289]

AIR 47. **T'amo tanto.** An air from *Ataxerxes* or *Ataserse*, an opera by Attilio Ariosti to a libretto by Apostolo Zeno (adapted by Nicola Haym) first performed in London on 1 December 1724 at the King's Theatre, Haymarket. Polly and Cawwawkee's paean to virtue would have suggested an erotic second meaning to listeners who recalled the original words—'T'amo tanto o mio tesoro' [I love you dearly, O my treasure]— and on stage could have looked like an expression of both same-sex and other-sex desire, depending on how the viewer 'saw' Polly, as male or female. [Lowell Lindgren, 'Ariosti's London Years, 1716–29', *Music and Letters* 62:3/4 (1981), 331–51]

AIR 48. **Down in a meadow.** Probably a song beginning 'As down in a meadow one morning I past', found later in *The Weekly Amusement* II, 460 (1735). A wry song about lovers' infidelity—ending, 'Most men are like Billy, most women like Sue, | And if men will be false, why should women prove true?'—Gay extends this cynical observation to politicians, who, like false lovers, also 'fawn and betray'.

AIR 49. **There was an old man, and he liv'd.** Opening words of a song titled 'The Jolly Broom-man' (*Pills* VI), about an old broom-maker whose son Jack starts out as a lazy good-for-nothing but discovers the rewards of hard work and an honest trade. Gay's use of the tune only underlines Ducat's utter lack of moral integrity. [Swaen 416]

AIR 50. **Iris la plus charmante.** Not yet traced.

AIR 51. **There was a Jovial Beggar.** First line of a song titled 'The Beggar's Chorus', probably written for a revival *c*.1684 of Richard Brome's play *The Jovial Crew, or The Merry Beggars* (first produced in 1641). It begins: 'There was a jovial beggar, | He has a wooden leg, | Lame from his cradle, | And forced for to beg. | And a begging we will go, we'll go, we'll go, | And a begging we will go!' The pirates' claim to military valour in Gay's version is satirically undercut by the connection the tune establishes between the pirate gang and a crew of beggars. [Simpson 40; Swaen 417]

AIR 52. **To you fair ladies.** Opening words of a ballad from 1664 by Charles Sackville, later Earl of Dorset, set to a tune originally titled 'Shackley Hay'. It opens: 'To you fair ladies now at land, | We men at sea indite, | But first would have you understand | How hard it is to write: | The muses now, and Neptune too, | We must implore to write to you, | With a fa la la . . .'. The tune was known in several different versions, and was used for a great many songs, and in many ballad operas. [Swaen 417; Simpson 647]

AIR 53. **Prince Eugene's march.** The music was composed by Jeremiah Clarke (1673–1707; see also Air 71), organist of St Paul's Cathedral until his death by suicide. Prince Eugene of Savoy won an important victory over the French (against whom England was also at war) to end the siege of Turin in 1706—a crucial turning point in the War of the Spanish Succession. Gay uses the heroic march tune, as before, to ironically undermine Macheath's 'heroic' call to arms. The tune was also printed in the 1728 *Dancing Master*. [Swaen 418]

AIR 54. **The marlborough.** A dance created by the famous dancing master Mr Isaac—to music probably written by his frequent collaborator James Paisible—in 1704/5 to celebrate the Duke of Marlborough, who, along with Prince Eugene (see Air 53), defeated the French forces at the Battle of Blenheim in August 1704. The tune was also printed in the 1721 *Dancing Master*. [Jennifer Thorp, 'Mr. Isaac, Dancing-Master', *Dance Research*, 24:2 (2006), 117–37]

AIR 55. **Les rats.** Not yet traced. The young dancers in training for the Paris Opera were known as 'les petits rats', and there are a number of nineteenth-century dances with similar names, such as the Rats Quadrille, so Gay's tune may be taken from a French contredanse (from the English 'country dance', on which the contredanse was based). According to an account from 1727 in the *Mercure gallant*, 'Les rats' was one of the contredanses included in the public masquerade balls held in the Théâtre de l'Opéra to mark the end of carnival. [Richard Semmens, *The Bals publics at the Paris Opera in the 18th Century* (Pendragon, 2004)]

AIR 56. **Mad Robin.** The tune was included in the supplement to the 1687 7th edition of *The Dancing Master*, and in later editions. Mad Robin is also the name of a country dance figure in which dancers circle their neighbours back to back while holding eye contact with their partners opposite: a figure to which the 'neighbours' in Gay's last line may refer.

AIR 57. **Thro' the wood laddy.** Title of a song which may date back to the mid-seventeenth century, but which is best known from Ramsay's version of 1724, which begins, 'O *Sandy*, why leaves thou thy *Nelly* to mourn?' The title phrase is sung in the last line of each stanza as part of the refrain. Ramsay's lyric expresses the sorrow of a woman waiting for her lover's return, and Gay's use of it here accentuates the romantic-erotic undercurrents of Cawwawkee's regard for Polly. [*Tea-Table* 85; Swaen 418; Simpson 705]

AIR 58. **Clasp'd in my dear Melinda's arms.** The song, attributed to the actor, singer, and dancer Matthew Birkhead or Burkhead (fl. 1707–22), appears in *Pills* from 1709. The first stanza runs: 'Claspt in my dear *Melinda*'s Arms, | Soft engaging, oh how she Charms; | Graces more divine, | In her person shine, | Then *Venus* self cou'd ever boast'. By using this tune for the moment of Cawwawkee and Polly's reunion after their separation in battle, Gay infuses their friendly or fraternal embrace with a homoerotic charge at the same time that the music unmasks the visibly male Polly as 'she'. [Swaen 418]

AIR 59. **Parson upon Dorothy.** A tune found in *The Dancing Master* from 1652 on, also known as 'The Shepherd's Daughter' or 'The Beautiful Shepherdess of Arcadia'. After a knight, Sweet William, has sex with the 'beautiful shepherdess', he rides off; but she pursues him, and enlists the king to compel him to marry her, refusing his offer of money: '"O I'll have none of your gold," she said, "nor I'll have none of your fee; | But I must have your fair body, the King hath given me"'. Luckily, the shepherdess turns out to be a duke's daughter, so 'He hath both purse and person too, and all at his command'. The story resonates at many points with that of Polly and Macheath. [Roxburghe ballads 2:30–1, transcribed in *English Broadside Ballad Archive*, http://ebba.english.ucsb.edu/ballad/30150/ transcription; Simpson 658; Swaen 419]

AIR 60. **The collier has a daughter.** Opening line of 'The Collier's bonny Lassie' in Ramsay's *Tea-Table Miscellany*. A Scottish laird, 'Rich baith in Land and Money', falls in love with 'the Collier's bonny Lassie' despite her humble station. At the end, he tells her, 'For I have Gear in Plenty, | And Love says, 'tis my Duty | To ware [spend] what Heaven has lent me, | Upon your Wit and Beauty'. Ramsay's sentimental bridging of the gap between rich and poor, high and low, is challenged by Gay's emphasis on the social price paid by those who 'fall from high condition' (152). The story is almost the inverse of 'The Beautiful Shepherdess', above.

AIR 61. **Mad Moll.** The tune is found in *The Dancing Master* from 1698. [Swaen 418]

AIR 62. **Prince George.** A tune found in *The Dancing Master* from the 1686 7th edition. It is most likely based on a song celebrating the 1683 marriage of Prince George of Denmark and Princess (later Queen) Anne; as with Airs 47, 57, and 58, the audience's awareness of the words of the original song would give Cawwawkee and Polly's duet a romantic-erotic second meaning.

AIR 63. **Blithe Jockey young and gay.** First line of a song probably written by Richard Leveridge and first published *c*.1700; later included by D'Urfey in *Pills* (1719–20). The original is a love song with a Scottish flavour: 'Blith *Jockey* Young and Gay, | Is all my Soul's Delight, | He's all my Talk by Day, | And all my Dreams by Night: | If from the Lad I be, | 'Tis Winter still with me, | But when he's with me here, | 'Tis Summer all the Year'. Polly's lyric is a dark, anguished elaboration of the fifth and sixth lines of the original song. [Swaen 420]

AIR 64. **In the fields in frost and snow.** First line of a song from Thomas D'Urfey's comic opera *Wonders in the Sun: or, The Kingdom of the Birds* (1706; see also Air 33 above), with the refrain 'We defy all care and Strife, | In a Charming Country-Life'. The tune was most likely composed by the violinist John Smith. [Swaen 420; Fiske 24]

AIR 65. **Whilst I gaze on Chloe.** Opening words of a late seventeenth-century song known variously as 'The Jealous Lover's Complaint' or 'The Lukewarm Lover'. Gay uses the tune written for the song by Lewis Ramondon *c*.1720, which was used in at least nine other ballad operas after *Polly*. Cawwawkee's, like the original, is a song of 'troubled', hopeless love; but here his sense of 'uneas[e]' and 'restless[ness]' is exacerbated by the shock of discovery of her sex. [Simpson 772; Swaen 420]

AIR 66. **The Jamaica.** A tune found in *The Dancing Master* from 1670, perhaps better known as 'My Father was Born before me' or 'The Prodigal's Resolution'. The original is titled 'Joy after Sorrow, Being the Sea-mans return from Jamaica', and was published in 1656, the year after England took control of Jamaica from Spain. It begins, 'There was a maid as I heard tell, which fell in desperation'; while the chorus ends, 'And my Love is gone to Jamaica'—making it well suited to *Polly*'s story and setting. [Wm. Bruce Olson, 'A Note on the Tune "Jamaica"', *Folk Music Journal*, 2:4 (1973), 315–17; Simpson 376]

AIR 67. **Tweed Side.** A tune used in several ballad operas. The version collected by Ramsay in the *Tea-Table Miscellany* begins, 'What beauties does *Flora* disclose', and has been attributed to Robert Crawford. It is a pastoral love song with a Scottish setting: 'We'll lodge in some Village on *Tweed*, | And love while the Feather'd folks sing'. Polly replaces the 'warblers' and 'flocks' of the original with a hunted stag—another rural image, but one that mirrors Polly's fears for Macheath. [Swaen 421]

AIR 68. **One Evening as I lay.** First line of a song known as 'Love in the Groves' from *c*.1710, later collected by Ramsay. It is a song of sexual revenge, which the singer convinces a grieving 'nymph' to take on the 'swain' who has left her alone, by having sex with the singer himself. At the end, we're told, 'Then she with smiles confess'd, | Her mind felt no more pain, | While she was thus caress'd, | By such a lovely swain'. [*Tea-Table Miscellany*, 9th edn., in 3 vols. (London, 1733), 309–10]

AIR 69. **Buff-coat.** The tune is found in every edition of *The Dancing Master* from 1670, and was used in at least a dozen ballad operas, sometimes as 'Buff Coat has no fellows'. As Simpson suggests, this last phrase likely comes from the refrain of a ballad that is now lost. Since the buff coat was part of early seventeenth-century military uniforms, that original song was probably a drinking song for and about soldiers. In the first edition of *Polly*, the music is marked 'Very slow', to emphasize that the jolly original song has been transformed into a dirge. [Simpson 72; Fiske 119]

AIR 70. **An Italian ballad.** Not yet traced.

AIR 71. **The temple.** The tune is found in *The Dancing Master*
from 1701, and is a variant of Jeremiah Clarke's well known 'Prince of
Denmark's March' or 'Trumpet Voluntary' of *c.*1700 (later misattrib-
uted to Henry Purcell). It's not clear what 'The Temple' refers to, but
John Playford, *The Dancing Master*'s original publisher, for many years
had his shop in the porch of Temple Church off Fleet Street in the City
of London, so he may have appropriated the music for himself.

EXPLANATORY NOTES

ABBREVIATIONS

NCD   *A New Canting Dictionary: Comprehending All the Terms, Antient and Modern, Used in the Several Tribes of Gypsies, Beggars, Shoplifters, Highwaymen, Foot-Pads, and all other Clans of Cheats and Villains* (London, 1725).

OED   *Oxford English Dictionary.*

Trivia   Clare Brant and Susan E. Whyman, eds., *Walking the Streets of Eighteenth-Century London: John Gay's* Trivia (Oxford: Oxford University Press, 2007).

THE BEGGAR'S OPERA

TITLE PAGE

1 *Nos haec novimus esse nihil*: 'We know these things to be nothing', from Martial, *Epigrams* xiii. 2. 8.

DRAMATIS PERSONAE

2 *Peachum*: like almost all the other character names, descriptive: to 'peach', from 'impeach', is to betray or inform against an alleged criminal—hence 'peach 'em'.

Lockit: an equally fitting trade name for the jailor of Newgate prison.

Macheath: i.e. 'son of the heath'. The heaths around London, such as Hounslow and Bagshot Heaths, were notorious sites of highway robbery.

Most of the other male character names allude to forms of criminality, many using eighteenth-century thieves' cant or slang: *Filch* (to steal); *Jemmy Twitcher* (*twitcher*, pickpocket); *Crook-finger'd Jack* (a pun on the two meanings of 'crooked'); *Robin of Bagshot* (a highwayman, from Bagshot Heath); *Nimming Ned* (*nim*, 'to steal, or whip off or away any thing' [*NCD*]); *Harry Padington* (*pad*, 'the High-way; also a Robber thereon' [*NCD*]; Paddington is also the London parish where the Tyburn gallows stood); *Matt of the Mint* (the Mint, a district in Southwark, was a haven for criminals and debtors); *Ben Budge* (*budge*, 'one that slips into an House in the dark, and taking Cloaks, Coats, or what comes next to Hand, marches off with them' [*NCD*]).

Apart from *Mrs Peachum, Polly Peachum*, and *Lucy Lockit*, all of the female character names signify sexual immorality or prostitution: *Diana Trapes* (*trapes*, 'a dangling Slattern' [*NCD*]); *Mrs Coaxer* (*coax*, seduce or persuade); *Dolly Trull* (*trull*, 'a Whore; also a Tinker's travelling Wife or Wench' [*NCD*]); *Mrs Vixen, Suky Tawdry*, and *Molly Brazen* have surnames that suggest sexual availability or excess (*vixen*, a female fox or, colloquially, a shrewish woman; *tawdry*, gaudy or cheap; *brazen*, shameless or insolent); *Betty Doxy* (*Doxies* are

'She-beggars, Trulls, Wenches, Whores' [*NCD*]); *Mrs Slammekin* (*slammekin*, like *trapes*, a slattern or slut). *Jenny Diver* stands somewhat apart, *diver* meaning pickpocket, although there may also be a sexual double meaning, as there is in 'Low-Dive Jenny', the character Brecht and Hauptmann based on her in their *Threepenny Opera* of 1928.

INTRODUCTION

3 *St. Giles's*: the London parish of St Giles in the Fields, near Holborn, was portrayed in the period as home to criminals, prostitutes, impoverished authors, foreigners, sodomites, and beggars.

Catches: popular songs in the form of a round, in which the voices enter in succession, singing the same tune and words; often sung as drinking songs.

James Chanter and Moll Lay: generic names for ballad singers. *Lay* can mean both a song and a criminal practice or speciality, and Gay links ballad singing to crime in his 1716 poem, *Trivia*: 'Let not the Ballad-Singer's shrilling Strain | Amid the Swarm thy list'ning Ear detain: | Guard well thy Pocket; for these *Syrens* stand, | To aid the Labours of the diving Hand; | Confed'rate in the cheat, they draw the Throng, | And *Cambrick* Handkerchiefs reward the Song' (*Trivia* 196 [III, 77–82]).

The Swallow . . . the Flower, &c.: conventional poetic similes, used (often to ironic effect) in several of *The Beggar's Opera*'s airs: the swallow in Air 34; the moth in Air 4; the bee and the flower in Airs 6 and 15; and the ship (or 'skiff') in Airs 10 and 47.

our two Ladies: the actresses playing Polly and Lucy, but alluding to the two most celebrated Italian female opera singers of the period, Faustina Bordoni and Francesca Cuzzoni, whose rivalry had led to blows onstage in 1727, parodied in the struggle between Lucy and Polly over Macheath.

Recitative: technique or style of performing passages of dialogue between fully composed arias and ensembles in opera, part way between speech and song, and rhythmically and melodically free; often accompanied by just one or two instruments. Many among English audiences of the period found this style of freely sung speech 'unnatural', as the Beggar says.

THE PLAY

5 *An old Woman cloathed in Gray, &c*: title of the ballad whose melody Gay has used for this air. See Appendix for notes on the originals of all the airs in *The Beggar's Opera* and *Polly*.

you will order Matters . . . bring her off: manipulate the evidence or bribe the justices so as to get her acquitted at trial.

plead her Belly: women convicted of capital crimes could not be executed while pregnant. If their claims or 'pleas' to be so were verified, they might be sentenced to transportation instead (usually after giving birth); in rare cases, the original sentence was carried out after childbirth, but more often the sentence was reduced or suspended.

6 *forty Pounds*: the reward paid for information leading to the arrest and conviction of male (but not female, as Peachum notes below) criminals.

Transportation: the practice of shipping convicted criminals to British North American and West Indian (and later, Australian) colonies as indentured servants, usually for a period of seven or fourteen years. To return to Britain before the term had expired was a capital offence.

Lock: 'a Warehouse where stolen Goods are deposited' (Gay, note to III.iii).

take her off: bring about her death by informing against her.

train'd up . . . Gaming-table: it was a commonplace of criminal biographies that young men were seduced into the 'business' of crime either by women or gambling.

We and the Surgeons . . . Professions besides: surgeons, doctors, and quacks were 'beholden' to women, notably prostitutes, for transmitting venereal diseases, whose treatment could be costly.

Newgate: the main criminal prison of London, built on the site of one of the old city gates, and located near the Old Bailey criminal court.

7 *Sessions*: terms when criminal trials are held; at the Old Bailey, in this period, there were eight sessions per year.

Six dozen of Handkerchiefs . . . Broad Cloth: along with watches and snuff boxes, these are items commonly stolen by pickpockets or shoplifters. Handkerchiefs of linen or silk were luxury items, as were men's periwigs or wigs (with a ribbon tie at the back); broad cloth is a fine quality cloth used mostly for men's clothes.

petty-larceny Rascal: one who steals goods worth less than a shilling, a non-capital crime (and of no use to receivers like Peachum). Theft of goods worth more than a shilling was grand larceny, a capital offence.

listed: enlisted.

Cart: the condemned were carried from Newgate to the gallows at Tyburn in an open cart.

Robin of Bagshot . . . Bob Booty: all of these names allude satirically to the first (prime) minister, Robert Walpole. Anti-government writers had already played on the similarity of *Robert* and *robber*, as Gay does here with *Robin* and *robbing*, reinforced by the connection to Bagshot Heath and its highway robbers. In thieves' slang, a *bob* was a shoplifter's sidekick; and booty is the goods stolen. *Bluff Bob* plays on *bluff*'s double meaning—outspoken (or blunt), and to deceive, especially boastfully—while *Carbuncle* (an ugly pimple or excrescence) and *Gorgon* (a hideous female monster) are rude insults, a common satirical weapon against political enemies.

8 *Black-List*: Peachum's list of those he intends to impeach and send to the gallows.

the Camp: that is, military service. Gay here satirically equates the lives and actions of criminals, on the one hand, and soldiers on the other.

8 *Venus's Girdle*: Venus, the Roman goddess of love, had a magic girdle or belt (or 'Zone') that made its wearer instantly desirable—or, as Mrs Peachum puts it, made 'her Face look wond'rous smuggly'.

Beneath the left Ear . . . an Adonis!: just as Venus's girdle turns an ugly 'Wench' into a beauty, so a hangman's noose around his neck transforms a lowly criminal 'Youth' into a Lord or Adonis (Venus's beloved).

9 *Bank-notes*: not paper currency as we know it, but receipts for money deposited in a bank and payable to the bearer. Thieves or receivers could cash such notes if the original owners had not yet stopped payment.

Quadrille: four-handed card game popular from the 1720s.

Mary-bone and the Chocolate-houses: the Marylebone district of London was known for its pleasure gardens, whose gaming-houses made it a popular haunt of gamblers. Similarly, the city's fashionable chocolate houses gave men a place to gamble while drinking chocolate and socializing.

10 *a Temple Coffee-House*: coffeehouses, like chocolate houses, were meeting places for men, and played an important role in eighteenth-century public life. Women, as Peachum suggests, were largely confined to working behind the bar, but if 'handsome' could profit from male attention. A Temple coffeehouse would have been located near the Inner Temple and Middle Temple Inns of Court, and would have been frequented mainly by lawyers and law students.

to make herself a Property: before the Married Women's Property Acts of 1870 and 1882, a married woman's possessions, money, and legal identity belonged and were subject to her husband by the law of coverture, so that she herself was to all intents and purposes 'a Property'.

like a Court Lady to a Minister of State: refers to the political connections between Walpole and women of the royal court, especially Queen Caroline, wife of George II, whom Walpole used as an intermediary to win the King's support.

rip out the Coronets . . . Cambric Handkerchiefs: remove the decorative embroidery (which could identify the original owner) from stolen handkerchiefs; *cambric* is a fine white linen.

Chap: a 'chapman' or pedlar.

11 *Oar*: variant spelling of 'ore'.

try'd and imprest: to 'try' is to refine or purify; to 'impress' is to stamp, as in coining.

Juggler: a sleight-of-hand artist.

ply'd at the Opera: practised his pickpocketing trade at the King's Theatre in the Haymarket, the London home of Italian opera.

Chairs: sedan chairs, enclosed one-seat vehicles carried on poles by two bearers; available for hire in the period.

Redriff: Rotherhithe, a dockland area on the south bank of the Thames.

12 *Fobs*: small watch pockets in men's waistcoats or breeches.

pumpt: held under the spout of a water pump, a form of popular justice for pickpockets caught in the act. See *Trivia* 196 (III, 73–4): 'Seiz'd by rough Hands, he's dragg'd amid the Rout, | And stretch'd beneath the Pump's incessant Spout'.

Hockley in the Hole: Clerkenwell site of a bear garden, where violent popular entertainments and sports—bear and bull baiting, cock fights, wrestling, and so on—were presented.

Old-Baily: the Old Bailey was London's principal criminal court.

go to your Book . . . Ordinary's Paper: the Ordinary was the chaplain of Newgate, responsible for preparing the condemned for death and testing prisoners who pleaded 'benefit of clergy', by means of which literate first-time offenders could have their sentences reduced. The test was to read a passage from the Bible ('your Book'), usually the opening of Psalm 51—the 'Catechism' Filch needs to learn. The Ordinary's papers or *Accounts* were pamphlets giving the life stories and last words or confessions of the condemned as told (supposedly) to the Ordinary himself.

13 *Court . . . Assembly*: the royal court and public assemblies were sites of fashionable sociability. Assemblies were less exclusive than the court, but were still largely limited to the higher ranks, who met there to converse, play cards, hear music, dance, and, Polly suggests, learn mercenary values.

thrown upon the Common: to become common property or fall into prostitution, with puns on common-land and common law.

Covent-Garden: known in the period both for its flower market and for its prostitutes, and thus the destination of 'pluck'd' flower and virgin alike.

Jade: a worn-out horse; used disparagingly of women.

14 *As Men should serve . . . herself away*: just as Polly has thrown herself away, despite the 'Care and Cost' her parents have spent on dressing her, by marrying Macheath, so men 'fling away' a dish of cucumbers, widely thought to be unfit for eating even when carefully dressed or prepared.

getting: growing richer.

ruin'd: reversing the word's usual sense of a woman who has lost her virginity before marriage, Peachum here means 'married'.

15 *squeezing out an Answer from you*: alludes to the legal torture of 'pressing' defendants who had refused to plead guilty or not guilty by placing heavy weights on their chests to force a plea out of them.

upon liking: on approval, or 'married' on a trial basis.

16 *nice*: particular; discerning or discriminating.

17 *Customers*: Peachum's 'customers' are robbery victims seeking to recover their stolen goods by paying him a fee to locate them and arrange their return.

17 *Repeating-Watch*: a watch that struck the most recent hour and quarter hour when a lever was pressed.

Drury-Lane: street and adjoining neighbourhood near Covent Garden, known as the centre of prostitution in London.

Tunbridge: Tunbridge Wells in Kent, a fashionable spa town in the period, and hence also attractive to pickpockets and thieves.

Fuller's Earth: kind of clay (hydrous aluminium silicate) used to clean fabric.

19 *Jointure*: legal arrangement by which property is jointly held by a husband and wife or is settled on the wife for her use in case of his death.

peach'd: from 'impeached', informed against or betrayed and so brought to trial.

nick'd the Matter: hit the mark, hit the nail on the head.

20 *For on the Rope . . . Depends poor Polly's Life*: audiences would have caught Gay's pun on 'depends', which in addition to meaning rely or be contingent on also meant to hang down.

Turtle: the turtle dove, a traditional symbol of conjugal love and fidelity.

particular: exclusively devoted to one person; overly fastidious.

For the sake of Intelligence: because of the incriminating 'intelligence' Macheath has on them.

21 *Stratagem*: cunning or ingenuity.

the Nosegay in his Hand: criminals en route to execution were often given a nosegay or small bouquet of flowers by friends in the crowd, especially in front of St Sepulchre's Church.

the Windows of Holborn: the road to the gallows at Tyburn led from Newgate along Holborn and Tyburn Road (now Oxford Street). Crowds lined the route and looked out from windows along the way, sometimes jeering but often expressing support ('extolling his Resolution') or pity ('Vollies of Sighs') for the condemned.

the Tree: Tyburn Tree, popular name for the gallows.

Jack Ketch: London executioner who died in 1686; later, the nickname for any executioner or hangman.

Conversation: company, including sexual intimacy, the loss of which will 'distract' or drive Polly mad.

22 *a Pension out of the Hands of a Courtier*: in this context, a pension is a regular allowance paid to a courtier to secure his political support; or, as Samuel Johnson put it in his 1755 *Dictionary*, 'pay given to a state hireling for treason to his country'.

25 *Poor Brother Tom . . . the Otamys at Surgeon's Hall*: the 'Accident' that befell brother Tom was death by hanging. Because he was 'so clever a made' (such a well-built) fellow, his body was taken by the surgeons for

use in an anatomy demonstration, and the skeleton or 'otamy' (from 'anat-omy') later put on display in the Barber-Surgeon's Hall.

26 *the Western Road*: the road connecting London to Bath and Exeter in the West Country, which crossed Hounslow Heath, a famous highwaymen's haunt.

27 *Bawd*: a brothel keeper; a pander or pimp.

Moor-fields: a London district with criminal associations, north of the City.

28 *See the Ball . . . Lead to Gold*: in the second quatrain of this air Matt compares the efforts of alchemists ('Chymists') and highwaymen to convert lead into gold. While the alchemists toil like asses, in vain, the highwaymen use lead in the form of a bullet or 'Ball', and the 'Fire' of their pistols, to obtain gold more effectively.

bit: smitten or love-struck, but also tricked or deceived.

The Town . . . would be uninhabited: by seducing young women, Macheath is 'recruiting' them to the ranks of 'free-hearted Ladies' or whores, for the benefit of the men of 'the Town', just as a recruiting officer enlists soldiers into the army. Soldiers and highwaymen alike—'us and the other Gentlemen of the Sword'—ensure that the brothels of Drury Lane are not 'uninhabited'.

29 *so strong a Cordial for the Time*: so powerful a stimulant for passing time pleasurably.

Vinegar Yard . . . Lewkner's Lane: sites near Drury Lane associated with prostitution; Jonathan Wild ran a brothel in Lewkner's Lane at one time.

I hope you don't want . . . Paint: I hope you don't require the cosmetics or 'Paint' that women of quality need to 'repair' their looks.

Strong-Waters: alcoholic spirits, such as gin, thought to be unhealthy and corrupting, unlike 'good wholesome Beer'.

Mrs Slammekin . . . affect an Undress: as 'slammekin' means slattern or slut, Macheath is ironic in calling her 'genteel', and in comparing all the women to 'fine Ladies' whose 'Undress' (from the French *déshabillé*) was a fashionably informal manner of dressing, associated with morning wear.

30 *Every thing she gets . . . a dozen Tally-men*: all the money she earns from whoring she spends on clothing, with a bawdy pun on 'on her back'. The tally-men she keeps in business sell goods on credit, such as clothes to prostitutes—the trade practised by Mrs Trapes (III.vi).

Turtle: the turtle dove, but here signifying amorousness rather than mari-tal fidelity (cf. I.x).

If Musick be the Food of Love, play on: the opening line of Shakespeare's *Twelfth Night*.

A Dance a la ronde in the French Manner: in this context, a burlesque of the formal dances of fashionable society, and of the ballets often included in Italian opera.

31 *Cholic*: colic, a stomach complaint.

Mercers: sellers of fine fabrics. Mrs Coaxer's 'Visits' are of course criminal, in competition with other shoplifting 'Interlopers', as in the following speech.

Lutestring . . . Padesoy: two fancy varieties of silk fabric.

the Ogle of a Rattle-Snake: an ogle is an amorous or lecherous look; rattlesnakes were thought to be able to hypnotize their prey (to 'rivet' their eye) by the power of their gaze—an odd, almost oxymoronic image.

Address: adroitness or skill.

32 *in keeping*: 'kept' as a lover or mistress.

is thereafter as they be: depends on how they behave.

bating: leaving aside.

A spruce Prentice . . . the Plantations: Mrs Vixen recommends lively, smart-looking apprentices as lovers because they 'bleed' or spend money freely (with perhaps a bawdy second meaning on 'bleed'). To keep their spending up, they turn to crime, and in the end are transported to the colonies—having likely been peached by Mrs Vixen herself.

33 *Souse*: sou, a coin of small value.

These: Macheath's pistols, as the following stage direction shows.

35 *Dear Madam . . . command me*: in this last exchange, Mrs Slammekin and Dolly Trull ape the manners of polite society in insisting the other take precedence; reinforced by the following stage direction.

Turnkeys: under-jailers.

Garnish: payments extorted from new prisoners as fees for the jailers and drink-money for the other prisoners (see *OED*, definition 1.5); as the ensuing scene shows, the amount paid determined how well one was treated.

nicest: most fastidious or refined.

36 *Basilisk*: mythical serpent which could kill with a look or breath.

load of Infamy: the child with which she is visibly pregnant.

37 *Bowels*: figuratively, feelings of tenderness or pity; thought to originate in the innermost parts of the body.

39 *Brother Peachum*: the repeated use of the word 'brother' in this scene confirmed, to the play's contemporary audiences, that it referred satirically to the enmity between Walpole and Charles, Lord Townshend, his brother-in-law and fellow Whig minister of state—a point reinforced by Peachum's later comparison of himself and Lockit to 'Great Statesmen' who profit from betrayal. In a letter dated 28 March 1728, Swift suggested to Gay that the scene was modelled on the argument between Brutus and Cassius in Shakespeare's *Julius Caesar* (IV.ii).

Arrear of the Government: delay in the government's payment of the reward money to those, like Peachum and Lockit, who informed against criminals.

Ned Clincher's Name: a 'clinch' is a pun, so the name could mean joker; *clinch* can also mean to grab hold (clench), so *clincher* could suggest thief. In 1726–7 Swift wrote the comic-satirical poem 'Clever Tom Clinch Going to be Hanged', whose protagonist is defiant to the end and refers to Jonathan Wild as a friend; given the two authors' friendship it's likely that Gay had the poem in mind here.

Condemn'd Hold: an area in Newgate prison where those already tried and sentenced awaited execution.

40 *Halter*: rope used for hanging; noose.

nimm'd: stole, from *nim*, 'to steal, or whip off or away any thing' (*NCD*).

41 *Weeds*: 'widow's weeds' or mourning clothes.

42 *Perquisite*: a 'perk' or tip paid for services rendered; in this context, a bribe.

43 *Sash*: sash window, behind which the male swallow is 'pent' or confined.

for th' Event: because of what has happened, or awaiting the outcome.

44 *Facts*: evidence, especially of evil doing.

bubbled: cheated or deceived; similarly, 'bit', just below, means tricked.

Fetch: ruse or trick.

45 *trapan*: ensnare or beguile.

46 *commit the Folly*: act foolishly; here, to have sexual relations (*folly*, 'a lewd action or desire', *OED*, definition 3b).

48 *burnt*: alludes to two forms of punishment in the period: convicted offenders who received 'benefit of clergy' were 'burnt' or branded on the right thumb, while women convicted of high or petty treason (including wives who had murdered their husbands) could be burned to death.

49 *to score*: to run a tab or keep an account.

are their own Bubbles: make fools of themselves.

50 *leaky in his Liquor*: talkative or indiscreet when drunk.

They fail of a Chap: they have no 'customers' or victims.

51 *a Quartern of Strong-Waters*: a quarter-pint of spirits (most likely gin).

a shotten Herring: a herring after spawning, worn out from excess of sexual activity.

Since the favourite . . . call'd down to Sentence: as female prisoners could not be hanged while pregnant, Filch is acting as a substitute 'Child-getter', since 'the favourite' has been 'disabled', presumably by venereal disease.

tip off: die.

his Lock . . . Crooked Billet: *lock* is 'a Cant Word, signifying, a Warehouse where stolen Goods are deposited' (Gay, note to this line in original text). The *Crooked Billet*, meaning a criminal occupation or place of work, is the sign that identifies his lock.

52 *One Man may steal . . . look over a Hedge*: proverb meaning that some men can get away with crimes while others get in trouble even though innocent.

The ironic implication is that Macheath is unjustly in 'Difficulties' while 'the vilest' of 'Gamesters' (denigrated as 'Mechanics' or manual workers, and thus 'servile' or low) are 'admitted amongst the politest Company'.

53 *deep Play*: high-stakes gambling.

Setting: setting upon or robbing.

Rouleau: a roll or packet of gold coins, loaned by the 'Money-Lenders' to needy gamblers at high rates of interest—condemned by Macheath as 'Extortion'.

in my Cash: has money that belongs to me.

The Coronation Account: the account or record of goods stolen at the coronation of George II in October 1727.

Instalments: the annual ceremony of inauguration of the new Lord Mayor of London—like the coronation, but on a smaller scale, an opportunity for thieves to work the celebrating crowd.

54 *Lady's Tail*: the train of a lady's gown.

she will make a good Hand . . . going into Keeping: Mrs Trapes will use the brocade to make fancy slippers and shoes for prostitutes who are becoming rich men's mistresses.

Pockets: pocket books or purses, tied round the waist and so easy to steal in a crowd.

the last Half Year's Plate: the gold or silver ware stolen over the past six months.

Gudgeons: small, easily caught freshwater fish; metaphorically, gullible fools.

55 *curious*: selective or choosy.

Blacks: mourning clothes.

Mantoes: mantuas, loose-fitting, fashionable gowns.

56 *The Act for destroying the Mint*: an act passed by Parliament in 1723 to do away with the extra-legal status that had made the Mint district in Southwark a haven for criminals and debtors.

the Act . . . Imprisonment for small Sums: a parliamentary act of 1725–6 that prohibited arrests for debts of less than ten pounds in a superior court or forty shillings in an inferior court.

when a Lady can borrow . . . the least Hank upon her: i.e. when one of her prostitute customers can obtain goods from her without fear of being sent to debtors' prison for what they owe—the 'Hank' or hold she had over them before.

under the Surgeon's Hands: under treatment, presumably for venereal disease.

58 *Rat's-bane*: rat poison. Prison scenes featuring poisoned cups were a staple of Italian opera, as in Handel's *Radamisto* (1720) and *Tamerlano* (1724), and are parodied in this and the next three scenes.

I can lay her Death . . . call'd in Question: Gin was very freely and cheaply available, especially in London, and was often of such poor quality as to be poisonous.

Spleen: the spleen was often represented as the seat of anger, melancholy, and low spirits. To have 'the spleen' was also sometimes taken as a sign of sensitivity or refinement.

Vapours: like 'the spleen', a term for ill humour; thought to be caused by exhalations of bodily organs and, like the spleen, particularly associated with women of fashion.

59 *Closet*: a small private room, usually adjoining or within a bedroom.

60 *particular*: devoted to one person.

Coquets: flirts.

chirping: cheering.

62 *Which way shall I turn me?*: Macheath's question echoes Antony's 'O Dolabella, which way shall I turn?' in John Dryden's heroic tragedy *All for Love* (1677), when confronted with the need to choose between his wife Octavia and his lover Cleopatra. Gay's scene may also allude to the classical myth of the Judgement of Hercules, called on to choose between two goddesses representing Virtue and Pleasure. William Hogarth's five paintings of this scene (from *The Beggar's Opera*), based on an early performance, emphasize the mock-heroic parallels to the Hercules story.

63 *sink*: suppress.

64 *Fry*: small fry, from a word meaning a swarm of fishes just spawned.

65 *Brimmer*: drinking glass filled to the brim.

66 *Busses*: kisses.

67 *Jemmy Twitcher . . . surpriz'd me*: since it is clear from III.vi that Mrs Trapes's information led to Macheath's arrest, Jemmy Twitcher must have given the testimony that led to his conviction.

Ship yourselves off . . . a Husband a-piece: this line may be seen to set up the scenario of *Polly*, in which the heroine does ship herself off to the West Indies in search of a husband, although not quite in the way Macheath imagines.

68 *All you that must take a Leap*: this is the only trio in *The Beggar's Opera*, and both imitates and parodies the operatic convention of concluding the action with an ensemble in which the main characters give vent to their feelings. The tune, fittingly, is from a ballad about a hanging. The chorus at the end of the trio may consist of the three protagonists, or may be offstage.

the Toll of the Bell: the bell of St Sepulchre's Church near Newgate, which started tolling a few minutes before the condemned were led from the prison to begin their procession to Tyburn.

69 *this kind of Drama*: Italian opera, often derided for its absurd or improbable plots; but also *The Beggar's Opera* itself, whose parodic, promiscuous mix of multiple genres is itself absurd.

70 *the Turk, with his Doxies*: may refer either to the Turkish custom of polygamy or, more likely, to the Turkish Sultan and his harem—figures of fascination to Europeans in this period. *Doxies* is criminal slang for 'She-beggars, Trulls, Wenches, Whores' (*NCD*).

POLLY

TITLE PAGE

71 *Raro antecedentem . . . pœna claudo*: 'Rarely does vengeance, albeit of halting gait, fail to o'ertake the guilty' (Horace, *Odes* iii. 2. 31–2). From *Horace, Odes and Epodes*, ed. and trans. C. E. Bennett [Loeb Classical Library] (Cambridge, MA: Harvard University Press, 1968), 177.

PREFACE

73 *Lord Chamberlain*: an officer of high standing in the royal household, he also traditionally had authority over the theatres and acted as censor. At this time the office was held by Charles Fitzroy, second Duke of Grafton, who was first appointed in April 1724.

litteral faults: misprints, usually minor errors involving the substitution of one letter for another.

75 *foul blotted papers*: manuscript pages containing errors, words blotted or crossed out, scrawled corrections, and so forth.

the present happy establishment: the current government under George II. Gay's antagonism to Walpole and his government was widely known or suspected, but he never took an explicitly oppositional stance.

76 *representation*: performance on stage.

I am engag'd . . . upon his Theatre: as is discussed more fully in the Introduction to this volume, *Polly* was never performed in Gay's or Rich's lifetimes; the first recorded performance was of George Colman's heavily revised and expurgated version, in 1777.

INTRODUCTION

77 *I hope . . . your last Piece*: refers to criticism (genuine or ironic) of *The Beggar's Opera* for the 'absurdity' or immorality of its 'catastrophe' or ending—which Gay, of course, was the first to point out.

78 *write in character*: i.e. creates a character who represents one or more 'follies and vices'.

79 *true kid*: leather made from the skin of a kid or young goat, valued for its softness, and used in making high-quality gloves; the tenor's insistence on these rather than 'clean lambskin' is a sign of his preciosity or over-refinement.

Signora Crotchetta: a crotchet is a musical note (a quarter note in North America), but also 'a whimsical fancy; a perverse conceit' (*OED*), whence 'crotchety' for eccentric or bad-tempered.

Tramontane: from the Italian for 'beyond the mountains'; applied to persons from any country north of the Alps, often with the connotation of uncivilized or barbarous.

little better than a fish: refers to the characters of two mermaids 'Dancing up and down in the Water' in Act II, scene 1 of Handel's opera *Rinaldo*, most recently performed in June 1717.

an Opera without singers: i.e. *The Beggar's Opera*, whose parts were taken by actors (also known in the period as 'Comedians') who could sing, rather than operatically trained singers.

DRAMATIS PERSONAE

As in *The Beggar's Opera*, but less consistently, most of the character names in *Polly* are descriptive. *Ducat* means a piece of money, from the name given to various gold and silver coins in the period. The name *Morano*—who is none other than Macheath in theatrical blackface disguise—alludes not only to *Moor* (and thus to Shakespeare's *Othello*) but also to *Marrano*, a term applied to the forcibly Christianized Jews and Moors of medieval and early modern Spain, especially those who only pretended to convert, and to *Maroon*, a term for fugitive and rebellious slaves in the West Indies.

The pirates' names derive from weapons or nautical devices: *Vanderbluff* suggests *blunderbuss*, a short musket but also, figuratively, a clumsy or stupid person; *bluff* also suggests outspoken or boastful. *Capstern* is an alternate spelling of 'capstan', an apparatus for winding in heavy ropes or cables on ships. A *hacker* could be any weapon or tool that hacks or cuts, and the term was also slang for a cut-throat or bully (*OED*, definition 1b). *Culverin* can mean either handgun or cannon, *Laguerre* is the French word for war, and *Cutlace*, an alternate form of *cutlass*, is a short sword much used by sailors.

The names *Pohetohee* and *Cawwawkee* are less easy to place. *Cawwawkee* may echo *Arawak*, name given to some of the indigenous peoples of the West Indies, who were effectively wiped out in that region in the wake of European colonialism. Similarly, *Pohetohee* may echo the Arawak word *bohito*, meaning priest or healer.

Trapes and *Jenny Diver* are discussed in the notes to the *Dramatis Personae* of *The Beggar's Opera*. Apart from Mrs Ducat, the only new female character names are *Flimzy*, insubstantial or weak, and by extension frivolous and shallow; and *Damaris*, whose name could only allude ironically to that of the early Christian convert named in Acts 17: 34.

THE PLAY

83 *younger brothers*: in the system of primogeniture prevalent in this period, the first-born son often inherited all or most of the family's money and property, leaving 'younger brothers' to seek their own fortunes or, as here, spend themselves into debt in order to fit into 'the polite world'.

83 *The disappointed Widow*: the title of the ballad whose melody Gay has used for this air. See Appendix for notes on the originals of all the airs in *Polly*.

Plantations: the sugar plantations of Britain's West Indian colonies; by extension, the colonial settlements in general.

84 *family lectures*: domestic squabbles or scoldings.

herring-pond: facetious term for the sea or ocean, especially the North Atlantic (the herring's native territory).

you shou'd break through . . . and keep ——: i.e. you should challenge your wife's 'usurpation' of your authority; the missing word would probably have been understood as 'whores'.

85 *my duty . . . hard upon me*: i.e. my wife's sexual demands are overtiring to me.

haply: perhaps.

numm'd in the brake: lying still or asleep ('numbed') in a thicket.

by the waggon: as seen in the first plate of Hogarth's *The Harlot's Progress*, the 'waggon' was a relatively cheap mode of transport that conveyed people (here, young women, commodified as 'fresh goods') from the various parts of England to London.

86 *pin-money*: an allowance, generally given to a wife by her husband, for personal expenses; here, with the sense of a bribe given in exchange for permission to take lovers.

88 *private conversations*: playing on a second meaning of 'conversation', i.e. sexual relations (as in 'criminal conversation' or adultery).

89 *want of parts*: lack of real abilities or talents.

90 *Death . . . they dye it seems too*: Death was 'oblig'd to' Peachum for delivering so many criminals to be hanged in exchange for the reward money; and likewise to 'the physicians', for killing so many of their patients.

Sessions-paper: list of cases due for trial at each session of a criminal court; also, as in the Old Bailey Sessions Papers, the trial reports from each session.

'Tis now . . . gone off with him: Macheath and Jenny were both transported to the West Indies as indentured servants or slaves (probably for a period of seven or fourteen years, but possibly for life), and Macheath was put to work on a sugar plantation.

91 *Thy shaft*: i.e. the shaft of Love's or Cupid's arrow.

tight: trim, tidy, shapely; also capable, lively.

92 *alderman*: a city official or magistrate ranking just below mayor; in London, chief officer of a ward.

93 *pistoles*: Spanish gold coins worth about eighteen shillings, or something under a pound; one hundred pistoles would have been a substantial sum in the period.

upon the nail: on the spot; without delay.

94 *racy*: delicious, exquisite.

95 *my least resort*: i.e. the place I'm least likely to be found.

restif: restive, impatient at restrictions and resistant to control.

freaks: perverse whims.

97 *separate maintenance*: financial support, typically provided by a husband to a wife, when the two parties have separated.

huffing: bluster, arrogance.

charge and cuffing: cost (or burden) and violence or blows.

99 *daw*: jackdaw, a kind of small crow; a common or dull-coloured bird of no interest to 'fowlers' or bird collectors.

teazing: here in the sense of annoying or bothersome.

naught: quiet or compliant.

102 *fling up your commission*: give up or relinquish your position. It was obligatory for all free men in the colonies to enlist in the militia at their own expense, in order to protect British colonial property from the threat of piracy, slave rebellion, foreign invasion, or native insurgency.

103 *succours*: aid, relief.

rapine: acts of pillaging or plunder.

105 *maid*: here, in the sense of virgin.

106 *smuglers in love . . . fair traders in matrimony*: just as smugglers of goods undermine the business and profits of 'fair traders', so 'strumpets' undermine or 'ruin' the happiness of wives.

nos'd: cheated or defrauded (a now obsolete sense of the verb 'to nose').

maudlin: tearfully sentimental or mawkish; drunkenly overemotional.

107 *grist*: in the figurative sense of profit or advantage.

108 *habit*: clothing, outfit.

110 *dead March*: piece of solemn music played at a funeral, especially a military or state funeral.

Symphony: instrumental introduction to the following song.

rod of incantation: magic wand.

111 *the privilege of travellers*: i.e. the right to make up stories or tell tall tales.

A sup or two of our cag: a swig (drink) or two from our keg.

112 *genius*: disposition or tendency.

rubb'd through: got through.

prefer'd: hired or appointed.

Pharaon-Bank: faro bank, a gambling house where faro (a card game) is played.

drunken bout: drinking binge, during which he 'was stript' or lost everything.

112   *recruit*: fresh supply of money.

    drawer: one who draws beer or fetches liquor in a tavern.

113   *tho' he is black . . . great man*: Morano's 'blackness' links him to such figures as the protagonists of Shakespeare's *Othello* and Thomas Southerne's
heroic tragedy *Oroonoko* (1695, adapted from Aphra Behn's novel-
romance), both of whom also have white female lovers. Gay both affirms
and undermines Morano's heroic glamour by attributing to him 'the air of
a great man', as 'great man' was an epithet often satirically applied to the
morally compromised Walpole.

    Cleopatra: Macheath-Morano's vacillation between love and heroic 'ambi-
tion' is modelled on that of Antony in Dryden's *All for Love* (1677; based
on Shakespeare's *Antony and Cleopatra*).

    flatt'ring: auspicious or fair-seeming, falsely encouraging hope (*OED*,
definition 2b).

    Can the bark . . . Pilot's blind: in this air's extended metaphor, 'Woman'
is the ever-changing ocean, her male lover a 'bark' or ship tossed on the
waves, and love the bark's blind pilot, mocked as 'silly' or foolish.

114   *Cartagena*: Spanish colonial settlement (founded 1533) on the coast of
present-day Colombia, and known as the treasure city of the Spanish
Main; target of numerous piratical attacks and invasions, including one
led by Sir Francis Drake, who seized Cartagena in 1586.

    Alexanders: one of several satirical allusions to the Macedonian king
Alexander the Great (356–323 BC), whose conquests could be regarded as
either civilizing and heroic or brutally criminal.

    mettl'd: mettlesome; spirited and vigorous.

115   *spawn*: contemptuous term for a brood or race—here, the 'race' of flattering courtiers.

    factory: colonial settlement or trading station.

    risque your fortunes: run the same risks as you.

116   *think war a widow, a kingdom the dower*: just as to 'win' a widow by court-
ship brings a man her 'dower' or dowry, so to win this war against the
colony would bring the pirates a 'kingdom'.

    game as deep as you please: gamble for stakes as high as you like.

117   *Have I ever betray'd you . . . to your self*: a reminder that it was Jenny who
betrayed Macheath to Peachum in Act II of *The Beggar's Opera*.

    competence: fortune sufficient to live off comfortably.

    nicest punctilio: most scrupulous attention to etiquette.

118   *gil-flirts*: variant of *gill-flirts* or *jill-flirts*, wanton or sexually forward young
women.

    woundy: extreme or excessive.

    compleat: complete, perfect.

119 *a boatswain must swear in a storm*: A boatswain is the foreman of a ship's crew. Proverbial.

   wheat-ear: small songbird known for looking under newly-turned earth for food, as well as for shelter from hawks or even the shadows of clouds.

   another-guess: altogether different in kind.

   keel-hawl: to punish by dragging or hauling under the keel of a ship.

121 *jarring*: quarrelling, clashing.

122 *try your mettle*: test your courage or spirit.

   those have always . . . ruin'd in their service: could mean either that women have a claim to men's protection, having been 'ruin'd' in men's service; or that men like himself have a claim to women's protection, having been 'ruin'd by women' in sexual or financial terms.

   the sex: in the period, used to mean the female sex, women in general; in this dramatic context, however, the sense is more evasive or ambiguous.

123 *stripling*: a male youth, at the point of crossing from boyhood to manhood.

   railly: variant of rally, to banter or tease.

125 *if he had been bred . . . his fortune*: the phrase sounds proverbial, but I have not been able to trace it.

126 *cat-o'-nine-tails*: whip with nine knotted 'tails' or lashes, used for flogging in the British navy and army until 1881.

   gibbet: originally another term for gallows, but by this period a post with a projecting arm from which the bodies of criminals were hung in chains after execution as a warning or form of debasement.

127 *Barbarians*: Morano's use of this term in response to Cawwawkee's paean to virtue is the first in a series of semantic ironies or inversions that run through this and later scenes, so that terms like *ignorant, civiliz'd, savages*, and so forth convey the opposite of their customary meanings.

128 *European*: Cawwawkee's use of this term in addressing Morano, who is meant to be an escaped African slave, expresses his contempt for the values Morano shares with the white colonials, but could also suggest that he sees through Macheath's disguise.

129 *Can madness this transcend?*: i.e. can there be any greater degree of madness than this?

   like the beaver . . . quit the chase: alludes to Juvenal, *Satires* xii, 34–6, in which the hunted beaver bites off his own testicles—thought to be the source of the musk-like substance castoreum for which beavers were hunted—in order to put an end to the hunt.

131 *I must go—But I cannot*: Morano's dilemma here echoes his alter ego Macheath's inability to choose between Polly and Lucy in *The Beggar's Opera*, as in Airs 35 and 53 ('Which way shall I turn me?—How can I decide?').

131 *<To her>*: in the copy text, the first four lines of this air have the stage direction 'to him', but these two lines seem to be directed to Jenny.

132 *a bubble's part*: the role of a fool, dupe, or victim (of a fraud or scam).

 in use of yore: practised long ago.

 the ready: ready money, wealth in hand.

134 *cancell'd faith*: broken a promise or pledge.

137 *stanch*: staunch, firm or determined; often in the sense of reliable or principled, and so ironic here.

138 *Camp*: temporary military encampment near the field of battle.

 touch: test or trial; related to *touchstone*, variety of dark stone used to test the quality of gold or silver, thus suggesting the two following lines.

139 *pass currant*: to pass current is to be in circulation or common use (as of money), or as here, to be regarded as genuine.

 will not dispense with my duty to my wife: i.e. will not exempt him from (military) duty despite his duty or promise to his wife.

140 *gauls*: alternate form of *galls*, irritates or annoys.

141 *horns*: hunting horns, used as signals in hunts on horseback, as trumpets (lines 6–9) are used in battle.

142 *Neger*: Culverin is clearly using this variant form of *Negro* (French *nègre*, from Spanish *negro*, black) in a negative or disparaging way.

 engrosser: one who engrosses or takes everything for himself.

 good afterwards: right afterwards.

 fling a merry main or two: play hazard, a dice game; the *main* is a number from five to nine that the gambler bets on before throwing the dice. In the lines that follow, a *nick* is a winning throw, and Culverin, having called seven as his *main*, can *nick* with either seven or eleven. When he rolls a winning eleven, Hacker accuses him of having cheated, using the thieves' slang term *cog*, for cheat.

144 *parts*: abilities or talents.

 mend its pace: goes more quickly.

145 *with a wide waste pursuing*: laying waste to the sheep as he pursues them.

 parley: discussion or conference with the enemy.

146 *Composition*: compromise.

 controll'd: commanded.

 unfold: reveal, display to view.

148 *spray*: a small, usually flowering, branch.

 fowler: bird hunter or trapper.

150 *betimes*: in good time; in advance.

 The men . . . Bound from the cord on high: acrobats or tightrope-walkers.

151 *consciousness*: i.e. conscience.

152 *newgate attorney*: one who works on behalf of prisoners in Newgate—conveying an implication of dishonesty.

157 *brake*: an area of densely growing shrubs and brush; a thicket.

stemming: crossing or swimming against the current.

160 *meet*: fitting, appropriate.

161 *foment the chace*: encourage or support the *chace* or hunt.